LIZZIE'S STORY

SEABURY SERIES COLLECTION: BOOKS 10-12

BETH RAIN

Copyright © 2023 by Beth Rain

A Quiet Life in Seabury (Seabury: Book 10)

First Publication: 14th July, 2023

All rights reserved.

Copyright © 2023 by Beth Rain

In A Spin in Seabury (Seabury: Book 11)

First Publication: 29th September, 2023

All rights reserved.

Copyright © 2023 by Beth Rain

Living The Dream in Seabury (Seabury: Book 12)

First Publication: 20th October, 2023

All rights reserved.

No part of this book may be reproduced in any form or by any electronic or mechanical means, including information storage and retrieval systems. Except for use in any review, the reproduction or utilization of this work, in whole or in part, in any form by any electronic, mechanical or other means now known or hereafter invented, is forbidden without the written permission of the publisher.

Published by Beth Rain. The author may be contacted by email on bethrainauthor@gmail.com

 Created with Vellum

A QUIET LIFE IN SEABURY

SEABURY - BOOK 10

CHAPTER 1

It was one of those spectacular summer days that made you feel glad to be alive. There wasn't a single cloud in the sky, and the waves were barely a ripple as they lapped at the shore of West Beach.

Lizzie Moore paused at the top of the stone steps that led down to the golden sand and stared around, doing her best to soak in every last drop of gorgeousness the day had to offer. It was only her third day back in town, and she felt as though she'd landed inside some kind of wonderful dream she never wanted to wake up from.

The soft air was rich with the tang of salty seaweed, and the gentle shushing of the waves was punctuated by the sharp cries of gulls as they swooped overhead.

Would she ever take Seabury for granted again?

Somehow, she very much doubted it – not after spending such a long time away from her beloved hometown.

Brushing a stray wisp of hair from her cheek, Lizzie ran lightly down the steps onto the beach, where she promptly kicked off her Converse. Next, she peeled off her socks – wobbling around on one leg and then the other in her haste to feel the sand between her bare toes.

Lizzie knew she was in Devon, but this morning it was hard to believe she hadn't somehow parachuted onto a Caribbean island. It wasn't even nine o'clock yet, but the sky was an intense blue, and the clear water shimmered with an alluring, dazzling turquoise that almost begged her to roll up the legs of her dungarees and have a quick paddle.

'Maybe later…' she murmured to the sea.

Lizzie could feel the sun warming her skin through the sleeves of her black and white polka dot shirt. It was going to be a scorcher at this rate! Closing her eyes for a moment, she tilted her face to the sky and took in a long, deep breath. She knew she probably looked like a prize idiot, standing there with her eyes closed, grinning up at the sunshine… but she didn't care. She was so grateful to be back, she could practically dance a jig.

It was hard not to hold onto a great big ball of resentment towards her husband for taking her away from Seabury in the first place. Her *ex*-husband, she should say. After all, it was already five years since they'd separated, and Mark was re-married. Their two grown-up daughters had flown the nest years ago and were off doing their own thing. Lizzie, however, felt like she was only just finding her feet again.

Still, she was *happy* that Mark was happy. She was *grateful* he'd found someone who loved him. It was *wonderful* he'd been able to move on so quickly.

Hmm... okay, maybe the whole gratitude thing needed a bit more work when it came to her ex-husband – but at least she was trying!

Lizzie opened her eyes again, determined to enjoy the moment – rather than getting caught up in the past all over again.

'Look where I am!' she whispered to herself.

After more than a decade away, she was finally back in the one place that truly felt like home. She'd been brought up here – living with her lovely grandparents in their little cottage just below the town's allotments. When her nan had passed away and left the place to her, she'd happily settled there with Mark. Their two daughters had arrived in quick succession... and life had felt pretty much perfect for a little while.

Lizzie shook her head, doing her best to clear her thoughts as she wandered along West Beach. *This* was something it was easy to be grateful for. After years of living in a bustling, grubby city that had never quite made sense to her, she was home - and she never had to leave again.

'I am grateful. I *am* grateful...' she murmured as she made her way towards a group of old-fashioned, canvas deckchairs that were lined up facing the sea. They were picture-postcard-perfect – so cute and vintagey that they looked as if they'd graced the sands of West Beach every summer since the 1950s at least! She knew that was a clever illusion, though. They certainly hadn't been around when the girls were little... or when *she* was little come to that!

She came to a halt next to the nearest chair and ran her hand over the gorgeous blue, cream and pink stripes – trying to resist the urge to sink into its depths.

Just five minutes won't hurt!

Lizzie glanced around, searching for someone to ask permission from - but the sunny beach was deserted. She shrugged. No doubt someone would be along if they wanted her to move! She tossed her shoes onto the sand and flopped down into the chair with a huge, happy sigh.

What a glorious morning! She couldn't believe she had the entire place to herself! That was one thing you could say for Seabury – it did get a few visitors, but most of the tourists seemed to jam themselves into the larger resort towns further down the coast. They were probably all over in Torquay, Paignton and Dunscombe Sands right now, setting up their windbreaks and laying claim to their little patches of beach for the day.

Frankly, those other towns could keep the crowds... though, if it was always this quiet, it was hard to see how anyone in Seabury managed to keep a business going.

A little thrill of excitement mixed with anxiety ran through her. Was she mad, thinking she could make a life here? Could she really make her grand plan work in such a sleepy little place?!

'It has to work!' she said, settling back and letting her eyes drift closed as the usual sense of certainty hit her, just like it did every time she thought about the brand-new business she was going to get up and running now that she was finally home. She just needed to get the Old Grain Store tidied up, some stock ordered, a name chosen, some marketing underway...

'I am grateful,' she whispered again in an attempt to stop herself from mentally reciting her ever-growing to-do list.

Lizzie sighed, her eyelids fluttering in the warmth. Blimey, if she wasn't careful she'd be fast asleep before long. She was absolutely exhausted from the move.

Packing up her flat in Bristol had seemed to take forever – and now that she was finally here, she'd barely even started the unpacking. There were walls of cardboard boxes all over the cottage, and scarcely enough room to squeeze between them. She knew it would take a while to get around to emptying all the boxes – but she'd decided to focus on the shop first. Once the Old Grain Store was ready for customers, then she could focus on the cottage.

At least the place had been left clean and tidy for her. Lizzie had felt awful about asking Lou, her lodger, to leave. Lou had been completely cool about the whole thing, though, and it had all worked out for the best as Lou had ended up buying Seashell Cottage, just across the field.

In fact - Lou had made sure Lizzie had a smile on her face the minute she arrived at the cottage by placing a lovely card and bottle of wine just inside the empty hallway, ready to greet her the moment she opened the door. It had been such a wonderful surprise after the long and stressful journey. She'd opened the card, only to laugh out loud as she read the note inside - "Imagine I'm a Bunch of Flowers." According to the postscript scribbled underneath, Lou hadn't wanted to risk her arriving to a vase full of dead blooms.

Lizzie couldn't wait to meet her new neighbour. They'd chatted on the phone a couple of times, and she had a feeling they'd get on like a house on fire. In fact – she couldn't wait to meet everyone here! She was pretty sure a lot of the old faces would still be around… though it was unlikely they'd recognise her after all these years. She'd changed – a lot.

The last time Lizzie had lived in town she'd been a worn-out mum doing her best to wrangle two teenage daughters single-handedly because Mark had worked away more than he was at home. Now... well... she was definitely still worn out – but this time it was because she was busy chasing her own dreams for what felt like the first time in forever.

Lizzie gave a little shiver of excitement, then yawned widely. The sound of the waves and the cries of the gulls were telling her that at last, she could relax... at last, she was home.

Lizzie frowned slightly as a shadow passed over the sun. She must have drifted off! She had no idea how long she'd been asleep... long enough for a cloud to appear, she guessed!

A gentle cough made her eyes fly open.

'Oh!' she said.

Oh didn't really cover it.

In front of her stood a man. She couldn't see his face because he was completely silhouetted against the sunshine, something that just served to outline beautifully strong arms, and ridiculously nice legs below a pair of cammo shorts!

'Erm, hi?' said Lizzie, trying to bring things into focus a bit better as she blinked and shaded her eyes.

'Hi!'

Ooh, he had a lovely voice too. Low and gravelly and... yum!

'It's a pound for the deckchair if you don't mind?'

'Oh… right!' said Lizzie, feeling slightly befuddled. 'Of course, hang about a sec… I know I've got some change here somewhere.'

She started to pat at the pockets of her dungarees.

'Here on holiday?' asked the man.

'No… no…' said Lizzie, completely distracted as she shifted onto one bum cheek to check her back pocket.

Ah Ha!

She triumphantly pulled out a handful of bits and bobs, only to find herself staring down at two clothes pegs, a couple of buttons, some hair grips and – randomly – a mint humbug.

How on earth did that get in there?

She peeped back up at the silhouette in front of her, doing her best to look apologetic, only to be met by a low rumble of laughter that made her bare toes curl into the warm sand.

'So… not visiting?' he said. She could still hear the laughter in his voice. 'Your first time in Seabury?'

'Nope. I lived here ages ago – but it's my first time back in about ten years.' Lizzie paused and sighed. 'Blimey, I seem to have lost a decade somewhere!'

'Happens to the best of us!' laughed the man. 'You must be Lizzie? Welcome home.'

'Thank you.' The words felt like a great big warm hug. 'Erm, how did you know...?'

'This is Seabury!' laughed the man. 'Anyway, see you around.'

He turned and started to wander off.

'Wait!' called Lizzie, trying and completely failing to get out of the low chair. 'I've not paid you yet – and I *know* I've got some change in these blasted things somewhere!' she added, tugging at the dungarees' straps.

'I'll get it next time,' he said. 'And I'll do my best not to wake you up in future!'

'I was just resting my eyes,' chuckled Lizzie.

'The customer always knows best,' came the amused reply.

Lizzie watched the man as he began to walk away again, and she couldn't help but admire the view. Broad, solid back, muscular arms and tanned legs that were clearly very at home pottering around - barefoot - on the sands of West Beach. He was exactly the kind of guy who'd have had her heart racing when she was younger... but she was well past all that kind of nonsense these days.

Okay, so her heart *was* beating a little faster than normal... but it was probably just from the shock of being woken up by a random stranger. Or... maybe she was just hungry. Yes – that's all it was – and the sea air was probably getting to her too. She was still acclimatising to it – that was all. She'd clearly been in the city for far too long.

Lizzie fanned her face with her hand, suddenly realising that, like an idiot, she hadn't even managed to get the guy's name. Even worse – he already knew hers, so it would be super-awkward to ask in the future. She let out a long sigh. Was she *really* so out of practice at being a normal human being? It certainly seemed like it!

Ah well – she couldn't do anything about it now. The man was already a dot in the distance as he headed in the direction of the Pebble Street Hotel.

Right. It was time to get on with her day. As lovely as it was to be lounging around on the beach in a deckchair, Lizzie had work to do. But first – she needed to get her hands on a coffee… and maybe a sugary treat. Anything to help her get over the shock of waking up to such a glorious sight!

Grabbing her shoes, Lizzie briefly thought about pulling them back on but promptly changed her mind. Why bother? She wanted to feel the sand between her toes for as long as possible. Instead, she tied the laces together and slung them over her shoulder. Now all she had to do was figure out how on earth to get out of this chair without it eating her alive!

CHAPTER 2

*A*fter executing one of the least graceful manoeuvres of her life, Lizzie managed to haul herself back to her feet. Despite her best intentions about getting on with her day, she completely failed to resist the draw of a quick paddle. She rolled her dungarees up to her knees and let the gentle waves soothe her tired calves and feet.

When she eventually dragged herself away from the beach and was back on the pavement, Lizzie realised she had a choice to make. Unlike years ago, there were now several places she could grab her morning coffee. The fancy new cafe on North Beach had looked pretty funky when she'd driven past it the day before, but frankly, its cool interior was a bit too much like something out of her old city life for her taste.

As for the Pebble Street Hotel, memories of the

miserable Veronica Hughes made Lizzie pretty hesitant about going anywhere near the place. Of course, there was a good chance that the old bat had moved on by this point, but just the idea of getting told off for being covered in sand and then force-fed the battery acid Veronica used to pass off as coffee made up her mind. That *wouldn't* be a positive start to the day!

That left The Sardine… and considering the gorgeous little place with its pretty, inviting yard was just across the road, Lizzie was more than happy with her decision!

'This is my life!' she murmured to herself, trying to shake off the feeling that she was just here for a visit and would have to head back to the drudge of the city at any moment.

This was *her* life. She could start every single morning like this if she wanted to – and no one could stop her!

'Morning!'

The café door opened just as she reached it, and the beaming face of an elderly gent appeared as he held it open for her.

'Lionel?' said Lizzie. 'Is that you?'

It certainly looked like the wonderful painter who used to live on the top floor of the hotel. The girls had loved to watch him paint whenever they bumped into him on the beach – and somehow he'd always managed to produce a little gift from his pockets for them – a new pencil each, or a bag of sweets to share.

'Well, goodness gracious me – if it isn't young Miss Elizabeth!' he said with a smile that seemed to reach all the way up to his bristling eyebrows.

'You know it's always Lizzie to you!' said Lizzie, taking his hand and giving it a delighted squeeze as the rush of happy memories greeted her. 'And… I'm not so sure about young these days!' she added.

'Let's have none of that,' said Lionel. 'You look wonderful – I have to say, I approve of the dungarees!'

'Thanks!' said Lizzie, pushing away the temptation to bounce up and down in delight - she couldn't help but feel secretly thrilled. She loved them – even if Mark wouldn't have been seen dead with her wearing a pair of dungarees in public! Not that what he thought mattered in the slightest anymore!

'I wonder if I could talk Mary into getting a pair,' said Lionel with a decidedly naughty twinkle in his eyes.

'Mary?' said Lizzie.

'My fiancé!' said Lionel proudly.

'What? Wow!' said Lizzie. 'Congratulations!'

'Well, thank you,' said Lionel, still beaming.

'Sorry - I hadn't heard…' she started, realising her surprise was probably more than a little bit rude.

'Hardly your fault,' said Lionel, 'you've only just

arrived back in town. There's an awful lot of Seabury gossip for you to catch up on.'

'More than ten years' worth,' sighed Lizzie.

For a brief moment, she felt a tug of sadness that she'd missed out on so many years here. So much had happened... so much life had flown passed... she couldn't help but wonder if the town would accept her as one of its own again. Maybe she'd only ever be a blow-in – someone who'd kept the house all this time without being an active part of the community.

With a frown, she gave herself a little shake, pulling herself together quickly. Now wasn't the time to be worrying about all that – not with Lionel watching her so closely.

'Don't you go worrying your head,' he said quietly, clearly reading more on her face than she'd said out loud. 'There are plenty of people around here who'll be delighted to fill you in. Give it a few days, and it'll feel like you never left!'

'Thanks Lionel,' she said, reaching out and giving his arm another squeeze.

'And how are the girls?' he said. 'I guess they've grown up a bit!'

'They're brilliant thanks,' said Lizzie with a fond smile, 'and hardly girls anymore – they're both in their twenties! Jenna's still floating around the world like the little fairy she always was. She's travelling around Morocco in her van at the moment.'

'And Megan?' said Lionel.

'Has her head down, working as hard as ever,' said Lizzie.

'I remember her serious little face,' said Lionel, nodding.

'Not much has changed,' said Lizzie with a sigh. 'I swear she was born with a five-year plan in that head of hers.'

Lizzie adored both girls, but they were about as different to each other as it was possible to be. Jenna – her youngest - never seemed to have a care in the world. She danced through life and troubles just seemed to bounce off her as she went.

Megan might be the one with all the plans - five-year plan, ten-year plan, plan to pay off her mortgage and marry the decidedly boring Owen by the time she was thirty - but Lizzie wasn't convinced her daughter was quite as in control as she liked to think she was. Lizzie had never said anything, but she'd been half-expecting Megan to start coming apart at the seams for years.

'Right, I won't keep you any longer,' said Lionel, 'but give them both my love when you speak to them, won't you?'

'Of course,' said Lizzie smiling. She didn't want to burst the bubble of happy memories by admitting that she rarely spoke to either of them these days. Nothing bad had happened – it was just that Jenna was usually far beyond the reach of mobile reception or in a completely different time zone, and Megan tended to be at work or too busy planning world domination for idle chitchat.

Plus, there was the fact that if either of them needed a parent, it was *always* Mark they turned to first. Lizzie swallowed down the familiar edge of hurt. It didn't matter it had been *her* who'd been there every day – feeding, clothing, taxying and caring for them – she'd quickly become the invisible mum they could just take for granted. Mark got the calls for advice. Not her.

Lizzie shook her head. She didn't want to go there. Not this morning.

'Coffee!' she muttered, making her way into The Sardine.

'That – we can do!'

The smiling face that greeted her wiped every single uncomfortable thought from Lizzie's head.

'Ethel!' she gasped, hurrying to the counter.

'Hello Lizzie, lovely!' Ethel bustled out from behind the counter and wrapped her up in a huge hug.

'You look wonderful!' said Ethel, pulling back again and looking her over from head to toe.

'I was about to say the same!' said Lizzie with a laugh. Ethel hadn't aged a day since she'd last seen her. In fact, Lizzie was convinced that if anything, she actually looked younger.

'Well, that's what being in love can do for you,' said Ethel with a grin.

'Wait… what?' laughed Lizzie. 'Has the entire town fallen in love in the decade I've been away?'

'Pretty much!' chuckled Ethel.

'I just bumped into Lionel, and he said-'

'Oh yes – *quite* the to-do, him and Mary,' nodded Ethel.

'Do I know Mary?' said Lizzie, wracking her brains.

'I should think so,' said Ethel, 'seeing as you went to school here, and so did your little ones.'

'Mrs Scott?!?!' said Lizzie, her eyes wide.

'You'd better believe it!' laughed Ethel. 'Now *that* was a love story decades in the making. Not like my Charlie. That was completely out of the blue.'

'Charlie… Charlie Endicott? Up at the allotments?' said Lizzie, thinking hard as all the old names started to come back to her.

'That's him,' said Ethel.

'And how long has this little fling been going on?' said Lizzie.

'Ooh, a little while,' said Ethel breezily. 'And it's a bit more than a fling. He asked me to marry him!'

'Not you too!' laughed Lizzie. 'I go and get unmarried, and you lot do the exact opposite.'

'Something in the water in Seabury, to be sure,' said Ethel. 'You'd better watch out.'

'Nah – thanks all the same,' Lizzie snorted. 'I'm done with all that.'

'We'll see,' said Ethel raising her eyebrows.

'No – really,' said Lizzie, more forcefully. 'I want my life back. I never wanted to leave Seabury – and now, there's not a single soul on earth who can make me leave again.'

'Good for you,' said Ethel with a little nod. 'I'm just saying… when the right person comes along, it doesn't mean you have to lose the other things you love.'

'Don't get me wrong, I'm really happy for you – and Lionel!' said Lizzie quickly before Ethel could go any further. 'But to be honest, I'm happy to spend the rest of my life having a torrid affair with Seabury, thanks!'

'Well – *that* I can understand,' said Ethel with a laugh. 'And how are the girls? I'm guessing all grown up by now?'

Lizzie nodded, grateful for the change of subject. 'Yup – they don't need me anymore – so I'm free to do what I want.'

'You're free… but the girls will always need you,' said Ethel, shooting her a soft look.

Lizzie felt her smile growing a bit tight. That had gone from one sticky subject to another in record timing!

'Let me get you that coffee!' said Ethel, clearly sensing her discomfort.

'That would be fab!' said Lizzie, glad to be on slightly less gnarly territory again. She took a deep breath. As much as it was lovely being in here, perhaps it was time to get back to work. Yes – what she really needed was to get busy bringing her new dreams to life. 'Any chance I could get it to take away?'

'Of course!' said Ethel. 'Anything to eat?'

Lizzie thought longingly of the pastry she'd promised herself for a moment before deciding that perhaps something a little bit more substantial might be a better choice.

'A sandwich, maybe?' she said doubtfully.

'We've got pretty much every filling imaginable,' said Ethel, 'so there's bound to be something you fancy!'

Lizzie had a quick look down the long menu Ethel handed her and opted for bree and grapes along with a fancy salad before plopping down onto a chair to wait.

'So... do you own this place?' she asked, watching as Ethel pulled together various ingredients on the counter.

'Not me – I'm just holding the fort!' said Ethel. 'Kate Hardy owns it – you remember her, I'm sure? She's a bit younger than you I think...'

'I remember her,' said Lizzie. 'Lived with her dad?'

'Yes!' said Ethel. 'Lovely man. So sad she lost him so young. Anyway, Kate and her other half are on holiday. Sarah – that's our young superstar baker – is doing the last of her coursework this next few weeks so she's not around as much either.'

'Blimey – and here I was thinking this place was quiet,' laughed Lizzie.

'Rarely,' said Ethel.

Lizzie grinned at her. Well, that certainly boded well for her plans!

'Doesn't Lou who rented my house work here too?' said Lizzie

Ethel nodded. 'Yup – she's off on the sandwich rounds at the moment. She splits her time between here and Pebble Street.'

'I can't wait to meet her,' said Lizzie. 'She seemed so lovely on the phone. I felt really bad about asking her to leave when I decided to move back.'

'Well, you mustn't!' said Ethel, wielding a vicious-looking knife as she chopped and sliced away merrily at the salad for her sandwich. 'She's happy as Larry in her new place – and I think being able to stay in your cottage was just the stepping stone she needed.'

'I'm so glad!' said Lizzie. 'She left me a gorgeous card, you know?'

Ethel nodded. 'She was desperate to leave you flowers too but she wasn't sure when you'd arrive!'

'Me neither!' laughed Lizzie. 'It took me way longer to pack than I'd been anticipating!'

'Always does,' said Ethel, adding handfuls of grapes to what was shaping up to be the biggest sandwich Lizzie had ever seen. 'Anyway, you're here now… you can take your time and settle in properly.'

'You're right,' said Lizzie with a happy sigh. 'You

know, I can't believe Lou works for Veronica Hughes!'

'Ooh, you really *are* out of touch,' said Ethel, placing a fat paper bag containing her sandwich onto the counter before turning to fill a puck with coffee. 'Veronica's long gone. Lionel owns Pebble Street now!'

'What?!' gasped Lizzie.

'Yes… didn't he tell you?'

Lizzie shook her head, her eyes wide. 'No – he was too busy telling me about his engagement!'

'Typical Lionel,' laughed Ethel fondly. 'Well yes – he bought the hotel, and his niece Hattie is head chef there. The food is wonderful – you'll have to try it!'

'Little Hattie who used to come down every summer holiday and cause mayhem?' said Lizzie, as an image of the wild little girl came to mind – always scruffy, always the ringleader.

'That's the one,' said Ethel.

'Blimey… and here I was thinking I could come back, safe in the knowledge that Seabury wouldn't have changed at all,' said Lizzie.

'Seabury might not have changed much,' said Ethel, 'but its people have.'

'So it seems,' sighed Lizzie. 'So it seems.'

CHAPTER 3

'Right, that's you all set, then?' said Ethel, handing over the biggest takeaway cup of coffee Lizzie had ever seen.

'I might be set for life with this monster!' she laughed, taking a sip and closing her eyes for a moment. She could almost feel the caffeine getting to work.

'Well... I'm guessing you probably need it,' said Ethel. 'Rumour is, you're going to be busy starting up a business?'

Lizzie's eyes flew open and she stared at Ethel in surprise. Was she just fishing or did she really know something? She'd barely told a soul about her plans for the Old Grain Store – she was far too superstitious for that. What if it all fell through?! There were several things she still wanted to get in place before she was ready to announce it to the world. After all, she didn't want to disappoint anyone – least of all herself.

Maybe Ethel was just fishing… but then again, that comment had been weirdly specific!

'I'm just a bit tired,' she hedged, hoping she might be able to escape without having to tell an outright lie.

'Well, maybe head home and put your feet up then?' said Ethel with a sly look on her face.

Lizzie grinned. Her old friend was clearly angling for more information, but right now she wasn't about to give in. Not yet. Then again, she did need to pick someone's brain about a few things, and who better to ask than Ethel?!

'I meant to ask,' she said, trying to sound innocent and unconcerned, 'does old Bob Jackson still do window cleaning?'

'No dear,' said Ethel. 'A young chap called Liam does that now – amongst other things. I can always ask him to pop around and see you if you'd like. Is this for your cottage… or the Old Grain Store?'

Lizzie had to fight the urge to gawp at Ethel's almost supernatural ability to gather information that simply wasn't available to the general public. She was going to *have* to tell her now, wasn't she?

Anyway, it wasn't like she was doing anything wrong. She'd bought the old building fair and square, and she was well within her rights to press it into service. She'd already jumped through all the hoops with the local council... ah... maybe that's where Ethel had been getting her information from! It was all meant to be confidential, of course, but she'd been warned that local set-ups could be about as airtight as a sieve!

'Yes – it's for the Old Grain Store,' she said, deciding to let Ethel in on that part of the secret at least. She'd keep the exact nature of her new venture to herself for just a couple more days... though she knew it wouldn't be long before it was all over town.

'Are you going to tell me what you're up to in there?' said Ethel with an air of amusement.

'Can I tell you in a couple of days?' said Lizzie, suddenly feeling like an awkward teenager rather than a budding businesswoman.

'Of course!' laughed Ethel. 'But if there's anything I can do to help, you know where to find me.'

'Thanks,' said Lizzie gratefully. 'Well, if you don't mind sending this Liam guy my way in the next few days, that'd be a huge help. The pigeons have made a right old mess. I mean – the windows are almost opaque – and that's just on the inside! I haven't managed to get the old wooden shutters open yet to see what the outside is like – that's a job for this morning. I sprayed the hinges with WD40 yesterday, but it's like the blasted things have been welded closed!'

'I'm not surprised,' said Ethel. 'They've probably

not been opened up for about fifty years. After all, I don't think anyone's used the place for…'

'Decades?' laughed Lizzie. She'd certainly never known it to be in use.

'It's been boarded up for so long, I don't think anyone around here even notices it's there anymore,' said Ethel. 'It's just part of the Seabury landscape… like the hills!'

Lizzie nodded. She could only pray that changed when she was ready to open her doors. She had grand plans for the old place… as soon as she'd finished evicting the spiders, sweeping up the pigeon poop and getting some light inside. With any luck, the town would welcome the change… though it wasn't exactly something the people of Seabury were known for!

'Don't worry,' said Ethel, clearly mistaking her frown as concern about the state of the windows rather than the magnitude of what she was undertaking, 'I'm bound to see Liam around later. I'll send him straight over.'

'Well… I'll be a bit busy this morning…' said Lizzie.

Her list of jobs for the day was so long, the last thing she needed was a curious stranger turning up and expecting a guided tour.

'Don't worry,' said Ethel. 'Liam's not likely to be free until late afternoon even if I do manage to pin him down. Anyway, it's due to rain in a little while, so he'll probably just stick his head in to arrange a time with you.'

'Rain? Really?' said Lizzie, turning to stare out of the café. It still looked pretty sunny out there to her!

'My Charlie's never wrong about the weather!' said Ethel. 'He's good with things like that. You can trust him to know everything about rain… and potatoes. You mark my words - we're in for a downpour at eleven twenty-three.'

'Right – I'll bear that in mind!' laughed Lizzie. 'Thanks Ethel.'

'Don't work too hard!' said Ethel cheerily, waving her out of The Sardine.

Lizzie barely registered the walk along the seafront to the Old Grain Store at the far end of West Beach. In her head, she was busy running through the list of things she needed to do before she could even consider opening her doors. She had an electrician booked in a couple of days to bring in new wiring and lights… and she knew that would make all the difference in transforming the space into the image she'd been carrying around in her head ever since she'd started on this hair-brained plan of hers.

As lovely as it would be to put her feet up for a couple of days and enjoy being back in Seabury, she simply wouldn't be able to relax and enjoy it. For one thing, she wanted to be up and running as soon as possible. For another - she was simply too excited to rest! Sitting still for more than a few minutes when she had a dream to bring to life just wasn't going to happen.

Slurping her coffee, which seemed to be practically bottomless, Lizzie came to a standstill opposite the Old Grain Store and rested against the railings for a moment, staring at the building she'd lost her heart to. She was sure it just looked like a total wreck to anyone else, but to her – it was the start of a dream come true.

Constructed out of huge slabs of local, grey stone, The Old Grain Store boasted two of the most marvellous wide, arched windows that looked out over the sea. Right now, they were still covered with the heavy wooden shutters... or at least, what was left of them. Lizzie would have to do some repairs to get them looking their best again – but it wasn't just about prettying the place up! The shutters were the perfect protection against winter storms blowing up from the sea – and they wouldn't hurt when it came to a bit of added security either!

'Right!' said Lizzie, gearing herself up ready for action. She'd get those shutters open if it was the only thing she managed to achieve before lunchtime.

Jogging across the road, she balanced her coffee on the wide stone doorstep. She couldn't resist giving the shutters a quick yank before she went inside... it was always possible she'd simply not given it enough welly the previous day. Maybe the spray had worked its magic by now!

'Come on, come on!' she muttered, wrapping her fingers around the edge of the wood and pulling with all her might. It was no use. Just like she'd said to Ethel – they almost felt like they'd been welded in place!

'Fine. I'm bringing out the big guns!' she said, digging out the huge old key from her shoulder bag and unlocking the wooden double doors. Flakes of red paint coated her hands as she pushed her way inside, but Lizzie simply brushed her palms against her dungarees. She was on a mission!

'Now… where did I put that can?' she said, pausing just inside the doorway. As her eyes started to adjust to the gloom, Lizzie broke into a slow, wide smile.

Heaven. She'd somehow managed to land herself in heaven.

A delighted shiver ran right down her spine, and Lizzie hugged herself in a moment of pure joy. This knackered, dusty old stone barn full of pigeon poop and goodness knows what else was the start of something incredible… she just knew it!

'Right,' she said again, pulling herself together and wandering over to where she'd set up a makeshift workbench. It was probably the only thing she'd managed to get organised since she'd arrived – but she'd needed somewhere to set out all her tools. Well... *most* of her tools. There would be plenty more to come!

Lizzie scanned the selection, hunting for the little blue can.

'Ah ha!' she cheered, spotting it hiding behind the box containing her hand-held compressor.

Lizzie grabbed it and gave it a shake. Good – it was still practically full. It might take the entire can to free those blighters up, but she'd have some daylight in here if it was the last thing she did today. Besides, if this Liam chap turned up, she'd need him to be able to actually *get* to the windows, wouldn't she?!

As an afterthought, Lizzie grabbed a lump hammer before hurrying back outside... just in case they needed a little extra *coaxing*. She liberally sprayed one set of hinges and had just turned to move over to the other window when she spotted an ominous bank of dark clouds marching across the sea towards her.

'Huh – maybe Charlie was right after all!' she muttered, raising her eyebrows. In that case, she'd better get on with it! If she was going to be stuck inside all afternoon, a bit of daylight would definitely be in order!

Lizzie quickly sprayed the hinges of the second set of shutters and then hurried back over to the first lot again, pocketing the can as she went. She took a firm hold of the ancient wood and gave it an experimental tug.

Nothing.

'Ah, come on you miserable git!' she growled. 'Fine... if that's the way you want it... you leave me with no choice!'

Lizzie grabbed the lump hammer. She knew it probably wasn't the best plan she'd ever had, but frankly, if she couldn't get the old things moving, she was going to have to cut them down anyway.

She'd just start light... nothing too full-on...

Lizzie tapped at the heavy, rusted metal right the way along the join. She did the same on the second hinge and then gave the shutter another tug. It shifted about a millimetre forwards, and then back again when she shoved it. Well, at least that was encouraging! She gave the hinges another, slightly more hefty tap or two with the hammer and then continued to wobble the shutter back and forth, easing it a little further each time.

Two minutes – and several more squirts later – and the shutter was open, leaving a little pile of rusty flakes on the pavement beneath it.

Not daring to stop for a victory jig, Lizzie quickly got to work on the other side, which didn't take nearly as long because she wasn't half as timid with the hammer this time. She was just about to head over to the second window when a large, cold drop of rain landed right on the back of her neck. In the time it took for her to turn around to eyeball the grumpy black clouds that were now almost directly overhead, the single drop had turned into a pelting curtain of rain.

'One window will have to do!' she laughed, bolting back inside just in time to hear the heavens open behind her.

Spinning on the spot to stare out at the downpour, Lizzie ran her grubby fingers through her already damp hair, then promptly cursed herself. Great – now she probably smelled like she'd washed her hair with WD40. Ah well – it was one of her favourite smells on earth, so why not! Besides, it wasn't like there was anyone else to be bothered by it, was there?!

Lizzie glanced down at her watch and grinned. She had to hand it to Charlie – he was spot on with his timing when it came to the weather forecast!

Glancing out through the curtain of rain again, Lizzie caught sight of a young couple on the other side of the road. They had their heads bowed against the rain as they dashed through the downpour, hand-in-hand. She could hear them giggling, and she couldn't help but smile.

Seabury really did seem to be full of loved-up couples… but that wasn't something that interested her in the slightest. Lizzie was done with all that nonsense. She would be quite happy here, tinkering in her new space and helping her customers.

A brief bubble of nerves surfaced as she wondered whether she'd really managed to make a go of this after all. What if there *weren't* any customers?!

'Don't be an idiot!' she said, rolling her eyes.

What she needed was a bit of positive action to get her back in the right frame of mind. Maybe it was time to do something symbolic.

Lizzie hurried over to her workbench and rummaged around until she found the old brass bell she'd brought with her. She'd bought it ages ago in an antique shop in Bath – hoping that one day she'd get to hear it go 'ping' the first time a customer entered her very own shop. She'd held onto the old thing for years, and it had become a talisman – a sign that she would make her dream come true... eventually.

Pocketing a couple of screws, Lizzie grabbed a pencil, her drill and a little stepladder. Sure – she was a long way from welcoming any customers just yet, but when she *did* finally open her doors, the little bell would remind her that she'd been brave and followed her dreams every time it sounded.

By the time she clambered back down the ladder, Lizzie was grinning from ear to ear. The bell certainly looked the part... now it was time to test it out.

She gave the door an experimental open and close, and couldn't help a *whoop* of pure joy escaping as a jaunty *ping* echoed across the Old Grain Store. It was perfect!

Now it was time to get back to a decidedly less symbolic job. There was nothing exciting or inspiring about the amount of pigeon poop she still needed to clear up before she could even think about bringing any stock in here!

Lizzie grabbed a broom and had just yanked an uncomfortable mask down over her nose and mouth when her newly installed bell rang out again. The unexpected *ping!* sent a shiver of excitement down her spine.

'Sorry!' she called over her shoulder, her voice muffled. 'I'm not open yet!'

'I can see that!' came a deep, amused rumble. 'I'm here about the windows.'

The voice was familiar…

Lizzie turned, dragging her mask back down.

Blimey!

'Hi!' she said, her voice several octaves higher than usual as she stared at the handsome face in front of her. She quickly cleared her throat. 'Hi!' she said again, this time at a slightly more human pitch. 'Sorry… erm… dust!'

'Right!' said the guy, quirking a grin at her. 'I'm Liam, by the way.'

'Hi!' she said again. Okay - that was her third *hi* in a row… what on earth was wrong with her?! Still, at least she knew his name now – because, of course, this was the same guy she'd met earlier on the beach.

Luckily, Liam didn't seem to have noticed that she was behaving like a total nutter. He was too busy staring around the half-cleared space, taking it all in.

'I'm Lizzie,' she said. 'Lizzie Moore.'

'Yes – I know,' said Liam, turning back to her with a grin that almost made her crumple to the floor in a jellified heap. 'We met earlier, remember? And anyway, Ethel told me. I have to say, it's lovely to see someone doing something with this old place.'

'Thanks,' said Lizzie. 'I've got quite a way to go yet, but I'll get there! Anyway – it'd be great to get the windows cleaned properly if you can fit me in sometime? I've only just managed to get the shutters open on one side so far – I'm afraid I was rained off midway – but I'll get the other one sorted out as soon as the rain stops.'

Lizzie closed her mouth, suddenly aware that she was gabbling. Why on earth was she feeling nervous? All she was doing was arranging for someone to clean the windows for heaven's sake!

'I can pop back tomorrow morning if that works for you?' said Liam.

'Yes please' said Lizzie with a nod. 'They'll need doing inside and out.'

Duh! Like that wasn't obvious!

'No problem,' he said with an easy shrug. 'And you're opening…?'

Lizzie wasn't sure if he was asking for the date, or angling to find out *what* she was planning to open.

'Soon,' she said with a smile she hoped was vaguely enigmatic rather than mildly deranged. 'Very soon.'

'Right. Brilliant,' said Liam, his eyes twinkling as he smiled at her. 'I'll see you tomorrow then.'

With one last grin in her direction, Liam ambled back out into the rain.

Lizzie reached out and put a hand against the wall to steady herself - she was feeling a bit weak at the knees, and more than a little bit dazed. What on earth was wrong with her? Probably just an overload of caffeine on an empty stomach. Maybe it was time to wash her hands and make a start on that sandwich!

CHAPTER 4

By the time she got home that evening, Lizzie was dusty, dirty, sweaty and exhausted. She was also happier than she could remember being in years.

She'd managed to clear the rest of the floor and had even made several repairs to the interior woodwork. Tomorrow, she would be ready to start painting and then... then it would be time to start ordering stock.

Shrugging out of her wet coat, Lizzie hung it on one of the pegs in the hall before doing a little jig of pure happiness. It burst out of her and she laughed at herself for being a total idiot.

The minute she stopped dancing though, a wave of pure exhaustion crashed over her. Okay – so it looked like she'd just used up her last scrap of energy.

Tonight was going to be about putting her feet up and nothing else!

Lizzie edged along the hallway, squeezing between the two towering walls of boxes that were piled high on either side. She knew she really should spend a bit of time finding new homes for everything and unpacking a bit, but frankly, she was far more interested in getting the shop up to scratch first. She didn't mind living out of boxes for a little while and camping in the cottage. There would be plenty of time to get this place sorted out after the shop was up and running.

In any case, Lou had looked after the cottage so well that it had been immaculate when she'd arrived. That had made things a lot easier for her. At least she hadn't had to do a deep clean on top of everything else.

As much as she just wanted to flop down onto the sofa and close her eyes, Lizzie forced herself to head into the kitchen first. There was one thing she needed to do before she crashed out completely. She knew she should forage in her meagre supplies for something to eat – after all, the sandwich had been hours ago - but the bottle of wine Lou had left for her was singing a siren song right now!

Even though the cottage had been her home twice before – when she was a kid living here with her grandparents, and then again as a newlywed – it definitely didn't feel like hers yet this time around. It wasn't just the cottage either. Lizzie had a feeling that it was going to take a bit of time for her to readjust and relax back into the slower pace of life here in Seabury after such a long time away. She was more than ready for it though.

Taking a moment to lean against the kitchen sink and peer out of the window, Lizzie marvelled that this was *her* view - and no one could ever take it away from her again.

To be fair, it hadn't really been Mark's fault they'd had to leave Seabury. His job in Bristol just became more and more demanding – they'd needed the money but he'd started to resent the time away from his family. So they'd made the decision that it would be best for everyone to relocate to be nearer to his office.

The girls had been over the moon of course. Yes, it had meant them both finding new friends and getting used to new schools, but the thrill of living somewhere there was so much to do more than made up for it – for them at least. Lizzie had simply gone into mourning for her old life in Seabury… and had never quite managed to escape that feeling.

Well, she was home now – and she didn't need to hold on to all that sadness anymore. Lizzie blew out a long breath, focusing on the view.

The horizon was filled with grey clouds and a choppy, slightly grumpy-looking sea – and she couldn't imagine anything more beautiful. This was exactly where she belonged.

'Right!' she said, doing her best to bully herself into action. 'What on earth did I do with that corkscrew?!'

Flinging open one drawer after another, she finally laid her hands on one - though she didn't recognise it. Maybe Lou had left it behind so that she had the bare essentials covered! She'd have to remember to thank her when she finally met the woman.

'Damnit!' she muttered. She might have a corkscrew in her hand, but there was no way she was going to sip her much-needed wine out of the coffee mug she'd used for breakfast. Or at least, not without a quick scout through a couple of boxes first!

Dragging her feet back into the hallway, Lizzie made a beeline for the first cardboard box marked "kitchen". Grabbing her house keys from the pocket of her dungarees, she used them to slice through the tape.

Opening it up, she rummaged through a bunch of cleaning products and roll upon roll of bin bags. Lizzie sighed, wishing she'd listened to the voice of reason in her head that had kept prodding her to label the boxes more carefully while she'd been packing. Unfortunately – that voice had sounded annoyingly like Mark – so she'd roundly ignored it!

Just as she was tunnelling through the fourth box

in the stack – that was looking decidedly more useful considering she'd just unearthed a bunch of tea towels wrapped around various breakables – she caught the muffled sound of her mobile vibrating.

'Who on earth can that be?!' she muttered, straightening up.

Now, where on earth had she left that blasted thing? It definitely wasn't in the pocket of her dungarees, otherwise she'd have hit the roof! Maybe in her old fleece that was hanging over by the front door?

Clambering over the mess of boxes, Lizzie managed to yank the phone out of the fleece, scattering bits of oily rag and old cable ties all over the floor in the process. Just as she went to answer it, the buzzing stopped.

'Typical!' she sighed, eyeballing the screen to see if it had been anyone important.

Missed Call: Jenna

Before Lizzie even had time to wonder what miracle was at work to make her youngest call her from halfway around the world, the phone started to vibrate again.

'Jenna?' she said in surprise.

'Hey, mum.'

It was a terrible line – and Lizzie felt like she could hear every single one of the miles between her and her daughter.

'How are you, love?' said Lizzie. 'And... *where* are you?'

'Still in Morocco!' said Jenna. 'And not good. The van's broken down again.'

Lizzie rolled her eyes. This was nothing new. That van had been a liability from the moment her daughter had set off in it. Luckily, Jenna took after her rather than Mark. She was good at fixing things and didn't mind getting her hands dirty, so she'd managed to keep it limping along far longer than anyone had expected.

'Oh dear – so how long will it take you to fix it this time?' said Lizzie.

'It's dead this time, mum!' said Jenna.

Lizzie paused. She was pretty sure that was a wobble she'd just heard in her daughter's voice.

'Surely it's not that bad?' she said, hoping she sounded sympathetic rather than dismissive.

'Erm… there was a lot of smoke,' said Jenna. 'And… well… fire actually. After a mini explosion under the bonnet.'

'What?!' gasped Lizzie. 'Are you okay? You're not hurt, are you?'

'I'm fine. Really I'm fine…' said Jenna, though it was now obvious she was crying.

Lizzie swallowed hard. Jenna wasn't prone to getting upset about anything… so now she was really concerned!

'I rang dad but I couldn't reach him,' Jenna continued with a sob. 'He's probably off with that idiot wife of his... why's he never there when I need him?!'

Lizzie bit her lip and did her best to ignore the spike of hurt as it hit her in the chest. As usual, Jenna had gone to her father first. As usual, Lizzie was the backup solution. Right now though, none of that mattered. She just needed to calm Jenna down and figure out how she could help.

'I'm stuck mum, completely stuck. I've run out of money and I don't know what to do and I just want to come home!' Jenna's voice got higher and higher as her words tumbled out.

'Okay, love,' said Lizzie calmly, 'take a breath. We'll get this sorted out, don't worry!'

Lizzie listened as Jenna blubbed on the other end of the line, clearly trying to regain control of her sobs. Her heart felt like it would break at the sound. Her youngest had always been so independent and confident – a cheerful, bouncy child who'd turned into a beauty with the biggest case of wanderlust she'd ever come across. It was rare she ever asked for anything - and now, here she was, sobbing her heart out, clearly exhausted and completely freaked out.

'What can I do?' said Lizzie, injecting as much calm into her voice as she could muster. She needed Jenna to breathe and think as rationally as she could.

'I've got nowhere to go, mum,' she said. 'I really need your help.'

'Just tell me what you need, and we'll sort it out,' said Lizzie.

'Can I come home?'

'Of course,' said Lizzie, her heart melting at how young Jenna suddenly sounded.

'I promise it won't be for too long,' said Jenna quickly, the relief evident in her voice. 'I just… need to regroup. Then I can gather enough money for a new van and get going again.'

'We'll sort all that out when you're back,' said Lizzie, desperately trying to remain the voice of reason in the chaos, even though she was already wondering how on earth she was going to clear enough space between all the boxes to fit another person into the cottage. Still - it would be wonderful to see her daughter – if totally unexpected.

'Love – just to warn you, it's a bit chaotic here. I'm still living out of boxes,' she said, figuring it was only right to give Jenna fair warning.

'Mum – I've been living in the back of a van for over a year!' said Jenna with a slightly soggy laugh. 'It'll be like paradise, no matter what state it's in!'

Lizzie breathed out a sigh of relief. It sounded like the carefree, easy-going Jenna was back in charge again.

'Okay,' she said. 'Book your flights home and let me know when you need picking up.'

'Right,' said Jenna. 'Erm… mum… I don't have any cash.'

'Right. Right,' said Lizzie. She'd somehow conveniently forgotten that bit of the conversation. 'Well... okay...'

Lizzie rubbed her face, trying to muster enough brain power to figure out what to do next. Considering she'd just moved house as well as coughing up the cash for the Old Grain Store, she wasn't exactly rolling in money right now either. The savings she had left were set aside for the renovations and new stock.

She'd just have to figure that out, wouldn't she? Jenna needed her help – and that had to come first. Besides, having her home for a little while would be wonderful. Not exactly restful... but that's what being a mum was all about, wasn't it?!

'Let me know how much your flight is going to be, and I'll transfer some cash to you tomorrow, okay?' she said. 'Enough to get you home, at least.'

'Thanks mum, you're the best,' said Jenna. 'But... can you do it now? I don't have enough left for food... or a taxi back to town.'

Lizzie let out a long sigh. It looked like that glass of wine was going to have to wait.

CHAPTER 5

Lizzie yawned widely, bowing her head against the rain as she ambled down the hill towards town. It would probably have been more sensible to drive considering she was going to be decidedly soggy by the time she got to the Old Grain Store. But she was having a hell of a job keeping her eyes open - so there was no way she'd trust herself behind the wheel. Besides... driving would have entailed knowing where her car keys were... and that was beyond her this morning!

Even though she'd been exhausted when she'd finally fallen into bed the previous night, Lizzie hadn't slept well. She'd spent several nerve-jangling hours dealing with international money transfers – no mean feat with her patchy internet connection! Then she'd had to make sure that Jenna actually *booked* her flight home, rather than just ambling off to another country now that she had some funds at her disposal.

Not that Lizzie would have minded - but there had been something in her youngest daughter's voice that had troubled her - and she wanted to make sure that everything was okay before Jenna continued her nomadic wanderings. After all, there was only so much parenting she could do at one in the morning when the child in question was on an entirely different continent.

And now... Lizzie had her own issues to face. There was so much she needed to do to the Old Grain Store, but after bailing Jenna out, her next job had to be wrapping her head around the numbers and what they might mean for her grand plans.

Lizzie blew out an irritable breath as the weight of a bad mood settled on her shoulders. She was frazzled and exhausted... and now she was worried about money too. Suddenly, her triumphant return to Seabury didn't feel like the idyllic lifestyle choice she'd been hoping for.

Resisting the urge to head straight for The Sardine for a giant caffeine fix, Lizzie forced herself on through the rain. She'd have much rather stayed at the cottage this morning while she juggled her books, but at the last minute, she remembered that she'd arranged to let Liam in to clean the windows... and that meant unsticking the second set of shutters too!

How she was going to make it through the day

without a decent coffee was anyone's guess, but she was going to have to watch every penny for a little while... and that included treats from The Sardine. Who knew that last-minute flights from Morocco cost so much!

As she approached the Old Grain Store, Lizzie spotted a bucket of soapy water under one of the windows. Then, with a little flicker of gratitude, she noticed that the second set of shutters was open. Liam had clearly arrived early and worked a bit of magic... before disappearing into thin air!

Shrugging, Lizzie yanked the keys out of her pocket, keen to see what it was like inside with both the windows open and about an inch of dust washed away. She had just pushed the doors open when she spotted a man heading towards her through the rain.

Lizzie waved, and Liam did a kind of half-hearted salute, raising two takeaway coffee cups in greeting. He was clearly unable to say anything because he had a paper bag dangling from his lips.

Feeling her mood lift at such a welcome sight, Lizzie grinned and hurried towards him. As she reached out and took the paper bag gently from his mouth, something inside her fluttered - the action was strangely intimate!

'Morning!' said Liam, grinning at her. 'For some reason, I thought you might fancy some caffeine... and a pastry?'

'You might just be my favourite person in the

whole world right now!' she said, doing her best not to go weak at the knees.

'I don't know about that!' laughed Liam. 'But Ethel told me what coffee you ordered yesterday, and the custard pastries were fresh from the oven... so I couldn't resist, could I?!'

Lizzie unrolled the top of the paper bag, and the scent of still-warm pastries floated up to greet her, instantly dissolving the last remnants of her bad mood.

'Yum,' she sighed. 'Thank you – *and* for getting the second shutter opened too – that saves me a job!'

'No probs!' said Liam, handing her one of the coffees. 'A bit of brute force and ignorance did the trick.'

'That and the entire can of WD40 I doused it in yesterday!' laughed Lizzie.

Liam grinned and grabbed the bucket with his spare hand before following her inside.

'Wow – it's really made a difference!' said Lizzie, staring around, finally getting to see the space in the daylight for the first time.

'You wait until I've done the inside!' said Liam. 'You won't know the place.'

Lizzie watched as he put his coffee down on one corner of her bench, clearly eager to get straight to work. She knew she should do the same... but that didn't stop her from watching as he began to sluice down the inside of the old windows, the water quickly turning grey with decades-old dust.

It was completely mesmeric – maybe not the gross water, but certainly Liam's rhythmic movements as he worked, squeegee in hand, drawing filthy water away from the glass and turning the world outside crystal clear, one swipe at a time.

If only it was so easy to wipe away the worries that were swirling around in her head again! Lizzie sighed. It was time to head through to the little back room she had earmarked as a staff room. She needed to focus, and there was no way she could do that while Liam's decidedly toned arms were busy at work right in front of her!

Grabbing an old pencil and scrap of paper from the workbench, Lizzie hurried through to the tiny room which currently only boasted a wooden stool and an ancient table that rocked slightly.

Sinking down onto the stool, Lizzie took a fortifying swig of coffee and then – before she could chicken out - she started to jot down the depressing figures that had been dancing around her head all night.

It didn't take long before she was frowning down at a long list of numbers. This was even worse than she'd thought. Now that she had the hard evidence right in front of her, she couldn't ignore the truth of the matter.

After paying for the extortionate flight, along

with the extra cash she'd sent so that she knew Jenna had enough in her account to keep her safe and fed until she got back to Seabury – Lizzie's precarious finances had now entered official disaster stage.

There wasn't enough money left for her to set up her business so that she'd be ready to open… at least, not in the way she'd planned. She might be able to stretch to about half the stock she had on her list… but there certainly wasn't enough for all the tools she wanted. There might be just about enough to cover the basic renovations the Old Grain Store still needed, but what good was a shop without the stock to fill it? And what use was a workshop minus the tools?

Had she really come this far, simply to be defeated by an exploding van in Morocco?

Lizzie dropped her pencil and sunk her head into both hands. There had to be a way around this… she just needed to figure out what it was. Not easy on so little sleep!

Heaving her head back out of her hands, Lizzie looked up only to find Liam standing in the doorway watching her.

'Sorry!' he said quickly. 'I was just wondering if you wanted me to do the windows back here too?'

Lizzie forced a smile and nodded. 'Yes please.'

'Okay. Cool.' Liam didn't move. He stood watching her for several long moments. 'Erm… is everything okay?'

Lizzie stared at him. She was desperate to have someone to share these worries with... but she'd barely told anyone about her plans for the Old Grain Store yet. Which was ridiculous considering she was planning on opening her doors in less than a month. Or... that *had* been the plan. Now everything was up in the air again, and there was a very real chance she might not be able to make this dream come true after all.

She desperately needed to talk to someone... and why *not* Liam. After all, he was standing there right in front of her and wasn't showing any signs of leaving her to it. Sure, the pair of them had only just met, but who else was there? Certainly not Mark... or the girls.

Liam *might* understand. One thing was for certain - she'd sat here in complete silence for long enough if his look of mounting concern was anything to go by.

'I want to open a bicycle shop,' said Lizzie. 'With bikes to hire, and a repair workshop too.'

She paused, not quite knowing what to expect now that she'd said it out loud. Lizzie wasn't really sure what she was waiting for – maybe for the sky to come crashing down, or for someone to start pointing and laughing. But Liam said nothing. There was no undermining smirk. No throwaway comment. He just stood there, patiently waiting for her to continue.

'Right,' he said when it became clear she wasn't

going to say anything else. 'Brilliant idea - so… what's up?'

Lizzie shrugged and then cleared her throat. It didn't work. She still couldn't get any more words to come out.

'I remember you, you know,' said Liam quietly, leaning his weight against the grubby door frame. 'As a kid, I mean.'

'You do?' said Lizzie in surprise.

'I went to school here too - just for a couple of terms. I stayed with my old aunt for a while and Mrs Scott let me join in with her lessons.'

'Oh wow!' said Lizzie, her eyes widening as the vague memory of a gangly, shy little boy rose to the surface. 'What were we then… about… ten years old?'

'About that,' said Liam with a nod. 'Anyway – I remember you. You were always zooming around on a bike… and when anyone's seat needed adjusting, or there was a puncture to be repaired, you were always the one to fix it! My chain came off once and I landed up in a hedge. You just whizzed over, pulled me out of the nettles – sorted out the bike and then zoomed off again.'

'I did?' laughed Lizzie.

Liam nodded. 'No one could keep up with you even though plenty tried. You were *so* cool - I don't think I even managed to get up the nerve to say thanks!'

'I'll let you off,' said Lizzie, feeling slightly dazed.

'Cheers!' said Liam. 'Anyway, if there's even the slightest hint of that awesome ten-year-old left in you – then I can't imagine a better thing for you to be planning!'

Lizzie smiled at him. He was right, of course – even her nan had called her Little Miss Fix-It when she was a kid. That's why her plans for this place had felt so much like a dream – it was her chance to embrace something that had always been a part of her.

'Erm… you're frowning again!' said Liam.

'Yeah…' sighed Lizzie.

'So it wasn't just a crisis of confidence then?' guessed Liam.

'More like a crisis of the wallet variety,' sighed Lizzie. 'I had everything worked out to perfection before I moved, but…'

'What happened?' said Liam.

'Daughter disaster!' said Lizzie with a weak smile.

'Now that's *definitely* something I can empathise with!' said Liam with a little smile.

'You've got daughters too?' asked Lizzie with interest.

'Just the one,' he nodded. 'And it's always… interesting!'

'I hear you there,' she laughed. 'I've got two girls. How old's your little one.'

'Definitely not little anymore!' said Liam with a wide smile. 'Mid-twenties.'

'Mine too,' said Lizzie. 'I'd love to say they're all grown up, but…'

'Not so much?' said Liam.

Lizzie shook her head.

'Amy is a junior doctor,' said Liam. 'She's probably more responsible than both me and her mum put together… but she's still my little girl, you know?!'

Lizzie nodded, though she couldn't help but register a pang of disappointment at Liam's casual mention of his other half. But then, of course someone like Liam was taken. He was gorgeous… kind… good company… caring… and why did she care anyway? It wasn't like she was on the hunt for someone new – she already had more than enough issues to contend with.

'So… does Amy live close by?' she asked.

'Nah!' said Liam. 'She still lives with her mum up in the Midlands. Lucy's place is close to Amy's hospital, so that works out pretty well.'

'You must miss her?' said Lizzie, doing her best to ignore the fact that her treacherous brain started to shout *He's single! He's single!* on a loop.

'I do, but neither of us really see much of her, to be honest! She's always so busy.' Liam paused and ran his fingers through his hair. 'Anyway… that's enough about me. What's going on with your errant offspring… parent to parent?'

'Bit of a long story,' said Lizzie with a rueful smile.

'Isn't it always?' said Liam.

Lizzie nodded. 'Okay – so the highlights include an exploding van in Morocco and a deep-dive into the *bank of mum* to get back home.'

'Is this both the girls?' said Liam looking wide-eyed.

'Crikey, no.' Lizzie let out a long sigh. 'Megan wouldn't dream of doing anything so reckless as having fun. Anything that's not on her ten-year plan is left well and truly alone. No, this is my youngest, Jenna. She's been travelling for ages and I think everything has just suddenly unravelled a bit.'

'Well... it's good you can help her out, I guess. So... is she moving back to Seabury to stay with you and your husband?'

'Husband?' Lizzie let out a loud hoot of laughter.

'Oh...' said Liam. 'Sorry... I just assumed... and I didn't want to listen to any local gossip.'

'Well, this time the local gossip is probably pretty accurate. The husband became an un-husband quite a few years ago now. It's just me. Just the way I like it!'

'Well... okay,' said Liam, ruffling his hair again. 'Erm – good for you. So Jenna...?'

'Yep – she'll be back with me for a bit,' said Lizzie. 'The cottage is still a total mess of boxes, but I'll sort it.'

'Right...' said Liam, still watching her closely. 'Right... but... that doesn't quite explain why I just found you staring at that piece of paper like the world was coming to an end!'

Lizzie smiled at him, grateful that he was pushing the point because she'd quite like to forget about the whole thing by this point. She might as well tell him the full story now she'd got this far.

'The money I just used to bail Jenna out was meant to be for this place – stock, tools, the hire bikes... I mean, I'll still get there eventually... I'm just trying to figure out how.'

Liam nodded and scratched his chin, looking thoughtful. Or maybe he was just bored. Lizzie took in a deep breath, instantly wishing she'd kept it all to herself. Poor bloke – he'd only come to wash her windows, not to run a therapy session!

'You know,' said Liam slowly, still rubbing his chin, 'I might just know someone who can help out.'

'You... you do?' said Lizzie in surprise.

'I'm not promising anything,' he said, 'but there's definitely someone you should meet. What are you up to this afternoon?'

CHAPTER 6

*L*izzie stared at the wild, rambling hedges that lined the road on the way out of Seabury. Colours flew past Liam's van - a rush of lush greens dotted with the vibrant pink of Campions and the warm yellow of tall Buttercups. The rain seemed to have made everything brighter somehow, the colours more intense.

Cracking open the window, Lizzie took in a deep breath of air, sweet and heavy with the threat of more rain. She had to admit, she felt a bit odd right now. She was immensely uncomfortable about the fact that she'd somehow managed to commandeer Liam for the afternoon, ruining his plans in the process. At the same time, she felt relaxed and totally at ease in his company – which was a bit bizarre considering he was whisking her off to an undisclosed location with a vague promise of "knowing someone who might be able to help."

'Are you really sure you've got time for this?' she said, turning to him.

Liam flashed her a quick grin from the driver's seat. 'Seriously, will you stop worrying? I finished off my rounds this morning, and I only had a meeting with Ben planned for this afternoon – and he's already been called away to sort out someone's leaking toilet cistern!'

'Ben…?' said Lizzie, wracking her brain.

'He was at school the same time as Kate from the Sardine… and he used to hang out with Hattie whenever she visited Lionel. Ben and Hattie are an item these days!'

'Ooh, I remember my nan talking about him!' said Lizzie. 'Didn't he used to take himself to school in a boat or something?'

'That's him!' said Liam. 'Anyway, you need to know Ben – I'll make sure I introduce you. He's Seabury's handyman extraordinaire. Not that you need one, of course - but if you could ever do with an extra pair of hands, he's brilliant. He's always super busy though… so you can always ask me instead!'

'Thanks,' said Lizzie. 'So… do you guys work together?'

'Not yet,' said Liam.

'Sorry,' said Lizzie, 'I don't mean to be nosy… I just couldn't help noticing the bits and bobs you've got in the back of the van – it looks like you're ready for any eventuality!'

She'd actually been pretty jealous when Liam had opened the back up so that she could pop her bag in there. Sure, it was a total mess – but it was like a little workshop on wheels. He had his window-cleaning kit stashed to one side, and what looked like a couple of very well-stocked toolboxes piled up at the back next to a large mystery object under a tarp. Two or three deckchairs were stacked on top of everything else, awaiting a bit of TLC before any unsuspecting holidaymakers got themselves stuck in the broken frames.

'You know – you're going to have to be careful when Jenna gets here,' said Lizzie.

'Erm... why?' said Liam, looking bemused.

'This is exactly the kind of van she loves!'

'What, completely knackered?' he laughed.

'No, no!' said Lizzie, 'I meant she loves anything where she can just bung a mattress in the back before zooming off for another adventure!'

'She'd have a job getting all my stuff out first,' said Liam. 'I don't think I've completely emptied the back since I first got her.'

'Why would you when you've got it all arranged just the way you like it?' said Lizzie with a shrug.

'Exactly!' said Liam. 'Finally – someone who gets it!'

'So... if you don't work with Ben... what do you

do?' said Lizzie. 'Other than the deckchairs… and the windows…?'

She couldn't help being curious about this guy who'd just offered to whisk her off on some weird, magical mystery tour at the drop of a hat.

'I've got lots of bits and bobs going on,' said Liam. 'Seabury is a bit like that. Frankly – *I'm* a bit like that. I did try the whole steady career, nine-to-five thing for a while, but I hated it. I get bored quickly and I love to be outdoors… so I'm just building my life around that, really!'

'Why not!' said Lizzie. She loved his attitude, even if the idea of piecing together an income from lots of little jobs made her shiver.

'So yeah,' said Liam, 'there's the deckchairs - though that's just an excuse to hang around on the beach a lot. And then there are the window rounds a few times a week. I do some bits of gardening, and Ben and I might be teaming up too.'

'Doing what?' said Lizzie curiously.

'He's got requests for odd jobs coming out of his ears, and he's simply not got enough hours in the day to get through them all,' said Liam. 'He'd do it all if he could, but he's also doing up an old boat over at Bamton Boatyard, and he drives the bus sometimes… and the fish van…'

'And I'm guessing poor old Hattie likes to see him sometimes too?' laughed Lizzie.

'Yeah. That!' said Liam with a grin. 'Luckily, she's

just as busy and nutty as he is, so it seems to work out. But I'm more than happy to take on some of the work. I can turn up in the evenings, and some folks seem to really like that if they're at work all day. Hopefully, it'll free Ben up a bit, as well as giving him someone else he can call out in an emergency.'

'Sounds like a great plan,' said Lizzie, feeling awful for dragging him away when he was clearly run off his feet. 'You know, you should have just told me how to get to Ted's place... I could have driven myself!'

'Give over,' laughed Liam. 'I love any excuse to go on an adventure! Besides, Ted's barn is hard to find unless you know where you're going.'

Lizzie nodded. She had to agree with that. Liam had headed out of town and set off towards the Old Schoolhouse to begin with, but then they seemed to have meandered through the lanes in ever-decreasing circles.

'And... why exactly are you taking me to Ted's mysterious barn?' said Lizzie. She'd been trying different variations of this question ever since he'd picked her up, but Liam was yet to give her a straight answer.

'You'll see!' he said with a grin.

'I can't believe I got in a van with a random stranger,' chuckled Lizzie. 'I mean – "heading to Ted's barn" – that's the start of every horror film I've ever heard of!'

'Erm... I'm hardly a random stranger, considering we've known each other since we were kids,' spluttered Liam.

'Well... okay... you do have a point,' said Lizzie. 'I'm not sure we really *knew* each other back then though. More like... aware of each other?'

'Yeah,' laughed Liam. 'You were way too cool to "know" me. I was a gawky little thing...'

'I can assure you I definitely *wasn't* cool!' said Lizzie indignantly. 'I've never been cool.'

As far as she was concerned, she'd been the weird kid who was happier on her bike than playing with the others. She'd never really cared whether she was on her own or leading a little pack behind her. As long as she had the wind in her hair and was pedalling like a lunatic - that's all she'd ever really cared about.

'I beg to differ,' said Liam. 'You didn't care what you looked like or what anyone thought of you. That's *exactly* what made you so cool!'

'Well... erm... thanks!' said Lizzie.

Liam shrugged. 'I was so desperate to hang out with you. I don't think I ever cycled so far in my life as I did back then, but I loved trying to keep up with you!'

'Well... it's nice to hang out now,' said Lizzie.

'Yup. Sure is,' said Liam.

'So... where exactly are you taking me?' she tried again.

'You're not very patient are you?' he laughed.

'It's not my strong point, no!' said Lizzie.

'We're going to see Ted Hatherleigh,' he said.

Lizzie waited for more of an explanation, but Liam just stopped talking and smiled serenely to himself.

'You told me that already,' she huffed. 'I meant – *why?!* Not that I'm not grateful, of course!'

'You'll see!' said Liam.

Lizzie tutted and crossed her arms. Liam chuckled, clearly not in the least bit bothered. It made a nice change. Mark had never quite been able to tell when she was mucking around and had regularly accused her of being in a mood – which then instantly became a self-fulfilling prophecy.

It really wasn't any wonder their marriage had imploded, was it?! In fact, Lizzie had a sneaking suspicion it would have disintegrated a lot sooner if it hadn't been for the girls. She blinked hard as the van clonked over a bump in the road, bringing her sharply back to the present.

'I hope you don't mind me doing the driving,' said Liam.

'Mind? laughed Lizzie. 'It's great, thanks! Anyway… I'm not entirely sure where my car keys are. I don't think I've seen them since I moved in!'

If she was honest, she was thoroughly enjoying being chauffeured around so that she could stare out of the window at the lanes. She couldn't wait to get out on a bike and explore. Of course – there was only one little hitch with that… she didn't currently own one. It was ironic really, considering she was about to open a bike shop.

Lizzie let out a long sigh.

'You okay?' said Liam, shooting a glance at her. 'Won't be long now!'

'I'm fine,' said Lizzie. 'Just wishing I had my bike with me, that's all.'

'Didn't you bring it down with you?' said Liam in surprise.

'It got nicked before I moved!' she huffed.

'Bummer!' said Liam. 'That's one thing you've got to say for Seabury – at least it's pretty safe.'

'Yeah,' said Lizzie. 'You know - I think that's half the problem. Seabury spoiled me. Even though I lived in the city for over a decade, I never quite got my head around the need to lock everything up. I guess I just wanted it to be like Seabury – safe and friendly.'

'Do you regret leaving?' said Liam with interest.

'Yes and no,' said Lizzie. 'I mean, I've got a feeling the teenage years would have been a bit less white-knuckle down here compared to shepherding two beautiful girls through puberty in a city full of exciting and interesting ways to cause havoc. But… at the time, moving up there was the right thing to do. It was breaking Mark's heart to be away from the girls so much.'

'And being away from you too!' said Liam.

Lizzie shot him a look.

'Sorry!' he said quickly. 'Sorry... I mean... I know you're not together anymore... I just meant back then... sorry...'

Lizzie reached out and patted his arm. 'Breathe!' she laughed. 'It's absolutely fine. Yeah – I mean, I think we'd already started to drift apart by the time I moved to Bristol - but there was no way I was ready to give up on us. I still thought we could make it work.'

'Wow, sounds really tough,' said Liam with a frown, turning down a lane that was so narrow, it almost felt as though the van was having to hold its breath and suck its belly in.

'Not tough,' said Lizzie, 'just really sad. We stayed together until Jenna left home – she's the youngest – and then, six weeks later, Mark moved out too.'

'What - so soon?' said Liam. 'That's harsh.'

'Not really,' said Lizzie with a shrug. 'It was inevitable by that point. It was a relief for both of us, to be honest. We got together when we were really young – and you do a lot of changing and growing up, don't you? Some people are lucky and grow in the same direction. Not us though. It didn't take long before our only common point was the kids. I think we'll always be close, though. We're just happier divorced than we were married.'

Liam let out a long, slow whistle through his teeth. 'I'm feeling very petty over here. As far as I'm concerned, my ex can go and swim with some eager jellyfish.'

'Ouch!' said Lizzie with a little wince.

'Ouch pretty much sums us up.'

'Sorry,' said Lizzie.

Liam shrugged. 'It is what it is. I married the egotistical, cheating…' He cleared his throat. 'I'm over it by the way. I just enjoy letting off a bit of steam sometimes.'

'Was it recent?' said Lizzie curiously.

'Nope – four… nearly five years now,' said Liam.

'About the same as me then,' said Lizzie.

She glanced at him, wondering if she dared ask if he was still single. No – maybe not. They might be sharing their sob stories, but that would make it sound like she was on the hunt – and she most definitely *wasn't*.

'So…' said Liam as he navigated a tight turn through a gateway that was half-covered with ivy, 'did your ex move on?'

'You'd better believe it!' Lizzie snorted. 'He jumped straight into an affair with one of the secretaries at the office.'

'Eww – cliché, much?' said Liam.

'Yep!' said Lizzie. 'Then, the minute our divorce came through, the pair of them were engaged.'

'Shiiit!' said Liam. 'How are you so calm about it all?'

'Because… I wanted him to be happy?' said Lizzie

with a shrug. 'He's a good guy. Mostly. And for some strange reason, Tiff makes him happy.'

'Again - I am feeling very, very small right now,' said Liam, pulling the van to a standstill in front of an immaculate stretch of grass. 'You're still really cool, you know!'

'Am *so* not,' laughed Lizzie. 'Trust me, I've had plenty of time to refine my story and leave out all the snot, tears and swearing that actually went on. I might not have loved Mark anymore, but it still felt like a thump in the chest.'

'Well thank heavens for that,' chuckled Liam. 'At least I know your human! And… are you seeing anyone now?'

'Hold that thought!' said Lizzie, spotting an elderly gent as he appeared around the corner of the huge, modern garage in front of them. He began hobbling towards them, leaning heavily on a stick as he went. 'I'm guessing that's Ted?'

'The one and only,' said Liam with a nod. 'Come on – let's get the pair of you introduced!'

CHAPTER 7

*L*izzie clambered down from the van and leaned against the side for a brief moment. She wasn't sure what Ted Hatherleigh might be able to do to help her with her current predicament, but she was intensely grateful that he'd appeared at that exact moment. She'd been enjoying her gossip with Liam, but that last question had made her heart leap into her throat, and she was more than grateful to escape the confines of the van and grab a couple of seconds to pull herself together!

Still… she didn't want Liam to think she was weird, so she forced a smile onto her face and started to make her way around the other side of the van to join him.

Lizzie couldn't help but peer around her as she went. After the overgrown lane and wild hedges, this was all quite a shock. The wide expanse of grass they'd pulled up to was manicured to within an inch of its life – complete with quintessential bowling-green stripes. The garden surrounding it, however, was completely tangled and wild – full of honeysuckle and crab apple trees.

As for the barn… well, when Liam told her they were going to drive to "Ted's barn", she'd been picturing something quaint and historic – not a modern blockwork garage complete with a roll-up, metal door.

'It's what's inside that counts! Don't let the appearance fool you,' muttered Liam as she came to stand next to him.

'What – do you mean Ted or the garage?' said Lizzie, shooting him a quick wink.

'Oi – I heard that!' said the old man with a barking laugh as he limped towards them across the immaculate grass.

'I'm so sorry!' said Lizzie, horrified.

How on earth had he caught that from all the way over there? The man must have the hearing of a bat!

'One of the perks of these new-fangled hearing aids!' said Ted with a wicked smile. 'That - and turning them off when Margie starts mithering on about something!'

'You know she does that to you too, right?' said Liam with a laugh, hurrying over to Ted to shake his hand.

'Where'd you think I learned the trick?!' said Ted

with a little shake of his walking stick. 'Now then, who's this firecracker?'

'I'm Lizzie,' she said, following Liam's lead and shaking the old man's hand.

'Lizzie Moore!' he said, his eyes twinkling. 'You're just as cheeky as you were when you were little.'

'You remember me?!' said Lizzie.

'Of course – you were a terror on these lanes – always leading a pack of kiddies with you on that snazzy little silver bike of yours!'

'I loved that bike!' said Lizzie with a little sigh. 'I can't remember what happened to it... nan probably gave it away when I got too big!'

'Sounds like your nan!' said Ted. 'Kind to a fault, that woman. I know Margie still misses her.'

'Yeah,' said Lizzie, 'I do too.'

Ted leaned forwards and gave her arm a gentle pat with his free hand. 'She thought you were the bee's knees, that's for certain. What brings you back to Seabury, Lizzie? Visiting?'

'Nope,' said Lizzie. 'I'm back for good.'

'What, to live in your nan's old place again?' said Ted. 'Below the allotments? Like before?'

'Yes. Back in my dream home,' sighed Lizzie. 'But not *quite* like before.'

'Lizzie's opening a bike shop!' said Liam, the words spilling out of him like a shaken can of coke.

Lizzie shot him a grateful smile. She wasn't sure if he was just trying to save her from the tricky subject of her missing husband or if he was just genuinely excited about her shop. Either way, she was glad for an excuse to exit memory lane.

'A bike shop? Are you indeed?' said Ted, his bushy eyebrows shooting up. 'Well then, I think you'd better come with me.'

'Oo…kay?' she said slowly. She turned to Liam with a questioning look, but he just grinned and nodded for her to follow.

What on earth were these two up to?

With a shrug, Lizzie decided to go with the flow. She was here now so she might as well find out what the big surprise was. Besides, she rather liked Ted and that mischievous twinkle in his eye.

'Stupid stick,' muttered Ted, tossing it away so that he could use both hands on the garage door. 'The blasted thing is Margie's idea and I can't stand it.'

Liam ambled forwards to help. 'Lawn's looking good,' he said as the door began to roll upwards

'Thanks!' said Ted. 'That's the *Bryant*. I've finally got it mowing a treat. Took a bit of doing, that did… I had to make a couple of the parts myself – they don't make them like that anymore. Not too many people have the skills anymore!'

If Lizzie was in any doubt as to what the *Bryant* was, they were cleared up the moment she peered inside the garage. There were dozens of ancient lawnmowers in there, in various states of disrepair.

'Ignore that,' said Ted, nodding to a rather snazzy

sign on the wall that said "The Barn" in swirly gold lettering. 'That's Margie's idea of a joke. I think she wanted to make the place sound grand. Poor old girl, getting stuck with me. She always wanted a big house, and instead, she got stuck with a grubby little cottage and a garage full of lawnmowers!'

'At least she got manicured lawns,' said Liam.

'Aye… poor girl, that she did!' said Ted, his eyes twinkling. 'Anyway, you follow me through here, young Lizzie, and see if you can't win me some brownie points with my wife while you're here.'

Completely at a loss again, Lizzie threw a pleading look at Liam, hoping that he might take pity on her and explain what was going on. Sadly, Liam was too busy admiring one of the ancient mowers to notice.

'Mind your head through here, there's all sorts hanging up to keep them out of the way,' said Ted from somewhere in the gloom in front of her.

Ducking her head and doing her best not to trip over any of Ted's treasures as she went, Lizzie picked her way towards the back of the garage.

'I'll get them all running eventually,' said Ted as she joined him. He patted the handle of yet another mower. 'Or - I will if Margie ever gives me a moment's peace!'

Lizzie smiled. The way Ted spoke about the mythical Margie made her think of her own grandparents – they'd been completely devoted to each other. They'd loved nothing more than to grumble and grouch, but Lizzie had known from an early age that it was a sign of their total love and adoration for each other.

'Right,' said Ted as the pair of them finally reached the back wall, 'bikes, you say?'

Lizzie nodded. 'At least, I hope so. I've hit a bit of a snag with getting all the parts and tools I need… but I'll make it work… somehow…'

'You follow me through here,' said Ted, opening a door in the back wall that Lizzie hadn't even noticed. She followed him through the doorway and then came to a dead stop.

'Wow!' breathed Lizzie.

So this was where bicycles came to retire! This hidden room was almost as large as the first - and it was full of bikes. They were, quite literally, everywhere she looked – hanging from the walls and ceiling, piled in bits in the corners, and standing upside-down in the middle of the room as though Ted was right in the middle of working on them.

Lizzie took in a deep breath and let the scent of metal and oil wash over her. Bikes had a special smell… maybe it was something to do with the tyres, but Lizzie always liked to think that it had something to do with all the adventures they'd been on over the years.

'Hey… wait a minute!' she gasped, moving towards a long workbench that ran along the entire

back wall. Above it, hanging from the wall was…
'Isn't that…?'

'Your old bike!' grinned Ted.

Lizzie gaped. The little child's bike was unmissable – it still had the silver tassels she'd tied to the handlebars and a tiny row of daisy stickers she'd pressed onto each of the peddles. 'How on earth…?'

'Whoever your nan gave it to must have left it in the hedge over near Mrs Scott's place,' said Ted. 'It sat there for about a month and then I thought I'd rescue it and bring it back here. I asked around, but no one claimed it, so it's just been here ever since.'

'And when you say ever since…?' said Lizzie.

'Time doesn't really exist in here,' said Ted with a laugh. 'That's why I like coming out here. Anyway, I expect I've got some other bits of your old bikes around here somewhere. Your nan asked me to take them when she was having a bit of a clear out – before you and your hubby moved in.'

'Ex hubby now, I'm afraid,' said Lizzie, figuring she may as well set him straight before they went any further.

'Ah. Well, I would say I'm sorry, but sometimes it's for the best,' said Ted.

'You're right!' said Lizzie, looking at him in surprise.

'Of course I'm right,' said Ted. 'Your nan always said he was a nice enough chap, but not the right one for you.'

'I know,' sighed Lizzie. 'She wasn't shy about telling me that, either.'

'I can imagine. She was a firecracker - just like you!' laughed Ted. 'Anyway – speaking of inconvenient spouses...'

'Oof, she'll hear you if you're not careful,' laughed Liam, coming through the door and catching them up at last.

'I don't mind if she does,' said Ted, grinning at him. 'Maybe it'd stop her mithering for a minute!'

'You realise this man adores his wife, right?' said Liam in a fake whisper.

'I got that impression,' laughed Lizzie.

'Too blummin' right I do,' said Ted, suddenly serious. 'That woman is my own personal angel. Just don't tell her I said that, or I'll never hear the last of it. Anyway – that's where you come in, young Lizzie.'

'Sorry, you've lost me!' she said in surprise.

'My old hands aren't what they used to be, and I don't do anything with the bikes anymore, fiddly beggars that they are. I much prefer spending my time on the mowers.'

Lizzie could feel her heart starting to patter, but she didn't dare interrupt.

'On top of that, Margie wants me to clear this place out so that we can get a caravan in here.' He paused and pulled a horrified face, making them both laugh. 'I've been putting her off for years, but I think she's finally worn me down. If any of this lot – the bikes, the parts, most of the tools – would come in handy, then they're yours.'

'What?!' said Lizzie, her voice coming out in a surprised gasp. She'd been hoping that he might let her nab a couple of spare parts and maybe her childhood bike for old-time's sake, but she hadn't expected him to offer her all of it. 'But... I'm really sorry Ted... I can't pay you... not yet, at least.'

'Don't be daft, girl!' said Ted, shaking his head. 'I've got a problem. I need this lot cleared out before my angel files for divorce – and it sounds like you might just be the solution I've been looking for. Two birds with one stone and all that? Besides, I'd love to see a bike shop open up in town. And if I ever need to borrow back any of the tools, I'll know where to find you, won't I?!'

'Are you sure?' she said, desperately trying to keep a sudden rush of excitement and gratitude under control.

'Sure as I need a cuppa and a sit-down!' chuckled Ted. 'If you can sort out taking it all away, then it's all yours.'

'Wow – I don't know how to thank you!' she said, swallowing down a sudden lump of emotion.

'Don't mention it,' said Ted gruffly. 'Bloody caravans... but anything to keep the wife happy, eh?!'

CHAPTER 8

'Quick!' hissed Lizzie, bouncing up and down in her seat. 'Go go go!'

'What?!' laughed Liam, taking his sweet time to get his seatbelt on before coaxing the old van into life.

'I don't want Ted to change his mind!' said Lizzie, crossing her fingers in her lap and trying not to look like she'd completely lost the plot.

'I don't think you need to worry about that,' said Liam, shooting her a smile. 'Did you see his face? He's just thrilled that you're taking everything and that all his treasures are actually going to be put to good use. I think he was dreading everything ending up at the scrapyard when Margie finally loses patience and empties the place herself!'

Lizzie let out a huge, exaggerated shudder. What a horrible thought!

Liam's van was now crammed to bursting with bike parts, all piled in on top of the broken deckchairs and around his window-washing kit and the mysterious object covered with the tarpaulin. He'd lifted the corner for a brief moment, and Lizzie had caught a glimpse of what looked like the gleaming back end of a vintage motorbike. She'd almost begged for a proper look, but Liam had been too busy wrapping a thick blanket around the whole thing so that it would be protected from the various bits of old bike frame she wanted to take back to The Old Grain Store.

It really had been the most amazing afternoon. With Ted and Liam's help, Lizzie had spent the last few hours picking out the best bits from amongst Ted's treasure hoard – the bits that would mean she could get her workshop open for business in her original timeframe.

Every single pile of "junk" – as Margie had put it when she'd appeared with a tray of tea and biscuits – held a surprise. She'd unearthed tools from her wish list, spare parts in every imaginable size and colour, and even an entire box full of brand-new innertubes.

Lizzie had checked and double-checked with Ted that he really was happy for her to help herself to anything she wanted, and in the end, Ted had brought Margie out again.

'Lizzie wants to know if it's really alright for her

to take what she wants?' he'd said with a knowing smirk.

Margie had folded her arms across her chest. 'Well, let's put it like this. If you don't take it, I'll be sending whatever's left to the tip. So... feel free!'

The idea of all those treasures being thrown away had sent a physical pain through Lizzie, and a fine sheen of cold sweat had appeared on her forehead.

'Don't worry,' Margie had chuckled, taking pity on her. 'Take what you want today and just pile up anything else you want us to keep for you.'

'There's no rush. Just come back whenever you're ready for the rest,' Ted had added.

Margie's parting shot had been a lot less gentle. 'Just remember, I know where to find you. If your stuff is still here when my caravan's due to arrive... then the countdown's on for a final tip-run!'

Lizzie grinned to herself. She'd make sure that she came back for the rest of the treasures before Margie even started to think about tip runs. Even if Liam was too busy to do any more trips, she'd beg, borrow or steal a van so that she could finish the job as soon as possible!

'Well,' said Lizzie with a long, happy sigh as Liam navigated his way back through the narrow, overgrown gateway and onto the winding lanes that would eventually lead them back to Seabury, 'it looks like the dream's well and truly back on track!'

'Brilliant!' said Liam. 'Did you get everything you needed?'

'And then some!' said Lizzie, stroking the fat ring binder that was sitting on her lap. 'Did you know it was Ted who designed and built that tricycle The Sardine uses for their deliveries?'

'Yep!' Liam nodded. 'Trixie is one of Ted's babies!'

'I know – how amazing!'

'Yeah – I think it was a real blow when his hands got too painful to carry on with that kind of work – he was so good at it! What's in the folder?'

'The original designs for the tricycle… and a bunch of designs for other projects he never got the chance to make before his hands seized up!'

'Wow – what a treasure!' said Liam.

'I know,' said Lizzie. 'I can't believe he let me have it!'

She didn't want to say it out loud yet, but a little seed of an idea had started to sprout while Ted had been leafing through the old, slightly yellowed drawings, explaining parts of the various designs to her as he went. Maybe she could have a go at making them herself. Maybe there were layers to this big dream of hers that she hadn't even started to explore yet.

Lizzie stared at her hands, resting on the folder. They were filthy – coated in oil and grease after sorting through piles of chains, handlebars and old-fashioned bike seats. A sure sign of an afternoon well-spent. She glanced across to where Liam's hands rested lightly on the steering wheel. Sure enough, they were exactly the same. He had nice hands. Strong and purposeful... a bit like him really. A little shiver ran down her spine, and Lizzie shifted slightly in her seat to mask the moment.

Liam had been just as excited as her as he'd helped her to sort through Ted's barn. They'd worked well together - organising the treasure trove that had been decades in the making. Lizzie had to admit that she hadn't met anyone she'd clicked with so easily in a long time... in fact, she couldn't remember ever feeling like this.

Oh crikey – she needed to take control of this before it took on a life of its own. She had a feeling she could be in serious danger if she spent too much time thinking about Liam's strong hands and easy-going company.

The whole dating and relationship thing simply didn't feature in her plans right now... she had too much to do! Sure... the future was full of possibilities, but first things first. Lizzie had a business to get up and running, and a grown-up daughter turning up in the next few days who sounded very much like she needed a bit of TLC. Liam - with his grubby hands, lovely legs and cheeky smile - was just going to have to wait!

'Thank you so much, by the way!' said Lizzie as Liam turned down the lane that would lead them onto the seafront at the North Beach end of town.

'What for?' he said.

'Are you kidding me?' laughed Lizzie. 'For introducing me to Ted, for driving me around when you had way better things to do with your time, for helping me find a way out of impending disaster… for letting me fill your van up with pilfered bike bits…'

'Oh. That!' said Liam, shooting her a smile that made her toes curl. 'Well – I'm glad to help. Though I've got a favour to ask you now!'

'Sure – anything!' said Lizzie. She winced slightly. Jeez, did she really need to sound quite so enthusiastic?!

'Cool. Well… if it's alright with you, can I drop this lot off in the morning instead of doing it now?' he said, pulling an apologetic face. 'It'll mean we'll be less likely to incur the wrath of the traffic warden if I stop by nice and early – so I'll be able to pull up on the pavement right outside. It'll make it a lot easier to unload!'

'Of course!' said Lizzie. 'Blimey – that's hardly a favour!'

For one thing, it had been such a brilliant day, she didn't exactly want to risk it ending with Liam getting a parking ticket. For another – she was absolutely exhausted – but in a good way. Her muscles ached from lifting and carrying and sorting, and she could really do with a long soak in the bath.

'So tomorrow then?' said Liam.

'Perfect,' said Lizzie. 'To be honest, it'll probably save me from myself. If we unloaded it all now, I wouldn't be able to resist getting it all organised and put away... and I'd probably still be at it at midnight!'

'I can just imagine!' said Liam. 'Anyway – thanks for today, it's been a real breath of fresh air.'

'What – hanging out in a mouldy barn full of broken bikes and old lawnmowers?' laughed Lizzie.

'That's the one,' said Liam, slowing down to let Lionel cross the road outside Pebble Street before continuing along West Beach. 'And you don't fool me – you were in seventh heaven, getting all grubby!'

'What can I say – I'm a happy little weirdo!' said Lizzie with a shrug.

'Me and you both,' said Liam, indicating and then pulling to a stop outside the Old Grain Store. 'Right, here we are. I'll be over around half eight tomorrow morning if that's okay?'

'Perfect. Thank you!' said Lizzie, undoing her seatbelt and tucking the folder under her arm as she hopped out of the van. She hurried around the front, not wanting him to drive off before she'd said thank you one last time. She tapped on his window, and he rolled it down, smiling at her.

'Thanks again,' she said, suddenly feeling a little bit shy now that they were face to face.

'No worries,' he said, his eyes twinkling. 'Right, I'd better head off before the locals start tutting at me for stopping on the double yellows!'

'Liam… you are one of the locals!' she laughed.

'Oh yeah!' he grinned. 'Well… so are you.'

Lizzie nodded in delight.

'Right, I'd better head off!' he said, as a car pulled up behind him, clearly waiting for Liam to get out of the way.

Lizzie quickly leaned forwards, ducking in through the open window to kiss his cheek, only for Liam to turn back to her just at the wrong moment.

Their lips met with a bump.

'Wow!' said Liam, his eyes wide as he pulled back to stare at her in surprise.

'Sorry!' gasped Lizzie, taking a quick step backwards. 'I was aiming for your cheek!'

'We'll talk about that tomorrow!' said Liam, starting to laugh.

'But-' gasped Lizzie.

She was too late. An irritable *honk* sounded from the car behind, and Liam set off, clearly not wanting to incur the wrath of anyone on the narrow seafront road.

Lizzie quickly scarpered to the safety of the pavement and raised her hand to wave. She couldn't help the huge grin that spread across her face as a grubby, oily hand appeared from Liam's window, waving back as he disappeared up the road.

CHAPTER 9

*I*n a daze, Lizzie turned to stare at The Old Grain Store. She was still clutching Ted's priceless folder to her heart as though it was some kind of comfort blanket that might soothe the mad fluttering that was going on inside her chest.

Why was she such an idiot? Just a nice, normal goodbye would have done the trick. A little wave. A smile. They'd had plenty of chat and banter on the way back to town… and then she'd gone and spoiled it all.

'Get a grip!' she muttered to herself, admiring the lovely clean windows before searching for the keys in the depths of her pockets. She just wanted to pop the folder somewhere safe and sound, close the shutters and then she was planning on treating herself to an early night.

Two minutes later, after a short-lived battle with

the shutters that were still decidedly stiff, Lizzie had locked up and was back out on the pavement. She eyeballed the front of her building with a critical eye. It wouldn't take too much more work to get ready for her grand opening. A lick of paint… a bit of work on the shutters… and a name.

Lizzie had been struggling with what to call her new shop for ages – after all, she couldn't just keep calling it the Old Grain Store, could she? It didn't exactly scream "bicycle shop!" Ah well - something would come to her eventually – she was sure of it! After somehow managing to dodge almost-certain disaster, figuring out a name suddenly felt like child's play by comparison.

Now that she knew her own big dream was still on, Lizzie needed to turn her thoughts to welcoming Jenna to the cottage. She'd need to move some boxes around so that she could find somewhere for her to sleep – but she quickly reminded herself that her youngest was used to living in the back of a van, so it wasn't like she was going to be too picky, was it?!

'Right… home time!' Lizzie muttered, crossing the road and staring out to sea for a moment. She loved the view from this end of West Beach back towards the centre of town. From here she could see the King's Nose jutting out into the sea behind the Pebble Street Hotel. Beyond that, high on the far point, stood the lighthouse where, according to Ethel, Seabury's two loved-up café owners now lived.

Lizzie let out a long sigh. Maybe she'd end up being friends with Kate... and Lou... she certainly hoped so. It had been wonderful spending time with Liam today simply because they seemed to be on the same wavelength. With any luck, she'd find plenty more people like that here too. If there was one thing she wanted, now that she was back, it was to fill her life with special people... because what else could be better than cramming every single day with as much friendship as she could get her hands on?!

As she started to climb the hill back towards the cottage, Lizzie couldn't help but run through the list of jobs she still had to do. Hopefully, she'd manage to get a second wind this evening so that she could clear enough space for Jenna. Then, perhaps she could head back down to the shop early tomorrow morning and get some painting done before Liam arrived with his van...

Lizzie's heart started to race as she wondered what Liam was like with a paintbrush. Suddenly her head was filled with the image of him with a pair of overalls tied around his waist and splatters of paint in his hair.

'Blimey!' puffed Lizzie, struggling to catch her breath. It was just the hill... and those flutterings were just because she was ravenous. After all, she hadn't eaten anything since that pastry Liam had brought her. She just needed some food... and to get her mind onto a safer topic!

The minute Lizzie reached the cottage, she let herself in and marched straight through to the kitchen, intent on finding something to eat in the vague hope that it might help her feel a bit more grounded and stop all this floaty nonsense she had going on in her head.

Hmm... not exactly inspiring!

That was the problem with being so busy and getting caught up with her plans and worries... she was completely losing track of the basics – like food shopping! She'd definitely need to rectify that before Jenna arrived.

For now, she'd just have to make do because she certainly didn't have the energy to hunt for her car keys and head out to buy groceries after the day she'd had!

After ten minutes of rooting around in the cupboards and the large cardboard box on the kitchen table marked "store cupboard", Lizzie started to throw together a quick meal. She piled up crackers, pickles and olives, along with the last remaining chunk of cheddar from the fridge, and one of the apples that had travelled down with her on the move. Lizzie quickly cut it in quarters and took a test bite. Not the best – but at least it hadn't quite turned into a tasteless potato yet.

Lizzie added the apple to the plate and stared down at her tea. Well... it certainly wouldn't win any awards for presentation - but at least it would fill a hole. She had to admit, she was looking forward to trying out the food at the Pebble Street Hotel. Ted had been telling her about it earlier, and even Margie had waxed lyrical on the subject. According to her, Hattie's cooking was nothing short of sublime – especially her puddings.

Carrying her plate through to the living room, Lizzie let out a huge groan when she spotted that the sofa had a mini mountain of fresh washing heaped at one end, and there were a couple of boxes piled precariously on the other end.

'Damnit!' she muttered.

Balancing the plate on the top box, Lizzie gathered the washing together in one giant, unruly armful, and proceeded to turn in a circle looking for somewhere else to put it. The loud, impatient growl from her stomach brought things to a head, and she marched out into the hallway and dumped the entire lot unceremoniously onto the floor at the bottom of the stairs. She'd sort it out later!

Stomping back through to the living room, Lizzie lowered herself carefully onto the sofa next to the boxes and grabbed her plate. She'd just managed to gather a bit of everything onto the corner of a cracker when her mobile phone begin to vibrate in her back pocket, making her jump. The laden cracker crumbled back onto the plate, and she sighed.

Ah well... small mercies... at least it hadn't landed on the floor!

Plonking the plate back on top of the box, Lizzie shifted her weight and yanked her mobile out of her pocket.

'Megan?' she said in surprise.

It was rare her eldest daughter ever called her – it was usually the other way around. Even rarer than that were the squeaking, sniffling sounds issuing coming from the phone.

'Meggie?' she said again, reverting to her pet name for her little girl, 'what's the matter lovely?'

Megan instantly started to jabber so fast that Lizzie had a hard time trying to figure out what she was saying. The reception in the cottage wasn't the best… but it definitely wasn't helped by the copious amounts of snotty tears going on at Megan's end.

'Slow down, Meggie,' she said gently, her heart hammering as worry mounted in her chest. What on earth could have got her steady, driven, focused daughter in such a tizz? 'Tell me what's wrong.'

'Focus mother!' blubbed Megan. 'I didn't get the promotion and I think Owen just split up with me!'

'Oh!' said Lizzie, secretly thinking that being rid of the most boring man in the world wasn't something to get upset about. And hadn't Megan been promoted just a matter of weeks ago?

'It's all such a mess,' she sobbed.

Lizzie was alarmed to hear her voice quivering again.

'What can I do, Meggie?' she said gently.

'I need to get out of here!' said Megan, sounding urgent now. 'Upstairs have got the builders in, they're renovating their flat. I mean – how am I supposed to concentrate and get my life back on track with that racket going on? Owen was meant to propose, mum – it's on my planner!'

Lizzie shook her head, feeling slightly dazed as Megan started off with another round of sobbing.

'When?' she said. 'Why?'

'It was part of my pl-a-a-n!' blubbed Megan. 'Now it's ruined and I've got to get back on tra-a-ack!'

Lizzie bit her lip, fighting down the horrifying urge to laugh. Maybe this was why the girls usually turned to their dad for support?! Before she could pull herself together and manage to get a word in edgeways, Megan was off again.

'I need a couple of weeks away from it all, mum – otherwise I don't know *what* I'm going to do!'

'Don't say things like that!' said Lizzie, horrified.

'I mean it! I might... I might... end up like Jenna!' she said, as though this was the worst thing she could possibly imagine.

This time, Lizzie couldn't help but let out a laugh.

'It's not funny,' huffed Megan. 'I'm serious! I'm coming down to stay with you for a couple of weeks. I tried calling dad and I can't get through so it's going to have to be Seabury. I'll be there the day after tomorrow.'

Lizzie did her best to fight down the customary

stab of hurt that - once again – she'd been the backup parental choice and that Megan, like Jenna, had turned to Mark first. She opened her mouth to warn Megan that her sister was also descending on Seabury in the next few days, but she was too late – Megan had already disappeared.

'Oh for goodness sake!' tutted Lizzie.

She wasn't sure whether to laugh or to cry, so instead she grabbed her plate. Staring at the crummy, less-than-appetising mess, she promptly changed her mind. It was time to dig out the emergency bar of chocolate.

CHAPTER 10

Lizzie yawned widely as she rinsed out the dregs of her morning coffee and set the mug down on the draining board. She scrubbed at her eyes with her still-damp hands. They felt gritty, and she had a sneaking suspicion that she had eyebags the size of suitcases - not that she'd know, of course, because she hadn't had a moment to glance in the mirror yet.

It had been another night that had included very little sleep. Lizzie's brain had insisted on running through her to-do list on a loop – it had grown substantially longer following Megan's phone call. The fact that darkness had also been punctuated by unsettling flashbacks of her accidental lip-bash with Liam definitely hadn't added a sense of calm to the situation!

In the end, she'd given up on sleep and had hauled herself out of bed early to see what she could do about moving enough cardboard boxes out of the way so that the girls would have somewhere to stay when they descended. Lizzie thought she might just about be able to clear one of the spare rooms in time, but there was no way she'd be able to sort the second one out. There were simply too many boxes – piled high from floor to ceiling.

There was plenty of room outside the front of the cottage of course, and Lizzie had briefly considered stashing some of the boxes under a tarpaulin… but she'd given up on that idea pretty quickly. She simply didn't have the energy to lug all her worldly possessions back down the stairs. Besides – what if it rained?

Her next bright idea had been to shift some of the boxes down to The Old Grain Store, but that would mean delaying opening the shop – and after risking the entire plan when she'd bailed Jenna out, she wasn't willing to do it again by turning the space into a dumping ground!

Lizzie had even considered calling Mark and asking for his help. Both the girls had mentioned they'd tried to reach out to their dad before calling her – and as much as that hurt - right now she could actually do with him pulling one of his "super-dad" moments. If they could just stay with him for the first week to give her a tiny bit longer to get herself sorted out, it would be a huge help.

Lizzie had bided her time, waiting until it was a more socially acceptable hour to call her ex and ask for a favour… but when the time came, she'd changed her mind. Even though she was still on excellent terms with Mark, the same couldn't be said for his new wife. The possibility of getting Tiffany on the phone at any time of day was enough to make Lizzie shudder in horror, and the thought of having to speak to her before she'd had the chance to sink a second coffee was simply inconceivable.

'Come on Lizzie!' she huffed, leaning heavily against the sink. There *had* to be a way to fit three adults into a house with three decent-sized bedrooms! If only her worldly goods weren't taking up every last inch of space, it would have been an absolute doddle. Instead, it was just a complete nightmare.

There wasn't time to organise it all, but she couldn't just abandon the girls. She *was* their mum after all – even if the pair of them were more than old enough to fend for themselves.

Urgh! She was officially too tired to deal with this right now!

Lizzie glanced at the kitchen clock and swore. She had precisely three minutes before she was meant to be down at the shop to help Liam unload the van!

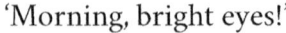

'Morning, bright eyes!'

Lizzie smiled wearily as she approached the van, and Liam climbed out to greet her. As promised, he'd pulled it right up onto the pavement outside the shop… though goodness knows how long he'd been waiting for her to turn up.

'I'm so sorry I'm late!' she said, puffing as she tried to catch her breath from her route-march from the cottage. At least it was all downhill – but that's about all that could be said in its favour this morning. She'd have brought the car… but she still hadn't managed to unearth the keys.

'You okay?' said Liam, raising his eyebrows in mild concern as he made his way around the back of the van to open the doors.

'Yeah – yeah fine!' said Lizzie, nodding. She suddenly felt a bit shy as she remembered their awkward bump-kiss from the day before. 'Erm… you've not been waiting too long, have you?' she said, fumbling in her cardigan pocket and praying that she hadn't managed to forget the keys to The Old Grain Store in her mad rush to get down here.

'Nah – don't worry about that!' said Liam. 'Though, I do need to get a bit of a wiggle on. Lionel gave me the heads up that a bunch of new visitors have just arrived at the hotel. It's not a bad day, so you never know - they might fancy a deckchair and a good lounge around on West Beach. I want to be ready to pounce!'

Lizzie smiled. She quickly dismissed the idea of asking Liam if he fancied joining her for breakfast in The Sardine when they were finished. She'd have loved nothing more than a bacon roll... and the chance to talk to him about a couple of things. Mostly, she wanted to apologise properly for that awkward kiss... but she also wanted to ask him for his advice about her daughter predicament!

Lizzie was glad to be back in Seabury – but she had to admit she was missing her friends back in Bristol this morning. She needed someone she could offload to - someone who knew her well enough that she could have a damn good whinge without the risk of any kind of judgement.

Ah well... maybe it was a good thing Liam was busy after all! To be fair to the poor guy, he'd already done *more* than his fair share of Lizzie-sitting for one week!

The pair of them worked in near-silence as they ferried box after box of bike bits into the shop in a kind of relay – one of them keeping an eye out for the parking warden while the other nipped inside.

The last piece to come out of the van was Lizzie's little silver bike – and just the sight of it brought a smile to her face. She might not know what her new shop was going to be called yet – but she knew exactly what the centrepiece of her first window display was going to be!

'Right – that's you all sorted,' said Liam, closing the van doors with a *thunk*. 'Have fun sorting it all out – and just let me know when you want to go and collect some more!'

'Oh I couldn't possibly ask you to-'

'Of course you can!' said Liam firmly. 'Right – I'd better be off!'

Before she even had the chance to thank him properly, Liam had hopped up into the driver's and was on his way.

Blimey... he really *was* desperate to get his deckchairs set up! Either that or Liam was scared she was going to attempt a repeat performance of yesterday's kiss!

'Oh shut up!' Lizzie huffed at herself crossly. The poor guy was just busy.

She turned and marched herself back inside, determined to get as much work done as humanly possible before tiredness forced her to go on the hunt for more coffee.

Closing the door carefully behind her so that she wouldn't be disturbed, Lizzie got to work, sorting through the goodies they'd just unloaded and arranging them on the shelves of her workshop area. She'd been looking forward to this, but she was so distracted that she worked on autopilot, her head full to bursting as she tried to figure out the logistics of having both the girls to stay at the same time.

Maybe she could just ask Jenna and Megan to share a room...

'Yeah right!' she muttered with a snort as she coiled a loose bike chain.

They'd given that a go when they'd first moved to Bristol and it had been an unmitigated disaster! It had lasted all of two weeks before they'd become so sick of the constant arguing that Mark had given up his home office so that Jenna could use it as her bedroom.

Of course, the girls were both in their twenties now, and - in theory – were grown-ups. But Lizzie had moved to Seabury for a quiet life, and she had a feeling that making them share a room would result in the exact opposite.

Perhaps she should just give up her own bedroom for a while? She could sleep in the living room, couldn't she? After all, Lizzie didn't care if there were cardboard boxes stacked up in the corners. That wouldn't work either, though, because Jenna was a complete night owl. She loved to stay up late, burning incense and listening to Joni Mitchel on repeat. She never got to bed much before two in the morning... and there was no way Lizzie could exist on so little sleep.

There was always the hotel...

Now there was a thought! Lizzie could just leave

the girls to fight it out between them and treat herself to a room at Pebble Street. Liam had said that there were a bunch of new visitors there, but the place was huge. Maybe Lionel still had a room available... it would have to be a really cheap room though, considering her bank account was already running on fumes!

Lizzie closed her tired eyes for a moment and allowed herself to daydream about a lovely hotel room where she could float around in a big, fluffy robe. Just imagine having a restaurant downstairs whenever she fancied something tasty - rather than having to raid her cupboards for increasingly stale crackers! Of course, Pebble Street was just down the road from the shop too... that would be an added bonus!

Lizzie opened her eyes and let the cold light of day pull her out of her delicious daydream. As much as it sounded like heaven to her right now, the girls both needed her. She couldn't just flake out and abandon them for a spot of luxury – no matter how tempting it was.

'Time for a spot of mum duty!' she sighed, running her hands through her hair. She only hoped they'd realise that she'd only just arrived in town herself and that she was still finding her feet.

Maybe they'd lend a hand when they realised how much she had on her plate with getting this place sorted out! They'd be understanding... wouldn't they? They'd see she was busy trying to build a business…

'Yeah, right!' laughed Lizzie, rolling her eyes.

No matter how grown-up her girls thought they were – Lizzie knew that she would always just be "mum" to them.

CHAPTER 11

About an hour into her sorting mission, Lizzie realised that she was wandering around The Old Grain Store in circles carrying the same box, while her thoughts did the same thing – swirling around her worries about the girls in ever-decreasing circles.

It was definitely time for a break! Lizzie promptly plonked the box down right in the middle of the floor and grabbed her bag. Coffee and a quick change of scene should do the trick and help her to get her head on straight again. At the very least the caffeine buzz should give her a bit of energy to get something useful done!

Locking the door behind her, Lizzie strode along the seafront, taking long, deep breaths. The weather was still a bit grumpy out here this morning, and she had a feeling Liam might have been a bit over-optimistic if he was expecting Lionel's new visitors to want to sit around on the beach for long. Sure, it had stopped raining, but there was a stiff wind whipping up from the sea. Tiny swirls of sand kept rising from West Beach and dancing along the surface.

Lizzie peered along the beach, keeping her eyes half closed against the stinging wind. Sure enough, Liam had set up his beautiful chairs on the stretch of sand below The Sardine. As far as she could see from here, only one of them was occupied, and it looked very much like that person was fast asleep, wrapped up in a huge coat despite the fact that it was the middle of summer.

If only she didn't have quite so much to do. Lizzie wouldn't mind a little doze on the beach herself. It would be even better if Liam joined her to keep her warm!

'Stop it!' she muttered. What was *wrong* with her this morning?!

Lizzie could feel a hot blush stinging her cheeks as she spotted Liam pottering up to the deckchairs. She needed to pull herself together.

Shaking her head as though it might help dislodge her troublesome thoughts, Lizzie crossed the little seafront road so that she was as far away from the beach as possible. It was all the distance she could put between herself and Liam right now… but maybe it would help!

What with the wind and her unsettled thoughts –

Lizzie felt thoroughly stirred up both on the inside *and* the outside, so she was super-glad when she reached The Sardine. She gave the door a gentle push, but it didn't budge.

Huh! The sign said "Open"...

Lizzie cupped her hands against the glass so that she could see inside, only to catch sight of Ethel's laughing face behind the counter. She seemed to be pointing to the spot just inside the door.

Looking down, Lizzie saw what the problem was immediately. There was a giant, fluffy roadblock lying just inside the door. She watched in amusement as Ethel came out from behind the counter, bent down and patted her knee with one hand, waving what looked like a Rich Tea biscuit with the other.

The fluffy roadblock heaved itself to its feet, and Lizzie watched as the huge Bernese Mountain dog mooched over towards Ethel, its feathery tail wagging as it went. The proffered biscuit disappeared with one, eager chomp.

'I'm guessing that must be Stanley?' laughed Lizzie, taking the opportunity to push the door open while he was otherwise engaged.

'The one and only!' laughed Ethel, tickling the big dog's ears as he stared up at her adoringly. 'Sorry about that – he knows Sarah's due at any moment with some fresh cake. It's like he's got a sixth sense for it, and he likes to lie in wait for her because he knows he'll get the crumbs when she empties the boxes!'

Lizzie smiled down at Stanley as he turned his big head towards her, panting lazily and swishing his tail slowly from side to side. She'd realised now that she'd seen him once before. She was sure she'd spotted his head sticking out of the sea, paddling for all he was worth directly away from the shore... and a pretty teenage girl had been hollering after him for all she was worth. At the time, Lizzie hadn't been entirely sure he was a dog or a seal!

'Erm, does Stanley like a swim by any chance?' said Lizzie.

'Ha! I'm not sure the word "like" covers it. It drives Kate to distraction because he loves heading out in search of seals to play with,' said Ethel, moving back behind the counter and washing her hands. 'She's had to call Ben to help her out so many times – he's got a little boat you see!'

'You monkey,' said Lizzie, holding out her hand for Stanley to sniff. He promptly leaned his entire head into her palm, demanding tickles.

'What can I get you?' said Ethel.

'Latte please,' said Lizzie, 'to have in, this time.'

'No problem,' said Ethel turning towards the gleaming vintage coffee machine. 'So... it's going to be a bike shop, is it?!'

Lizzie gaped at Ethel, wondering if she'd just heard that right over the whirring of the coffee beans being freshly ground... but given the twinkly look of curiosity Ethel was sending her over her shoulder, she didn't think she'd been mistaken.

Lizzie sighed. Liam must have said something... and she had to admit, she wasn't entirely sure how she felt about that! It wasn't as though she'd sworn him to secrecy or anything, but still...

'Now, don't you go blaming Liam,' said Ethel quickly, showcasing her usual knack for mindreading as she spooned fine coffee grounds into a huge metal puck before tamping it down efficiently. 'We had Margie Hatherleigh in here earlier, and she was all excited because you cleared out so much of Ted's barn yesterday.'

Lizzie opened her mouth to say something but shut it again. She wasn't really sure *what* to say if she was honest. It didn't *really* matter that the news was out... did it? It would have just been nice to at least have a name for her new shop before the whole town knew about it!

'I know you've been away for a good while, Lizzie love,' said Ethel kindly, 'but don't forget that news travels fast around Seabury!'

'You're right there!' Lizzie laughed, nodding. 'I was just thinking I wished that I had a name for the place sorted out. I've been struggling with what to call it.'

Ethel cocked her head for a moment. 'You're using your maiden name again now, aren't you?'

Lizzie nodded.

'Well, that's easy then,' said Ethel. 'How about Moore Bikes?'

'Ethel… you're a genius!' said Lizzie.

'So I've been told,' said Ethel with a grin, popping a perfect latte on the counter.

Lizzie jumped to her feet to grab it, only to hear a mad, drumming sound coming from behind her. She turned around to discover that it was Stanley's tail thumping against the floorboards as he stared avidly at the café door.

Through the glass, Lizzie spotted a young girl balancing a bunch of cake boxes in front of her. She hurried over to open the door.

'Cheers!' said the girl, throwing a grateful smile at Lizzie as she ambled in. She was obviously an expert at keeping her balance while managing to avoid treading on Stanley's paws, because he was now dancing around her in excitement. 'Down!' she said, and Stanley promptly sat on Lizzie's feet.

'So, you must be Lizzie?' said the girl, plonking the boxes down on the nearest table and then turning to smile at her. 'Are you here trying to sell Ethel a Penny Farthing?'

Lizzie snorted in amusement. Wow – the news was *really* spreading fast!

'Young people these days,' huffed Ethel. 'So cheeky!'

'You'd better believe it!' said the girl, giving Ethel

a kiss on the cheek and earning herself a one-armed squeeze. 'I'm Sarah, by the way,' she added, grinning at Lizzie.

'Sarah's Mike Pendleton's daughter – Mike owns New York Froth,' said Ethel.

'Oh!' said Lizzie, beginning to fit the pieces of the puzzle together. 'So you live up at the lighthouse with your dad and Kate?'

'That's me!' said Sarah. 'But those two are off gallivanting around Italy at the moment. Dad decided Kate deserved a break... though he had a right job getting her to leave Seabury - even for five minutes!'

'I'm not sure if it was Seabury or Stanley she was more reluctant to leave behind,' laughed Ethel.

'It's only for a couple of weeks!' said Sarah with a shrug, ruffling Stanley's fur. 'And she knew we'd look after this idiot! Anyway – I know who you are of course – Lou told us! Your new shop sounds exciting!'

'Erm... thanks!' said Lizzie, getting caught up in the girl's infectious blast of energy.

It *was* exciting! She'd just allowed herself to get caught up in all the stressy nonsense and lost sight of the fact that this was her dream.

'So what have you got for us today?' said Ethel. 'The Chilly Dippers will be in any moment-'

'Chilly Dippers?' said Lizzie.

'Mad bunch of cold water swimmers,' said Sarah. 'Lou goes out with them. Total nutcases, the lot of them... and they always need a good sugar fix afterwards!'

'Oh!' said Lizzie with a shudder at the thought of sea swimming when it was so windy outside.

'Right,' said Sarah, turning back to the boxes. 'I've got toffee apple cake, classic red velvet, fudge-butter scrumdiddlyumptious, and a Deep, Dark and Interesting!'

Lizzie felt her eyes grow wide as Sarah whipped the top off of each of the boxes as she went, revealing one perfect cake after another. The toffee apple cake boasted a shiny, red toffee glaze, the red velvet had perfectly piped poppies coating every last inch of it, and the fudgy-thingummy looked like it would just melt in your mouth.

'What's the deep and dark one?' asked Lizzie, eyeballing the pure-white cake that looked like it had been dusted with charcoal.

'That's one of her newest creations,' said Ethel. 'Folks can't get enough of it.'

'Of course they can't!' said Sarah. 'Bitter chocolate, espresso... with a hint of mystery.'

'What's the mystery?' said Lizzie.

'Ha – good luck with that one!' said Ethel.

'Magic!' said Sarah, wiggling her eyebrows. 'Wait... unless you have any allergies?'

Lizzie shook her head. 'Nope.'

'In that case... magic!' Sarah said again with a laugh. 'So... which one are you going to try?'

'Oh... erm...'

Lizzie hadn't been planning on adding cake to her morning indulgence, but the sweet scent of fresh cake had set her stomach rumbling. Of *course* she was going to have a piece of cake... but how on earth was she going to be able to choose between them!

She watched as Sarah carefully transferred each of the ginormous cakes from their boxes onto the empty stands on the counter, doing her best not to dribble – and still none the wiser.

'How about you have a little bit of each of them?' said Ethel, coming to her rescue with a knowing smirk.

Lizzie was about to come over all polite and protest that *no, she couldn't possibly*, but instead she found herself nodding eagerly.

'Oooh yes please... I can't resist!'

'See, that's music to my ears!' laughed Sarah. 'Do you reckon I can borrow you... you can come into college, sit behind the examiners and whisper nice things like that in their ears!'

'I'll do anything for cake!' laughed Lizzie.

'Sounds like we have a deal!' said Sarah.

'Sarah, love - can I just say you're not going to need any kind of favours to blow those examiners away,' said Ethel, carefully cutting thin slices of each of the magnificent cakes and arranging them on an embarrassingly large dinner plate. 'You know your stuff, young lady! You've had so much hands-on experience, you could probably teach them a thing or two by this point! I mean, look at this glaze – I could use it as a mirror!'

Sarah grinned and tried to wave away the compliment, but Lizzie could see that she was thrilled.

'Here we go!' said Ethel, placing the huge plate full of cake in front of Lizzie.

She picked up a fork and, after a long moment of deliberation, tried a piece of the toffee apple cake with its crisp glaze first.

'Oh my... YUM!' she mumbled, trying not to spray cake crumbs everywhere.

'My point exactly!' said Ethel with an approving nod. 'Our Sarah's going to be famous.'

'I'd have to agree with that!' said Lizzie, scooping up a bit of the fudge cake next.

It was such a shame that neither Megan nor Jenna had any interest in cooking. She had a feeling if they could bake like this, she'd happily shift boxes out of the way until the cows came home. Sadly, the pair of them took after her when it came to cooking... and she could just about use a tin opener.

She wasn't sure if it was the sugar hit or the lovely company that was working its magic, but Lizzie felt like all her worries were fading away as sat in the little café, working her way through her plateful of cake. She'd just made a start on her second coffee when Lizzie became aware that someone was trying to catch her attention.

Looking down towards her feet, she came face to face with Stanley. His big, brown eyes held hers as he stared at her intently. He licked his lips. He didn't blink. It was pretty clear he was waiting for *his* piece of cake from her treat plate.

Lizzie smirked and glanced at her plate to choose a morsel for her new friend. She'd been circling around, taking a bite out of each slice in turn, so there were still three tiny pieces remaining. Hmm... maybe she'd just give him a tiny bit of her least favourite... but no – that was impossible. They were all amazing – completely dribble-worthy in fact. There was nothing for it – she'd just have to close her eyes and pick one.

Her fork landed on the red velvet cake, and she stuck out her bottom lip. But a deal was a deal! Lizzie picked it up and dropped it next to Stanley.

It really was a case of *blink and you'll miss it!* The dog's head dashed down and the cake was gone in a split-second. After a quick polish of the floorboards with his big, pink tongue, Stanley flopped down right across her feet. He was surprisingly heavy – but there was something incredibly comforting about his warmth, even though she could feel the blood being squeezed out of her toes.

'Now you've done it!' laughed Ethel. 'Looks like you've got a friend for life!'

CHAPTER 12

By the time Lizzie stepped out of The Sardine, she was riding high on far too much cake and coffee. She felt about one thousand percent better... and now she couldn't really get her head around what all the fuss had been about.

If she didn't know better, Lizzie would bet anything that Sarah had spiked the Deep, Dark and Interesting cake with something decidedly dodgy – but she felt pretty confident that there was no way the straight-talking Ethel would let anything like that happen under her watch!

The wind seemed to have become even stronger while she'd been busy loading up with sugar and caffeine, and Lizzie paused to pull on her cardigan. She was almost done when a group of decidedly damp women appeared from the direction of the beach.

The Chilly Dippers swirled around Lizzie, clearly intent on warming up inside The Sardine. They were wrapped up in everything from oversized jumpers to towels with wellington boots sticking out underneath.

Suddenly, she realised that one of them was waving in her direction. Lizzie turned and peered over her shoulder, assuming there must be someone behind her – but the pavement was empty. She turned back to the woman - who was wearing a brilliantly mad swimming cap with dozens of bright plastic flowers stuck all over it – and smiled at her tentatively.

'I'm L… L… Lou,' she stuttered as she reached Lizzie. Her lips looked slightly blue. 'L… L… Loved your house. C… C… Catch up soon when I've got more c… c… clothes on?'

'I'd love that!' said Lizzie, thrilled to finally meet her old lodger. 'You know where to find me!'

Lou gave her a juddering nod. 'C… c… cottage or b… b… bike shop!' She forced a smile onto her shivering lips and gave Lizzie the thumbs up - almost dropping her towel in the process.

'Go! Warm up!' said Lizzie, ushering her in the direction of The Sardine and then shaking her head in amusement as the rest of the group rushed past her and piled into the tiny café behind Lou. Something told her Sarah's delicious cakes stood no chance of survival against that lot!

Well – if Lou knew about the bike shop too, it looked like the news was well and truly out. Lizzie tilted her head for a moment, testing out how she really felt about her secret travelling around the Seabury grapevine at warp speed. She promptly came to the conclusion that she didn't mind in the slightest. In fact, she was rather impressed. It wasn't even ten in the morning and she'd only visited the Hatherleigh's barn yesterday!

Well, at least it boded well for when she wanted to do a bit of marketing – maybe she should see if Margie wanted a bit of work! Thank heavens Ethel had given her the heads up that it was Margie who'd let the cat out of the bag – at least it would save her from making an idiot out of herself by accusing Liam of saying something.

Thinking about Liam made her want to say hello again, and now that she had all that sugar coursing through her system she was feeling a lot braver about it than earlier. Maybe she'd just stop by briefly on her way back to The Old Grain Store. After all, she needed to carry on with her mammoth task of sorting all those goodies out so that she'd be ready to fetch the next load from Ted's barn as soon as possible.

Lizzie crossed the road and ran lightly down the steps onto the sandy beach. Well – there were the chairs… or at least *most* of the chairs! It looked like a gust of wind had got hold of one of them and was busy whisking it along the beach, with Liam hot on its heels.

Huh – maybe now wasn't the best time after all!

Liam hesitated, clearly catching sight of her, but with a quick wave, he continued the chase. For a brief moment, Lizzie wondered if she should join in – but promptly decided against it. Her feet hadn't quite re-gained full circulation after playing dog-bed for Stanley for the past half an hour… and besides, she'd never been much of a runner anyway.

Lizzie was watching Liam pelt along the sand, trying not to be too blatant about the fact that she was admiring his bum, when one of the deckchairs nearest her collapsed, making her jump out of her skin. She spun around to stare at it.

The wind was whipping the canvas of the empty chairs into a frenzy, and she hurried over to put a hand on one just as it tried to lurch off down the beach and follow its friend towards the sea. Somehow, she doubted Liam was going to get many customers today – the sky might be blue, but there was a good chance this little lot were going to take off at any moment.

'Hey!' Liam called in greeting as soon he was back within shouting distance. The wayward deckchair was now neatly folded and tucked under his arm – though it seemed to be acting a bit like a sail. Every couple of steps, Liam stumbled sideways as the canvas billowed and threatened to pull him off his feet.

'Hi!' said Lizzie, grinning over at him. 'Erm – that chair fainted and this one seems to want to go for a wander too!' she laughed, taking a slightly firmer hold on the wooden frame and wincing slightly as one of the others decided to fold in on itself.

'Yep – time to give it up as a bad job for the day,' said Liam, tossing his burden onto the sand and quickly moving to dismantle the front row of chairs before any of them could make a break for it.

Without thinking about it, Lizzie started to do the same with the back row. 'Where do they need to go?' she said, raising her voice slightly as the wind roared past her ears.

Liam pointed to a little cabin near the pavement. It was a little garden shed that had been decorated to resemble a tiny beach hut. It had been beautifully painted and firmly strapped down to several heavy concrete blocks – clearly a precaution against it ending up in the sea.

Lizzie quickly gathered a couple of the chairs together and hauled them towards the hut with her head bowed in an attempt not to get a mouthful of swirling sand while she was at it.

The minute she stepped inside the shed, she let out a sigh. Just to be out of the wind for a second was a huge relief.

'Blimey!' laughed Liam as he joined her, squeezing

into the cramped space. 'That's a bit much for July in Devon! I wouldn't be surprised if we're in for a storm later at this rate.'

'You might be right!' said Lizzie, pushing back her hair and removing several strands from her eyes and mouth before smiling at him. 'Hi, by the way!'

'Hello!' said Liam, smiling at her broadly. 'And thank you!'

'Are you kidding me?' snorted Lizzie. 'I think I owe you so many favours before we're anywhere near even that this one barely even counts!'

'Nah,' said Liam with a shrug. 'It doesn't work like that!'

'I like it in here,' said Lizzie, peering around just to give herself something other than his beautiful smile and lovely crinkly eyes to stare at.

'Yeah – I was lucky that the council agreed for me to have it down here in the summer,' he said. 'They're happy as long as it's off the beach before the end of September.'

'Fair enough,' said Lizzie. 'I mean, that'll be a bit of a pain but…'

Liam shrugged. 'Sean who built it for me said he's happy to stash it at his place over winter, and he'll do any repairs it needs before next year while it's there too.'

'That's brilliant!' said Lizzie. 'Actually… it's given me an idea.'

'Oh yeah?' said Liam.

Lizzie nodded, doing her best to ignore the fact that his eyes seemed to be twinkling at her.

'I don't think I mentioned it earlier – but I've now got both girls descending on me in the next few days,' she said. 'Problem is, I'm up to my eyeballs with moving boxes, and I haven't got time to finish unpacking before they turn up and shifting them all somewhere else would be a nightmare.'

'Especially when you want to be sorting the shop ready to open!' said Liam.

'Exactly!' said Lizzie, shooting him a grateful look that he'd come to that same conclusion quite so quickly and matter-of-factly.

'So… what's your plan?' he asked in amusement. 'You're going to shove them both in a beach hut?'

'Not quite,' said Lizzie shaking her head, 'but not too far off! I've got that big space outside the cottage, and if I could get my hands on a caravan – just for the short time the pair of them are with me – that could be the answer! I bet I could hire one from somewhere… and it's got to be cheaper than staying at the hotel while they're here!'

Liam stared at her silently for a moment, chewing on his lip, and Lizzie started to fidget. Why on earth did she have to go and mention the hotel? Now all she could think about was Liam in a fluffy robe!

'Tell you what,' said Liam at long last, 'you help me with the rest of these blasted chairs… and I reckon I might just have an idea!'

CHAPTER 13

*L*izzie picked at her cuff. She was wearing her favourite yellow jumper under her trusty dungarees – but at this rate, she was going to shred it to pieces if she wasn't careful.

No – she absolutely hadn't dressed up just because Liam was on his way over to the cottage to pick her up. Nope – not at all... that would just be sad.

'Shut up, Lizzie!' she muttered to herself.

This wasn't her. She was calm... collected... allegedly cool! She didn't get worked up about such mundane things as collecting a caravan with her new... new... what, exactly? Friend she'd managed to accidentally bump faces with?

Catchy!

Lizzie sucked in a deep breath in a bid to calm herself down. She knew what the problem was, of course... this morning, it was a case of Liam to the rescue yet again. She hated feeling like she was a burden and she couldn't help but feel more than a little bit bad about dragging him out on yet another mission.

That said, the man simply wouldn't take "no" for an answer... which was just as well if she was being completely honest. Even if she could find her car keys in the disaster zone that was the half-tidied cottage, there was no way her little car would cope with towing a caravan along the narrow Seabury lanes.

Still... it meant accepting yet another favour from Liam, and Lizzie couldn't help the fact that she was struggling a bit when it came to embracing the damsel in distress vibes. Hence the dungarees and favourite jumper. This was what she wore when she wanted to feel more like herself - comfortable and capable and not even slightly in need of rescuing.

Lizzie still couldn't quite believe that Liam had managed to magic up a caravan for her to borrow with just a couple of phone calls. Yet again, the solution to her problem had started with Ted and Margie Hatherleigh - who she was quickly starting to view as her fairy god-grumps.

As it turned out, the caravan Margie wanted to buy needed to be moved from its current owners' yard asap as there was some muttering about it being sold to a dealer. As the Hatherleigh's lane needed a fair bit of work before they'd even be able to think about fitting a caravan down there, Liam had easily managed to convince both parties for Lizzie to borrow it for a couple of weeks. Suddenly, everyone was happy - Margie wouldn't miss out on her caravan, Mrs Watkins would see the back of it at long last, and Lizzie would have a bit more space while the girls were in town.

Lizzie took a deep breath as she watched Liam's van trundle towards her. Her treacherous heart had started to do annoying little backflips every time she set eyes on him. She plunged her hands into the pockets of her dungarees and dug the toe of her heavy boots into the compacted mud of the driveway. She was about as awkward as any fifteen-year-old waiting to be picked up for a date... and this *wasn't* a date. Not by a long shot. Lizzie didn't *do* dates!

As the van got closer, Lizzie spotted a familiar, furry face sitting next to Liam.

'Hello, you two!' she said as they pulled up next to her.

'Hey!' said Liam. 'Hope you don't mind, but Stanley decided he wanted to come for a ride. I stopped by The Sardine to grab us a takeaway coffee and the next thing I knew, he'd hopped up into the van!'

'Of course I don't!' said Lizzie, grinning at Stanley's panting face. 'Won't Ethel mind though? Or Sarah?'

'Nah,' said Liam, shaking his head. 'Sarah's at college today, and Ethel and Lou are run off their feet in the café. Ethel actually said it would be a relief not to have to worry about him making a break for it and going for a swim while they weren't looking! The courtyard was packed, and Stanley kept nipping out every time one of the visitors opened the door.'

'You're a monkey,' said Lizzie, scruffing Stanley's head as she climbed up next to him, getting a big, wet nose in her ear in the process.

'Right... let's go fetch this caravan!' said Liam, expertly manoeuvring the van so they were heading back towards the town. 'I think Mr and Mrs Watkins are thoroughly excited to see the back of the thing! They've got big plans for the bit of garden it's parked on, apparently.'

'Like what?' said Lizzie, settling back and smiling as she felt Stanley lean his entire weight against her side.

'Well... Mrs Watkins wants a conservatory, but from what I could make out, Mr Watkins fancies a trampoline... supposedly for the grandkids.'

Lizzie grinned. 'A bit of trampolining can't hurt!'

'Well... it can when you're in your eighties and you're already rocking a plastic knee,' laughed Liam as they made their way up the hill past the allotments.

'Okay, you might have a point there,' said Lizzie.

'Yep... I've got a feeling Mrs Watkins is going to

win this particular battle!' he said. 'You're coffee's down there in the door by the way.'

'I seriously can't believe how nice it is!' said Lizzie, peering in the passenger wing mirror to take another peep at the smart little caravan that was trundling along merrily behind the van.

For some reason, she'd been expecting a rusty shed on wheels – something with moss growing in the seams and dandelions sprouting along the narrow window ledges… but it was pristine.

Mrs Watkins had shown her where to find all the nifty storage spaces, where everything was tucked away in the tiny but perfectly formed kitchen, and how the dining table folded down into a double bed if the single bunk wasn't quite big enough.

'Yeah,' said Liam, 'they've definitely looked after it. I can see why Margie's so keen to get her hands on it.' He shot a look at Stanley, who was now flopped down between them, fast asleep with his head in Lizzie's lap. He'd had a grand time chasing after cheeky rabbits in the Watkins's garden. 'Do you think it'll make things easier when the girls turn up?'

'Definitely!' said Lizzie with a nod. 'In fact, the state the cottage is in at the moment, I think the three of us will be fighting it out as to who gets to stay in it!'

Liam laughed. 'Well good. I'm glad – and not bad going… two disasters averted in as many days!'

'Yeah,' said Lizzie, feeling suddenly awkward. 'Thanks so much. You've been really kind.'

'Ah, get away with you!' said Liam with a shrug. 'I just happened to know the right people to point you at, that's all.'

'Erm… it's a bit more than that!' said Lizzie. 'I'm really grateful.'

'It's just what friends do,' he said, sounding awkward.

Lizzie raised her eyebrows.

Friends. Right.

Suddenly, she was thinking about that accidental kiss again. Neither of them had mentioned it… and now it would just be weird to bring it up. Still, a tiny splinter of disappointment had just lodged in her stomach when he'd dropped the "F" word so casually. Which was completely ridiculous. They *were* friends… and she should be grateful to have such a good friend so soon after moving back to town.

'Hey… I don't suppose I can tempt you to join me for a meal in The Pebble Street Hotel sometime?' she said, the words tumbling out before she could stop them. 'I mean… just to say thank you for everything!' she added quickly. 'I really want to find out what the food's like…'

Liam glanced at her, and Stanley stood up too, turning to stare at her with his eyebrows quivering.

Lizzie let out an uncomfortable laugh.

'What... you mean like a date?' said Liam.

Stanley turned to eyeball him.

'No!' said Lizzie quickly, feeling a blush hit her full force in the face. 'Not a date... I mean... just a-' she broke off as Stanley turned back to her and gave her a judgmental frown.

'It's a date!' said Liam.

'No... really - it isn't,' persisted Lizzie, doing her best not to laugh at the ridiculous dog, who now looked like he was watching a very slow tennis match as his head bobbed back and forth between them. 'More like a thank you, that's all.'

'Sounds like a date to me!' said Liam.

'You're impossible!' said Lizzie. 'It's *not* a date.'

'Can I wear my shorts?' he said.

'No,' said Lizzie.

'See – that makes it a date!'

'Honestly, men!' spluttered Lizzie.

Stanley let out a little *woof* of protest, and she snorted with laughter.

'Right... onto scarier things,' said Liam, as he turned down the lane that led towards her cottage.

'Uh oh,' said Lizzie, 'that sounds ominous.'

'I just mean reversing this monster into the right spot for you!' said Liam. 'Can you direct for me?'

'Sure!' said Lizzie with a shrug.

Liam came to a halt a little way from her drive, and she hopped down – making sure that Stanley stayed safely in the cab. All she needed to do was give Liam the heads up if he got too close to the ditch on one side or the hedge on the other – but as long as he kept it straight to start with, he shouldn't have any problems.

Two minutes later, Lizzie had broken into a cold sweat at the number of times Liam had nearly lost a wheel into the ditch. He'd come very close to taking a chunk out of the hedge several times too!

'THE OTHER LEFT!' she yelled, wheeling her arms frantically in the air. Every move he made seemed to be making matters worse.

Liam came to a halt and she heard the handbrake going on. Hurrying to the window, she peered in.

'You okay?' she said.

'Sorry!' laughed Liam. 'I'm making a total hash of this. My brain doesn't like working in backwards mode at the best of times... especially not when I'm towing anything.'

'Why didn't you say something?' said Lizzie, raising her eyebrows.

'Erm... I've not tried it for ages... and I thought I might have miraculously got better somehow?'

'Right,' said Lizzie. 'Switch places! All I need you to do is give me a sign if I get closer than about a foot to the ditch, okay?'

She was half expecting Liam to protest. That's what Mark had always done. If it had anything to do with driving... or fixing things... or decorating... or washing the car... he'd always wanted to take the lead - even though he was totally crap when it came to anything practical. It was just a simple fact that out of the pair of them, she was the one with the practical brain, had a knack for fixing things and genuinely enjoyed doing it.

To his credit, Liam didn't even hesitate. In fact, a look of pure relief crossed his face as he hopped gleefully down to make way for her behind the steering wheel.

'Right boy, let's get this job done,' said Lizzie, putting the van into reverse, adjusting both the rear-view mirror and the wing-mirror on her side, before making sure that Liam was nice and visible.

One minute later, she had the caravan sitting neatly outside the cottage - exactly where she wanted it. Leaving the van running, she hopped down and moved around the back to help Liam with the tow-hitch.

'Okay... that was officially impressive!' he said, grinning at her.

'Nah!' said Lizzie. 'I'm just one of the lucky ones whose brain works well in reverse.'

'Well, I'm jealous!' said Liam. 'And relieved! That was getting embarrassing. It's always the way when you're trying to impress someone!'

Lizzie straightened up and was amused to see that the cool, unrufflable Liam was blushing. He clearly hadn't meant to say that last bit out loud.

'Anyway,' he muttered, making a beeline for the driver's seat again. 'I'd better be going. Lots to do!'

'Okay!' said Lizzie in surprise. She'd been half-hoping to talk him into a cuppa before he left. Instead, she watched as he quickly clambered back into the van. 'Well, thanks again. I'll book that table at the hotel, shall I?'

Liam nodded. 'For our date!'

Then he put his foot down and took off, leaving Lizzie staring at the back of the van as it disappeared down the lane.

'It's *not* a date!' she said to no one in particular.

CHAPTER 14

Considering tonight *definitely wasn't a date*, Lizzie was finding it ridiculously hard to choose what to wear for her meal with Liam. The minute he'd zoomed off after delivering the caravan, Lizzie had dashed inside to call the hotel and book a table before she chickened out of the whole thing.

As luck would have it, it was Lou who'd answered. As even *more* luck would have it, someone had just cancelled a table for two for the next night.

'It's perfect for a date,' Lou had added, with a definite smirk in her voice.

With much awkward spluttering, Lizzie had firmed up the booking, and done her best to dodge Lou's inquisitive questioning (otherwise known as the third-degree). In the end, she'd simply given in and told her that she was treating Liam to a meal to say thank you for all his help.

'Like a date?' Lou had said.

'Definitely *not* a date!' Lizzie had replied firmly.

Now, though – with the huge laundry bags containing her clothes upended all over the living room while she tried on outfit after outfit – even Lizzie had to admit to herself that it was starting to feel a *lot* like a date.

Still, it wasn't a crime to want to look her best, was it? Plus, it gave her a great excuse to unpack her clothes. Lizzie really wished she'd just binned half of these things before she'd moved. Instead, she'd followed the path of least resistance and bunged them into the huge tartan bags with a promise to herself that she'd have a proper clear out once she'd settled in.

Picking up something pink and sparkly, Lizzie frowned, absolutely convinced it wasn't hers. It wasn't that she had anything against pink… or sparkles come to that… but she'd never actively choose to wear either!

'Oh my god!' she laughed, holding up the tent-like smock in front of her.

How on earth had she managed to keep this for so long? It was a maternity top her old nan had given her when Megan was little more than a bump. She couldn't remember ever actually wearing it – favouring voluminous men's shirts of ever-increasing sizes instead – but because it had come from her nan, she'd never had the heart to get rid of it.

'Well, I'm not wearing you!' she laughed, tossing it over the back of the sofa and staring forlornly at the heap in front of her.

This was ridiculous. Shouldn't she just pick whatever she was most comfortable in and settle for that? A pair of dungarees would definitely make life easier – she could change things up a bit and go for her bottle-green, cropped cord ones for a change? But no – that wasn't fair on Liam after she'd banned him from wearing shorts!

A little flutter of nerves hit Lizzie in the chest and she straightened up for a moment, taking a deep breath. At least he wasn't coming to the cottage to pick her up – that would have been excruciating! Even if Liam *did* want to go in for anything quite so soppy, there was no way they could arrange it because she didn't even have his mobile number. In fact… she wasn't sure if he'd turn up at all!

Lizzie had left a note pinned to the door of the deckchair hut with their booking time, and then she'd left a message for him in The Sardine for good measure – asking him to meet her at the hotel. Then she'd spent all day with her eyes peeled, hoping to bump into him… but typically, he seemed to have vanished into thin air.

Blowing out a long breath in an attempt to calm herself down, Lizzie shrugged. There was nothing she could do about it now. She'd just have to hope that he'd got the message… and was able to come!

'What's the worst-case scenario?' she muttered, rooting around in the pile of clothes again.

Well... that was easy enough to answer. If Liam didn't turn up she'd just have to sit at her table for two like Billy-no-mates and enjoy a meal for one instead. Frankly, on a normal day, that wouldn't bother her in the slightest. If it happened tonight though – she had to admit she'd be pretty gutted. And something told her Lou probably wouldn't ever let her live it down, either!

'Think positive, woman!'

All being well, in just over an hour she'd be sharing a meal at a swanky restaurant with the cutest guy she'd set eyes on in... well... decades!

Okay... so... if this *was* a date... what would she wear? It had been a very long time since she'd even considered that question... but surely she could figure something out!

Pulling the front door of the cottage closed behind her, Lizzie took a deep breath, willing the butterflies in her chest to bog off. She knew she was being ridiculous – and frankly, this wasn't like her at all. She didn't go all gooey and silly... but right now she was doing just that.

Still, at least she'd finally found something to

wear. Plus, one good thing had come out of turning the living room into a complete bomb site – she'd found her car keys at long last. They'd managed to get wedged down between the sofa cushions and, by a stroke of luck, they'd got tangled up in a cardigan sleeve and leapt out on her when she went to try it on.

Not that she was going to take the car this evening. For one thing, she wanted to have the option to help herself to a bit of Dutch courage if she needed it, and for another, she was already feeling way too giddy to be in charge of a vehicle. Hopefully – a nice breezy walk down to The Pebble Street Hotel should knock a bit of sense into her... and it would give her an excuse for looking a bit pink-cheeked and windswept when she got there too! Lizzie really did feel like a teenager again... silly, giddy and very alive. She had to admit, it felt pretty bloody wonderful.

Anyway, this was her last night of freedom. Both the girls were due to descend on Seabury the next day, and their arrival would shake everything up all over again... but Lizzie was looking forward to seeing them. Perhaps they'd get the chance to meet Liam while they were here. Not that he was her boyfriend... or her *anything* really, but... well... he *was* her friend, so that counted, didn't it?

For a moment, Lizzie's head filled with Liam as

she wondered what the girls would make of him. They'd like him, of course – who wouldn't? It was hard not to, with his wild, tousled hair and his ever-present shorts and mischievous smile.

'Breathe!' she muttered, slowing down a bit as she neared the seafront and the butterflies took flight again.

She paused in front of a little cottage, trying to catch a glimpse of her reflection in the window... just to check she still looked okay. Part of her wished she'd had the balls to go all-out and wear her little black dress... but that was *way* too try-hard for a casual meal with a friend. The other part of her wished she'd just stuck to her dungarees.

Instead, here she was, stuck in the middle somewhere, wearing her skinny black jeans and a cute black top that with its wide boat neck in a skull and crossbones print. She'd pulled her hair back with one of her red and white bandanas and even added a touch of red lippy. That was the bit she felt most uncomfortable about... but the over-excited teen that seemed to have body-snatched her had insisted. Still... at least she wasn't wearing heels. Her feet were comfy in her usual beaten-up old Converse.

Resisting the urge to grab a tissue and wipe off the lippy, Lizzie forced her steps onward towards the hotel. Why did this evening feel like it could be the start of something... new? Something... big? There was a strange weight of expectation around the whole thing.

'Urgh,' she groaned, stopping again when she came within sight of the hotel's front door. This had been a bad, bad idea. What if he didn't turn up? What if he hadn't got her messages?

He must have.

She'd left them all over town.

Lizzie willed herself to move forward and go inside the hotel, but she seemed to be rooted to the spot.

Why was this such a massive deal all of a sudden? This was just two friends meeting up for a casual meal. If Liam didn't turn up… it wasn't a big deal! Except it was. She'd be crushed!

Lizzie knew she was fooling herself – she knew exactly why this was so important to her. It was the first time she'd even bothered to look at another man since her divorce. In that time, Mark had moved on, dated and got married again. But she'd needed the time to grieve – not for her marriage - but for her little family unit that seemed to have dissolved overnight.

And now… she was ready to move on. She'd already taken huge steps to change her life into the one she wanted… but these little flutterings she felt every time she thought of Liam? They were new… and frankly, they were terrifying!

'Are you going to stand out there all night?'

The voice made Lizzie jump. She'd been gazing absently beyond the Pebble Street Hotel across the King's Nose, where the point jutted out to sea. Now her attention snapped back to the hotel. The door had been flung open and a face was grinning out at her. It had to be…

'Lou?' said Lizzie. 'I barely recognised you minus the swimming cap!'

'The one and only!' laughed Lou. 'I'll let you off… especially as you look a bit like someone's clonked you over the head this evening – you're in that much of a daze!'

Lizzie grinned at her. 'Yeah… just a bit preoccupied.'

'Well, don't get your knickers in a twist,' said Lou. 'Your date's here!'

'*Not* a date!' said Lizzie, even as she blew out a breath of pure relief.

'If it looks like a date and wiggles like a date, then it must be a date,' said Lou blandly. 'Besides – if it's not a date, why do you look quite so hot right now?!'

Lizzie's grin widened even as she felt her cheeks flame at the compliment. It was a very long time since anyone had told her she was hot… in fact, this might be the first time ever!

'Erm… thanks?' she said, feeling awkward.

'Just stating a fact,' Lou shrugged. 'Anyway, the question still stands… are you just going to hang around out here making poor Liam sweat, or are you going to come in and have something to eat?!'

'Oh!' said Lizzie. 'Right… yeah. I'm coming in.'

'Excellent,' said Lou with a wide smile. 'Follow me – I'll take you to your table.'

CHAPTER 15

*L*izzie paused for just a second before following Lou through the gleaming doorway - she couldn't help taking a moment to admire the neatly clipped, narrow strip of front garden, polished menu holders, and neat welcome mat. The Pebble Street Hotel gleamed golden and welcoming in the evening air.

It was very different to what she remembered from when the girls were little and Veronica Hughes had ruled the roost. Then it had been scruffy, run-down and vastly overpriced.

'I know!' said Lou, grinning at Lizzie as she followed her into the foyer, only to stop again.

Okay – this was far beyond welcoming. This was stunning!

'Erm... so it's changed a bit in here, then!' said

Lizzie, running a nervous hand down her top and skinny jeans. Clearly, a beaten-up pair of her favourite shoes had been a very poor choice. This place deserved designer heels at the very least!

The last time she'd been in here was when Jenna was tiny, and one of the mothers had booked the dining room for her son's birthday party. The poor woman was new in town, so it wasn't her fault that she'd inadvertently subjected the kids to an hour and a half of pure torture as they'd all sat quietly on sticky, grubby chairs, not daring to make a sound in case they invoked the wrath of Veronica.

'Lionel's done a gorgeous job, hasn't he?' said Lou. 'Just wait until you've tried the food too. Hattie's a genius.'

Lizzie shot her a nervous smile. She normally had the appetite of a horse, but she was so worked up right now, she had a feeling she'd struggle to eat a single bite.

'Right,' said Lou, tugging at her elbow, 'don't leave that poor guy waiting any longer. He's been here for ages.'

'Oh don't!' said Lizzie, pulling a face.

'Okay… ten minutes!' said Lou, shooting her a naughty wink.

Lizzie grinned back. She might not be quite in the right frame of mind to fully appreciate Lou's friendliness and banter, but she had a sneaking suspicion she might have just met a kindred spirit. Lou's smile was infectious, and she clearly didn't believe in taking life's little moments too seriously.

'Right... let me at him!' said Lizzie, blowing out a breath and squaring her shoulders.

'That's more like it!' said Lou approvingly.

Lizzie followed her new friend into a beautiful dining room. Parquet floor gleamed underfoot, and the cream-clothed tables were surrounded by merry-faced diners. Light spilled into the room from the wide doors at the far end, and Lizzie could suddenly see why the place had such a good reputation these days. If you were going to splash out on a nice meal, this was the perfect place to do it!

Considering it was still pretty early, the restaurant was already packed, and there was a lovely, light buzz of chatter in the air. As her eyes danced around the room, trying to take everything in, Lizzie spotted Liam at a cosy table for two near the windows. The minute he saw her, he got to his feet.

Lizzie let out a low gasp of pure appreciation.

'Scrubs up pretty well, eh?' breathed Lou over her shoulder as she led Lizzie towards the table.

Lizzie just widened her eyes. There was *no way* she was going to let the fact that she heartily agreed with Lou escape her lips. Not when she was this close to Liam, and the man in question seemed to have his eyes glued on her as she approached him.

'Hey!' he said as they came to a standstill next to his table.

Lou was beaming like a Cheshire cat as she stared from Lizzie to Liam and then back again.

'Hi,' said Lizzie, smiling at him nervously and doing her best to ignore the over-excited Lou, who was practically vibrating next to her.

'You look amazing,' said Liam.

'Aw!' said Lou with a squeak. 'Sorry... I mean... I'll leave you to your date.'

'It's not a date!' they both chorused as Lou scuttled away.

Lizzie turned an amused smile on Liam. 'Thanks, by the way. You look fab too.'

'No shorts, as promised,' he said with a shrug.

'Well... you look great,' she said awkwardly. Because he really did scrub up remarkably well. It wasn't like he was wearing a suit – thank heavens - but his dark blue shirt looked like it had seen an iron relatively recently, and he was wearing a pair of light chinos.

'Here,' he said, hurrying around to her side of the table and pulling her chair out for her.

'Thanks!' said Lizzie in surprise. As she sat down awkwardly, she got a waft of something woody and spicy and ridiculously delicious. Probably Liam's shower gel. The scent practically made her shiver. Blimey... considering this really *wasn't* a date, it was off to an excellent start.

'Want to hear something weird?' he said, grinning at her as he sat back down.

'Always!' she said, smiling at him and feeling some of her nerves start to melt away.

'I'm nervous,' he said, looking slightly sheepish. 'I've been nervous ever since I picked up your message earlier.'

Lizzie smiled at him broadly. 'Yeah. Me too.'

'You?' said Liam in surprise, rubbing the back of his neck. 'I didn't think anything fazed you!'

'Are you kidding me?!' laughed Lizzie. 'Pretty much *everything* fazes me. You saw what I was like when I thought I might not be able to open the shop!'

'That's different,' said Liam quickly. 'That's your dream! And anyway – you were still super-cool about it all.'

'I think it was you who was cool – swooping in with a solution,' said Lizzie. 'And again with the caravan.'

'It was nothing,' said Liam. 'Both times!' he added with a laugh. 'Anyway – have you decided which one of the girls is going in there?'

'Probably Jenna,' said Lizzie, finally deciding that she couldn't possibly wait a single second longer to give into her grumbling stomach. It looked like her appetite was back with a vengeance. Liam seemed to be intent on ignoring the warm, herb-scented bread that was sitting in the basket between them, but there was no way she could last another second.

Choosing a roll, she ripped off a chunk and spread it with a thick layer of creamy butter.

'Though,' she said, glancing up at Liam, 'the caravan is such a nice space, I was serious when I said I might commandeer it for myself and leave those two to fight it out in the cottage!'

She took a bite of her bread and rolled her eyes, a small groan of pleasure escaping her lip.

'Okay, that's it!' laughed Liam, grabbing a roll for himself. 'I'm starving!'

'Me too!' said Lizzie.

'Good,' said Liam. 'In that case, shall I get Lou over and we'll get our orders in... and... from previous experience, I can recommend the Pebble Street pudding.'

'Shall we share one?' said Lizzie.

'Share?' said Liam. 'No. Definitely not. Or at least, not the first portion. I'd say we order three... one each and the third to share.'

'It's that good?' said Lizzie.

'You'd better believe it. Anyway, if you don't like it, I'll gladly clear up the extras!' said Liam.

'Right... in that case, you're on!' said Lizzie, turning to wave to Lou.

Lizzie leaned against the railings for a moment, letting the cool air from the sea dance across her pink cheeks. It had been an unexpectedly wonderful evening. Of course – she should have known it would be fun because Liam was such easy company. But… this had been more than fun.

Their cosy table had been like a private little island – a bubble that contained just the two of them. After the initial awkwardness had passed, the pair of them chatted away as though the rest of the diners didn't even exist. In fact… three hours later and they really *didn't* exist – the pair of them had closed the restaurant… even though Lizzie could swear the entire meal had only lasted ten minutes.

In the end, it had taken some seriously heavy hinting from Lou about her tired feet and the fact that were already on their third coffee to get them to pay up and leave. Lizzie made sure she left a generous tip… and she had a feeling Lou would be in touch for all the gossip tomorrow anyway!

Lizzie closed her eyes for just a moment, relishing the memory of every time their knees had touched under the table… and that moment Liam had reached across and rested his hand on hers… just for a moment. It had felt like the most intimate, exciting thing that had ever happened to her.

But… as with all good things, it had come to an end. She had the long walk back up to the cottage, and Liam needed to head back to his own place… wherever that was.

'Okay – slightly awkward question,' she said,

turning to face him and watching as he pulled on his jacket.

'O-kay?' said Liam.

'Where do you live?!' she said.

'How very forward!' he said, his eyebrows shooting up in mock surprise.

Lizzie stuck her tongue out at him, her pleasant, wine-haze leading the way. 'I didn't mean that!' she laughed. 'I just meant – are we walking together for a bit or are you in the other direction?'

'And why's that awkward?' he said curiously.

'Because you know nearly everything about me – where I live, why I'm back, why I'm divorced… you know all about the girls arriving… and helped me to find somewhere for them to stay… and I don't even know where you live!'

'Oh!' said Liam. 'Well, I'm on Sand Piper Lane. But I'm walking you back up to your cottage first. It's far too late for wandering around the lanes on your own!'

'This is Seabury!' said Lizzie with a shrug.

'I don't care,' said Liam. 'Don't worry, I'll be a gent. I won't even come through the garden gate.'

'Shame,' said Lizzie, then promptly clapped a hand over her mouth.

'Lizzie Moore!' he laughed. 'I thought this wasn't a date?'

Lizzie cocked her head, staring at him for a moment. 'It's not,' she said, pushing away from the barriers and moving slowly towards him. 'But not because I don't want it to be.'

'Oh?' said Liam, his eyes widening slightly as she came to stand right in front of him.

She looked down, making sure her Converse were toe to toe with his boots.

'So…' he said quietly when she looked at him. 'So… why isn't it a date again?'

'Because,' said Lizzie, 'I quite like the idea of another – official - first date.'

'You do?' said Liam.

'I do,' she said, holding his gaze. His eyes were a soft grey, but this close, she could see the dark, navy ring around his irises. 'What about you?'

'Me?' said Liam. 'I think I'd like to kiss you right now.'

'Here?' breathed Lizzie.

Liam nodded.

'Okay!' said Lizzie, her heart going into overdrive even as the most ridiculous smile spread across her lips. She stared at him, and he stared right back, not moving. Lizzie shrugged, and leaning in, she kissed him very lightly on the corner of the mouth before stepping back, still smiling.

'Coming?' she said, holding out her hand.

Liam nodded and, reaching out, threaded his fingers through hers.

Warmth seemed to spread up her arm as the pair

of them wandered along the seafront hand in hand in complete silence.

They only got as far as The Sardine before Liam drew her towards him. Smoothing her hair away from her face with his free hand, he kissed her under the street light.

CHAPTER 16

All Lizzie really wanted to do right now was spend the morning lazing around in bed... but as much as she'd love nothing more than to curl up with the duvet and imagine it was Liam's arms wrapped around her, she really had to get up.

Today was the day she had to pick both the girls up from the train station in Plymouth. By some complete fluke, they were arriving on the same train... though typically, they'd managed to book seats at opposite ends of the thing!

Lizzie knew she should be over the moon about seeing them. This was her chance for some quality family time – a rare thing these days! Right now, though, all she wanted to do was re-live the night before.

Liam had walked her all the way home – and just as he'd promised, he hadn't even set foot inside the garden gate. That didn't mean they hadn't kissed like teenagers all the way up the hill from town, though.

It must have taken them over an hour to reach the cottage, and then they'd stayed outside for ages, snogging against the side of the caravan. It had taken every last drop of Lizzie's willpower not to drag Liam inside when she'd finally retreated into the cottage. Now wasn't the time to rush things, though. She wanted to savour every last second of whatever this was.

Considering it hadn't been a date, it had been pretty bloody wonderful! Lizzie shivered and curled her toes at the thought. Who was she kidding? Of *course* last night had been a date. One of the best dates she'd ever had, in fact. Even so, she couldn't wait to see what came next. Liam had promised her that their *official* first date would be special. All she knew was that it was going to have to go some to beat last night!

Sadly though, all that was going to have to wait.

Glancing at the clock on her bedside table, Lizzie realised that she needed to get a wiggle on. There were still a few boxes in her car left over from the move, and she needed to drop them off at the Old Grain Store before heading to Plymouth – otherwise there wouldn't be enough in there for the girls and their bags!

With a groan, Lizzie pushed the duvet back and clambered out of bed. She needed at least two buckets of coffee before it was time to go. All that kissing might have made her feel like a randy teenager – but her ability to deal with late nights definitely hadn't got the memo.

Lizzie was just emerging from the Old Grain Store when Liam's van appeared, heading in her direction. She grinned as he slowed down.

'I enjoyed our date!' he shouted out of the window as he trundled past.

'It wasn't a date!' she called back, laughing as he disappeared towards North Beach. 'Idiot!' she added with a giggle.

It wasn't long before she was ensconced in her own car and heading out of town in the opposite direction, wishing that she could spend some time with Liam later on. There was no way she was about to abandon the girls the moment they got here, though!

Lizzie sighed. She wasn't entirely sure when they'd be able to grab some time alone together, but they'd work something out.

'Get a grip!' she chuckled.

It was like the man had somehow managed to set up camp in her head. She blamed those kisses... especially the ones where he'd pressed her up against the side of the caravan!

Good grief!

'Maybe not while you're driving!' she gasped, winding the window down so that she could get some fresh air. The little car seemed to be incredibly warm all of a sudden!

The drive to the station didn't seem to take as long as usual... but perhaps that was because her mind was full of her new boyfriend.

Boyfriend!

That might be taking things a little bit too far! Liam was definitely *not* a boy. Boys didn't kiss like that.

Blimey!

Maybe it was a good thing the girls were about to descend on her after all. This really was the last thing she'd been expecting when she'd moved back to Seabury, and she could do without completely losing her head over the poor guy! Even so, she had to admit that the previous evening had been... exciting. Stupidly, wonderfully exciting. She couldn't wait to do it all over again as soon as she could pin Liam down.

That was possibly the worst choice of words she could have gone with... and they'd made her all hot and bothered again. Lizzie rolled her eyes at herself, fanning her face with her hand.

Right... it was time to go and meet the girls... and push all sordid thoughts out of her head while she was at it!

Lizzie managed to reach the platform just as the train doors were opening, and a swoop of excitement ran through her. It might have presented her with a bit of a logistical nightmare, but having her little family all back under the same roof was going to be wonderful. Well... kind of under the same roof... and Mark wouldn't be joining them, would he? But... that was okay!

Suddenly, after all these years, it really *was* okay. Mark would always be her friend, but the dark hole in her heart that had been reserved for them as a couple had miraculously disappeared. In its place was a huge bubble of gratitude – for Seabury, for her new friends and new business... and for the possibility of something else new... hinted at by an entire evening of stolen kisses.

As the commuters started to stream from the train, their heads down, eyes glued to their phones like a hoard of zombies, Lizzie stared around, trying to catch sight of the girls.

'Jenna!' she yelled, raising her hand in the air to catch the attention of her youngest as she stepped down from the train. Jenna's face creased into a wide smile, and pushing her mane of tangled, strawberry blond hair over one shoulder, she floated in Lizzie's direction.

Lizzie couldn't help but smile. With her long white cotton dress and patchwork jacket, Jenna stood out like a beacon against the rest of the passengers.

Even though she'd been travelling for hours and must be stressed out of her brain, she looked relaxed and happy. Her eyes glittered with life as she dumped her bags onto the ground and threw her arms around Lizzie in a tight hug.

'Yay! Mum!' she squealed, right in her ear.

Lizzie grinned, sinking into Jenna's embrace for a moment, only to let out a little cough and step back quickly.

'Sorry,' laughed Jenna. 'Everything about me smells like burning van!'

Lizzie nodded, wriggling her nose, trying to rid herself of the weird scent of burning electrics.

'Meggie!' squealed Jenna, almost bursting Lizzie's eardrums in the process.

Sure enough, there was Megan… but not the Megan she remembered from their last catch-up over coffee in Bristol. Her eldest daughter looked like she'd deflated somehow. Her usually immaculate dark bob was lifeless, flat and pulled back behind her ears. Megan wasn't wearing a scrap of makeup – not a bad thing in itself, but Lizzie didn't think she'd seen Megan's bare face since she was about thirteen.

Also missing in action was the usual sharp blazer, neat pencil skirt and ballet pumps. Instead, Megan was wearing a tired old pair of jogging trousers, battered trainers and a motheaten sweatshirt with a glittery cat on the front. Lizzie frowned. She recognized that cat – she'd bought it for Megan as a joke when she was about sixteen. Her daughter had been horrified. The fact she was wearing it now didn't bode well.

'Don't call me that,' Megan grouched as she made her way over to her little sister.

Lizzie smiled. She might not look like her old self right now, but that response was classic, old-school Megan.

'Why not, Meggie-Moo?' said Jenna with a beatific smile as she wrapped her arm around her sister's neck in a hug that was nearing head-lock territory.

'Get off!' said Megan, struggling to break free whilst completely failing to keep a tired smile off her face as Jenna planted a sloppy kiss on her temple.

'Hi love,' said Lizzie, stepping forward to give her daughter a hug. It was nothing like the all-enveloping cuddle she'd just received from Jenna. A quick double pat on the back before she was pushed away again.

'Jeez mum, what are you wearing?!' said Megan, staring in mild horror at Lizzie's cord dungarees.

'I think you'll find she looks fabulous!' said Jenna enthusiastically. 'Whereas you look like...'

'*Girls! Quit it!*' said Lizzie, sensing a quarrel brewing at ten paces. They weren't even in the car yet... it wasn't a good omen for what the few weeks were going to be like! Any hope she had that the girls might rub along a bit better now that they were older promptly disappeared.

'Can we get going?' said Megan. 'I'm knackered.'

'*You're* knackered?!' laughed Jenna. 'I'm the one who's been on all the planes in the entire world!'

'Don't exaggerate!' huffed Megan. 'Anyway – it's not our fault you haven't got an ounce of ambition and keep disappearing all over the place.'

Lizzie rolled her eyes and decided that she didn't have the energy to step in between them again. She grabbed Megan's large suitcase – ominously heavy considering she'd said she'd only be staying for a couple of days - and started to lead the way back to the car.

'Shotgun!' said Jenna, the moment they reached it.

'No way, I'm sitting up front,' said Megan. 'I'm the one that gets car-sick.'

'Give over,' said Jenna. 'You've not been car-sick since you were eight – and that's only because you stuffed your face with too much candyfloss and then went on the big wheel!'

Lizzie grimaced. She remembered that journey far too well, even though it had been Mark who'd cleared up the violent pink puddles from the back of the passenger seat!

'Anyway,' said Jenna, 'I've been away for longer and I want to tell mum about the van blowing up.'

'No way – I-'

'You can *both* sit in the back!' said Lizzie, quickly pulling rank before the girls descended into all-out war in the car park.

While the pair of them muttered and mumbled their way into the back seat, with plenty of elbowing on the way in, Lizzie hefted the big case into the front seat and buckled it in. At least it wasn't Jenna's case... though she could already smell the fumes wafting towards her from the boot. Something told her that her little car would always have a slight whiff of burning van from now on.

Lizzie barely had to say a word all the way back to Seabury – the girls were too intent on quarrelling about every single little thing. She was just turning down the lane that led down into the town when she remembered something.

'Have either of you heard from your dad yet?' she said, shooting a quick look in the rear-view mirror. She caught a look pass between them that she didn't quite understand.

'Nope,' said Jenna.

'Me neither,' said Megan.

'I'm a bit worried,' said Jenna.

'Yeah...' said Megan.

Lizzie bit her lip. She knew it had precisely nothing to do with her these days, but the fact that Mark hadn't messaged either of the girls or returned their calls was definitely odd.

'Well... shall we try him again over the weekend?' she said.

'Yeah,' said Megan. 'I've left about a dozen messages, but he's not even seen some of them.'

Lizzie frowned. 'Erm... either of you tried calling Tiffany?'

'Hell no!' laughed Jenna.

Megan shook her head.

'Right... well, maybe that would be a good plan?' she suggested.

'Can you do it?' said Jenna.

Seriously? She hadn't signed up for calling her ex-husband's new wife just because he'd gone incommunicado. But then... she *was* starting to get a bit worried.

'Let's see if we can get hold of him... if not, then we'll call Tiff.'

'Eww!' said Jenna.

Lizzie smirked. Her daughter's sentiment just about covered it.

'Right!' said Lizzie, 'here we are!'

She slowed the car down, ready to pull up next to the caravan.

'Mother,' said Megan, 'what the *hell* is that?!'

'Cool!' said Jenna.

'That... is going to be a bedroom for one of you,' said Lizzie, bracing for the storm of complaints.

'Me!' said Megan.

'No – me!' said Jenna.

'I asked first,' said Megan.

Lizzie let out a sigh, killed the engine and hopped out of the car. She needed coffee. She'd leave those two to fight it out between them.

'Take a look before ripping each other's hair out,' she laughed before making her way towards the cottage. 'I'll put the kettle on.'

'But mum...' said Jenna.

'If my case is in there, it's mine!' crowed Megan.

Lizzie closed her eyes briefly, wondering how she'd somehow managed to travel back in time during the drive back from Plymouth.

Coffee – that was the only answer – before she started to tear her hair out. She pushed her way through the garden gate and then broke into a wide smile.

There, leaning against the front door, was a beautiful bunch of wildflowers, tied together with what looked like a piece of old deck-chair fabric.

Suddenly, Lizzie was firmly back in the present. Even if her daughters were squabbling behind like they were back in primary school... Lizzie was ready to stride into her future - and it was bright and full of first dates and toe-curling kisses.

THE END

IN A SPIN IN SEABURY

SEABURY - BOOK 11

CHAPTER 1

*L*izzie closed her eyes and pursed her lips as she paused at the bathroom door to listen. There was the unmistakable sound of water cascading from the shower into the bathtub.

'Give me strength!' she muttered. One of the girls had beaten her to it yet again.

It's not a big deal.

Not. A. Big. Deal!

Sucking in a long, deep breath, Lizzie paused for a second before letting it out again, sounding like a deflating balloon. She needed to get her temper under control – it was way too early in the morning to be flying off the handle! The past week had brought her mood to an angry simmer that seemed to be constantly bubbling away just beneath the surface. Right now, she was about ready to boil over.

It had been a little over a week since Megan and

Jenna had descended on Seabury. Lizzie knew she should be in seventh heaven. After all, the unexpected company of both her adult daughters was a rare thing these days, and definitely something she should be making the most of.

Instead, their visit was starting to feel more like a cruel and unusual form of punishment!

Her house was in chaos.

Her life was in chaos.

Every single day was chaos.

From the moment Jenna and Megan had stepped off the train, Lizzie's wonderful new start in Seabury had turned into a whirlwind of frustration set to the soundtrack of their bickering. They might be in their twenties, but they seemed to have regressed by at least a decade!

Lizzie knew they were both facing challenges... but that's what being an adult was all about, wasn't it? As much as she wanted to be their safe haven - somewhere they were both welcome when they needed a bit of TLC – she couldn't help wishing they'd do the same for her.

Instead of the nurturing, bonding mother-and-daughter time she'd been hoping for, Lizzie felt like she'd somehow time-travelled back to the *terrible teen* years... and she didn't like it one bit! She hadn't much enjoyed being the exasperated mother of two teenagers the first time around – not when they'd tried her patience at every turn.

She really didn't think she could handle a do-over!

One thing was for certain – the quiet life she'd been craving when she'd moved back to Seabury just a handful of weeks ago had taken one look at her girls and done a bunk.

Lizzie had been doing her best to take things one day at a time… or even one moment at a time… but right at *this* moment, she needed a shower! The girls might be in holiday mode, but she had a business she was trying to get on its feet.

'Oh, come *on!*' she sighed, reaching out to give the bathroom door handle an experimental rattle. As expected, it was locked.

'Mother! How about a little bit of privacy here!'

So… it was Megan in there, was it?

Lizzie frowned. It was bad enough that she had to shift all Jenna's candles and grubby joss-stick holders out of the way every time she wanted to use the bathroom, but at least her youngest was actually *staying* in the cottage.

Megan, however, had taken up residence in the snazzy little caravan Lizzie had borrowed and parked up outside… a caravan that boasted an equally snazzy little shower room! The girls had fought tooth and nail over it, too!

'Megan!' she hissed, tapping on the door. 'The caravan's got its own bathroom! Couldn't you have used that? You know I've got to get to work!'

'Ew, no!' spluttered Megan. 'I'm not going in there. Now... kindly bog off, you're ruining my morning success meditation!'

Lizzie bit her lip to stop herself from swearing.

Coffee. She needed coffee.

Turning on her heel, Lizzie stomped downstairs, snuggling her chin down into her ancient towelling robe as though it were some kind of comfort blanket.

'Morning mum!'

Jenna was already in the kitchen, standing on her tiptoes as she rummaged deep inside one of the cupboards. This vision of her youngest – wearing a long white Victorian nightdress with her blonde ringlets tumbling down her back - was practically angelic. But, instead of it warming her heart, Lizzie felt her simmering anger threatening to boil over.

All the cupboard doors were open, and there were various jars and tupperware boxes spread across every available surface – most of them minus their lids.

'Jeez mum - don't you ever shop?' said Jenna, screwing up her nose as she took a sniff of the last bit of Lizzie's precious ginger marmalade. Ethel had given it to her when she'd first arrived, and she'd been eking it out. She was saving this last bit as a special treat for when she really needed a pick-me-up!

'I've been a bit busy,' sighed Lizzie, watching as Jenna dumped the open jar on the counter before turning to give the uncut remains of a loaf of bread a good squeeze before putting it down again.

'I hope you're going to eat that now you've manhandled it!' said Lizzie.

Jenna just shrugged and wrinkled her nose as she headed to the fridge and pulled out the glass bottle of milk. She swirled it around and gave it a sniff.

'Don't you have any oat milk?' she said.

'Does it look like we do?' said Lizzie.

'Alright, alright, keep your wig on!' said Jenna, swigging milk directly from the bottle.

Lizzie closed her eyes, sending up a little prayer to whoever might be listening to lend her some patience. Wearily, she cracked them back open and her gaze landed on the bunch of wildflowers Liam had left for her on the doorstep the day after their "date that wasn't really a date."

Suddenly, Lizzie was smiling again. Liam. He was one good thing she could hold onto right now, wasn't he?

Jenna jogged the table as she moved back towards the cupboards to continue her rummaging, and Lizzie sighed as several golden petals drifted down onto the wooden surface. The flowers had almost had it - but she couldn't bear to get rid of them while there was still the tiniest bit of life and colour left in them.

Lizzie hadn't even told the girls she had a boyfriend yet - that could be tricky! For one thing, she didn't really want to unleash them on him – it was too soon for him to be exposed to the weirdness that was her family. For another – she'd definitely lose her cool if they criticised him!

Besides, what would she say? Actually saying the word "boyfriend" out loud would sound ridiculous… and there was nothing ridiculous about Liam. Lizzie sighed. If only she could spend a bit more time with him…

Ever since the girls had arrived, Lizzie had only managed to sneak moments with Liam here and there. Megan and Jenna had developed an annoying habit of turning up unannounced and loitering around… not quite knowing what to do with themselves.

Still… she'd be able to go on a proper date with him sooner or later, wouldn't she? Lizzie grinned idly at the fading flowers. Even though their stolen moments had been a bit few and far between, they'd certainly been memorable – Liam's little deckchair shed on the beach had certainly become one of her favourite places in Seabury!

Lizzie felt a tingle creep down her spine and she shivered.

'Go and get dressed if you're cold!'

Megan's sharp voice made Lizzie jump, and she glanced up to find her eldest daughter calmly spreading the last of her precious ginger marmalade onto two pieces of toast, her wet hair piled up on top of her head in a towel turban.

'Oh good, you're out of the shower,' said Lizzie, heaving herself to her feet.

'Yeah,' said Megan. 'But I think Jenna's on her way up.'

'What!' said Lizzie, staring around and realising that while she'd been daydreaming about Liam, the girls had managed to pull the old switcheroo on her. 'No no no! I *have* to get in there - I've got to get to work!'

'Mother! You're constantly lecturing me on getting my priorities right... but I think it's you who seriously needs to take a chill pill!' said Megan, rolling her eyes as she nibbled the edge of her toast. Two seconds later, she pulled a face and slid the entire lot into the bin. 'Oh – did you want that?' she added, with an unconcerned shrug as Lizzie let out a little squeak of protest.

Lizzie took a deep breath, swallowed hard, and decided that the safest option would be to leave the kitchen without saying a word. She shook her head tightly and left the room.

Jogging upstairs in the vague hope she might reach the bathroom before Jenna got into the shower, Lizzie's hopes were dashed the minute she reached the top step. The door was closed and Jenna was already warbling some kind of folk tune in the bathroom.

Lizzie bustled over and tried the handle.

'Locked!' came Jenna's cheery voice.

Lizzie opened her mouth in a silent, infuriated scream and then stamped her foot for good measure - not that Jenna would hear it over the roar of the shower.

'Love,' she said loudly, doing her best to keep her voice sounding cheerful rather than axe-murder-y, 'I really need to get in there so I can go to work!'

'Sorry mum,' came Jenna's floaty, laughing voice, 'if ya snooze, ya lose!'

Lizzie stuck her tongue out at the bathroom door. How was it that neither of her *supposedly* adult daughters had even considered that *maybe* someone else's need was greater than their own?

Just as Jenna started to belt out the opening lines of her French folk song again, the whine of a hairdryer drifted up the stairs. Lizzie lifted her hands and covered both her ears for a second. She'd been promising herself mornings filled with the calm of the seaside – not this cacophony!

Well… there was nothing for it. She needed to escape before she blew a fuse!

Lizzie stomped back into her bedroom. It was time to throw some clothes on and head into work - she'd just have to forgo her much-needed shower. Maybe she'd grab some breakfast first… preferably somewhere where the bread hadn't already been fondled by one of her ungrateful daughters!

CHAPTER 2

As soon as Lizzie left the cottage and caravan behind her, she felt better.

'Breathe!' she murmured, staring over the hedgerows dotted with ripening hawthorn berries, towards the glittering waves far below. The sight brought an instant smile to her face, and she felt a heavy weight lift from her shoulders. This was why she was back in Seabury. The place always had a magical effect on her - irritating offspring or not.

Lizzie gave herself a little shake as she strode along, doing her best to ignore the fact that she felt a bit grubby and crumpled having left the house without her usual morning ablutions.

Still... in a way, Megan *was* right. Lizzie would never admit it to her infuriating daughter – but she *did* need to chill out a bit. The girls would drift back to their own lives before she knew it. In the meantime, Lizzie knew she should be doing her best to enjoy having them there with her.

The little town was at its best right now, cloaked in a jacket of late summer sunshine. The air had a hint of crisp, autumnal tang to it - a taste of the golden days to come. Right now though, the sun still had a bit of warmth to it. For once, the weather forecast was right – they were in for a beautiful day.

Frankly, Lizzie didn't really mind what the weather was up to. Seabury was gorgeous whatever the weather - rain, frost, wind or snow – and she was glad to be back, ready to experience it all.

By the time she reached the seafront road that would lead her to the Old Grain Store - or Moore Bikes as she'd renamed her soon-to-be shop – Lizzie was smiling from ear to ear. As usual, Seabury had delivered, and she was ready to face the day.

Even so, her smile slipped a little only to be replaced by a frown of confusion as she neared the Old Grain Store. There, piled against the heavy wooden doors were dozens of rusty old bikes. They were propped up against each other, blocking the pavement.

'What on earth..?!' laughed Lizzie, hurrying towards them.

Moore Bikes wasn't even officially open yet - Jenna and Megan's arrival had put her behind schedule a bit. She had no idea where this lot had come from!

'Morning lovely!' came Ethel's voice as she bustled past on the other side of the road.

'Hi Ethel!' said Lizzie in surprise. 'Where'd you spring up from?'

'Just back from a nice breakfast with Charlie up at the allotments before I start in the cafe!' said Ethel, with a dreamy smile. 'It's so beautiful up there at this time of the morning.'

'But... then you must have just followed me all the way down the hill?' said Lizzie.

'Yep!' nodded Ethel. 'I did try calling your name, but you were in your own little world, and I'm afraid to say I don't *do* running anymore!'

'I'm so sorry!' said Lizzie, cursing herself for being so wrapped up in her own head that she'd missed a walk into town with her friend.

'Don't you think on it!' said Ethel with a kind smile. 'I'm sure you needed a few minutes to yourself. You've got quite a houseful up there with your two in town.'

'Don't I know it!' said Lizzie with a rueful grin.

'Ah well, I'm sure it's lovely to have them home for a bit,' said Ethel. 'Anyway... looks like you've got a busy day ahead of you!' she added, nodding at the pile of bikes.

'Erm... yeah!' said Lizzie, frowning at them all. 'I've got no idea where this lot came from, though...'

'I promise I didn't say anything,' said Ethel,

suddenly looking more than a little bit shifty. 'Or at least… not much!'

'Not much - *to who?*' said Lizzie, raising her eyebrows.

Ethel pulled a face. 'Well… I *did* mention that you'd be opening soon. Only to Charlie - but then the old fool went and spread it around the allotments. You know what that lot are like up there - tell one of them anything and they all know by tea time.'

'Right,' laughed Lizzie, 'so… these are all from people up at the allotments?'

'Could be,' muttered Ethel, looking slightly sheepish. 'Anyway, can't stop… I'll be late for work!'

Lizzie shook her head and grinned as she watched Ethel beetle off towards The Sardine.

'Well… they'll definitely keep me out of trouble for a while!' she chuckled to herself. First things first, she'd need to shift a few of them out of the way so that she could get inside.

Lizzie grabbed the handlebars of a gorgeous bike. It had a real vintage-vibe - complete with a cute front basket. She spotted an old-fashioned cardboard luggage label dangling from the bell. Flipping it over, she stared down at the elegant, copperplate handwriting.

Needs a new chain and the brakes adjusting please.
Erica – plot 15c

Lizzie propped the old thing gently against the wall before shifting a few more of the new arrivals so that she could unlock the shop.

Propping both doors open as wide as they would go, Lizzie began wheeling the bikes inside, two at a time, and carefully lining them up against the far wall of the workshop. Sure enough, every single one of them had a note taped or tied somewhere – they dangled from handlebars, saddles and even the wheel spokes.

Darting back outside for the next pair, Lizzie paused to pick up a piece of paper as it fluttered from a brake lever onto the pavement.

'Oh no you don't!' she said, grabbing it before it had the chance to blow away. It would be a total nightmare if this lot got mixed up! This one had been scrawled on the inside of a torn seed packet.

Ben.
Hattie's Ben.
Puncture!

Lizzie had just wheeled the ninth and tenth bicycles inside, feeling like it might take all day at this rate, when a glimmer of hope appeared in the distance. A scruffy white van was heading her way from the centre of town, surrounded by its very own halo of grey smoke.

Liam.

Lizzie couldn't help an idiotic smile from spreading over her face – it grew wider and wider until she was practically beaming at the approaching vehicle. This... whatever *this* was... was still so new and exciting that it made her toes curl with pleasure.

'Hey you!' called Liam as he pulled up next to the curb and grinned at her across the passenger seat through the open window. 'Need a hand?'

'I'm not going to say no!' laughed Lizzie.

'Right... let's do this!' Liam killed his engine, hopped down and then jogged around to join her on the pavement. He promptly wrapped her in a bear hug and lifted her right off her feet as he planted a kiss on her lips.

Lizzie let out a surprised squeak.

'Morning!' he said, setting her back on her feet, though he kept his arms wrapped tightly around her.

'Hi!' said Lizzie, grinning up at him and doing her best not to ruin the moment by glancing over her shoulder to check no one had seen. Liam smelled divine – all citrusy and clearly fresh out of the shower. It was enough to remind her that she wasn't!

'You might want to take a step or two backwards,' she muttered.

'Why?' he said in surprise, letting go of her and peering around. 'Have you spotted the traffic warden... or the girls?'

'Nope!' she laughed. 'But you smell practically

edible... and I definitely don't, considering both girls beat me into the shower this morning.'

She wrapped her arms around herself, slightly self-conscious now that she'd mentioned it. Wrestling with a bunch of ancient bikes in the morning sunshine definitely wouldn't have helped matters!

'Like I care!' chuckled Liam, pulling her towards him again and snuffling his nose playfully into her neck, making her squeal.

'Traffic warden!' she giggled.

'Where?' he demanded, stepping back and staring around as though she'd just announced the arrival of a dangerous beast.

'Made you look!' she winked.

As much as she loved being wrapped in his arms, Lizzie *really* didn't want Jenna or Megan spotting them canoodling in public before she'd had the chance to tell them she was seeing someone.

'So!' said Liam, grabbing the nearest bike and wheeling it inside as Lizzie followed up with two more, 'are the girls settling in okay?'

'Mmm!' she muttered.

'Ah... right. Sore subject?' laughed Liam.

'Could say that,' she huffed, only half joking.

'Right... change the subject, Liam,' he said with a comical look on his face. 'So... where did all these bikes come from?!'

'Well, from what Ethel said just now, it looks like

they're from the plot holders up at the allotments!' said Lizzie. 'Though I haven't actually had the chance to look at all the labels yet.'

She watched as Liam flipped over the scrap of paper that was attached to the handlebars of the knackered bike he was pushing.

'Kathleen. The one with all the flowers,' he read. 'Yep - that's got to be Kathleen up at the allotments!'

'But… how will I know which one she is?' said Lizzie, suddenly worried that she'd never be able to match all these bikes back up with their owners once she was done with them.

'Well…' said Liam, leading the way back outside and taking another hasty look up and down the road, 'I'm guessing she's…'

'Do not say "the one with all the flowers",' laughed Lizzie.

'Fine. I won't!' said Liam, grabbing hold of her and kissing her again.

'Not out here!' giggled Lizzie, putting up a completely pathetic fight.

'Why?!' said Liam, 'I didn't know we were having a secret affair!'

Lizzie felt her face start to flush and she grinned at him. What was it about the word affair that made her think of the decidedly naughty moments they'd shared in the little deckchair shed down on the beach?!

'Not a secret… but you know I haven't told the

girls about you yet!' she said, shivering as he leaned in and kissed her neck.

'Embarrassed about me?' Liam mumbled in her ear, his breath tickling her skin and making her squirm. Lizzie could hear the grin in his voice.

'Nope,' she sighed, curling her toes as he kissed her again. 'Definitely not embarrassed!'

'Good,' he said.

At this rate, she was going to end up pinning him up against the wall of Moore Bikes and having her wicked way with him in full view of the entire town. That would definitely set Seabury tongues wagging!

Lizzie reluctantly pulled away from him.

'To be honest - I've barely had the chance to tell them much at all about what's going on with me... not even about the shop. They're just... just...'

She paused and made a gesture of pure frustration.

'A bit wrapped up in their own problems?' said Liam gently.

'Bingo!' said Lizzie, pointing at him.

'I'm sure they'll calm down,' said Liam. 'Sounds like they just need to be the centre of their mum's attention for a bit, that's all.'

Lizzie let out a huge sigh. Liam was probably right - but why did the thought of that make her feel like she wanted to climb back under a duvet and hide? She adored her girls - but she'd come to Seabury to do things on her own terms for the first time in forever. Only, that was starting to make her feel like the worst mum on the planet!

'They won't be here forever,' said Liam gently, 'which is *definitely* a good thing, because I'd rather like to take you on a proper first date... and that's a bit hard when we have to sneak around!'

'I'd hardly call snogging me in front of my shop in broad daylight *sneaking around*,' laughed Lizzie as he reached for her again.

'Well, I'd *love* to take this inside where it's a bit more private!' grinned Liam, 'but I'm already late to meet Ben over at Bamton Boatyard - and I really don't want to get caught by that blasted traffic warden... I think he's got it in for me!'

'Go! Go!' laughed Lizzie, giving him a playful shove towards the van.

'But what about all the bikes?!' said Liam.

'I can manage the rest,' said Lizzie. 'You should have said you were in a rush!'

'And miss the chance to do this?' said Liam, grabbing her hand and pulling her in for one last kiss that forced all the breath and sense out of her in one fell swoop.

'Yes,' she said when he finally pulled away again, 'that would have been a tragedy!'

'Sure you're going to be alright with this lot? I mean, you're not even open yet. This is a lot of work... especially as you've got the hire bikes to finish checking over,' he frowned at her in concern.

'Finished with them yesterday!' said Lizzie proudly. 'They're good to go!'

'Still, I'm guessing you're going to need some help in here if you're going to be this busy!' laughed Liam.

'Yeah, you're probably right,' said Lizzie.

A tiny part of her wished that he'd volunteer his services - but she knew he had way too much on his plate already. Not only was he helping Ben out with renovating his boat, but the pair of them were also in cahoots covering all the handyman-style odd jobs that came up around town.

'I wish I could stay...' he said again, looking decidedly torn.

'Go go go!' laughed Lizzie. 'Seriously, stop worrying! You should know by now that a bunch of rusty old bikes to keep me busy all day is basically my version of seventh heaven! And say hi to Ben for me!'

'Will do,' he said, leaning in and giving her one last smooch before clambering back into the van.

Lizzie sighed as she waved him off. Wrapping her arms around herself, she indulged in a goofy smile. That man seemed to have the power to turn her into a human marshmallow!

Lizzie turned her attention back to the bikes. She needed to get the rest of these inside and then make a list of what belonged to who - and what needed doing on each bike - just in case the labels got mixed up. It was time to get her hands dirty... and she could hardly wait!

Liam was right. Everything back at the cottage would settle down soon enough, and the girls wouldn't be in town forever. They had their own lives to lead... but... in the meantime, maybe they could help her out at the shop?

'Ha! As if!' chuckled Lizzie, instantly dismissing the idea as she started to untangle the next rusty offering from the pile. She glanced at the note cello taped to the saddle.

Plot 19B - the pink shed with the green roof

'This is going to be fun!'

CHAPTER 3

Lizzie was having the time of her life. She really hadn't been exaggerating when she'd told Liam how much she enjoyed being at the shop. Things might be a bit rocky up at the cottage, but down here in the newly christened Moore Bikes, Lizzie was in her element. She felt like she'd somehow managed to get her hands on her own slice of heaven on earth.

After getting all the bikes indoors, Lizzie did her best to stack them neatly along one wall, keeping them well away from her new hire bikes in their snazzy rack. Not that there was much chance of them getting mixed up. The hire fleet looked ridiculously shiny compared to this morning's arrivals – which seemed to be equal parts mud, rust and dust.

Next, Lizzie drew up a list – jotting down all the

details from the labels along with a fool proof description of each bike. It took ages – but at least it would come in handy when it came to figuring out what spare parts she'd need to forage for!

With that job done, Lizzie turned on the spot, surveying her little kingdom. She wasn't quite ready to open to the public just yet - but she was getting there. The final layout for both the shop and workshop was sorted, and she knew exactly how she wanted her tools set out. At the moment, they were all lined up neatly on her workbench – but Lizzie wanted to add more hooks to the walls so that everything had its own special home.

On top of that, she needed at least one more bike rack – especially if she was going to get this many repairs in one go! She'd also need to order in some more spare parts… but both those things would have to wait until she'd managed to get her cash flow… well… flowing again!

For now, though, there were probably enough spares in the goodies she'd already managed to bring over from Ted Hatherleigh's barn to get the majority of the work done on this morning's arrivals.

Lizzie turned to eye the massive pile of spare parts that currently took up the back corner of her workshop. Some bits were still in boxes, but most of it was jumbled up, waiting for her attention. It was another job that desperately needed doing.

'One thing at a time,' she sighed, choosing a bike at random and checking her sheet. 'New saddle… we can definitely do that!'

Lizzie wandered over to the mountain of spares and began to pick her way tentatively through the tangle. It was tricky going, clambering between wheels and discarded inner tubes and random bits of frame.

It was definitely a test of nerves. What if she lost her balance and ended up trapped underneath it all? She'd have to call for help and hope someone heard her!

'Idiot!' she laughed.

None of this stuff was very heavy, after all. Grubby? Yes. Heavy? No! Besides she was rather enjoying this bicycle-themed game of twister.

Lizzie was just steadying herself with an old pair of handlebars while she hopped over a snaking pile of chains when she stiffened. She could swear someone had just cleared their throat right behind her.

Very carefully so as not to lose her balance, Lizzie turned her head, hoping it might be Liam.

'Lionel!' she said, forcing a smile onto her face as the vague hope of grabbing a few more of those stolen kisses promptly disappeared.

'Lizzie!' he said, smiling and nodding at her. 'Erm… would you like a hand to escape that lot?'

'Not to worry!' she said, grinning at him. 'I got myself into it on purpose… I'm quite happy!'

'Yes, I can see that!' he said, his kind eyes crinkling in amusement.

'So… what can I do for you?' said Lizzie, shuffling around so that she could face him properly without actually clambering all the way out. After all - it had taken quite a bit of effort to get this far! 'Are one of those bikes yours?' she added, nodding to the new arrivals. 'I can always bump it up to the top of the list if you need it in a hurry?'

'Oh no, nothing like that,' said Lionel, looking decidedly awkward for some reason. 'No, no, I haven't brought my bike in yet… though that's actually quite a good idea…'

Lizzie watched him curiously as he trailed off and started to fidget.

'Lionel are you okay?' she asked at last when he did nothing more than readjust his braces, fiddle with the brim of his hat and smooth his hair back.

'I'm fine… I just need to talk to you about something…' he paused again and glanced over his shoulder. 'Something a little delicate,' he added, his voice low.

'Oh,' said Lizzie in surprise. 'Well… that's okay - there's no one else here.'

'It's about your, erm…' Lionel frowned. 'Forgive me… your ex-husband?'

'Mark?!' said Lizzie in surprise. That was the last thing she'd been expecting him to say.

Lionel nodded. 'He's at the hotel.'

'What hotel?' said Lizzie, feeling like her brain had just turned into cotton wool.

'My hotel!' said Lionel with a little laugh. 'He's at Pebble Street. He arrived quite late last night.'

'Mark's at Pebble Street?' said Lizzie again. For some reason, her brain was taking a ridiculously long time to catch up.

Lionel nodded.

'Just Mark... no Tiffany with him?' she said.

'Quite literally just him,' said Lionel. 'He doesn't appear to have any luggage... or his wallet, come to that. He said you'd vouch for him.'

'Oh,' said Lizzie. A feeling of dread settled on her chest as she tried to wrap her head around yet another part of her old life showing up just as she was trying to get to grips with her new one. She took a deep breath.

'The hotel's pretty busy at the moment and he didn't have a booking,' said Lionel. 'I've put him in Hattie's old room for the time being. I usually keep it empty for emergencies... like this one, I guess...' He trailed off again, watching her with concern.

'Well... of course I'll vouch for him,' she said quickly. 'I'll make sure any bills are covered and all that - but I'm afraid I've got no idea what he's doing here... or how long he'll stay.'

'There's nothing for you to worry about on my account,' said Lionel with a shrug, 'I'm sure it'll all come out in the wash. I really just wanted to give you the heads up that he's here and throwing your name around.'

'Thank you!' said Lizzie. 'I appreciate that.'

Lionel gave her an old-fashioned little bow. 'Sure you can manage to get yourself out of there without any help?'

'I'm sure!' said Lizzie, smiling at him. 'Thanks, Lionel.'

He smiled and nodded again before turning and disappearing into the morning sunshine.

Lizzie stood frozen to the spot for a long moment. What the hell was going on?! She felt as though her world had just tilted on its axis, and it had nothing to do with the fact that her left foot was caught up in a tangle of old bike chains.

Maybe she just needed some breakfast! That always helped her think straight. A nice big fat pastry and a vat of coffee would help her gather her wits and figure out what Mark's arrival in Seabury meant for her... if anything.

First things first, though - how on earth was she going to extricate herself from this lot?!

Lizzie shuffled on the spot and was just about to start clambering back over the frames when she spotted the perfect saddle a few meters away.

Maybe she'd just grab it while she was there -

after all, it was why she'd ventured into the pile in the first place, wasn't it?! The question was, how was she going to reach it?

Duck... swerve... mind her arm on the sharp bit... hmm, this could take a bit of thinking about!

CHAPTER 4

By the time Lizzie had rescued the saddle and then managed to escape the heap of bike parts, her stomach was grumbling and she was starting to feel decidedly grouchy again. She stomped out of Moore Bikes and turned towards The Sardine. Only sugar and caffeine had the power to lift her out of this funk. Or Liam, of course... but in his absence a double-shot cappuccino would just have to do!

Instead of sinking into a delicious daydream about Liam as she trudged along the seafront, Lizzie found her mind far less pleasurably engaged.

What was Mark doing here?!

Even more pressing than that - why the hell was he here on his own? Mark never went anywhere without Tiffany as far as she knew!

Lizzie glanced at her watch. She was going to have to head over to Pebble Street herself and get to the bottom of what was going on, but there was no point doing that right now. Mark had never been an early riser, and he never made much sense until he'd had some toast and marmalade and plenty of time to read the paper. Still... she *could* just turn up, knock on his door and demand some answers, couldn't she?!

Blowing out an exasperated sigh, Lizzie paused for a moment. Of course, she *was* relieved that Mark had turned up safe and sound considering he hadn't been answering texts or calls from either of the girls for a couple of weeks now. Lizzie herself had even called his landline – something that had taken quite a bit of bravery considering the likelihood she'd end up with Tiffany on the other end.

Mark's second wife wasn't her greatest fan... but Lizzie didn't take it personally. She had a feeling that might just be the woman's default setting. Still, that hadn't stopped her from breathing a sigh of relief when she'd reached their answer machine. Mark hadn't returned her call though.

'And now he's here,' she sighed. Should she go and try to rouse him before grabbing a coffee? 'No point,' she muttered.

Besides... it wasn't something she was particularly looking forward to... and she'd much prefer to be full of buttery calories and hot coffee before facing her ex-husband!

Lizzie hot-footed the last few meters towards The

Sardine. Pushing her way inside the tiny café, she slumped down at one of the little tables, suddenly feeling more than a bit dejected. Hadn't she got divorced so that she wouldn't have to deal with all this rubbish anymore?!

'Oookay!' said Ethel, glancing across at her. 'That's definitely not your happy face... I'll get you your favourite, shall I?'

'You. Are. A Star,' sighed Lizzie.

'Speaking of faces...' said Sarah, peering across at her before tapping her own cheek.

'Huh?' said Lizzie, completely non-plussed.

'Just there...' said Sarah, tapping the same spot again, 'and a bit there too!' she added, tapping the point of her chin.

'Sorry...?' Lizzie shook her head in confusion.

Ethel glanced across at Sarah and then stared at Lizzie. 'You've got something on your face!' she said, pointing at the same spots Sarah had just indicated.

'Nice,' laughed Sarah. 'Blunt as a spoon there, Ethel. At least I was trying to be subtle about it!'

'Oh!' said Lizzie, raising her hand to her face and giving it a cursory rub. 'Did I get it?'

Sarah shook her head. 'I think it's oil... unless the seagulls are about,' she said with a wink.

Oil sounded about right, not that it bothered Lizzie in the slightest... or it wouldn't normally, anyway. But after Lionel's bombshell, the fact that she was going to have to go and face her ex-husband with oil on her face made Lizzie's bottom lip give a bit of a wobble.

'Hey!' said Sarah gently, frowning at her in concern. 'It's okay - we'll get you sorted out. Here!' She grabbed a fresh tea towel, ran it under the hot tap, wrung it out and then hurried around the counter.

'Thanks!' said Lizzie, feeling a bit pathetic as she took the towel and proceeded to scrub at various bits of her face while Sarah directed proceedings.

'One last bit... a bit further up,' she said. 'That's it... wait, no, that's made it worse.'

'Honestly, you're going to end up looking like you've got a black eye if you keep doing that,' said Ethel, setting a frothy cappuccino down in front of Lizzie along with one of her favourite almond pastries. Then she stole the damp towel from her.

'There's no need, seriously...' said Lizzie, as Ethel plopped herself down onto the chair beside her.

'Oh hush,' laughed Ethel, 'it'll only take me a second.'

And that was that - Lizzie suddenly found herself sitting with Ethel holding her chin gently with one hand while she scrubbed at her cheek with the other.

'Nice!' laughed Sarah, whipping out her mobile to take a couple of photos.

'Don't you dare, young lady!' said Ethel seriously.

'I need photos to take with me to college,' she said indignantly. 'I'm going to miss you all so much.'

'Oh,' said Ethel softening, wiping at something just above Lizzie's eyebrow. 'Well as long as you're not putting it on the interwebs.'

'I wouldn't dream of it!' said Sarah. 'But this one's priceless, so I might have it printed up nice and big!'

Sarah let out a delighted squeal as Ethel shot to her feet and whipped the damp tea towel at her. Lizzie grinned at them both.

'Ooh, you look much better,' said Sarah.

'Did you manage to get it all off?' said Lizzie, rubbing her face.

'I did… but I don't think she's talking about that,' said Ethel.

'Nope… I meant you've stopped looking like you're about to dissolve,' said Sarah, cocking her head. 'Are you okay?'

Lizzie smiled and nodded, feeling a bit daft. She had to admit, having the pair of them fussing around her felt really nice… they were a lot less shrill than her daughters… and they actually seemed to care about how she was feeling.

'I'm okay,' she added quickly, noticing they were both still peering at her with identical looks of concern.

As much as she'd love to offload about Jenna, Megan – and now Mark - she didn't think it was fair. Ethel and Sarah didn't need her dragging them down, and as for Mark, she hadn't even set eyes on him yet.

'Nothing a nice coffee and a sugar fix won't sort out, eh?' said Ethel gently.

'Exactly!' said Lizzie. She went to pick up her pastry but paused as she caught sight of her hands. So that's where all the oil had come from!

'Here!' said Ethel, tossing the tea towel back to her.

'It's going to get ruined if I wipe this lot on it!' said Lizzie.

'Don't worry about that,' said Sarah. 'Kate's just about to upgrade them all anyway.'

Lizzie nodded her thanks, but the towel didn't do much good anyway - the oil was engrained around her fingernails and into the lines of her palms. She'd have to use some of the special grit soap she had back at Moore Bikes.

'Ah well,' she said, smiling down at Stanley as he appeared next to her. 'It won't stop us, will it, boy?! I'll just go and give them a quick wash.'

Stanley panted up at her. He was damp and seemed to have quite a bit of seaweed stuck in his fur. Lizzie reached out and after giving his ears a good tickle, she started to pick the slimy weed out of his coat, one piece at a time.

'There, that's better, isn't it?' she crooned. 'I'll just wash my hands and then you can have a bit of my pastry.'

It was already too late for that, though. The

minute she stopped fussing with him, Stanley flopped down right across her feet.

'Erm... right,' laughed Lizzie, realising she was anchored to her chair whether she liked it or not.

With a shrug, Lizzie grabbed the paper napkin from beside her plate and wrapped it around one end of the pastry so that she could pick it up without actually coming into contact with her sweet treat.

'Here!' laughed Sarah, clearly pre-empting the mess she was about to make as she handed her a small stack of extra napkins.

'Cheers,' said Lizzie with a grin. 'Sorry to be this morning's nightmare customer.'

'Are you kidding me!' laughed Sarah. 'You've got a seriously long way to go before you even qualify as a mildly annoying customer, let alone one of the nightmare ones.'

'Oh, well... thanks!' said Lizzie, feeling weirdly chuffed at the non-compliment.

'You'll learn once you've dealt with plenty of your own!' she said, in a tone wise beyond her years.

'I'm sure I will once I've finally managed to get the shop open!' said Lizzie.

'Wait,' said Sarah in surprise, 'I thought Ethel said-'

Sarah promptly shut her mouth as Ethel shot her a wide-eyed look, complete with a tiny shake of her head.

'What?' said Lizzie, looking between them.

'Oh... nothing!' said Sarah. 'My mistake... I thought you were already open, that's all.'

'Not quite... though I might as well be!' laughed Lizzie. 'There was a huge mountain of bikes waiting for me when I got there this morning.'

'Do you have room for another one at some point?' said Sarah. 'I'm pretty sure I spotted an old bike of dad's when we moved into the lighthouse, and it'd be handy to be able to get into town without relying on those two for lifts!'

'Of course!' said Lizzie. 'Bring it down whenever you want and I'll check it over for you.'

'See... that's the way to do it,' said Ethel with an approving nod.

'What do you mean?' said Sarah, raising her eyebrows innocently.

'Nothing... nothing...' said Ethel.

'Spit it out!' said Lizzie in amusement.

'Well... I was just worried those girls of yours had already put a dampener on your big dream... and you might not open at all,' she said, looking sheepish.

'Oh!' said Lizzie, suddenly realising this morning's massive pile of bikes might have been Ethel and Charlie's idea of a gentle bit of encouragement to get on with it. 'Don't worry - nothing's going to stop me from opening Moore Bikes!'

'Excellent,' said Ethel with a nod. 'It would be such a shame to disappoint all those customers, wouldn't it?'

Sarah snorted. 'Yeah Lizzie... no pressure or anything!'

Lizzie grinned at them both even as a jolt of nerves flip-flopped in her stomach.

She could do this... couldn't she?!

CHAPTER 5

Feeling about a million times better with breakfast inside her, Lizzie headed back out of The Sardine. It had taken quite a bit of wrangling to encourage Stanley to leave his snoozing spot on her feet, and she turned to give Ethel a grateful wave as she held onto the big dog's collar.

The sight of Sarah, Ethel and Stanley all watching her go made Lizzie smile. She might have only been back in town for a couple of weeks, but everyone at The Sardine already treated her like an old friend, and that felt incredibly precious.

Glancing at her watch, Lizzie sighed. It was probably still too early to go over to Pebble Street - deep down, she knew it would be a total waste of time. Mark simply wouldn't be out of bed yet, and she didn't much fancy waiting around in reception long enough for him to wake up, get dressed and finally deign to see her. Besides, even if she *did* get to see him, it would probably just ruin her new-found calm, and she didn't fancy coming back down from her caffeine high with such a bump!

There was nothing for it but to head back to the shop and make a decent start on some of those repairs. She'd deal with Mark when she surfaced for another break… when it suited *her*.

Lizzie forced herself to make the most of the short stroll back to the shop. She'd been dreaming about being back in Seabury for long enough – and it would be ridiculous to stomp around and miss it now that she was finally here.

Just to be by the sea - to be able to wander along next to the beach on a weekday morning was such a thrill. Lizzie didn't ever want to take it for granted. She sucked in a deep breath of the soft sea air and let it out slowly.

By the time Lizzie reached Moore Bikes, she had an easy smile on her face. She was excited to get back to work - and Mark was a mere irritation somewhere right at the back of her mind. Her smile flickered as the sound of angry voices drifted out of the shop's open doors.

Wait… she'd pulled them closed behind her… hadn't she?!

Lizzie frowned. She really needed to get into the habit of locking up properly now that she had other people's property inside - even if she *was* just nipping over to The Sardine for coffee.

Crossing her fingers that the uninvited guests weren't quite as stroppy as they sounded, Lizzie hurried inside.

Her heart promptly sank. It was Megan and Jenna and - as usual – they were busily griping at each other. Even worse, caught between the pair of them and looking like he'd rather be *anywhere* else in the world, was Liam.

Lizzie watched for a moment, completely speechless. Her feet seemed to have glued themselves in place. Megan was busy wrecking her beautifully organised tool bench by piling everything swiftly into a cardboard box.

'Come on, come on, you need to get these bikes organised like I told you!' Jenna snapped at Liam. 'I want them in size order. God knows why mum's got them all over the place like this.'

'Don't be ridiculous!' said Megan, sweeping all Lizzie's allen keys into one pot and tossing them into the box. 'Do them by colour!'

'Colour - what use would that be?' said Jenna. 'Oh – hey, mum. We thought we'd come and help you out.'

'You thought... help...?' Lizzie said faintly, catching Liam's eye. He shot her a little grimace but didn't say anything as he turned to move a couple of the newly arrived repair bikes back to their original spots while Jenna wasn't watching.

'Jeez,' said Megan, joining Lizzie and watching Liam with a look of distaste on her face. 'You seriously need some help hiring better staff, mother... I mean, he's not exactly quick on the uptake, is he?!'

Lizzie stared at Megan, not sure whether she wanted to laugh or cry. They thought Liam was a member of staff?! She had no idea what he was doing there, but now definitely wasn't the time to introduce them all... especially when he'd clearly been on the receiving end of a Jenna versus Megan bickering marathon.

Somehow, Lizzie had a feeling she'd have some apologising by proxy to do when the girls buggered off.

'Meggie's right,' said Jenna with a frown. 'I've been trying to get him to organise the bikes for at least ten minutes, and he just won't listen.'

'He wouldn't even help me put your tools away!' said Megan. 'You know, mother, you really need to be more methodical... fancy leaving them all over the place like that!'

Lizzie swallowed. In the few seconds she'd been back, her heart had once again plummeted into her shoes. Having the girls around should be such a joy, but they had an uncanny talent for undoing everything she was trying to put in place - both when it came to organising her shop – and her new life here in Seabury too!

'Just... give me a second!' she said quietly, holding up her hands to shut them both up.

'You show him who's boss!' said Megan.

Lizzie ignored her daughters as they promptly started to squabble like a couple of toddlers again and headed over towards Liam.

'Hey,' she said, quietly.

'Hi!' said Liam, raising his eyebrows. 'I was just on my way back from seeing Ben, and I thought I'd pop in and see if you needed a hand with anything before heading over and setting up the deckchairs.'

'Oh,' said Lizzie, 'thank you!'

'Have to admit... I sort of wish I'd just kept driving,' he added with a low mutter.

Lizzie felt her heart sink even lower until she spotted the smile dancing on Liam's lips.

Phew. He was just pulling her leg!

'I think they think I'm your shop boy!' he added in an amused whisper.

'I'm so sorry!' said Lizzie, cringing slightly.

Liam shrugged good-naturedly. 'Maybe I should take it as a compliment!' he grinned, displaying cheeky dimples.

The urge to reach out and pull him in for a kiss nearly floored Lizzie... but that might add one complication more than she could handle, considering the girls didn't even know who he was yet, let alone his relationship to her.

'You look like you're about to jump on me!' whispered Liam, looking amused... and maybe a little bit hopeful.

Lizzie kept her eyes locked on his for several long seconds. Did she dare just go for it - and sod how the girls felt about it?

No. Maybe not! She wasn't that selfish... was she?

Lizzie shook her head. Nope. She wanted to tell her daughters about Liam when *she* was ready. Kissing him now – as wonderful as it would be – would just be a cheap shock tactic to get them to shut up. A lot of fun... but not exactly fair on any of them!

What she really needed to do was get rid of her daughters for a few minutes - mainly to stop them from completely undoing the hours of work she'd put into getting everything organised! Plus, it would give her a moment to do a bit of damage-limitation with Liam... and maybe grab a quick kiss or two while she was at it!

'Girls,' she said, turning to them, 'your dad's arrived in town.'

'What?!' said Jenna.

'When?!' demanded Megan.

'Late last night, apparently,' said Lizzie. 'Look - why don't you go over and find him. He's staying at the Pebble Street.'

'You're kidding?!' said Jenna.

Lizzie shook her head.

'Is *she* there?' said Megan.

'Apparently not,' said Lizzie - guessing that Megan was referring to Tiffany.

'Excellent!' said Jenna.

'Brilliant!' said Megan. 'God mother, you should have told us straight away.'

And just like that, the pair of them bundled back out onto the seafront and headed off to bug Mark. Lizzie could hear them chatting excitedly as they went.

'You wouldn't believe they're in their twenties sometimes,' sighed Lizzie, slumping back against the edge of her workbench.

Liam snorted.

'I'm so sorry,' she said again.

'Don't worry!' laughed Liam. 'Though you might want to consider turning the key in the door next time you nip out for a coffee... to keep the girls out! That's if you ever want to be able to find all your tools!'

He peered into the box that Megan had "tidied" away.

'I was thinking exactly the same thing,' sighed Lizzie. 'It took me ages to set that lot out where I wanted them. The sooner I get some hooks and shelving sorted out, the better. Maybe that'll stop Megan's urge to tidy up!'

'I wouldn't bank on it!' chuckled Liam.

'Thanks for coming back to help, by the way,' she said.

'No worries,' said Liam, taking a step towards her and reaching out as if to take her hand. Then he shot a nervous glance at the door and thought better of it. 'Man - watching out for those two is worse than keeping an eye on the traffic warden!' he laughed.

'Tell me about it!' said Lizzie.

Liam glanced at his watch and swore.

'I'd better go,' he said, reluctantly. 'Sorry... I need to get the deckchairs out!'

'Don't apologise!' said Lizzie.

'Catch you soon?' said Liam, giving her a swift peck on the cheek.

Lizzie nodded again before watching him hurry off, feeling more than a bit deflated.

CHAPTER 6

As silence descended on the shop, Lizzie stared around. It was a mess. The girls could only have been here for twenty minutes at most, but in that time they'd managed to undo most of the morning's work.

Liam had clearly been trying to stop everything from getting mixed up, but several of the bikes that had come in for repairs were now abandoned on their sides near the doorway. Others had been jumbled in along with her hire bikes in their rack.

Lizzie went to move towards her tool bench when something crinkled under her foot. Bending down, she picked up the brown cardboard label with its fancy handwriting. Thank goodness she'd already made that list, otherwise this could have been a disaster!

'Right,' she said, straightening back up. 'First things first!'

Lizzie delved into the box of tools Megan had removed from her workbench and began to set them back in their rightful places. As she worked, Lizzie's brain began to whirr.

Maybe she should be more grateful that the girls had come down to the shop. After all – their hearts had been in the right place. At least they'd wanted to help, even if it had been a bit misguided. Sure, it was unfortunate that they'd just happened to manage to time it to coincide with Liam's surprise visit, but that wasn't their fault. She really needed to get on and tell them about Liam.

If she was being honest though, it was such early days between them that Lizzie couldn't really say she was in a relationship, could she?! After all – they'd only been on one non-date so far. What would she say… that they were *seeing each other?!* Lizzie shuddered. She hated that phrase. Maybe she was overthinking it.

Then again… she still hadn't got to the bottom of why Megan had been in such a state when she'd arrived. Jenna seemed to have recovered now that she'd had some decent sleep, but there were moments when Lizzie felt like her eldest daughter's mask slipped and showed something wistful and maybe a bit sad lurking underneath. The last thing she wanted to do was make anything worse by making any surprise announcements!

Lizzie sighed. Maybe she'd tackle telling them about Liam when she was sure that Megan was okay... and after she got to the bottom of why exactly Mark was in town.

'Ah... shit!' she breathed, pausing with a wrench in hand and staring into the middle distance. She hadn't explained to Liam why Mark was here, had she?! Poor Liam - what was he going to think?! She should have explained!

'But how?!' she demanded of the empty shop.

How on earth was she supposed to explain to Liam what Mark was doing in Seabury when *she* didn't even know the answer to that particular mystery.

'Bloody Mark!' she sighed.

Having her ex-husband in town was one complication she could have done without. Especially as he expected her to vouch for him... which she could only assume meant that he expected her to pay for his hotel bill.

The thought made her turn cold. Lizzie's funds were still pretty overstretched after bailing Jenna out and coughing up to get her home safe and sound. Then, of course, she'd *had* to pay for the hire bikes and a few essentials to get the shop up and running. She really didn't know where she'd be without lovely

Ted Hatherleigh and all the goodies he'd gifted her from his barn.

If it was just her, Lizzie knew she could cope. Barring the odd emergency coffee and pastry run, she could happily survive off noodles and her store cupboard essentials for a few weeks while she got herself back on a bit of an even keel. But the girls were currently eating her out of house and home, and that really wasn't helping the situation!

If she ended up having to pay for Mark to stay at the hotel too… well… she was *really* going to struggle. It was incredible of Lionel to be quite so laid back about the whole thing - but that was the exact reason she'd make sure that he was paid fair and square. If Mark didn't cough up, then she'd find the cash… somewhere.

A feeling of pure overwhelm bubbled up, and for a moment Lizzie felt completely paralysed. Had she bitten off more than she could chew by moving her entire life back to Seabury and starting a new business at the same time?

'No - pull yourself together!' Lizzie muttered, giving herself a little shake.

She'd got this far, hadn't she? She just needed to face any problems head-on… and preferably one at a time rather than all at once! First things first, she needed to get everything in here re-organised. If her tools were tidy, then her brain would follow… hopefully!

Lizzie had just reached the bottom of the cardboard box when a tentative knock on the open door of the shop made her turn.

'Hello...?'

A man was staring in at her.

'Hi!' said Lizzie. 'Can I help?'

'Erm... maybe?' said the guy. 'I was just over at The Sardine, and the old lady in there said you might have some bikes for hire... but...'

Biting her lip, Lizzie did her best to stop herself from laughing at hearing Ethel described as an old lady. She'd love to put him straight but... the customer was always right!

Lizzie watched as the man stared around the shop, looking mildly unconvinced. She couldn't blame him. The nicely organised hire fleet was punctuated by rusty repair bikes, and she still hadn't shifted the others from where they'd been abandoned in the middle of the floor.

'You'll have to excuse the mess,' said Lizzie quickly. 'I'm not officially open yet - and I had a massive delivery of repairs arrive this morning!'

'Oh,' said the man looking disappointed. 'Not to worry...'

'The hire bikes are ready, though! I'm sure we can find one that's right for you,' she said quickly. There was no way she was going to risk losing a customer when he'd appeared as if by magic. Talk about the universe throwing her a bone the moment she needed it!

'Actually... I'm after five for the day, if you can manage it?' he laughed. 'My wife and the three kids are just making a start on breakfast!'

'We'll get you all kitted out,' said Lizzie decisively. 'If you can give me a minute to get organised and grab some paperwork?'

'No problem!' said the man. 'We'll have breakfast and then pop back in about an hour?'

'That's perfect!' said Lizzie. 'Then we can make sure you're all set up and everyone's got the perfect bike for the day!'

'And you're sure it's no bother?' said the man.

'It will be my pleasure!' said Lizzie, meaning every word. 'You guys will be my first official customers!'

'Can't wait!' said the man, grinning at her. 'I'm John, by the way.'

'I'm Lizzie,' she said, returning his smile with interest. 'Enjoy your breakfast... and I'll see you in a bit.'

The minute John ambled off, Lizzie jumped into action. Her earlier frustration disappeared in a rush of excitement. After dreaming about this moment for such a long time, she was about to welcome her first official customers to Moore Bikes.

'Have the best time!' said Lizzie.

'What do you say?' demanded John, giving the three little girls in their bright bicycle helmets a proud smile.

'Fanks Lizzie!' they all chorused, grinning at her from the backs of their borrowed bikes.

It had been a mad morning. Lizzie had sorted all the bikes out only to realise that the rack for the hire fleet would be better if it was right next to the doors. She wanted it to be somewhere nice and easy to get to. There was no way she wanted paying customers to have to perform any kind of acrobatics just to get to the back of the shop!

Lizzie thanked her lucky stars that she'd bitten the bullet and used the last of her precious funds to buy the hire bikes. At the time it had felt like a huge gamble, but now she knew it had been the right decision. It meant that she could serve her very first customers – confident in the knowledge that the bikes were all in perfect condition - even if the rest of the shop wasn't quite as polished as she'd like it to be!

John, his wife Minnie, and their three little girls had reappeared after just forty-five minutes - both parents apologising profusely for being early, but explaining that everyone was so excited, they'd been unable to string breakfast out any longer.

Lizzie hadn't minded and had spent a fun time with the little family, helping them to choose the perfect bikes, and adjusting the saddles and handlebars so that they were just right.

'Actually… can you grab a photo for us?' said Minnie, looking just as excited as the girls as she rummaged in her backpack for her mobile.

'Of course!' said Lizzie. 'Anything for my first customers!'

'Thanks!' said Minnie, handing her the phone and scootching in with the other four, all of them grinning widely.

Lizzie took several shots and then checked the screen. They were the perfect family holiday photos… and she couldn't help but feel a flutter of pleasure that she'd played a part in making their little adventure happen.

'Right… wish us luck!' said John with a grin.

'Good luck!' she laughed, watching as the girls zoomed up and down the pavement, getting a feel for the bikes just as she'd taught them in the twenty minutes she'd spent fussing around them, making sure they were all completely comfortable.

'Oh - by the way, our friends are arriving in town later,' said John. 'Is it okay if we send them over?'

'Please do,' said Lizzie, trying to sound chilled at the idea of more customers turning up before she was even meant to be open. Inside, she was jumping up and down in excitement that this first, completely unofficial first day of business was turning out so well. 'I'll look forward to it!

She stood and waved them off, feeling proud as punch to see the little girls riding away along the seafront so confidently, flanked by their lovely parents.

Lizzie was just about to head back into the shop to continue sorting things out for her next batch of potential customers when she spotted Megan and Jenna heading towards her. She paused and smiled in their direction. After such an unexpected bit of good fortune, she was ready to put her frustrations behind her.

'Who were they?' demanded Megan, nodding at the retreating bikes.

'My first customers!' grinned Lizzie.

'See mum,' said Jenna, 'all you needed was a bit of help from us to get you sorted out, and the customers just start turning up as if by magic!'

Lizzie bit her lip to stop herself from pointing out that the customers were actually down to Ethel's magic wand. If anything, the disastrous mess the sisters had left her with had almost put John right off the whole idea. She managed to swallow the retort though. She was too happy right now to spoil things with an argument.

Thrusting her hand into her dungaree pocket, Lizzie closed her fingers around the bundle of cash John had just handed over. The folded notes felt like a talisman - a sign that her dream was busy coming true.

'So!' she said, as the girls trailed back inside the shop behind her. 'Any luck with your dad?'

'No,' said Megan. 'We got sick of waiting in the lobby.'

Lizzie watched as Megan frowned down at the bench where the tools had magically reappeared. Megan sniffed and turned her back on it without comment, and Lizzie had to fight the impulse to apologise for undoing all Megan's hard work. This was *her* shop, after all!

'Yeah,' said Jenna, leaning on the hire rack and idly ringing the bell on the nearest set of handlebars. 'We wanted to go up and surprise him, but that mad woman in there wouldn't let us.'

'Mad woman?' said Lizzie in surprise.

'Lil… or something,' said Jenna vaguely.

'Lou?' said Lizzie.

'That's her,' said Megan. 'Came in wearing wellies, a towel and a swimming hat.'

Lizzie snorted. It sounded like Lou must have popped in on her way to or from a swim with the Chilly Dippers!

'I mean… I don't even know if she worked there,' said Megan. 'Totally nuts, but she wouldn't let us upstairs. She called dad from reception and then handed the phone over and disappeared!'

'Oh,' said Lizzie, trying and failing to keep a grin off her face at the image of Lou wandering around

Pebble Street in her swimming cap. 'So... what did he have to say for himself?'

'Nothing much,' said Megan with a frown still on her face. 'He just said it was too early - that he's tired - and that he's booked a table in the restaurant for this evening.'

'Well, that'll be nice for you,' said Lizzie, wincing at the thought of a three-course meal for three people being added to the bill.

'You're coming too,' said Jenna. 'He's booked for all four of us.'

Lizzie sighed. She'd been afraid of that. Surely it was bad enough that her ex-husband had rocked up in town and used her name to get away with staying in the hotel without a means of paying for it, without actually having to spend time with the man. Sure, they were on good enough terms... but there *was* a good reason they were no longer together!

'I don't get why he's got to stay at the hotel at all,' muttered Megan, turning back to the workbench. She started to gather Lizzie's carefully sorted spanners into a pile again, no doubt ready to sweep them back into the cardboard box.

Lizzie hurried to her side and gently batted Megan's hand away before lining the spanners back up again.

'I need them like this,' she said quietly.

Megan just shrugged and wandered over to stand next to Jenna.

'You know, I'm with Meggie,' said Jenna. 'Why's dad in the hotel when he should be with us at the house?! It's just daft.'

'Yes,' said Megan. 'It's our family home, after all!'

Lizzie opened her mouth to point out that it *definitely* wasn't their family home. It might have been once upon a time… but that was a lifetime ago. She didn't have the chance to get a word in edgeways, though.

'There's plenty of room,' Megan continued. 'He could share with Jenna.'

'Or maybe you could get your selfish butt out of the caravan?' said Jenna sweetly.

'Or maybe you could move to the couch!' said Megan.

'Or maybe mum and dad can share a room - and then neither of us have to move!' said Jenna.

'*Excuse me?!*' said Lizzie, suddenly very happy that Liam wasn't around to hear this decidedly surreal exchange.

'No funny business mum,' laughed Jenna. 'I mean… he *is* married, even if the woman is a… is a…'

'Is a Tiffany?' said Megan helpfully.

'Exactly,' said Jenna. 'And I mean… wouldn't it be great?!'

'It would!' said Megan nodding. 'The whole family back under one roof again. It'd be like old times.'

'No,' said Lizzie. 'No…'

Lizzie was frantically searching for the perfect

words to explain just how much she *hated* the idea of things going back to the "old times" when she noticed a movement over by the doorway.

'Morning! Can I help?' she said, making shushing motions at the girls before heading over to the newcomer.

'John said you'd be able to sort us out with a couple of bikes for the day?' said a pretty woman with a bright red braid wrapped around her head.

'Sure!' said Lizzie in delight.

This was why she was here in Seabury. *This* was what was important right now. Mark, and the girls - and their insane plans - would have to wait.

'Come on in.'

CHAPTER 7

An hour later and Lizzie hadn't had a second to worry about the fact that she was being forced to have a meal with her ex-husband later that evening. Jenna and Megan had retreated to the little back room and were no doubt busily plotting the renewal of her and Mark's vows if their comments earlier were anything to go by!

Right now though, Lizzie didn't really care. Things had been so busy that she already knew for certain that she was going to need a second pair of hands to run the shop. If it was just the repair side of things, she knew she'd be able to keep up with those, no problem. She simply hadn't expected word to get out so quickly about the hire bikes! All but one of them were currently out and about on the lanes around Seabury!

At one point, Lizzie had even considered digging

the girls out of the back room to give her a hand... but then, she'd promptly decided against it. They'd probably just cause more work for her in the long run!

'And you'll be able to sort out new brakes for me before we go away at the weekend?' said Robbie, the barista from New York Froth.

'Sure thing!' said Lizzie. 'I've got some arriving in tomorrow's delivery.'

'That's brilliant!' he said.

'You working tomorrow?' she asked, moving Robbie's expensive bike carefully into position at the back of the shop.

'Yep,' said Robbie.

'Great!' said Lizzie. 'In that case, I can bring it over as soon as I'm done with it if that works for you?'

'That would be amazing!' he said gratefully. 'Cheers, Lizzie!'

'My pleasure!' she said, walking him to the door and waving him off with a huge smile on her face.

The minute he disappeared, Lizzie turned her back to the door and gave her face a hard rub with her hands. Blimey, she was tired! Lunchtime had been and gone without her noticing and she hadn't eaten anything since her breakfast pastry at The Sardine. Maybe that was the problem!

'Who was that?!'

Lizzie blinked as Jenna and Megan reappeared

from the back room. 'Another customer - Robbie from New York Froth.'

'Oh,' said Megan with a sniff of disinterest.

'I really need to get some lunch,' said Lizzie.

'Don't look at us,' said Jenna quickly, 'we're going shopping.'

'Can you bring me something back?' said Lizzie.

'No - I mean... we're going *out of town* shopping,' said Jenna.

'Oh,' said Lizzie. 'Right.'

'Yeah,' said Megan. 'If dad's going to be around the house, we need to make sure we've got some decent food. Your cupboards are truly crap, mother.'

'Well... thanks for that!' sighed Lizzie.

'My pleasure,' said Megan with a raised eyebrow.

Lizzie wished she had it in her to be as unapologetic as her eldest daughter sometimes!

'Anyway,' said Jenna, 'can I grab your keys?'

'Huh?' said Lizzie. She was so tired she was starting to feel a bit fuzzy around the edges.

'Car keys, mother - so we can go shopping?' said Megan, rolling her eyes.

'But you don't drive, Meggie!' said Lizzie.

It was true. Megan had never bothered to learn – she'd said it wasn't worth her time and attention because she never intended to live anywhere she couldn't just grab a taxi. Besides, she was planning to have her own driver by the time she was thirty!

'Yeah, but I do!' said Jenna, holding out her hand expectantly.

Lizzie raised an eyebrow as every fibre of her being resisted the idea of handing over her car keys to the daughter who'd just left her own van gently smoking on another continent.

'No,' said Lizzie, shaking her head. 'If you want to go, you can catch the bus.'

'Give over,' spluttered Megan.

Lizzie shrugged. 'It's a shorter walk for you to the bus stop than all the way back to the cottage to get the car. It's just outside the Pebble Street Hotel. Though, I bet if you ask the driver on the way back, he'll drop you off at the top of the hill to save you the walk.'

'But...'

'Customer!' said Lizzie, turning to a girl who'd just appeared in the doorway.

Lizzie did her best to hold back a smile as the girls grumbled and elbowed each other as they left the shop. Then – peace descended and she let out a little sigh of relief.

'Hi!' said the girl. 'Are you Lizzie?'

Lizzie nodded.

'Cool! Robbie asked me to come over - from New York Froth?'

'Oh!' said Lizzie in surprise. 'Did he forget something?'

The girl shook her head and held out a brown

paper bag. 'He told me to bring these over for you. He said you were run off your feet!'

Lizzie opened the bag and her mouth instantly started to water as the scent of two fresh iced fingers wafted up to greet her. Either Robbie was a mind reader or he'd heard her stomach growling while she'd been serving him.

'What do I owe you?' said Lizzie.

'Nothing,' she said, shaking her head. 'It's a thank you for doing his bike so fast!'

'That's so kind!' said Lizzie, a little taken aback.

'And I wanted some fresh air, so I volunteered for the walk!' she added with a smile.

'Well... thanks!' said Lizzie.

The girl shrugged, flicked her hair as she shot a look towards the back of the shop, blushed, and then scarpered.

'What on earth?' laughed Lizzie, taking one of the cakes out of the bag as she turned to see what had just prompted such a weird reaction. She was about to take a massive bite of the soft, lemon-scented bun with its perfect crust of white icing when she paused, staring.

There, kneeling just behind the pile of repairs that had arrived that morning, was a young lad. At a guess, she'd put him roughly around the same age as Sarah from The Sardine. What really had her flummoxed though was the fact that he was calmly working away on one of the bikes, spanner in hand.

'Erm... hello?' she said, dropping the bun back into the bag with a pang of regret and moving towards him.

'Hey!' said the lad, looking up and shooting her a quick smile before continuing to remove the front wheel of the bike he was working on.

Lizzie watched for a moment in bemused silence. What on earth was going on?! Had she somehow managed to hire a member of staff without noticing it?

'Erm... who are you?' she said, hoping she didn't sound mean.

'Liam sent me!' said the lad, peeping up at her again. 'He said you might need a hand. I heard you telling those two stroppy girls that you needed to work through these repairs, so I thought I'd make a start for you on some of the basics.'

'Those two stroppy girls are my daughters!' said Lizzie with a laugh, watching him work.

'Oops... sorry,' he said.

Lizzie shrugged. 'No need to apologise - it's an apt description. I'm Lizzie by the way.'

'Yup!' said the lad with a nod.

'Want a bun?' she said with a small smile.

'Sure!' he said.

'Here,' said Lizzie, removing the one she'd already fiddled with before handing over the bag. 'Look... would you mind holding the fort for five minutes? I need a breath of fresh air... and something a bit more than a bun for lunch!'

'Sure thing, boss!' said the lad.

Lizzie grinned. That had a nice ring to it!

'There's a bunch of hire bikes out, but they're not due back for hours yet.' She paused, wondering if she was making a huge mistake leaving him on his own considering she didn't even know his name, let alone anything else. But Liam had sent him... and Lizzie trusted Liam... so she figured she'd be safe for five minutes. 'I won't be long - I'm heading up to The Sardine if you need me.'

'Cool!'

Lizzie grabbed a sheet of paper from her workbench and quickly scrawled down her mobile number.

'Just in case,' she said, handing it over.

'Go,' laughed the lad. 'It'll be fine!'

Lizzie nodded and with one last, backwards glance, she headed out onto the seafront. She'd *definitely* head to The Sardine, but not without a quick detour to see if Liam was still at the deckchair shed.

Jogging across the road, Lizzie peered towards the far end of West Beach. Sure enough, she could see Liam's deckchairs nestled on the golden sand.

'Brilliant!' she said with a smile. She hurtled along the front and dropped down onto the sand the minute she came to the first set of steps.

'Hey you!' said Liam, looking delighted at the sight of her. 'Stopped for a break?'

Lizzie nodded, bending over and clutching her knees as she tried to get her breath back from practically sprinting along the beach.

'Got a minute?' she said at last, straightening up and nodding at the little wooden shed where Liam stashed the chairs overnight.

'Blimey,' laughed Liam, his eyes shining, 'I love a woman who knows what she wants.'

'Oh hush!' laughed Lizzie, feeling her cheeks flame as he shot her a suggestive wink. 'I need to talk to you a minute.'

'Sounds ominous,' said Liam mildly.

Lizzie shrugged and beckoned for him to follow her, which he did, pulling the door closed behind them.

In the gloom of the cosy little space, it was as much as Lizzie could do to stop herself from reaching for Liam and pulling him in for a kiss, but she was more than aware that – right now - a random stranger was looking after Moore Bikes.

'What's up?' said Liam watching her closely.

'Well... two things, actually,' said Lizzie. 'First... I wanted to explain about Mark being in town.'

'Oh!' said Liam.

Lizzie watched him straighten up slightly, the half-smile disappearing from his face.

'Look... basically... I *can't* explain,' said Lizzie

with a laugh. 'According to Lionel, Mark turned up at the hotel last night. None of us had heard from him for over a fortnight... and now he's here!'

'Right,' said Liam, ruffling his hair. 'Well... it's good news he's okay, I guess? Have you talked to him yet? Is there anything he needs? Anything I can do?'

Lizzie gazed at Liam, fighting the urge to wrap her arms around him. It was so like him to ignore his own feelings and worry about everyone else's well-being first!

'I've not spoken to him yet,' she said. 'The girls went over there earlier, but he didn't come down from his room. I'm guessing there might be some kind of issue with Tiffany...'

'Wife number two?' said Liam.

'Yeah her,' Lizzie nodded. 'That's just a guess though – because she's not with him. Anyway, he's gone and booked a meal at the hotel for tonight and according to the girls he expects me to go...' Lizzie trailed off, feeling awful. 'Look, I just wanted you to know that I had no idea he was coming here.'

'Hey,' said Liam, reaching out and giving her hand a squeeze, 'you worry too much.'

'Yeah well, I think it's a side-effect of having the girls around!' she laughed.

'I can see why!' said Liam with a grin. 'But seriously, it's fine. At least you'll be able to get to the bottom of what's been going on with him. And... if there *is* anything I can do, just yell, okay?'

Lizzie nodded gratefully. 'I'll text you when I get home from Pebble Street and fill you in on the gossip.'

'No point,' said Liam, shaking his head. 'My mobile's dead. I managed to wallop it with the strimmer when I was at a job yesterday!'

'Oops!' said Lizzie.

'Yeah... I said something a bit stronger than that, I must admit,' said Liam. 'Anyway, how about we have an early breakfast at The Sardine tomorrow? You can tell me everything then!'

'Sounds like a plan!' said Lizzie.

'Great! So... what was the other thing you wanted to talk about?' said Liam.

'Well... since you asked...' said Lizzie, 'who on earth is the kid currently looking after my shop?!'

Liam stared at her for a long moment and then started to laugh.

'What?' she demanded.

'Didn't he even give you his name?' said Liam.

'No!' said Lizzie.

'Honestly, typical Jason,' said Liam, shaking his head with a look of mild despair on his face. 'The lad's brilliant - a hard worker, and amazing at fixing anything he turns his hand to... but he's quite quiet. Not shy, exactly, but not very forthcoming with words!'

'I noticed!' said Lizzie. 'Right... so... Jason?'

'Jason Eaves,' said Liam with a nod. 'He's the son of the guy who keeps bees on The King's Nose.'

'O-kay...' said Lizzie. 'And... you sent him?'

Liam ruffled his hair again. Lizzie was quickly coming to realise it was something he did when he wasn't feeling entirely comfortable.

'Look... I'm really sorry if I overstepped the mark,' he said, pulling a face. 'He works with me and Ben sometimes, and when I saw how busy you were earlier with all those bikes turning up at once, I thought you might need an extra pair of hands. After meeting them this morning, I had a feeling the girls weren't very likely candidates!'

'You could say that!' Lizzie laughed. 'I mean, Jenna's amazing at fixing stuff, but Megan definitely wouldn't want to get her hands dirty. Either way, they're just visiting... and you saw what complete chaos monsters the pair of them are at the moment!'

'Yeah,' said Liam with a grin. 'I was going to mention Jason to you earlier, but with the girls there, it went right out of my head. Then I bumped into him, so I thought I'd send him over to introduce himself.'

'He just got straight to work!' said Lizzie with a laugh. 'He must have been at it for ages when I finally spotted him!'

Liam ruffled his hair again and Lizzie smiled.

'I can always talk to Jason if you don't need him.

It's not a big deal - Ben can find plenty of work for him - I just thought... I thought it might help. Sorry.'

'Your turn to stop worrying!' said Lizzie. 'And it's definitely *not* that I don't want him... it was just a surprise, that's all.'

'Noted,' said Liam. 'I won't spring any more random teenage boys on you in the future without checking first!'

'Deal!' said Lizzie, as Liam took her hands and pulled her in for a gentle kiss.

After a couple of seconds, Lizzie pulled away again. It was the last thing she wanted to do. 'Speaking of teenage boys, I'd better head back.'

'He's a capable lad,' said Liam with a decidedly wicked twinkle in his eye as he tugged her back towards him. 'I'm sure he can manage for a little while longer!'

CHAPTER 8

Lizzie's heart was hammering as she jogged up the steps that led off West Beach. As much as she wanted to look back at the little shed, she forced herself to stare straight ahead as she made her way across the road towards The Sardine. She'd already been away from Moore Bikes far longer than she'd been anticipating. That said… she hadn't been expecting to spend so much time snogging her secret boyfriend!

The thought brought a smile to her face, and Lizzie was hard-pressed not to add a little skip to her step. She knew she really should head straight back to the shop, but she'd already been gone for so long, a couple more minutes to grab a roll and a cup of coffee wouldn't make a blind bit of difference… she hoped!

Lizzie quickly glanced down at her mobile. Nope

– there weren't any missed calls from Jason. From what Liam had told her, he was more than capable of looking after the place. Still... it really didn't excuse her skipping out on him for so long!

Grabbing the door handle, Lizzie was about to push her way inside the little cafe when she finally gave in to temptation and peeped over her shoulder. There was Liam, standing next to the furthest deckchair. He was so far away, she couldn't be sure... but she had a feeling his eyes were glued to her. Just the thought made Lizzie wriggle with happiness.

They'd been like a pair of teenagers when it came to sneaking out of the shed. Agreeing that it would be the safest bet to stagger their exits, Lizzie had made a break for it first - but not before she'd peeped around the edge of the door to make sure the coast was clear. After all - the girls might have missed the bus... or even worse, Mark could very well have managed to get himself out of bed by now.

'You look happy!' said Lou, grinning at her as she bounded towards the counter.

'A lot happier than earlier, anyway!' Sarah chipped in, peering at her from beside the coffee machine.

'It's been a mad day so far,' said Lizzie, beaming at them both. 'Really busy... and unexpected!'

'Busy in the shop, you mean?' said Sarah.

Lizzie nodded. 'Nearly all the hire bikes have gone out and I've probably got enough repairs to last me about three weeks!'

'Ethel will be thrilled,' said Sarah.

'Yeah,' laughed Lou. 'I think her and Charlie have been on a mission to make sure you're so busy, that you don't even consider giving up on your shop.'

'Why would I give up?' laughed Lizzie.

'Plenty of people do, right before their dreams are about to come true,' said Lou seriously. 'Remember that young lady,' she added, glancing across at Sarah.

'No chance of that with me!' said Sarah. 'I'm living the dream!'

Lizzie grinned at the young girl and Sarah winked.

'Anyway - what can I do for you before we end up with a riot on our hands?' said Lou.

'Huh?' Lizzie glanced over her shoulder only to find a queue had formed behind her and was now snaking right out of the door and around towards the little courtyard. Blimey, how long had they been talking for?! She could swear it had only been a few seconds.

It was certainly a busy day in town... unusually so... but long may it last. If Seabury kept this up, she'd have no problems getting her shop off the ground.

'Wow!' she said, turning back to Lou. 'Right... cheese toasty and a takeaway cappuccino for me, please. And... I don't suppose you know what Jason Eaves drinks, do you? I know it's a long shot but he's in helping me out and...'

'Black coffee and he likes the sausage rolls,' said Sarah promptly.

'Oh he does, does he?' said Lou wiggling her eyebrows.

'Look... it's not my fault I've got a good memory for customer orders,' said Sarah, her face unusually impassive all of a sudden.

'Especially when they're seriously cute and have the whole silent, mysterious thing going on?' said Lou.

'Whatevs!' laughed Sarah, already working on the coffees while Lizzie paid Lou and then quickly shifted out of the way so that she could get to work on the rest of the queue.

'Hey Jason,' said Lizzie, hurrying into the shop and grinning at the young lad, who was knee-deep in the pile of spares in the corner. 'I'm sorry I was so long. I grabbed you some lunch and a coffee.'

'Ta!' said Jason, picking his way towards her with far more ease than she'd managed earlier.

'Wait a sec!' she said, staring at the junk pile... which was no longer a jumbled heap. 'You organised all that while I was out?!'

'Yeah?' said Jason, turning to look behind him. 'I really hope that was okay. I just thought it'd be easier for you to find stuff if it was grouped together a bit.'

'It's... amazing! But... blimey, how long was I gone for?!' she said, staring at him in wonder. 'Thank you!'

Jason grinned at her. 'No worries.' He took the bag from her and his eyes lit up when he opened it. 'Hey - you got my favourite!'

'That was Sarah's work,' said Lizzie.

'Cool,' said Jason, cool as a cucumber as he took a bite.

'Here's your coffee,' she said. 'I'm guessing Sarah got that right too...'

'Black?' said Jason.

Lizzie nodded.

'Spot on,' he said, taking it from her and taking a grateful swig.

'So...' said Lizzie. 'You got on okay?'

Jason nodded. 'Two bikes came back early. I wrote down their names. They said they'd already paid you earlier, so I figured that was that. Bikes were fine. I checked them over - they're back in the rack over there. Oh - and another repair came in.'

'Show me?' said Lizzie.

Jason pointed at the bike leaning against her workbench.

'Thought I'd better keep it separate from the rest until you'd seen it,' he said. 'I made a note on that bit of paper on the bench.'

Lizzie wandered over and picked it up.

Jean.
Plot 23a.
Just look for the broad beans.

'Another one of Charlie's flock from the allotments!' laughed Lizzie.

Jason nodded.

'So… thank you so much for turning up and helping… I was getting a bit desperate for a breather!' she said.

Jason shrugged.

'Is today a one-off or do you fancy coming back?' she said.

'I'd love to,' said Jason.

'Perfect,' said Lizzie with a wide smile. Somehow, she had a feeling she was going to get on like a house on fire with this polite teen. 'How does three days a week to start with sound? Start with a month's trial and go from there?'

Lizzie wasn't sure where the money was going to come from, but she'd find it from somewhere. She had a sneaking suspicion Jason would prove to be worth his weight in gold.

'What do you reckon?' she prodded when he didn't answer.

'Anything you say boss!' said Jason, shooting her a grin before stuffing the last of the sausage roll into his face and turning to the next bike waiting for his attention.

CHAPTER 9

It had already been one of the longest, most tiring days ever... and that was saying something considering Lizzie had just moved house. Sadly, it wasn't over yet!

Lizzie was practically dropping by the time she'd hauled herself back up the hill to the cottage. All she wanted to do was change into her PJs, pour herself a glass of wine and then celebrate her unexpected - but brilliant - first day of business from the comfort of her sofa. Instead, she was going to have to get ready for the weirdest family dinner of her life.

'Ah well!' she whispered with a tired grin, pushing her way into the cottage. She would do her best to face the evening with good grace - if not enthusiasm. After all, she had Moore Bikes to hold on to like a talisman this evening. She'd taken more money in one day than she'd forecasted for an entire week during her first few months of opening. She had a new member of staff who'd appeared as if by magic... and with his help, she'd already made excellent progress with all her repairs!

Lizzie hadn't seen her daughters since pointing them towards the bus stop, which could only mean one of two things - they'd either managed to catch it, or they'd retreated back here to sulk the afternoon away.

Intent on grabbing herself a glass of wine to take up to the bath, Lizzie wandered through into the kitchen and then stopped dead to stare at the table... and the worktops... and the floor.

'Girls?!' she yelled, her eyes wide as they flitted from bag to bulging bag of groceries. Some of the stuff had been half-heartedly unpacked and lay strewn all over the place. This had to be *hundreds* of pounds worth of shopping!

'Hey mum!' said Jenna, bouncing down the stairs, looking relaxed and pretty in a long purple sundress, her hair flowing around her in freshly washed waves.

'Ooh, you smell nice!' said Lizzie, distracted for a moment as Jenna glided into the room.

'Same can't be said for you, mother!' said Megan, appearing behind her sister, wearing a little black dress.

Lizzie raised an eyebrow. She wanted to point out that it had something to do with a *very* hard day of work on top of the fact that she hadn't been able to muscle her way into the bathroom earlier because the pair of them had been hogging it... but she bit her tongue.

For one thing - she wanted the evening to be as pain-free as possible. For another, this was the first time she'd seen Megan really looking like her old self since she'd come to stay. Her hair was a glossy, dark sheet across her shoulders, and she looked properly rested.

Lizzie took a long, slow breath and then smiled at them. 'You both look gorgeous.'

'Aw, thanks mum,' said Jenna, bouncing on the balls of her feet.

'Yeah - it's a bit of a miracle after the afternoon we've just had!' said Megan.

'Looks like you've been busy!' said Lizzie lightly, wandering over to the nearest shopping bag and having a bit of a rummage.

Oh heaven help her!

Lizzie delved through an entire deli counter's worth of cured meat, pre-sliced cheeses, pots of fat, juicy olives, and little containers of rice and pasta salad. The next bag was full of organic goodies that were all free from something or other - gluten-free, sugar-free, fat-free. Not exactly stuff she'd have chosen... but then, as she hadn't been the one to shop and pay for all this, it wasn't really up to her.

'We thought we'd treat you,' said Jenna.

'Well... that's erm... very thoughtful,' said Lizzie.

She *was* grateful – even if a much better way to treat her would have been to top up on the basics... like tinned tomatoes, pasta, and potatoes... the kind of thing that wouldn't be out of date in a matter of days.

'It must have been a nightmare for you to carry all this back on the bus!' she added, suddenly feeling guilty for being so stingy with the keys earlier.

'Nah,' said Jenna.

'Come on, mother, there was no way we'd manage to carry this lot back,' said Megan, opening a pot of olives and nibbling on one before popping the stone down onto the table. 'We got it all delivered.'

'Well that's... good?' said Lizzie. She had no idea the big supermarket would deliver all the way over to Seabury without it costing an arm and a leg.

'Yeah,' said Megan. 'They were really cool. They set up an account in your name no problem, and just added the delivery charge to that. I gave them your email address, so you can pay any time!'

Lizzie stilled. 'Wait... you... you what?!'

'Well - we didn't have your card with us, and there's no cash around here,' said Jenna with a shrug.

'What else were we supposed to do?' said Megan.

Lizzie's ears started to buzz. She needed a moment on her own... otherwise she was going to blow a fuse.

'I'm going up for a bath,' she said, her voice suddenly quiet.

'Good luck with that,' huffed Megan. 'Jenna used all the hot water. You'll have to grab a shower like me.'

Lizzie closed her eyes and started to count to ten very *very* slowly.

'You know mum, you seriously need to chill,' said Jenna. 'You look stressed. I'm not sure your little bike shop is doing you any good. I got you a couple of bath bombs while we were in town.'

The irony of what she'd just said seemed to be completely lost on Jenna.

'Great. Well... maybe I'll get to use them when you go home,' said Lizzie with a little growl.

Jenna shrugged and started to look sulky.

'Put this lot away,' she said, pointing at the devastation surrounding her. 'I'm going upstairs.'

'You seriously expect us to do that after doing all the shopping?' said Megan.

'No Megan. I expect you not to spend money I don't have on things I don't want while I'm at work.' Lizzie paused and took a deep breath before her voice went ultrasonic. Both girls were now looking mutinous.

Lizzie sighed. She seriously didn't have the energy for this. Suddenly, she wasn't sure if she wanted to laugh at the ridiculousness of having to tell off her grown-up daughters as though they were naughty kids, or cry because the day's earnings would be completely wiped out by their little shopping trip.

'Just put anything that needs to go in the fridge away for me, then,' she said. 'I don't want it to go to waste... and I *really* don't have time for food poisoning right now.'

'Fine!' muttered Megan, grabbing the nearest carrier bag and heading to the fridge, where she bundled the entire thing onto one of the shelves before forcing the door shut.

Turning on her heel, Lizzie legged it upstairs before she exploded.

Lizzie caught the light tap on her bedroom door just as she turned her hairdryer off.

'Mother - we're going to be late if you don't hurry up.'

'Two minutes,' said Lizzie, relieved that her voice didn't sound anywhere near as narky as she felt.

To be fair, the shower had helped her calm down a lot - the water beating down on her scalp had been just what she'd needed. It wasn't quite the long, relaxing soak in the tub she'd been fantasising about, but she'd been so angry she'd have probably managed to bring bathwater to a rolling boil!

Yanking a comb through her hair, Lizzie peeped at herself in the bedroom mirror.

That would do. It was only Mark and the girls.

Lizzie sat on the edge of the bed and thrust her

feet back into her heavy boots, taking her time to tie the colourful laces before heading back downstairs.

'Oh mum,' said Jenna, staring at her wide-eyed, 'you can't wear dungarees out for a meal!'

'Who says,' growled Lizzie.

'And you haven't got a scrap of makeup on,' said Megan. 'Let us choose something for you and I'll do your face.'

Lizzie felt herself starting to waver under their two-pronged attack... mainly because she was simply too tired to argue.

'What's dad going to think - you turning up looking like that?!' said Megan.

The throwaway line was enough to snap Lizzie out of it.

'I don't care what he thinks!' she said, forcing a smile onto her face as she strode towards the front door. 'Come on, let's get this over with. I'm starving!'

CHAPTER 10

For the first time since moving back to Seabury, Lizzie didn't enjoy the walk from the cottage down into the town. It should have been idyllic. The late summer sun was low in the sky, tinging the fluffy clouds a peachy pink. They reflected in the gentle ripple of the waves so that the sea twinkled with amber accents. This was Seabury at its best. There was barely a breath of wind, and the air smelled sweet and salty.

Sadly, Lizzie wasn't in the mood to appreciate any of it. The evening should have been the perfect family snapshot - the chance to enjoy the company of her two grown-up daughters as they all wandered into town for the pure indulgence of sharing a meal together at the Pebble Street Hotel. Instead, she was trailing along behind the girls, wishing she could be almost anywhere else.

Jenna and Megan hadn't stopped arguing since they'd left the cottage. As much as she was doing her best to ignore it, their constant squabbling was grating on Lizzie's nerves. She thought she'd left this part of being a parent far behind her!

'I'm going to tell her,' said Jenna.

'Don't you dare,' snapped Megan, 'we said we'd wait until we were all together. I want dad there too!'

'But why do you get to decide everything,' said Jenna.

'Because I'm the oldest!' said Megan, sounding like a bossy primary school kid.

'Tell me what?' said Lizzie, suddenly on high alert. She didn't like the sound of that one bit. So far, any surprises the girls had sprung on her had cost her a great deal of money.

'Oh, nothing!' said Megan in a singsong voice, shooting her a smug smile.

'It's *not* nothing!' said Jenna, looking excited. 'It's a brilliant surprise.'

Uh oh!

'Well you'd better tell me before we get there, then,' said Lizzie. She sounded exhausted even to her own ears... but then, she *was* heading for a meal with her ex-husband who'd reappeared in town – uninvited - after being AWOL for a good couple of weeks.

'No, we're saving it until dad's with us too,' said Megan, aiming a sharp elbow at Jenna's ribs just as she opened her mouth to spill the beans.

Lizzie rolled her eyes. 'Fine,' she sighed. She didn't have the energy left to argue. If she did, she'd be tempted to use it to head straight back up the hill to the cottage. She quite fancied the idea of hiding out in her darkened bedroom until they all cleared off and left her alone!

Lizzie paused for a moment and turned to stare back up the hill.

Nope. No way. She needed something to eat first!

'What are you doing, mother?' said Megan, noticing that she was no longer following along like a grumpy shadow.

'Oh nothing,' said Lizzie lightly, 'just admiring the clouds.'

'Well,' said Megan, 'best get your head out of them, otherwise we're going to be late!'

Lizzie poked her tongue out at the back of Megan's head, only for Jenna to spot her and shoot her a wink. 'Meggie... you've got no romance in your soul, that's your problem!'

'And you've got no sense of responsibility,' snapped Megan.

'Oh hush, the pair of you!' sighed Lizzie.

'I'm hungry!' whined Jenna.

'That makes two of us!' said Lizzie.

'Three,' said Megan. 'What's the food like at this place, anyway?'

'Really good,' said Lizzie with a little smile as she thought of her amazing "not-a-date" with Liam.

They'd kept poor Lou there until she'd practically had to throw them out at the end of the night. 'The Pebble Street Pudding is divine - absolutely glorious.'

'Trust you to go straight for the pudding!' laughed Jenna.

Lizzie shrugged. 'When it tastes that good, you'd be an idiot not to!'

'Speaking of tasty things... have you *seen* your bus driver?!' demanded Megan.

'Hey, hands off,' said Jenna, 'I saw him first!'

'Erm... nope!' said Megan, glaring at her sister. 'I believe I spotted him, went *phwoar* really loudly, and then you cottoned on. I've got dibs. Anyway, do you know him?'

'Ben?!' Lizzie laughed in spite of herself. 'Yes, I know him. He's lovely.'

'Told you he would be!' said Jenna primly.

'No you didn't,' retorted Megan. 'You said anyone that good-looking was bound to be a total dimbleweed.'

'No one says "dimbleweed" Meggie!' spluttered Jenna. 'Other than my complete dork of a big sister, of course!'

'I still saw him first,' said Megan.

'Sorry to have to tell you this,' said Lizzie, ushering the girls ahead of her down the narrow path towards the front door of Pebble Street and lowering her voice as they went, 'but I'm afraid Hattie spotted Ben first... and she definitely has first dibs!'

'Who the hell's Hattie?!' demanded Megan.

'That would be your chef for tonight!' said Lizzie with an amused smile, 'and Ben's girlfriend.'

'All the pretty ones are taken,' sighed Jenna.

'How do you know what she looks like?' asked Lizzie curiously.

'I think she was talking about Ben,' said Megan, rolling her eyes.

'Well… that settles it,' said Jenna, 'I'm going to need champagne to get over the disappointment!'

'Absolutely,' said Megan with a curt nod. 'And anyway, we're celebrating.'

'We are?' said Lizzie following the girls into the hotel. 'What are we celebrating?' she added in a whisper as Lou beetled towards them with a smile.

'You'll see!' said Jenna, shooting her a wink.

'Hi guys!' said Lou, coming to a halt in front of them all. 'Nice to see you again.'

'Have we met?' said Megan coolly.

Lizzie instantly wanted to give her a nudge and tell her to behave nicely.

Lou just grinned. 'I was the one wearing a swimming hat!'

'Oh. Yes,' said Megan with a slight sneer as she swept a look over Lou, making Lizzie cringe. 'Hello.'

Completely unperturbed, Lou turned and led them towards the dining room.

'I've given you the table over by the doors - I thought you'd enjoy the sunset,' said Lou.

'How romantic!' sighed Jenna.

'Idiot,' muttered Megan. 'Bags-I that chair!' she added, dashing across the packed room to commandeer the seat with the best view, with Jenna hot on her heels.

'You okay?' whispered Lou. 'You've just turned puce.'

'Yeah…' sighed Lizzie. 'I just feel a bit like my life's been rewound by about fifteen years, that's all.'

'Deep breath,' said Lou, patting her arm gently.

'Thanks,' she said with a weary smile. 'Is Mark not down from his room yet?'

'I've not seen him,' said Lou, grabbing four menus and leading the way through the other diners towards their table.

Lizzie bit her lip. She didn't want to start bitching about her ex in public - but this was *classic* Mark. He was staying just upstairs, the whole evening was his idea… and yet he was late.

'Is Liam joining you guys?' asked Lou curiously.

Lizzie shook her head frantically, grabbing her arm and drawing her to a halt.

'What?!' said Lou in surprise.

'I haven't told them about him yet!' whispered Lizzie, not wanting the couple at the table nearest them to hear.

'You're kidding?' said Lou, matching her volume.

'No!' said Lizzie. 'I really want to tell the girls - but it's so new and…'

'You want to enjoy it for a bit longer?' said Lou with a naughty wink. 'No matter how sly you think you are, I spotted you coming out of that shed'

'Nooo!' said Lizzie, feeling her cheeks flame.

'Don't worry, I'm the soul of discretion!' laughed Lou.

Lizzie cringed as her friend's volume returned to its usual booming tones. 'It's not even that,' she said quietly. 'I just want to figure out what Mark's doing here first.'

'You don't think he's after some kind of reconciliation, do you?' said Lou, her face turning serious.

Lizzie shook her head in horror. 'Nope. No. Nope – definitely not. Mark's-'

'Shh!' said Lou, cutting her off. 'Ex-husband arrival at your two o'clock.'

Lizzie spun around only to spot Mark standing in the doorway of the dining room, scanning the tables.

'I'll bring him over,' muttered Lou, ushering her over to the table to join Megan and Jenna, who were waving madly as they tried to get Mark's attention.

Grateful for a moment to gather her wits, Lizzie sank down into the chair next to Jenna, poured herself a glass of water and took a sip. Two seconds later, Mark appeared at the table bringing with him the overwhelming waft of the same old cologne he'd worn for decades.

Blimey, he must have bathed in the stuff!

Lizzie blinked hard, willing her eyes not to start

watering at the stench. It took her right back to when they'd been married.

'Well, look at this!' said Mark, beaming at the three of them and then wrapping an arm around each of the girls as they hurried to hug him. 'How wonderful to have my three girls back together again.'

Lizzie felt her smile tighten on her face. Lou – who was hovering just behind Mark – widened her eyes.

Oh no... oh no!

What if Mark really *was* here hoping for some kind of reconciliation?! Well... she'd just have to let him down, wouldn't she? And right now, she wasn't in the mood to be particularly gentle about it either. Mark was a nice enough guy, but their relationship had come to an end for a very good reason – he drove her potty. That hadn't stopped Lizzie from feeling like she'd been punched in the heart when he'd married Tiffany so soon after the divorce, though!

'Good of you to turn up!' she snapped, instantly going on the defensive.

'Mum!' hissed Jenna, giving her a horrified look.

'What?' said Lizzie. 'Your dad's been awol for more than a fortnight.'

'Mother!' said Megan, shaking her head at her.

'It's okay girls, your mum's right,' said Mark.

'Of course I am!' said Lizzie, earning herself an

approving little nod from Lou as she handed out the menus. 'We were all worried sick about you.'

'You were?' said Mark, looking delighted.

'It's not something to be proud of,' snapped Lizzie. 'Where were you? What happened?'

Mark glanced at Lou, clearly embarrassed, but Lou carried on blandly dishing out bread rolls for each of them.

'Can we *not* this evening?' muttered Mark.

'Yeah, give him a break, mother,' said Megan.

'You *are* okay though, dad?' said Jenna with a little frown.

'I'm okay, darling,' said Mark. 'Just a little hiccup with Tiffany, that's all. We needed a bit of time apart. I've been staying at the office a lot and with my mate Barry the rest of the time.'

'But-' said Lizzie, getting ready to gear up and launch a full interrogation.

'*Mother!*' said Megan in a warning tone.

'Let's just enjoy the evening, shall we?' said Mark, looking at her pleadingly.

Lizzie narrowed her eyes and peered at him.

Fine. Round one: Mark.

But only because she couldn't handle an all-out row in public. The girls were both glaring at her, clearly ready to shout her down loudly if she took things any further.

'Fine,' sighed Lizzie with a little shrug.

Mark winked across at her, and she scowled at

him. If he thought he was going to get away without answering any of her questions this evening, he had another thing coming. But… maybe she'd get a drink and some food inside her before starting in on him again!

'Let's get champagne!' said Jenna. 'We've got so much to celebrate.'

Lizzie shook her head. 'Sparkling water for me, please Lou.'

'Okie dokies!' said Lou. 'And the rest of you?'

'Champagne and four glasses,' said Mark, looking smug. 'Like Jenna said, we're celebrating!'

Lou gave a terse little nod, shot a sympathetic look at Lizzie and hurried off.

'What exactly are we celebrating?' huffed Lizzie.

'Erm… how about the fact that you're amazing, have followed your dreams and opened your business?' said Mark.

Lizzie opened her mouth to argue back before she'd even realised that he'd just given her a compliment - and had actually managed to sound sincere while doing it.

'Well… thanks,' she said, feeling like he'd just whipped the rug out from beneath her feet.

'Yeah,' said Megan. 'She's been so wrapped up in that stupid shop we've barely seen her. Anyway, that's nothing compared to our news!'

Just like that, Lizzie's little bubble of surprised pride popped. She gritted her teeth. She loved her daughters... but liking them was something she was having to work quite hard at right now!

'Yeah - sorry mum,' said Jenna, shooting her an apologetic look, 'but we've got a surprise for you both. It's huge!'

'And *not* your surprise to tell, Jenna!' hissed Megan, making Jenna roll her eyes.

'Well get on with it then!' said Jenna.

Mark shot a questioning look at Lizzie, and she shrugged. She had no clue what was going on. For a brief moment, Megan's appearance when she first appeared flashed into her head. Tired, pale, decidedly waxy and wearing slouchy sweats...

She couldn't be pregnant... could she? No... she'd have said something... surely?!

Straightening in her chair, Lizzie gave herself a mental smack around the head for being so impatient with her daughters since their arrival. She'd thought they'd been so selfish... but maybe she was the selfish one here.

'Okay, Meggie,' she said gently, smiling at her eldest. 'We're listening.'

'Well...' said Megan, looking unusually shy all of a sudden. 'When we went shopping earlier, I decided to visit a local builder in town.'

'A builder?' said Mark, looking confused.

Lizzie eyed him and then turned to Megan again. Of all the things she'd been preparing herself to hear... that had *not* been one of them.

Megan took a deep breath. 'Now we're all back together... and the family's getting bigger... I figured it would be a good idea to get the cottage extended.'

'What cottage?' said Lizzie, now completely lost.

'Duh - your cottage!' laughed Jenna.

'Who's telling this story?' demanded Megan.

'I don't see why you-'

'Girls!' snapped Mark, pinching the bridge of his nose.

Well... at least he was on the same page as her about something!

'Sorry dad!' they chorused.

'Megan - explain,' said Lizzie carefully, not wanting to jump to any conclusions. 'How exactly is the family getting bigger?'

'Because dad's home,' said Megan rolling her eyes, as though Lizzie was being dense just to irritate her. 'He'll be moving out of the hotel and back up to the cottage with us, won't he?!'

'It'll be brilliant!' said Jenna. 'Just like old times!'

Oh no... not those Old Times again!

Lizzie stared between her daughters. Was she really hearing this right?

'So the builders are going to come and visit next week to draw up some plans!' said Megan, looking excited.

'No. No no no!' said Lizzie, half getting to her feet and then sitting back down again.

'Don't make a fuss,' said Mark, looking embarrassed.

'A fuss?' she said, noting that her voice had risen to a shriek. She cleared her throat and ducked her head as several of the other diners glanced in her direction. 'Your dad's married *to another woman*,' she said.

'Not. Now!' said Mark.

Lizzie stared at him for a long moment. His face was white and strained. There was so much she wanted to say - about his behaviour… about this little charade the girls seemed to have cooked up… but maybe Mark was right. This was not the time.

'Okay, fine,' she hissed. 'But this isn't over.'

For a brief moment, Lizzie considered getting to her feet and leaving, but that would only create a scene. Besides, she was hungry.

'Let's order,' she said, her voice coming out in an exhausted monotone. 'But *absolutely* no champagne.'

'Spoilsport!' sighed Jenna, rolling her eyes.

CHAPTER 11

Lizzie tiptoed down the hallway. Careful to avoid the creaking floorboard, she cracked the front door open and slipped outside. Then, taking care that the light breeze didn't snatch it out of her hands with a bang, she pulled it closed behind her with the least noise humanly possible.

Considering the fact that she really wanted to slam the door repeatedly in its frame until both girls – and their hangovers – were wide awake, she was actually quite proud of herself.

It was so tempting… but she managed to hold off. Because Lizzie was an adult. Perhaps the *only* adult to have graced their family meal the previous night. No matter how hard she'd protested, a bottle of champagne had arrived at their table… closely followed by a second.

Lizzie clenched her fists. She'd promised herself

she wouldn't get all worked up again this morning… but that was proving to be much harder than she'd been expecting!

Letting out a long sigh, Lizzie did her best to let the crisp morning air calm her frazzled nerves. She crept past the little caravan where Megan was presumably dead to the world and turned her steps towards town. It was still a bit early for breakfast, but it was better to be out here than sitting in the cottage, quietly fuming!

When she'd climbed into bed the previous night, Lizzie had been so angry she'd practically been quivering. The meal had been a disaster from start to finish. Knowing that Mark was hiding something from them, Lizzie hadn't been able to relax. She'd eaten her starter in silence and then had promptly resumed trying to get the truth out of him.

Mark hadn't given in to her prodding though, no matter how many times she led the conversation back to his absence and the real reason he was in town. He'd countered with everything from humorous excuses to changes of subject. In the end, he'd resorted to one of his trademark strops which had resulted in Megan begging her to shut up.

Well… Mark could keep his weird little secret if he wanted to. The thing that was really getting under her skin was the fact that Megan and Jenna seemed to be hell-bent on playing a strange, slightly dangerous game of pretending the divorce had never happened. Even worse - Mark seemed to be playing along with it!

Lizzie had spent most of the meal wishing she was anywhere else... which was a shame, as the food had been divine. If she was honest though, she hadn't enjoyed a single bite. In the end, she'd turned down dessert, feigned a headache and made a break for it before the girls had even started on their vast portions of Pebble Street Pudding.

Lizzie had stomped all the way back up the hill to the cottage, and the beauty of the last hints of colour on the horizon and the fact the sea was singing her a lullaby had been completely lost on her.

All she'd wanted to do was text Liam... but of course, his phone was dead. She *could* have invited herself over to his place... but she'd quickly decided against that. There was no way she'd been willing to infect him with her awful mood.

Instead, she'd set her alarm, fallen into bed and eventually drifted off into an uneasy sleep that had been full of dreams of the girls when they were little... and every argument she'd ever had with Mark.

Lizzie blew out a long raspberry and picked up her pace.

'Not this morning!' she said, giving herself a little shake. She was off to meet Liam for their breakfast date, and she wasn't going to ruin it by worrying about Mark and the girls for a second longer.

Lizzie couldn't wait to feel Liam's strong arms around her. With any luck, he'd do that thing where he pulled her close and kissed the top of her head. Maybe that would help her feel like her wonderful Seabury dream was still real.

Yawning widely, Lizzie gazed across the sea as the sun peeped through a fine veil of lacy mist. It was going to be another beautiful day. With any luck, it would be another busy one at the shop too. Jason had promised he'd join her at the shop first thing - so at least that meant she might get the chance to get properly organised rather than chasing her tail all day!

As she ambled down the hill towards town, Lizzie focused on trying to let all the tension go from her body. It wasn't something she was particularly good at – but she knew a bit of gratitude for all the good things in her life would put a smile on her face. After all – she'd moved to Seabury to help her escape stress, not add to it!

'Time for this old dog to learn some new tricks!' she mumbled. There was always loads to be thankful for… she just needed to make sure she noticed it all. 'Open your eyes, idiot!'

There was the beautiful blue sky promising another stunning day.

The soft sound of the waves, far below her on West Beach.

Her new shop - and all those wonderful

customers Ethel and Charlie had sent her way the day before.

Then there was Liam. The man had an almost magical ability to put a huge smile on her face, no matter what else was going on.

A laugh escaped her, and Lizzie rolled her eyes. It had taken just thirty seconds of thinking about all the good things in her life - and here she was, practically skipping down the hill with a big smile on her face. Well, it certainly beat grumping around like grumpy grump-face!

As she neared the town, Lizzie scanned the sandy beach all the way along towards The King's Nose, searching for any sign of Liam. He was often down there early, and she wondered whether he was planning to set the deckchairs up before joining her for breakfast.

So far, there was no sign of him or the chairs. Maybe he was planning to start a bit later today. That would be nice - they'd be able to take their time in The Sardine and have a good catch-up before diving into their busy days.

Sucking in another deep breath of sea air, Lizzie made a pact with herself. She wouldn't spend breakfast moaning and complaining. Sure - last night had driven her to distraction - but that was no reason to taint today with it as well, was it?! She wanted to hear Liam's news. He was always full of stories - and she'd much rather kick the day off that way rather than listen to herself moaning!

As she reached the door of the Sardine, Lizzie glanced at her watch and had one last look around in case Liam was on his way. She was still a bit early... but the open sign was hanging in the door and the lights were on.

'Coffee!' she whispered with a grin. She might as well wait for him with a cappuccino in her hands!

'Hello?' she said, pushing her way inside only to find the little café completely empty.

'Hello!'

Lou appeared from beneath the counter like a jack-in-the-box, making Lizzie jump and let out a little shriek of surprise.

'Sorry!' giggled Lou. 'I was just trying to get organised back here!'

'No worries!' grinned Lizzie, resting her hand on her hammering heart.

'I've got a message for you,' said Lou.

'Oh?' said Lizzie.

'Liam can't make it,' she said, sticking out her bottom lip in sympathy.

Lizzie felt a tiny pinprick of disappointment pierce the floaty bubble of positivity she'd been working so hard to inflate.

'Oh,' she said. 'Is he okay?'

Lou nodded. 'He stuck his head in about half an hour ago to let me know.'

'But… why?' said Lizzie, trying not to let her good mood evaporate completely.

'Something to do with his daughter?' said Lou vaguely. 'He said it's nothing to worry about, but something's come up at the last minute and he's got to head off to help her out. I'm not sure where she lives? Anyway - he said he might be away for a couple of days.'

'Oh… well…' Lizzie felt herself flail for a moment and then decided it was time to take a leaf out of Liam's book. 'Well… as long as everyone's okay?'

'I think so,' said Lou with a little shrug. 'He said it was urgent but not serious.'

'Daughters, eh?' sighed Lizzie with a little laugh.

'I wouldn't know,' said Lou with a wide smile. 'Mind you, I feel like I've got time-share in young Sarah these days, and that's enough for me. But then I think the whole town feels a bit like that towards Sarah – the kid's got enough honorary parental units to sink a battleship!'

Lizzie grinned - she knew exactly what Lou meant. She'd not been here long at all, and she already felt like that about Sarah too. She was so close to going off to college, it was like everyone in Seabury needed to get their fix before she spread her wings and became the world-famous pastry chef they all knew she was going to be.

'I really hope she's okay,' said Lizzie. 'Liam's daughter, I mean.'

'How old is she?' said Lou.

'Twenties-something, I think,' said Lizzie. 'She's a junior doctor – though from what Liam said, she still lives with her mum because her house is convenient for the hospital.'

'Well, he said not to worry,' said Lou, 'and that he's really sorry he couldn't tell you in person.'

'Broken phone,' said Lizzie with a nod, suddenly realising she couldn't even give him a quick call to check everything was okay.

'Yeah,' said Lou. 'I think he was pretty happy that I'd come into work early! He was going to brave coming to the cottage otherwise. I don't think he wanted to risk seeing Megan and Jenna, though.'

Lizzie pulled a face. How awful that he'd disliked them so much that he didn't want to see them!

'He didn't mean it like that,' chuckled Lou, clearly catching sight of her downcast expression. 'He said they don't know about you two yet and he didn't want to make your day a nightmare before it had even started!'

'Oh!' said Lizzie, the smile returning to her face.

'He did say he's going to try to get a new phone when he gets there too,' said Lou, 'so you never know - keep an eye on your mobile for smexy texts! You've got a good one there.'

'I'm not sure I've "got him",' chuckled Lizzie.

'Are you kidding me?' said Lou, 'the man is head over heels.'

Lizzie felt the blush hit her cheeks, and Lou watched her with interest.

'I know it's not my place...' she said slowly, 'but he's definitely an improvement on the ex!'

Lizzie's eyes widened and then she started to laugh as Lou promptly clamped a hand over her mouth.

'Sorry... sorry!' Lou muttered.

'No - you're right!' said Lizzie. 'Definitely right.'

'Did you guys manage to sort anything out before you left Pebble Street last night?' said Lou, clearly deciding that as she'd already put her foot in it, she might as well keep on stomping.

Lizzie shook her head, casting a quick glance over her shoulder just to make sure she was still the only customer in the little cafe.

'Nope. He wouldn't tell me what he was doing here, and in the end, I got bored asking and being treated like an annoyance,' she sighed. 'It's nothing to do with me anyway.'

'I saw you leave early,' said Lou sympathetically. 'I wanted to check you were okay, but I was caught up with a couple of tourists who wanted to know everything from the best walks to where they could get a couples massage!'

'Nice!' laughed Lizzie. 'Anyway, probably a good thing... I wasn't in the best mood by that point!'

'I'm not surprised,' said Lou. 'They were all being total dicks.'

Lizzie snorted and Lou covered her mouth again.

'Sorry. I shouldn't have said that,' she said through her fingers.

'It's fine,' said Lizzie with a grin. 'Did they stay long after I left?'

Lou nodded, still looking apologetic. 'Long enough to get through another bottle of wine, puddings, multiple coffees… and then they moved over to the bar and had a nightcap or three.'

'Oh no,' sighed Lizzie, her shoulders slumping.

'It's okay,' said Lou, 'Mark's put everything on his tab, so you're fine.'

Lizzie nodded. She didn't really want to admit to her friend that the dreaded tab was highly likely to head her way when Mark finally left the hotel.

'Right,' said Lizzie, trying to wrap her head around the fact that her wonderful morning treat of breakfast with Liam wasn't going to happen after all. 'As I'm already down here, I think I'll make the most of it and head over to the shop early. Jason's coming in again this morning – so… two coffees and a couple of pastries to go?'

'You've got it!' said Lou, cheerfully.

CHAPTER 12

*P*ausing on the pavement outside The Sardine, Lizzie readjusted the cardboard tray carrying the two takeaway coffee cups. For a moment, she gazed down at the little deckchair shed on the beach.

'Come home soon!' she whispered, then looked around in horror as she realised the words had actually escaped her lips.

Uh oh! She was in danger of turning into a lovesick teenager if she wasn't careful!

It was time to pull her big girl pants on and get on with the day. Liam was away – so she'd just have to pour all her energy into Moore Bikes!

Lizzie had just set off towards the shop when a little red car came storming along the road towards her. She paused again to stare as it streaked past her, going way too fast for the centre of town.

'Wait a second...' she gasped, her hands tightening on the cardboard tray. It could just be the early morning light playing tricks on her eyes... but wasn't that...?

It couldn't be...?

Could it...?

The car had already zoomed past the hotel, hurtling in the direction of North Beach. Lizzie really hoped she was mistaken, but that had looked an awful lot like Tiffany behind the wheel!

Blimey, if Mark's second wife was in town, then things were about to get... exciting... or explosive... or something equally as unsettling!

Lizzie stared after the car for a long moment and then shook her head. Maybe it wasn't Tiffany at all. Perhaps she was just seeing things because her head was still full of Mark after the meal the previous evening. If that *was* Tiffany though, it didn't have anything to do with her anyway, did it?!

Moore Bikes. That's what was important right now. And Liam. But as Liam was out of reach... the shop came first! Turning her back firmly on North Beach and Pebble Street, Lizzie marched towards Moore Bikes.

When she reached the shop, Lizzie balanced the coffees on the stone doorstep and rummaged in her pockets for the keys. She was just unlocking the doors when she spotted a figure cycling in her direction.

Straightening up, Lizzie shielded her eyes with her hand only to break into a wide grin. It was Jason, and he was pelting down the middle of the road - carrying a coffee in each hand – and looking super-cool considering he wasn't holding onto the bike at all.

'Unbelievable!' she laughed, completely unable to stop herself from being impressed.

'Coffee boss!' he grinned, somehow managing to come to a neat stop right next to her without spilling a drop.

'You - young man - are a genius!' she laughed, pointing to the tray bearing the takeaways she'd picked up at The Sardine. 'Great minds think alike!'

'Excellent!' said Jason. 'I've just about finished mine already!'

'Let's get inside and grab a bit of breakfast, then,' she said. 'There are pastries in the bag. I have no idea what you like, so there's almond or chocolate - and I like both equally.'

'Chocolate,' said Jason, his eyes lighting up. 'Always chocolate!'

'I'll remember that,' said Lizzie.

'By the way, someone was looking for you over at the Froth just now,' said Jason, following her into the shop.

'Oh?' said Lizzie, her heart sinking. She didn't need to hear anything else... she just *knew* who it was going to be.

'Yeah - I was just leaving and she screeched to a halt in the parking spot outside,' he paused to gulp down the last mouthful of his first coffee before grabbing a fresh cup from the tray Lizzie had just placed on the workbench.

'Right stroppy she was,' said Jason mildly. 'Not local - never seen her before - said her name was Tiffany.'

'Urgh!' said Lizzie before she could stop herself.

Jason chuckled. 'Yeah - I had a feeling you might say something like that!'

'You... didn't tell her where I was, did you?'

'No way, boss,' said Jason, shaking his head. 'None of my business.'

'And Robbie?' she said.

'He wasn't in yet. It was a girl I don't know – someone new Mike's training up to cover holidays. Don't think she knew who you were... either that or she did an excellent job of acting dumb!' he said cheerfully. 'Last thing I heard, this Tiffany was going to head over to the hotel. No idea why.'

'Mmm,' said Lizzie, nibbling her pastry, though her appetite seemed to have taken a back seat.

'Moody baggage, isn't she?' said Jason. 'Sorry... if she's a friend of yours...?'

'Not a friend,' said Lizzie, shooting him a smile. She didn't want Jason worrying about offending her when it came to Mark's second wife. 'And really - she's none of my business.'

'Right!' said Jason, perking back up. 'So... what are we starting with today?'

Lizzie grinned at him and decided to follow his example - he had the right idea.

Whatever trouble Mark was in, it had nothing to do with her - after all, she hadn't asked him to come to Seabury, had she?! With any luck, Tiffany turning up would mean that his impromptu visit was about to come to an end.

'Hire bikes!' she said, turning her attention quickly to what mattered. 'Can you give them another quick look over and double-check they're ready to go out again? With any luck, we'll have another day like yesterday.'

'Cool,' said Jason, heading straight towards the rack.

As for her, Lizzie was going to check over the repairs he'd completed for her the day before and then make a list of exactly what was needed to work their way through the rest of the list!

Lizzie screeched to a halt outside the shop with a grimace. The new chain was spot-on, but going by that awful sound, Jean's brakes needed seeing to before her bike would be ready to head back up to the "allotment with all the broad beans".

Kneeling down on the pavement, Lizzie was just

about to have a closer look when someone stepped into her light.

'I thought I'd find you here!'

The voice sent a little shiver through Lizzie and the smile froze on her face. Straightening up, she came face-to-face with the last person she wanted to see.

'Tiffany.' Lizzie was quite pleased with herself, considering what she really wanted to say was *"duh, of course you found me at my own shop!"* 'What can I do for you?' she added, doing her best to make sure she sounded calm, cool and in control.

'It's your stupid husband!' snapped Tiffany, crossing her arms over her chest and tapping one pointy, heeled boot on the pavement.

'Hold on,' said Lizzie, 'he's *your* stupid husband these days. He divorced me and married you - remember?!'

'Worst day of my life,' hissed Tiffany.

Lizzie felt her calm begin to crack. 'Yeah, well, it wasn't the best one I've had either!'

Tiffany glared at her, and Lizzie braced herself, ready for an explosion. Wasn't it just typical that it was going to happen right in front of the shop, in full view of anyone who happened to be around? Thank heavens it was still pretty early – though Lizzie had no doubt someone was bound to make sure the whole thing was witnessed and submitted straight to the gossip mill - this *was* Seabury after all!

Lizzie watched Tiffany as the moment lengthened - becoming taut. Even the wind seemed to pause and hold its breath - waiting for the eruption.

Then, to Lizzie's surprise, Tiffany's bottom lip began to tremble. She spotted it immediately because it was exactly what Jenna had done when she was a little girl. It had always been the first warning sign that she was gearing up to bawl the house down. But, in Jenna's defence, she'd been in her terrible twos at the time - and Tiffany definitely wasn't!

As if in slow motion, Lizzie watched Tiffany's entire face crumple as she burst into tears.

Staring around, feeling slightly helpless, Lizzie caught Jason's eye as he peered out of the shop – clearly checking everything was okay. He pulled a face at her, and she shrugged.

Lizzie glanced back to Tiffany - and something seemed to give way inside her. She might not know the woman very well - for obvious reasons - but these weren't crocodile tears. Her entire body was shuddering as violent sobs wrenched themselves from her throat.

Striding forwards, Lizzie wrapped her arms around her ex-husband's new wife and held her tight, while Tiffany promptly drenched the shoulder of her tee shirt.

A full two minutes later and Tiffany wasn't showing any signs of calming down. A couple of early customers had paused to stare at them curiously before Jason had swooped to the rescue and ushered them inside the shop. Without letting go of Tiffany, Lizzie peered over towards the doors, hoping to catch his eye. She was in luck.

'Can you hold the fort for a bit?' she said apologetically. 'I think there's a few things I need to sort out.'

'No problem!' said Jason easily. He nipped out of the shop, grabbed Jean's bike from the pavement next to Lizzie and glanced at her with a raised eyebrow.

'Chain's good but the brakes need sorting out,' she said.

'Got it,' said Jason.

'New hire forms are on the workbench if you need them,' she added, over a renewed wave of sobs from Tiffany.

Jason gave her the thumbs up, and with a slightly scared look at Tiffany that almost made Lizzie laugh, he disappeared back inside the shop.

Right... it was time to take control of this situation before she actually ended up drowning in the flood of tears.

'Tiffany!' she said, her voice firm but gentle. 'Come on, pull yourself together.'

Lizzie placed her hands gently on her shoulders and stood her upright, holding her there until she was sure Tiffany was steady on her feet.

Tiffany scrubbed at her sodden, red eyes with the

back of her hands, sniffing and hiccupping as she did her best to draw a breath.

Oh, good grief!

The woman was in a state. Lizzie's heart squeezed as she stared at the trails of melted mascara and snot that were now spread all over Tiffany's usually impeccably made-up face.

'Here,' said Lizzie, grabbing a clean spotted handkerchief from her pocket. 'Blow your nose and sort yourself out a bit. I'll be right back.'

'Alright,' said Tiffany, sounding like a lost little girl as she took the vast red hanky.

Lizzie paused for a split second, trying to decide what she should do next. Then - making up her mind - she dashed inside the shop, grabbed her wallet from the workbench and thrust it into her pocket. Then she waved at Jason to indicate she was heading out. Jason gave her a brief nod of understanding before continuing to fill out a pair of hire forms for their first customers of the day.

As Lizzie stepped back outside, she was happy to see that even though Tiffany was still a mess, there was a lot less snot in evidence.

'Right - let's go,' she said. 'Follow me.'

She had a feeling it was going to be another long day... but for the first time since Jenna had called and announced that she needed to come home - Lizzie felt like she was in control of the situation.

Now all she needed to do was to get to the bottom of what the situation actually was!

CHAPTER 13

*L*izzie led Tiffany all the way to the other side of town. As they scurried past the Pebble Street Hotel, she crossed her fingers in her dungarees pockets that Mark wouldn't break the habit of a lifetime and emerge early. She needn't have worried though - there wasn't any sign of him - not that it had been very likely if Lou's report of him and the girls propping up the hotel bar and working their way through Lionel's spirits collection was anything to go by!

The two women barely spoke as they made their way along North Beach in the direction of New York Froth. Lizzie would have much preferred the shorter walk to The Sardine, but as much as she loved the little café, it really wasn't the place to go if you needed any kind of privacy.

The joy of New York Froth was that it was large

enough that you could remain slightly anonymous if that's what you wanted. It was easy to ensconce yourself at a table towards the back where you were far less likely to be spotted by anyone who happened to be out for a stroll along the seafront. Today - it would serve her purposes down to the ground.

'Here again?' mumbled Tiffany.

Lizzie nodded. 'Come on - coffees are on me.'

Tiffany sniffed then gave a defeated little shrug as she pushed her way inside.

'Hey Robbie!' said Lizzie, glad to see the familiar face had turned up.

'Lizzie! Got my bike already?' he grinned.

'Gotta wait for the postie first, I'm afraid!' she laughed. 'But I'll have it back to you before the end of the day. I'll get Jason to drop it over the minute we're done.'

'Cool!' he said, shooting a curious glance over her shoulder at Tiffany.

Lizzie turned, only to find the tears had made a comeback.

'Cappuccino for me,' she said quickly. 'Tiffany - you want a cappuccino?'

Tiffany stared at her, a look of complete confusion on her face for a moment before she shook her head.

'Hazelnut decaf macchiato triple whip no sprinkles with rice milk,' she said.

Robbie stared at her in surprise and then gave a single bemused nod.

'You actually got all that?' whispered Lizzie, leaning towards him.

'Yep. I'm afraid so!' he grinned. 'It's my superpower!'

'Okay - that's impressive!' she said, digging out her debit card with a sinking sensation in the pit of her stomach.

'On me,' said Robbie, shaking his head. 'As a thank you for fast-tracking my bike before you're even open for business.'

'Oh no... you don't have to-' she started.

'It's fine,' he said quietly. 'Anyway - I think you might have your hands full.'

He nodded in Tiffany's direction and Lizzie turned only to find the silent stream of tears was taking over again, and the shuddering sobs were making a reappearance.

'Oh crap,' sighed Lizzie.

'I'll bring them over,' said Robbie, looking concerned.

'Cheers,' said Lizzie, taking Tiffany by the arm and steering her towards a private little table right in the back corner of the cafe.

Lizzie deposited a damp and snivelling Tiffany in the chair that faced away from the rest of the café - just to give her the benefit of a bit of extra privacy in case anyone else came in while she was still doing her human waterfall impression.

'Okay - get that hanky to work,' said Lizzie kindly, sitting back and waiting for Tiffany to pull herself together enough to be able to speak.

'Sorry,' said Tiffany unexpectedly. 'Thanks.'

Lizzie just nodded and glanced around before adding, 'remembering to breathe is always good too, by the way.'

A little bubble of laughter erupted from Tiffany as she mopped her face with the hanky. It didn't last long, however, and the poor woman was back to looking like a heartbroken mess in less than a second.

'Right - I'm going to have to ask... what's this all about?' said Lizzie, realising that if she waited for the tears to stop, she could be there for hours.

Tiffany swallowed.

'Take it slow and remember to breathe,' Lizzie added with a smile.

Tiffany sucked in a shaky breath.

'Me and Mark have been married for four years now, right?' she said.

'Right...?' said Lizzie.

'And for the first three years, he forgot our wedding anniversary,' she said, glancing down at the table with a frown.

'Uh-huh,' said Lizzie. 'Sounds about standard.'

'Well, this year he remembered,' said Tiffany.

Lizzie noticed her bottom lip was starting to

wobble again. She didn't want to rush the woman, but perhaps a little chivvying along might stop another full-blown eruption… if she was lucky.

'Go on,' she said, leaning forward in what she hoped was an encouraging manner.

'He brought me flowers, booked us a long weekend away… made a huge fuss!' said Tiffany with a sniff.

Lizzie frowned in confusion. 'So… what's the problem?' she said. 'That all sounds great!'

'It does, doesn't it?!' said Tiffany, her voice coming out on a sob as fresh tears tumbled down her cheeks.

Lizzie braced herself… she had a feeling she was about to discover the real reason Mark had disappeared for a fortnight before gate-crashing her perfectly lovely new life.

'So…?' she prompted as Tiffany just sat there crying silently.

'It wasn't our anniversary he remembered - it was y-y-y-o-u-r-s!' she howled.

Lizzie flinched at the sound even as her jaw dropped in horror. Any vague sense of sympathy she felt towards Mark vanished in an instant.

For some reason, she'd assumed that Tiffany was more likely to have been the one to have sent their relationship off the rails… but this… well, this was classic Mark taken to a whole new level. To forget your wedding anniversary three years in a row was bad enough, but then to rub it in by getting the date mixed up with your first wedding? Well... it was just inexcusably crap, wasn't it?!'

Tiffany let her face fall into the hanky and Lizzie sighed. She stared around the cafe, checking to see if there was anyone around she might have to apologise to later on, but the only other person present was Robbie.

As she caught his eye, the friendly barista pulled a face at her that clearly said *uh oh!* Lizzie held her hands up in a gesture that was half-apology, half-desperation.

Robbie pointed at the tray bearing their newly made drinks, clearly asking if it was okay to bring them over, and Lizzie nodded. At least it would give her something to do while she waited for Tiffany to calm down again. Robbie's arrival might even help her to snap out of it... though looking at the soggy mess in front of her, that was probably wishful thinking.

'Here,' said Robbie quietly. 'And I've added a couple of triple chocolate cookies... in case it might help?'

'You're a sweetheart,' said Lizzie sincerely. 'Thank you.'

'Thank you!' snuffled Tiffany from behind the hanky.

Lizzie winked at Robbie as he straightened up and gave him a subtle thumbs-up.

'You okay?' Lizzie said eventually, after spending

about five minutes sipping her coffee in silence and nibbling one of the biscuits as she waited for Tiffany to pull herself together a bit.

Tiffany nodded. With a final blow of her nose, she reached for her coffee. She took a sip and let out a sigh.

'That's so good.'

'You probably need the fluid!' said Lizzie. The joke slipped out of her mouth before she could stop it. She could have kicked herself - now really wasn't the time!

Tiffany stared at her for a long moment before breaking into a watery grin. 'You're probably right. This has been going on for weeks.'

'I figured,' said Lizzie. 'When the girls said they couldn't reach Mark, I guessed something was going on.'

Tiffany nodded, biting her lip the minute it started wobbling again. 'I said it wasn't on... and he just bailed out. He said *you'd* never have a go at him about something so trivial. He... he... he said he was coming back to you!'

Lizzie snorted. 'He might be back in Seabury, but I can promise you he is *not* coming back to me.'

Tiffany nodded, sipping her coffee again, holding onto her cup with both hands as though it was the only thing keeping her anchored.

Lizzie was about to tell her that this was all classic Mark behaviour when a weight in her lap made her jump. She looked down, only to come face to face with a big, concerned-looking Bernese Mountain Dog.

Stanley had arrived.

'You swapped cafes for the day?' laughed Lizzie in surprise, tickling his head.

He wagged his tail, his orange eyebrows twitching as he shot a look over at Tiffany and then back to her again.

'I think Stanley wants to know if you want a hug,' laughed Lizzie. 'He takes his role as the town therapy dog rather seriously!'

'I'm... not sure I like dogs that much!' said Tiffany, wide-eyed as she stared at the massive pile of fluff who'd just extricated himself from Lizzie and was now eyeballing her instead.

'Well... Stanley's kind of part dog... part seal... part human. And he's very friendly,' said Lizzie watching with interest.

'How about just a pat?' said Tiffany nervously. She slowly stretched her hand out and laid it on Stanley's head. The big dog closed his eyes lazily and began to pant. 'Oh, you *are* lovely!' said Tiffany.

Lizzie grinned as she watched the worry and sadness drain right out of the woman. She could swear Stanley had superpowers sometimes!

'Look,' said Lizzie, deciding that it was probably down to her to take some kind of action if she ever wanted peace to descend again, 'I think I know what we need to do. You stay here and finish your coffee with Stanley. Give me half an hour - then come over and find me in the hotel?'

For one brief moment, Lizzie thought Tiffany was going to tell her where to go... which would have been fair enough considering she'd decided to pull her bossy pants on. She watched as Tiffany got to her feet, and braced herself once again for the impending argument, but it didn't come.

'Thank you,' said Tiffany quietly, before dropping to her knees next to the table and wrapping her arms around Stanley, burying her face in his fur.

Lizzie smirked as Stanley shot her a look that was almost an eye roll.

'All yours, boy!' she chuckled, grabbing her biscuit from the plate and making a beeline for the door.

CHAPTER 14

For one brief minute, Lizzie stood in front of the cafe in the sunshine and contemplated hot-footing it back to Moore Bikes… but then she squared her shoulders and marched along the seafront towards the hotel. There was a job to do, and it looked like it was down to her to sort the whole mess out!

Opening the grand door to the Pebble Street Hotel before she could wuss out, Lizzie stared around the lovely reception. There didn't seem to be anyone around, but she could hear the gentle clink of cutlery and the burble of soft conversation coming from the breakfast room just along the corridor.

Lizzie hesitated. Should she just wander through and see if Mark was already down from his room? Somehow she doubted he would be in there, sipping tea and eating toast and marmalade with the other guests. She glanced at her watch and shook her head. Nope - it was definitely still too early in the day for Mark to have emerged - especially if he had any kind of hangover.

Maybe she should just head straight upstairs and hammer on his door. But then... she didn't know which room he was in. Lizzie sighed, cursing herself for not asking the girls if they'd figured that out the previous day.

She was just contemplating sticking her head around the door to the breakfast room to see if Hattie was around when someone cleared their throat on the stairs.

'Hello Lizzie!'

'Lionel!' she said, a rush of relief running through her at the sight of his friendly face.

'All well?' he asked looking concerned.

'Yes,' she said quickly, 'actually no... or... maybe?'

'Well... that clears that up!' chuckled Lionel.

'Sorry,' she said, shaking her head. 'I was wondering... has Mark come down for breakfast?'

'No,' said Lionel. 'I believe he has a *do not disturb* sign on his door. Not surprised after the amount of drink he added to his tab last night!'

'Uh oh!' said Lizzie. 'I hope they weren't a nuisance?'

'Not at all,' said Lionel, his eyes shining. 'Custom is custom is custom! Though I think it was definitely time for them to retire to bed by the time Lou bundled your girls into a taxi!'

'Taxi!' gasped Lizzie. That was new!

Lionel nodded. 'There was absolutely no way we were going to let them walk back up to the cottage - they'd have ended up in the sea... or maybe a ditch. Hattie called Ben, and he played taxi.'

Lizzie pinched the bridge of her nose and shook her head. 'Lionel - I'm so sorry... my family seems to be causing you no-end of havoc right now!'

'Not at all!' chuckled Lionel. 'You know, we had another member of your... ah... party here earlier too.'

'My... party?' said Lizzie, dreading what he was going to say next.

'Mark's wife, I believe,' he said delicately. 'Obviously, we wouldn't allow her upstairs because we didn't want her disturbing the other guests... so she hung around down here. Mark refused to come down. I did try to call him several times.'

'Oh god,' groaned Lizzie.

'Don't fret,' said Lionel kindly. 'She got bored in the end and wandered off.'

'I know,' said Lizzie. 'She turned up at the shop.'

'Ah,' said Lionel.

'Ah indeed!' laughed Lizzie. 'You've been brilliant. I can only apologise for my... erm... *extended* family...'

Lizzie paused, silently cursing the lot of them. She'd come back to Seabury for a quiet life – one where she could make new friendships and rekindle old ones. The last thing she needed was for her out-of-control family to wreck it all so soon.

'It's funny how things work out, isn't it?' said Lionel gently. 'And it *will* work out, Lizzie. If there's anything I can do to help... anything at all... you name it.'

Lizzie smiled at him gratefully, and for a moment she had to blink back a few tears of her own.

'You know,' she said, as soon as she was sure she was in full control of her voice, 'it's funny you should say that... because I really need to ask for a favour. Or... maybe two?'

'Ask away!' said Lionel, looking intrigued.

'Well... do you reckon Ben might be up for playing taxi driver again?'

Lizzie took a deep breath to steady her nerves before reaching out and knocking sharply on the door of room 324.

She paused, listening hard.

Nothing.

'Mark, you epic waste of space!' she hissed, thumping on the door a bit harder and then pressing her ear up against the wood. There was still no answer, but she could hear the sound of bare feet padding around.

So... he was definitely listening!

'I know you're hiding in there,' she said. 'I've spoken to Tiffany, and I know what this is all about.'

Lizzie paused again, hoping he might say something.

'Listen,' she said, her voice sounding hard and cold, 'I don't care how bad your hangover is. I don't care that you haven't had your precious toast and marmalade. I don't care if you've not finished your effing newspaper either. I'm calling a family meeting down in the dining room in exactly ten minutes. The girls will be there too. If you aren't there, I will come up here and personally drag you downstairs myself.'

Lizzie went quiet again, listening hard. There was the sound of a nose being blown on the other side of the door. Lizzie rolled her eyes. What was it with these two?!

'Lionel's been good enough to let us use the dining room, so we won't be disturbed,' she said. 'But these people are my friends and you two are starting to make me look ridiculous. It's not on - got it? We're sorting this out. And no sniffling - blow your nose!'

'Okay...' came the sheepish reply from just behind the door.

Lizzie was sitting at the head of one of the long dining tables, feeling uncomfortably like some kind of mafia boss as she waited for the others to join her. All it would take was for someone to hand her a long-haired white cat, and the image would be complete.

Unfortunately, though, Tiffany had bogarted Stanley, and Lionel didn't own a cat, so there was nothing to do other than pick at her nails and repeatedly tell herself that everything would be fine. One thing was for sure, for better or for worse, she was *definitely* about to shake things up a bit!

The girls appeared first, both of them looking bleary-eyed and decidedly worse for wear as Lionel ushered them into the room. Jenna's blond curls stood out from her head in a halo that was more like a fright wig, and she looked pale and washed out. Megan was still wearing a pair of pyjama trousers. She'd pulled on an old tee shirt and a fleece that Lizzie recognised as one of her own.

'Mum?' said Jenna, her eyes wide. 'That taxi-driver guy said it was urgent. Is dad okay? Is he ill?'

'Sit down,' said Lizzie, not unkindly. 'He'll be down in a second.'

Hopefully! she added silently to herself.

Jenna threw Megan a look, and her big sister just shrugged at her and then flopped down onto one of the dining chairs, burying her face in her hands.

Jenna took the chair opposite her. 'You said this was urgent?'

'It is,' said Lizzie, catching sight of Tiffany hovering in the doorway. 'Come on in,' she added.

'O-kay,' said Tiffany, sidling in and staring at the girls for a long moment before opting to take the seat next to Jenna having clearly decided that it was the lesser of two evils.

Lizzie sighed as her daughters shot daggers at the newcomer before turning worried eyes back towards her.

'If she's here...' said Megan.

'And she's been crying...' added Jenna.

'What's wrong with dad?!' demanded Megan.

'Oh no, it's serious, isn't it?!' said Jenna, looking as though she might start to cry.

'He's fine!' snapped Lizzie. 'But he won't be for much longer if he doesn't get his behind in here!'

Tiffany caught her eye and Lizzie quickly looked away as she felt a giggle threatening to escape. It would definitely spoil the moment - she really needed to keep hold of her mafia-boss energy until this unholy mess had been straightened out once and for all!

Glancing at her watch, Lizzie scrambled to her feet.

'I'll be right back,' she growled. 'So will Mark. None of you move a muscle.'

She only got as far as the door when Mark appeared in front of her.

'You're late,' she hissed.

'Give me a break!' he mumbled, sounding like a little kid.

'You don't deserve it,' she said. 'Go sit next to Megan.'

For a brief moment, Mark looked like he'd quite like to argue, but then his entire body deflated as though he simply didn't have the energy.

Good!

'Right, first things first,' said Lizzie, getting back to her seat and picking up a large jug of water Lionel had brought in for them. She started to slowly pour four glasses of water, and the tension around the table ramped up with every clink of ice cube hitting crystal.

'Pass them around,' she said quietly.

Okay, so Lizzie had to secretly admit that she was kind of enjoying herself! Still... why shouldn't she? They all deserved what was coming... and by the looks on their faces, they all knew they had a damn good bollocking coming their way... and she was very nearly ready to deliver it.

'Right. Everyone take a sip of water - you all look like you need it!' she ordered, taking her seat again.

Obediently, all four of them took a mouthful of water as she glared at them.

'Right. Mark - apologise to Tiffany for being an idiot!' she demanded, keeping her tone even.

Both Jenna and Megan's eyes went wide as they turned in unison to stare at their father.

'It was a mistake,' huffed Mark.

'I don't care,' said Lizzie, glaring at him. 'Apologise this instant.'

'Sorry,' muttered Mark, not looking up from his glass.

Tiffany folded her arms and Lizzie sighed.

'Mark - apologise properly. To. Your. Wife. What you did sucked.'

Tiffany shot her a grateful glance and Lizzie felt herself soften. Out of all four of them, the poor woman didn't deserve any kind of harsh treatment. The only thing she was guilty of was falling in love with her idiot of an ex-husband - and there was no accounting for taste.

'I'm sorry,' said Mark again, and this time he looked across the table towards Tiffany.

'What for?' demanded Lizzie, earning herself an angry glance from Mark. She just about managed to refrain from poking her tongue out at him.

'I'm sorry for forgetting our anniversary... and then... when I did remember... for getting the date mixed up with my first wedding.' He paused. 'Our wedding,' he added, growling at Lizzie.

'Oof!' gasped Jenna.

'Jeez dad,' muttered Megan. 'Dick move!'

Tiffany looked pleased. Clearly, the girls' reactions backed up Lizzie's.

'I'm *also* sorry for running away,' said Mark with a sigh. 'Especially for coming here. You deserve better... and I promise I'll do better... and I love you and-'

'Alright, alright, that'll do!' said Lizzie, cutting him off. It was all starting to go a bit mushy for her liking, and knowing Mark, if she let him get into his stride, it would take forever to shut him up again.

'Tiffany - are you satisfied with the apology?' she demanded

From the gooey look Tiffany was now giving Mark, Lizzie didn't really need to see her nod to know that he was well and truly forgiven. All that drama - for nothing. He could have just apologised weeks ago, and then none of this would have happened.

Well... that was round one done... but she wasn't finished yet!

'Girls,' she said, turning her attention towards them.

Lizzie noticed that they both flinched ever so slightly – and once again she had to rein herself in from enjoying this too much. Usually, she hated confrontation more than anything else. Right now though, the feeling of being in charge was coursing through her veins... and it felt good!

'Look,' she said, softening her voice slightly. 'You know you're my daughters, and I love you both very much. I will do anything for you - within reason.'

The two girls smiled at her uncertainly, and it was as much as Lizzie could do not to bundle them both in for a hug and forget everything. But... they needed to hear this.

'But... and it's quite a big but...' She paused and took a deep breath. 'You're both adults - but you're behaving like spoiled brats. You've got your own lives to get back on track... but you need to stop ruining mine while you're at it!'

Lizzie paused again. Maybe she'd gone too far because the girls looked horrified. She blew out a long, slow breath.

'I came here for a new start,' she said. 'I came here for some peace and quiet. I came here to build my business and discover stuff about myself... but since you've come home, I feel like I've been babysitting two very stroppy toddlers.'

Megan had now turned bright pink and Jenna's eyes were shining with tears as she stared at Lizzie.

'I love that you're here,' she continued, suddenly realising the truth of it, 'but I want you here as adults. I don't have *time* for babysitting right now – but I'd love to be a part of your lives – and to help you both with whatever you're working through!'

'I'm really sorry, mum,' said Megan.

Lizzie smiled at her eldest in surprise.

'Me too,' said Jenna.

'Right. Well... that's okay,' said Lizzie. She wasn't quite done yet, though. 'Oh – and just so you know - we won't be getting builders in to make the cottage bigger. Because you two are visiting - not moving in.

And there's no way your dad's ever coming back to the cottage for more than a cuppa when he and Tiffany pop in for a visit.'

Tiffany looked surprised and rather delighted at this and shot her a smile. Lizzie grinned back.

'Also, your dad and I are *definitely* not getting back together!' she added - just to make sure that the rather horrible notion never came up in conversation again. 'For one thing, he's happily married.'

Lizzie paused. 'You *are* happily married, right?' she demanded.

The pair of them nodded and started making gooey eyes at each other again across the table. It was as much as Lizzie could do to stop herself from making barfing sounds.

'Just making sure!' she said. Then she turned to eye the girls. 'Besides, I'm seeing someone anyway.'

'Who?' said Megan in surprise.

'Liam,' said Lizzie. Even mentioning his name seemed to have a strange effect on her, and the hard mafia-boss shell she'd donned started to melt.

'What, that old bloke from the shop?' said Jenna curiously.

The mafia-boss promptly re-formed, and Lizzie turned to glare at her youngest daughter.

'Sorry mum,' she muttered, dropping her eyes to the table.

Suddenly, Lizzie let out a laugh. Being stroppy was too exhausting to keep up. 'You'll like him,' she said. 'Both of you will, I hope. He's away at the moment, but I'd really like you to get to know him a bit while you're here, if you're up for it?'

'We'd love to, mum,' said Megan quietly.

Jenna nodded enthusiastically.

'Great,' said Lizzie, feeling like a weight had just been lifted from her shoulders. 'So... we're all good?' she said, staring around the table. 'Everyone's sorted... everyone's alright?'

Everyone nodded.

'Perfect,' said Lizzie with a happy smile. 'Because I've got a shop to run.'

Lizzie burst out of Pebble Street with a huge smile on her face. The sun was beating down, and there was a decidedly triumphant theme tune running through her head. Frankly, it was a miracle she didn't break into a song and dance routine as she strode along the seafront.

The world felt like it had righted itself. She'd stood up for herself and told her family a few home truths... and in the process, it felt like several barriers between them had dissolved. Maybe they'd all find it a bit easier to talk to each other from now on!

Lizzie took a deep breath as she grinned out across the sea - her heart hammering with a mixture of excitement and possibility. Now, maybe she could get back on track with her dreams.

Sure - she didn't expect miracles. There were bound to be a few more hiccups while the girls were still in Seabury – but at least now that the air was clear, perhaps they'd get the chance to talk properly at long last. As adults.

Lizzie's steps slowed and she came to a halt beside one of Seabury's ornate lampposts. This was where she'd shared her first kiss with Liam – and she'd been coming from the Pebble Street Hotel then too. Wrapping her arms around herself, Lizzie closed her eyes and tried to imagine he was with her right now.

If only she could call him or message him – just to tell him how much she wanted to see him!

'Sod it!' said Lizzie, opening her eyes with a grin. She rummaged in her pocket and pulled out her mobile. She'd send him a message - then it would be waiting for him when he managed to get his phone sorted out.

I'm standing under our lamppost thinking about our first kiss. Girls and ex (plus second wife!) all sorted. Details later. Can't wait until you're home so we can have that breakfast date! Hope everything's okay. Lx

Lizzie hit send before she could think better of it and was just about to pocket her phone again when it buzzed to life in her hands. Jumping, she fumbled with the handset and only just managed to save it before it clattered down onto the pavement. Peering at the screen, Lizzie laughed out loud.

New phone! Picked it up in the service station on my way to play super-dad. Details later, but everything fine. Sorry to disappear with no warning. Daughters eh?!
P.S. How about making it breakfast in bed?! ;)

THE END

LIVING THE DREAM IN SEABURY

SEABURY - BOOK 12

CHAPTER 1

Lizzie leaned against the ancient wooden doorjamb and gazed towards the centre of Seabury. She couldn't see much. The Sardine, Pebble Street, and even the King's Nose were barely visible behind a heavy curtain of rain. It had been pelting down all morning. Huge drops danced on the surface of several deep puddles that were trying to turn the little seafront road into a water feature.

There wasn't a soul in sight - not that Lizzie could blame everyone for staying snuggled up inside on a day like this! Just a week ago, the sun had been shining and the little town had been buzzing with late-summer visitors, all intent on exploring the lanes on her hire bikes. Today couldn't be more different though. They hadn't had a single customer through the doors of Moore Bikes all morning.

It might be quiet, but Lizzie couldn't help but feel a bit… fidgety! She let out a long sigh and turned to peer in the other direction – up the hill that led past the turning to her cottage and then on towards the allotments and the main road.

There wasn't anything to see that way either - other than more rain.

'Boss?'

Lizzie jumped and turned to find Jason peering at her with an amused expression on his face. She couldn't blame him… she'd spent a good portion of the morning propping up the shop doors and staring into the middle distance. It wasn't like she didn't have plenty of work to be getting on with. They'd had customers coming out of their ears for days - and there was more than enough to keep the pair of them busy until bonfire night!

'You okay?' prompted Jason.

'Yeah, sorry!' laughed Lizzie. 'I'm being a total slacker today, aren't I?!'

'I thought you said Liam wasn't due back until this evening?' said Jason, cutting straight through her apologetic waffle.

'Yup,' said Lizzie, feeling daft as her cheeks rapidly started to heat up. 'That's right.'

Damn the boy for his razor-sharp memory and attention to detail!

Still, that's what made Jason the perfect member of staff, so she couldn't exactly complain when he turned his superpowers on her, could she? Besides - he'd just hit the nail on the head. Jason had caught her in the act of mooning around after a boy... and at her age too!

There wasn't much point in trying to deny it. After a whole week away, Liam was finally due back in Seabury by the end of the day - and Lizzie had been like a love-sick puppy all morning.

More like all week!

Even though Liam wasn't due to reappear in town until well past closing time, Lizzie couldn't help herself from keeping half an eye out for his arrival... just in case he rocked up early. She longed to see his battered old van trundling towards the shop.

'Anyway,' she said, clearing her throat and feeling like a bit of an idiot, 'where are we up to?'

'Hire bikes are all clean, checked over and ready to go again,' said Jason, scratching his nose. 'So I'm going to head home for lunch if that's okay? I was just wondering if you'd like me to take Heather Landry's bike back while I'm at it. She's only just up the road from our place.'

'You're not going to walk home in this weather, are you?' said Lizzie with a frown. 'I'm happy to grab us both something to eat from The Sardine to save you from getting soaked?'

'Dad still isn't feeling that great,' said Jason, pulling a face. 'I just wanted to check in on him... but only if that's okay with you?'

'Of course it is!' said Lizzie quickly. 'It's so quiet today, you're welcome to take the afternoon off if he needs you at home?'

'It's just a really sucky cold,' said Jason, shaking his head. 'He doesn't really need me there - I just thought I should make sure he eats some lunch. He was all over the place this morning - completely out of it to be honest. I'm guessing he's got a temperature or something.'

'Poor thing!' said Lizzie. 'Take as much time as you need.'

'Thanks Boss,' said Jason. 'I won't be too long. I'll just heat up some soup if he's not had anything... I don't want him feeling worse!'

'I wish I had the car so I could give you a lift and save you a soaking!' said Lizzie as she watched Jason pulling on his jacket.

The lad was so ridiculously capable - able to do pretty much anything he turned his hand to – that it was almost too easy to forget that he was still just a kid. From what she'd picked up on the town grapevine, it was just Jason and his dad at home.

Lizzie bit her lip. Her mother-hen antennae were tingling... but she hadn't known Jason long, and she wasn't entirely sure how he might react if she started to fuss. Still, she'd not reached her age without learning to follow her instincts!

'Jason... if you ever need anything...' she said, not quite knowing where she was going with this. 'I mean - I know we haven't known each other long - but if you or your dad ever need anything, you can always call me, okay?'

Jason held her eye for a long minute and then smiled.

'Cheers,' he said.

'I'm serious,' said Lizzie.

'I know,' said Jason quietly, giving her a nod. 'Thanks.'

'Anytime. Just shout,' she said. 'As for Heather's bike - leave it here for now. She said she's not in a rush for it, and it'll get drenched in this. Bad enough that you will too!'

'Who's getting drenched?'

Lizzie turned only to find Jenna standing behind the pair of them, a half-folded umbrella held at arm's length so that it didn't drip down her leg.

'Jason - he's got to walk home for lunch!' said Lizzie.

'I can give you a lift if you'd like?' said Jenna, glancing at Jason.

'It's fine,' said Jason, somehow managing to look hopeful and awkward at the same time. 'I mean - I'm just across town... it's not a big deal!'

'Lift?' said Lizzie distractedly. 'You drove down?'

'I hope you don't mind!' said Jenna with a nod, looking a bit awkward as she jangled Lizzie's car keys in her free hand. 'Megan found them down the side of the sofa when she was tidying up earlier!'

'It's fine,' said Lizzie faintly. The idea of her eldest daughter tidying up without being asked had temporarily put her into a state of shock. 'Where are you going?'

'Oh!' said Jenna. 'Only down here to see you and bring you this.' She rummaged around inside her shoulder bag for a second before producing a large Tupperware box. 'I made you some lunch. I didn't think you'd want to head out to the cafe in this weather. Plus - I know what you're like - you'd probably get so caught up in whatever you're working on, you'd just forget to eat anything.'

'Sounds a bit like my dad!' laughed Jason.

'Aw, Jenna!' said Lizzie, smiling gratefully as she took the box. 'That's really kind of you!'

'I would have walked down…' said Jenna, feeling around in the bag again before handing over a bottle of elderflower fizz.

'And got soaked to the skin just to save me from the rain?' laughed Lizzie. 'Don't be daft! Anyway - it's brilliant timing if it saves Jason from getting wet through!'

'Only if you're sure you don't mind?' said Jason, looking strangely shy.

'Course!' said Jenna. 'Better be quick though - there was a traffic warden mooching down the hill just now, and he looked like he was in a foul mood… not that I can blame him. There was rain dripping off his nose!'

'Go go go!' laughed Lizzie. 'Otherwise, this'll be the most expensive packed lunch of all time!'

'Won't be too long!' said Jason as he gave her a quick wave before following Jenna out into the rain.

Lizzie watched the little car splash away towards the centre of town, and then sighed as her eyes scanned the road yet again for any sign of a beaten-up white van.

'Idiot!' she laughed.

She just needed to keep herself busy - the afternoon was bound to fly past if she did that... and then Liam would be back before she knew it! Lizzie couldn't believe how much she'd missed him considering they weren't even officially an item yet... but then, who needed official? She was old enough to know exactly how she felt about him.

Totally crazy.

At least they'd managed a couple of quick chats since he'd dashed off to help Amy move into her new home at the last minute.

'Bloomin' daughters,' she muttered with a grin.

Lizzie didn't really mean it, though. Liam clearly doted on his girl – a hard-working junior doctor roughly the same age as Megan. As for Megan and Jenna, they were still very much at large, but the cottage had been unnervingly quiet since their little family show-down at the Pebble Street Hotel.

If she was honest, Lizzie hadn't really expected her intervention to work so well - but giving everyone a good talking-to seemed to have worked some kind of magic. For starters, Tiffany had insisted on paying for Mark's stay *and* the meal they'd all shared - and Lizzie's sigh of relief had been more than heartfelt.

More importantly though, since then she'd been able to get in for a shower before the girls *every single morning*. Even if that was the only change, it would have been nothing short of a small miracle... but the girls seemed to be determined to make up for being total brats – and Lizzie definitely wasn't complaining!

If she wasn't afraid of jinxing things, Lizzie might even go so far as to say that she was starting to enjoy having them around. Now that she was getting to grips with things at Moore Bikes, she was looking forward to spending some quality time with both of them.

Besides... she wasn't convinced that Megan was quite as *fine* as she was pretending to be, and she wanted to get to the bottom of what was going on while they were all together. Whether she liked it or not, Megan was going to get all the moral support she needed!

Still, there was nothing Lizzie could do about that right now. Thanks to Jenna, though, there was *definitely* something she could do about her growling stomach!

Turning her back on the rain, Lizzie headed over

to her workbench and perched on the wobbly chair tucked in behind it. After a brief fight with the lid, she peered inside her lunchbox and her mouth instantly started to water.

'Wow Jenna!' she breathed.

Her daughter had sectioned off the inside of the box using smaller tubs and had crammed them with a lunch fit for a very hungry queen. There was a gorgeous, colourful salad, a smoked salmon and cream cheese bagel, a lemon quarter to squeeze into it, and a fork rolled up in a couple of napkins. The pièce de résistance was a chocolate brownie, carefully wrapped so that it wouldn't end up tasting of salmon.

Lizzie twisted the top off her drink and took a long, thirsty sip. It was her absolute favourite.

Definite brownie points!

As she bit into the bagel, Lizzie let out a little groan of delight and wondered if Liam was getting the same royal treatment from his daughter!

'For heaven's sake,' she laughed, shaking her head at herself. She'd only managed to think about something else for about thirty seconds - before getting straight back to her favourite subject - Liam.

CHAPTER 2

'Yum!' sighed Lizzie, tossing her fork into the empty Tupperware box before snapping the lid back in place. There were packed lunches… and then there were *packed lunches*. This one was most definitely the latter. She wasn't sure if Jenna was a genius, or if the bagel had simply tasted divine because she didn't have to go out into the rain to fetch it. Either way, Lizzie made a mental note to thank her daughter for being so thoughtful.

'Back to work, slacker!' muttered Lizzie, hauling herself to her feet and staring around the shop. In a way, she was glad of this rain. She'd adored the sunny days that had brought so many customers through her doors already, but this weather meant she might actually get the chance to catch up a bit.

Turning to eyeball the wall behind the workbench, Lizzie decided she'd start by getting the rest of the hangers and brackets screwed into position so that she'd be able to stash most of her tools up out of the way when she wasn't using them.

Lizzie had just dragged her stepladder into place and climbed to the top when she heard a car pull up right outside. Wondering if Jenna might have come back for some reason, Lizzie craned her neck to take a peek, only to spot Mrs Hatherleigh dashing towards the door bearing a slightly soggy cardboard box in front of her.

'Give me a hand, Lizzie love?' she said, striding inside and plonking the box down on the workbench before Lizzie had even had the chance to budge an inch.

'Hi Margie,' said Lizzie in surprise as she hurried back down to ground level.

'I thought I'd get some more of these boxes down to you,' she said, bustling back out into the rain.

'You didn't need to do that!' said Lizzie, hot on her heels and suddenly feeling guilty that she hadn't managed to collect the last of the bike parts from the Hatherleigh's barn as she'd promised. What with Jenna and Megan being around, and then Mark and Tiffany descending on Seabury, she simply hadn't had the chance to pick them up.

'I absolutely *did* need to!' laughed Margie. 'Don't worry – I'm not about to make good on my threats of taking everything to the tip… it's just… Ted's starting to drive me mad!'

'How so?' said Lizzie, grabbing a box from the boot and dashing back inside. She felt a bit like she'd missed a step in the conversation somewhere.

'Well... let's put it like this – I needed to bring you these boxes before the old fool empties them all out again,' said Margie, rolling her eyes. 'It's just as well you took away that file of designs of his, otherwise I think he'd be back at it!'

'Oh no,' said Lizzie, her heart sinking. She'd been worried Ted might regret handing over his incredible collection of goodies to her.

'Don't look like that, love!' said Margie, shaking her head and letting out a long sigh. 'He's over the moon that you're going to be able to put all his junk to good use. He just misses tinkering around with it himself. Hearing about your plans and getting excited for you...well... it's just stirred him up a bit, that's all!'

'Oh,' said Lizzie, not quite knowing what to say. 'Poor Ted.'

'Don't you *poor Ted* me!' laughed Margie. 'I definitely don't miss having greasy old bits of bike lying around here there and everywhere. I'm looking forward to when he finally gets around to sorting out our lane so that we can have the caravan at ours – once you're done with it, of course! In the meantime... the man's driving me nuts.'

Lizzie frowned as she grabbed another box from Margie's car and hefted it inside the shop. She'd just had an idea… but she wasn't sure if she should broach it yet. Perhaps now wasn't the time. She had the feeling one wrong move on her part could cause all manner of grouching between the Hatherleighs. Perhaps she'd mention it to Ted first… after she'd had the chance to think it through a bit further.

'I'll make sure I get up to yours as soon as I can to grab the last few boxes,' she said.

'For your own sake – that's probably a good idea,' said Margie, smiling at her. 'Before the old fool squirrels any more of it away. He thinks I don't notice, but I swear he's emptied at least two boxes and hidden the bits in behind those old mowers of his.'

Lizzie grinned. Ted Hatherleigh was a man after her own heart.

'I thought his hands were too sore to be able to do much now?' she asked, doing her best to make it sound like a throwaway comment.

'If he fiddles around in that cold barn day after day, then yes – his hands do get sore,' sighed Margie, pausing just inside the shop out of the rain. 'But the thing is, I think he misses the people… he always had someone turning up for something or other. He loves a good gossip – you probably noticed.'

Lizzie nodded, doing her best not to look too excited. This was sounding better by the second.

'Anyway, I'd better skedaddle – I'm off to bridge club over in Dunscombe Sands,' said Margie, giving her arm a friendly pat. 'Anything for five minutes' peace from him indoors. I tell you Lizzie – I'm not used to it! He used to be out in that barn all hours… but now he's under my feet from morning till night!'

'I'm sure you'll get used to it!' said Lizzie.

'I don't want to!' said Margie looking horrified. 'Anyway… see you soon.'

As soon as she'd waved Mrs Hatherleigh off, Lizzie clambered back up the ladder, drill in hand, intent on getting at least one job finished before Jason reappeared from his lunch break. She'd just got into position to start on the first hole when she felt her mobile buzz to life in her pocket.

'For heaven's sake!' she muttered, switching off the drill and hurrying back down the ladder. She'd learned the hard way that playing with tools and mobile phones at the same time didn't mix. There was a fresh scratch right across the middle of her screen where she'd tried to read a text while tightening up a pair of handlebars… it hadn't gone well.

'Hello?!' she gasped, desperately tapping the screen to answer the call.

Damnit! It had already gone to voicemail. Maybe whoever it was would call back…?

Lizzie sighed impatiently as she stared at the screen, waiting for it to spring to life in her hands. A couple of seconds later it buzzed with a voicemail notification.

"Hey, Lizzie. You don't know me… it's Amy… dad's… I mean, Liam's daughter…"

Lizzie sucked in an involuntary breath as a bolt of fear shot down her spine.

"Look, dad's broken down on his way home. He says he's really sorry he can't call you himself, but his phone's in the van - and the van's on the back of the tow truck on the way to the nearest garage. He borrowed the driver's phone. He couldn't remember your number - so he called me and I had to call The Sardine to ask for your number!"

Lizzie grinned as she imagined poor Amy having to phone her way around Seabury just to reach her.

"Anyway, someone called Sarah gave me your details. I've left a message at your house too. Dad's hoping to get back tomorrow sometime as long as the garage can do some kind of temporary fix."

Amy went quiet and Lizzie wondered if that was the end of the message, until she heard a long, tinny sigh.

"Look, I know we've not met yet and he'd probably kill me for saying this - but dad's the happiest I've seen him in ages. Be nice to him. He's a good guy. Hopefully meet you soon. See ya!"

Lizzie couldn't help the goofy smile that promptly spread across her face. Was she really making Liam as happy as he was making her? She was suddenly very glad she was alone in the shop... because it meant there was no one to witness her doing a little happy-dance on the spot.

Then a wave of pure disappointment hit her as

the other part of what Amy had just said sank in - Liam wasn't going to be back today after all.

Still... maybe it was a good thing. He was safe and sound, and with any luck, the van wouldn't take too long to sort out. In the meantime, she'd just have to get her head down and get as much work done here as possible so that she could skive with a clear conscience when he did finally get home!

With a newfound burst of energy, Lizzie grabbed her drill and headed back up the ladder. She'd just managed to get back in position when she felt the familiar buzzing in her pocket again.

'What now?!' she growled, heading back down the ladder again. At this rate, she'd have thighs of steel from all the extra exercise!

'Hello?' she huffed.

'It's Megan! You okay? You sound out of breath!'

'I'm fine!' laughed Lizzie. 'I was up a ladder.'

'Ah - sorry,' said Megan. 'I've just picked up a message from Amy - Liam's daughter and-'

'I got one on my mobile too,' said Lizzie.

'Oh, cool. So you know Liam's not back until tomorrow?' said Megan.

'Yeah,' sighed Lizzie.

'Gutted!' said Megan.

'A bit!' said Lizzie.

'Amy's really nice, you know,' said Megan.

'I'm sure she is!' said Lizzie in surprise. 'But how'd you get that from an answering machine message?'

'I called her back, duh!' laughed Megan. 'I wanted her to know I'd picked up the message so that she didn't worry.'

'Oh!' said Lizzie. 'That was really thoughtful - thanks Meggie!'

'No worries,' said Megan. 'Anyway, she's really nice. She was telling me about her new place - I'm actually quite jealous!'

'It *does* sound lovely,' said Lizzie. 'Last time we talked, Liam said he was surprised she'd finally moved - but it sounds like Amy had had enough of living with her mum.'

'Well... not everyone's mum is as cool as you,' said Megan.

Lizzie's jaw dropped. Blimey - that was one hell of a compliment coming from Megan!

'Thanks, love!' she said, surprised to find her voice had gone thick with emotion.

'Don't get all soppy on me!' snorted Megan. 'Anyway - you bog off and do whatever you were doing with that poor ladder. I've got a kitchen to clean!'

Lizzie opened her mouth to form some kind of half-baked protest, but Megan had already gone.

'Well... I'm not going to stop you!' she said with a grin, turning to eye the ladder again. 'Right... third time lucky!' Or maybe it was the fourth? She'd lost count!

This time, Lizzie managed to get all three holes

drilled before climbing carefully back down to grab the bracket and screws.

'You know, Boss - you really shouldn't be playing on the ladder when you're the only one here.'

Lizzie jumped and spun around, only to find Jason standing just inside the doorway, watching her.

'Blimey! How long have you been lurking there?' she gasped, resting her hand on her thumping heart.

'Since the first hole,' said Jason. 'I didn't want to make you jump – at least not while you were at height!'

'Well... thanks?' laughed Lizzie.

'I'm serious, Boss - you shouldn't be up the ladder when there's no one else around,' said Jason, stripping off a heavy waterproof jacket and hanging it over the corner of one of the doors before running his hands through his wet hair.

'Okay - noted!' said Lizzie, deciding not to tell him how many times she'd climbed up and down in the last few minutes. 'When did you become so wise?!'

'Dad's often out on his own with the bees,' said Jason with a shrug. 'He's always taught me to work safely – especially when you're on your own!'

Lizzie nodded. The kid did have a fair point.

'How's your dad doing?' she said, keen to change the subject.

'Not great,' said Jason. 'He said he's all achy. I

made him soup and got him some pills and more water. He's gone back to bed.'

'Poor guy!' said Lizzie.

'Yeah,' said Jason with a shrug. 'I mean... I don't think it's serious or anything... he's just feeling rough.'

'Are you okay?' said Lizzie, eyeing him closely. He certainly looked fine - no coughing or spluttering - not pale or ridiculously flushed either.

Ah - to have a nice, youthful immune system!

'Fit as a fiddle, Boss!' said Jason.

'And you've had lunch?' she said. She wouldn't put it past him to just look after his dad and forget about feeding himself.

'Yep - cheese on toast for me, so I'm all sorted!' said Jason with a grin. 'Thanks to Jenna giving me that lift, I had plenty of time.'

'That was perfect timing!' said Lizzie.

'I like her,' said Jason. 'She's really cool. She was telling me a bit about her travels!'

'Uh huh,' said Lizzie, raising an eyebrow as she made a mental note to ask Jenna not to put too many ideas into the impressionable head of her one and only member of staff!

'Yeah,' said Jason. 'And she's got some brilliant ideas for this place too... but I guess you know all that.'

'For this place?' said Lizzie.

'Yup!' said Jason. 'If she hasn't told you yet, you should definitely ask her about them.'

'Maybe I'll do that!' said Lizzie.

Knowing how impulsive Jenna could be, Lizzie figured she'd better find out what was going on in that head of hers as soon as possible… otherwise, she might well rock up at the shop one morning only to find it had been transformed into a roller-disco or something equally as nuts!

'Shall I?' said Jason, waving the bracket she'd been about to install in front of her to get her attention.

'Go for it!' said Lizzie with a nod. 'Mrs Hatherleigh dropped off some more boxes while you were out - I'll see what new goodies we've got in this lot!'

CHAPTER 3

'Hellooooo? Anyone home?' Lizzie closed the front door of the cottage behind her with a thump and inhaled deeply.

YUM! Someone was cooking something nice!

'Hey mum - I'm in the kitchen!' Jenna's voice drifted along the hallway to greet her.

Slipping out of her jacket, Lizzie hung it on a peg to dry out. The rain had eased off a bit, but the walk home had still been decidedly damp. Pottering through to join her daughter, Lizzie came to an abrupt halt in the doorway.

'Blimey... who stole my kitchen?!' she gasped. The room was immaculate, barring a neatly stacked pile of dishes next to the sink waiting to be scrubbed. 'And what's that smell?!'

Jenna straightened up from the oven, her face

flushed, and grinned at her. 'It's either paint... or lasagne.'

'Ooh, my favourite!' said Lizzie, her mouth instantly starting to water. 'Wait though... paint?!'

'Megan got a bit... *enthusiastic* with her cleaning earlier,' laughed Jenna.

Lizzie's eyes widened as she looked around. Not only had the kitchen been cleaned to within an inch of its life, but the slightly scuffed lavender blue that had graced the walls since the girls were little had disappeared. In its place was a fresh coat of primrose blush, along with rich, Jersey-cream accents. The room looked like it was full of sunshine despite the heavy rain clouds still bruising the horizon.

'She did all this today?!' gasped Lizzie, admiring the neat paintwork. It was the exact colour combination she'd been dribbling over in one of Megan's glossy household magazines just a couple of days ago.

'Yeah,' said Jenna, rolling her eyes. 'You know what she's like when she gets going.'

'And the lasagne?' said Lizzie, shaking her head, feeling like she'd slipped into an alternate universe.

'That was me!' said Jenna with a grin. 'It's always been my favourite... yours too... so I thought you might fancy it?'

'Are you kidding me?' laughed Lizzie. 'Yes please! Blimey - if you don't watch out I could get used to all this. I feel thoroughly spoiled.'

Jenna looked pleased but a bit sheepish at the

same time. 'Well yeah... I mean, after how the pair of us behaved when we first got here... you deserve it.'

'Thanks Jenna,' she said, moving over to her and giving her a big hug. 'And thanks for lunch too - and for giving Jason a lift.'

'Was his dad okay?' said Jenna, pulling back and ushering Lizzie towards the sink so that she could wash the grime off her hands.

'I think the poor man's either got a really bad cold or a dose of the flu,' sighed Lizzie. 'Bless his heart, Jason was desperate to head home and check on him.'

'Yeah I know,' said Jenna. 'Seems like a nice kid.'

Lizzie nodded as she lathered her hands thoroughly, doing her best to get as much of the filth out from around her fingernails as possible - though she had a sneaking suspicion that some of this grease was now a permanent feature.

'Jason's lovely - you'd never believe he's just eighteen, would you?' She shot a look over her shoulder at Jenna. 'Seemed to be quite taken with you, though! He said you were "cool!"'

'Aw blimey!' laughed Jenna. 'That's quite a compliment... but why does it make me feel about a hundred years old?'

'Welcome to my world!' said Lizzie, snagging a fluffy hand towel she'd never seen before and drying her hands before waving it at Jenna. 'Yours?'

'Megan again,' said Jenna, laying a tray with napkins and cutlery. 'She said she wanted to treat you

– and don't worry about the paint - she got some kind of special deal on it.'

'I don't doubt it!' said Lizzie. 'I think people are too scared of her to say no!'

'Idiots!' laughed Jenna. 'Anyway - I thought we could eat in the sitting room. It still smells of paint in here.'

'Good plan,' said Lizzie, nodding. 'Sofa for three, then? Shall I go get Megan in?'

'It's just you and me this evening,' said Jenna, shaking her head.

'Why - where's Meggie?' said Lizzie in surprise, watching as Jenna opened the oven and drew out a huge glass casserole dish of lasagne, complete with a bubbling, cheesy top that had her weak at the knees with hunger.

'I think she said she wanted to go for a walk,' said Jenna once she'd set the hot dish carefully down onto a board. 'She disappeared off to the caravan after finishing in here. She said she wasn't up for a meal this evening.'

Lizzie frowned and then noticed that Jenna was doing exactly the same thing.

'What's up?' said Lizzie.

'There's something not quite... right... with Meggie,' said Jenna, pausing in her search for a long serving spoon. 'And I don't mean the usual pain-in-the-behind grouch we're used to.'

'Yeah,' said Lizzie. Something uncomfortable

squirmed in the pit of her stomach as she thought back to how bedraggled and exhausted Megan had looked when she'd first arrived in town.

'You've noticed something too, haven't you?' said Jenna, watching her closely.

Lizzie nodded, not completely sure how much she should say. The last thing she wanted was for Megan to feel like they'd been gossiping about her behind her back.

'I mean, it's obvious why I came back here,' said Jenna slowly, as she started to load two dinner plates with massive portions of steaming lasagne, 'but what did Meggie say?'

'Erm... she said that her upstairs neighbours were doing work on their flat, and she couldn't hear herself think,' said Lizzie, wracking her brain as she tried to remember the details of that bizarre phone call. 'She said that she'd missed a promotion-'

'Typical Megan to be upset about work,' said Jenna cutting in.

'Yeah, well... it *is* understandable,' said Lizzie gently.

'For complete control freaks,' said Jenna.

'For most people, to be fair!' laughed Lizzie. 'And then... she said Owen had dumped her... or she thought he had.'

'The most boring man in the UK,' said Jenna with a shrug. 'No great loss.'

'Well... yeah. I mean... we both know he wasn't exactly thrilling company, but if Megan loved him-'

'I don't think she did,' said Jenna, licking the serving spoon before turning to toss it into the sink.

'That's a bit harsh,' said Lizzie.

'Nah - it's not,' Jenna shook her head. 'Personally, I think it only lasted as long as it did because he put up with her bossing him around.'

'Hmm,' said Lizzie, deciding that it was probably safest not to comment.

'Well, I guess any of those things could have put her in a bit of a huff,' said Jenna, grabbing the plates and nodding for Lizzie to pick up the tray before leading the way through to the living room. 'But it's not like Meggie to mope, is it? I mean, did you see the *state* of her when we got off the train?! *I* looked more pulled together than her - which never happens.'

Lizzie set the tray on the low coffee table, grabbed a fork and took one of the plates from Jenna before curling into her favourite corner of the sofa.

'Meggie would normally have planned her way out of it by now,' said Jenna, 'but she's still moping when she thinks we're not looking.'

'We'll get to the bottom of it,' said Lizzie, 'don't worry. Maybe she just needs a bit of TLC - maybe all three of us do!'

Jenna nodded and took a huge bite of lasagne. Her eyes promptly started to water.

'Oh Jenna - don't worry lovely!' said Lizzie quickly. 'She'll be fine - we'll make sure she is.'

'It's not that!' spluttered Jenna. 'Cheese! Hot!!'

Lizzie snorted. 'I'll grab some water!' she said, dashing back through to the kitchen.

'Ta!' said Jenna, grabbing the glass the moment Lizzie was back and chugging half of it straight down, making panting sounds and fanning her face with her free hand.

'You always used to do that when you were little, too,' said Lizzie. 'You were always the one burning your tongue or getting brain freeze from ice cream!'

'Guzzle-guts, that's what dad used to call me!' said Jenna, picking her plate back up and taking a much smaller forkful - dutifully blowing on it this time.

Lizzie followed suit and let out a low groan of appreciation as she took the first bite.

'See, I'm not completely useless,' said Jenna.

'I never said you were!' said Lizzie in surprise.

'No, but growing up with Megan, it felt a bit like that,' said Jenna. 'She's the high achiever – all I want to do is fit in as many adventures as possible - and meet as many people as I can before settling down… if I ever do!'

Lizzie watched her. Suddenly Jenna wouldn't meet her eye.

'Hey - Jenna,' she said, reaching out and prodding her on the knee with the handle of her fork to get her attention. 'I'm proud of you.'

'Really?' said Jenna, pulling a face.

'It's impossible not to be!' said Lizzie. 'I'm constantly amazed by how brave you are. You're completely fearless, and you go after what you want more than anyone I've ever known.'

'But I don't have a plan like Megan...' said Jenna.

'You don't need one. That's what's so amazing,' said Lizzie with a smile. 'You're resourceful - and you've never once let anyone or anything stop you.'

'Apart from calling you when my van blew up!' said Jenna.

'That's just a blip,' said Lizzie with a shrug. 'You needed a break. All you need now is a new van and you'll be off again. In the meantime, you're here - and I get to spend some time with you. Which I love - by the way. I want to hear every single story about the adventures you've been on.'

'Really?' said Jenna, perking up a bit.

'Of course!' laughed Lizzie.

'I think you're brave too, mum,' said Jenna. 'Doing your thing with the shop like you've wanted to for so long.'

Lizzie swallowed down a lump in her throat that had nothing to do with hot cheese.

'Thanks love,' she said with a smile. 'Actually, that reminds me - Jason said you had some "cool" ideas I really should ask you about.'

'Hmm... so the boy's a blabbermouth!' laughed

Jenna, scooping up another great big gob-full of lasagne.

'Poor Jason - I don't think so,' said Lizzie with a fond smile. 'I think he meant it as a compliment. Like I said, he was a bit taken with you.'

'Aw shucks!' laughed Jenna. 'Well... I do have some ideas if you really want to hear them.'

'Shoot!' said Lizzie.

'Okay - so I got one of them from Liam's shed down on the beach,' she said. 'I was thinking you could do some bicycle-powered tours of Seabury. Like - either have someone on a bike to lead groups around the place, or you could get hold of some of those trikes like Kate at The Sardine has or... wait wait wait! I've got it - how about a rickshaw so you're cycling and the visitors are sitting in a thingy on the front.'

Lizzie bit her lip to stop herself from laughing. Jenna was getting more excited the more outrageous her ideas became. It was taking some effort to keep up with the slightly frantic stream of ideas... but Jenna's excitement was contagious, and Lizzie could feel the fizz of possibility in the air. Even though a lot of what her daughter was saying was absolutely insane... there were definitely several grains of inspiration lurking in there somewhere.

'Where does Liam's shed come into the equation?' said Lizzie, when Jenna paused to take a breath.

'That's where I come in,' said Jenna. 'I thought I

could have a little hut like that down on the beach too. I could sell tour tickets for you!'

'Right!' laughed Lizzie.

'I don't want to do the actual cycling,' she added quickly. 'That's more your thing. I mean - have you seen some of the hills around Seabury?! But I could wear a cute outfit and drum up some customers!'

'A cute outfit, huh?!' said Lizzie.

'We could get matching dungarees!' said Jenna, her eyes going wide. 'Or… overalls with the Moore Bikes logo on them!'

'I like the idea of overalls,' said Lizzie lightly, glancing down at her current pair of dungarees and noticing that they were covered in smears of rust, oil and other random grime from the bikes she'd been working on that afternoon. 'And I definitely need to sort out a logo!'

'But you don't like the other ideas,' said Jenna, sounding downcast.

'I didn't say that,' said Lizzie. 'Tell me more about those rickshaw things?'

'Well, I saw them when I went to Thailand,' she said.

'Wait,' said Lizzie, relinquishing her empty plate with a sigh of contentment. 'You didn't make it to Thailand… I thought you said all the driving routes were way too dangerous and you didn't fancy trying to across China on your own.'

'Right… right…' said Jenna distractedly as she did

her best to scrape up the last flecks of herby sauce from the edge of her plate. 'Yeah… so I saw them in one of the brochures when I was researching.'

'Have you still got it?' said Lizzie with interest.

'It's in my emails somewhere,' said Jenna. 'I can forward it to you if you'd like?'

'Perfect,' said Lizzie. 'I can't remember if I told you, but Ted Hatherleigh gave me his designs folder along with all the rest of his stuff. He's the one who built Trixie - Kate's tricycle.'

'Oooh!' said Jenna, her eyes shining. 'I feel rickshaws in my waters!'

CHAPTER 4

'Hey Boss!'

'Hi Jason - ooh thanks!' said Lizzie, as he handed her a giant New York Froth takeaway cup.

'No worries,' he shrugged. 'I was desperate for a coffee and I didn't think it was fair to turn up without one for you too!'

Lizzie smiled at him, noticing that he looked pale and exhausted.

'You okay?' she said.

Jason nodded. 'Yeah – just didn't sleep that well, that's all.'

'Okay – well, I'll return the favour later!' she said, taking a grateful swig of coffee as she peered down the road towards the centre of town.

'This is total déjà vu, you know!' said Jason.

'What is?' said Lizzie, reluctantly following him inside.

'You - staring down the road, looking for Liam!' he said.

'Cheeky blighter!' laughed Lizzie, feeling her cheeks colour.

He was right, of course. She'd got a text from Liam first thing. He'd managed to get his hands on his errant mobile after a long, uncomfortable night in a grotty motel. According to the mechanics, the part they needed for the van would be arriving on the early delivery, so all being well, Liam should be back in town before the end of the day.

'How's your dad?' said Lizzie, wincing as Jason started to cough.

'Rough still,' he said.

'And you're sure you're okay?' she asked, raising her eyebrows.

'I'm fine, I think it's just-' he cut himself off by coughing again.

'Woooow,' she said, her eyes going wide even as she took a subconscious step away from him. 'You - young man - are most definitely *not* fine.'

'I'm fine if I'm not gossiping,' he said with a weak smile.

Lizzie winced. The poor lad had turned even paler.

'Nope,' she said. 'As much as you like to think you're invincible... I'm afraid you're in for it. I want you to head home and take the day off. You need a break.'

'But I-' started Jason.

'Nope. Absolutely no buts,' said Lizzie firmly. 'I can handle things here. We're not even meant to be open yet - so I can always just close the doors and get on with things.'

'But-'

'No buts. Full pay - but only if you go home and put your feet up this instant!' said Lizzie, more than aware that she was using her "mum voice". 'I mean it. I prescribe tons of fluids, some truly mindless movies, and just chilling on the sofa, okay?'

Lizzie watched as Jason seemed to deflate in front of her. It was like he'd mustered the last bit of his energy just to get to work, and now that it was spent, all he was good for was a day in bed.

'Come on,' she said. 'I've got the car just around the corner. I'm taking you home.'

'You've got the car?' said Jason, his voice low.

Lizzie nodded. 'I was going to leave you in charge this afternoon and head over to the Hatherleigh's to see Ted and bring a few more boxes back. But that can wait!'

She half expected Jason to put up another argument, but instead, he seemed to sway on the spot as he rubbed his face.

'That settles it. Stay put a second,' she said, dragging a stool over for him to perch on. 'I'll bring the car around.'

'Okay,' he said, his voice coming out even quieter.

Lizzie glanced at him to check that he wasn't about to pass out in the thirty seconds it would take her to fetch the car. Still, she'd have to risk it - there was no way he'd manage the short walk to the parking spot around the corner.

By the time she pulled up outside the shop and popped her hazard lights on, Jason had gone from white to grey and was shivering violently.

'Bloody hell!' she said. 'Come on - that sofa's calling your name!'

Without thinking about it, Lizzie put an arm around the lad and helped him out to the car. She could feel his whole body shaking against her.

'Sit tight,' she said, as he practically dropped into the passenger seat. 'I'll just lock the doors a second.'

Lizzie hurried to pull the shop doors closed. She wouldn't be long, but she'd learned her lesson about leaving the place open. You never knew what - or who - would be waiting for you when you got back, otherwise!

'You're up the hill past North Beach, right?' she said, pulling on her seatbelt and then making sure Jason had done the same.

'Yeah,' said Jason, his hands now covering his eyes.

'You going to throw up?' said Lizzie.

'Nope,' said Jason. 'Just dizzy.'

'Okay - let's get you home. Your dad's there isn't he?' she asked.

There was no way she was leaving him on his own in this state. If Mr Eaves wasn't there for any reason, she'd just have to take Jason back up to the cottage and make him a bed up on the sofa.

'He's there. On the sofa under a duvet,' said Jason.

'Sounds like the pair of you'll have to fight it out over the remote control, then!' said Lizzie.

Jason shook his head and then frowned, clearly wishing he hadn't. 'No TV,' croaked.

Lizzie raised her eyebrows but kept her mouth shut. After all, it had nothing to do with her - but she wasn't sure how she'd get through a bout of flu without the medicinal value of watching her favourite sitcoms with her eyes closed.

'Lemsip... flu powders... multivitamins... extra strength vitamin C...' Lizzie muttered to herself as she meandered around the grocery store, tossing half the medicine aisle into two baskets.

She'd made sure Jason was safely inside his house before leaving him there. The poor lad had gone downhill really quickly, and after watching him fumble with his house keys for a couple of very long minutes, she'd ended up hopping out of the car to let him into his own house.

After knocking loudly - just in case Mr Eaves was wandering around in his PJs - she finally managed to get the door open. It hadn't been particularly easy considering she'd been practically holding Jason up by that point. A grey-faced badger of a man had appeared, looking confused. Though he hadn't looked much healthier than poor old Jason, Mr Eaves had had enough wits about him to instantly spot that his son was poorly.

Lizzie had offered to help get Jason inside, but Mr Eaves had gently taken his son's arm and thanked her for bringing him home – before firmly shutting the door in her face.

'Totally normal,' she muttered to herself, adding several boxes of tissues into each basket. She kept telling herself that – after all, there was nothing worse than having someone else in your space when you felt like death warmed up, was there? Still, she couldn't help but feel concerned for the pair of them in that state!

Instead of heading straight back to the shop, Lizzie had made an executive decision to nip to the nearest grocery store and stock up on two care packages. The one for Jason and his dad was already bursting with cans of soup and other easy-to-grab bits of food to keep their strength up - as well as all the cold and flu remedies she could lay her hands on. Her plan was to do a drive-by of their house on the way back to the shop and leave the groceries on their doorstep.

The second basket was for her and the girls - and included everything she could think of to help boost their immune systems. After all, both her and Jenna had been in close contact with poor old Jason over the last few days, and when an illness like this hit a small community - it tended to run rampant!

'I don't have time for the flu!' she muttered. 'Oranges... blueberries... ooh - a bottle of tea tree oil!'

'Helloooooo?'

The hammering on the closed shop door made Lizzie laugh... because there was simply no mistaking who could be on the other side!

'Mother? Are you in there?!'

'Two secs, Meggie!' laughed Lizzie, hurrying over to the doors and removing the heavy block she'd put behind them to keep them from blowing open.

'Wow!' she said, blinking as afternoon sunlight came streaming into the shop. 'It's brightened up a bit since this morning, then!'

'Erm... yeah!' said Megan, eyeing her. 'Are you okay? How come you're not open... and why have you barricaded yourself inside?'

'Well,' said Lizzie, beckoning for Megan to follow her in, 'for one thing, we're not officially open yet.'

'Well no - but you'll *never* be officially open unless you... well... open?!' said Megan, cocking her head to one side.

'You do have a good point!' laughed Lizzie. 'Anyway, I decided to get on with some of the jobs I needed to catch up on with the doors closed.'

'Why does it smell funny in here?' said Megan frowning and wrinkling her nose.

'Funny?' said Lizzie distractedly, picking up the glass from her workbench and taking a long slurp.

'And what on earth are you drinking?' said Megan, eyeing the fizzy concoction.

'Extra strength vitamin C,' said Lizzie, licking her lips. 'And I'm guessing the smell is tea tree oil.'

'But... why?' said Megan.

'I had to take poor old Jason home earlier,' said Lizzie. 'The walk into work almost finished him off. He was all grey and shivery.'

'Uh oh,' said Megan. 'And Jenna gave him a lift yesterday, right?'

Lizzie nodded and rattled the tube of soluble vitamin C at Megan. 'Fancy one?'

'Don't mind if I do!' said Megan gratefully, grabbing them and making a beeline for the little back room where Lizzie had stashed a few cups and plates and some bottles of drinking water.

Lizzie trailed after her, swigging her drink. It

really was repulsive - and probably far too late to do much good... but then, there was something to be said for the placebo effect.

'Hey Meggie,' she said, 'I'm glad you're here! I'm so sorry I missed you last night!'

Megan turned and eyed her over the rim of her glass as she chugged the fizzy orange drink far too quickly.

'Don't worry about it,' she said eventually, letting out a burp and then looking horrified. 'Pardon. Sorry mum!'

Lizzie grinned at her. 'I wanted to say thank you for painting the kitchen!'

'Oh,' said Megan. 'That.'

'Don't say it like that!' laughed Lizzie. 'It's amazing. Thank you so much - it was an incredible surprise to come home to.'

'I know I should have asked first, but-'

'Then it wouldn't have been a surprise!' said Lizzie, shaking her head. 'Seriously - very sneaky way of getting me to choose a colour scheme by leaving your magazines lying around and then making secret notes when I told you what I liked!'

'Worked pretty well, eh?' said Megan, looking relieved. 'You really like it?'

'Love - it's incredible. If it was left to me, it would be waiting for at least a decade for me to get around to it, and then it would be completely half-arsed. I can't believe how fast you did it – and it's so beautiful, it looks like the painting fairies have been!'

Megan shrugged, but she looked thrilled and had gone pink with pleasure. 'I wanted to do it as a thank you - for letting me stay. And for making me realise I was being a dick.'

'Hardly a dick...' said Lizzie.

'Ah, come on. Dick where dick's due!' said Megan seriously.

Lizzie snorted, and she saw Megan's eyes widen as she realised what she'd just said.

'Whatever!' she added quickly. 'Do *not* tell Jenface I just said that.'

'Promise!' giggled Lizzie. 'So - it's nice to see you... did you erm... did you come down to chat or...'

'If you've got a sec, I've got something important I'd like to talk to you about.' Megan paused and did her head cocking thing again. 'Actually, two things. But only if you've got time?'

'For you?' said Lizzie. 'Always!'

'Thanks mum,' said Megan. She paused and scuffed the floor with her toe.

'Shall we sit down a sec?' said Lizzie, wondering if she was about to discover what had been bugging her daughter for so long.

Megan plopped down into one of the ancient chairs and wobbled as it failed to settle properly on its wonky legs.

'You seriously need a decent staff room when you get everything else sorted out!' said Megan.

'On the list already!' sighed Lizzie. 'With about a million other things!'

'Right… so…' Megan paused and took a deep breath.

'Are you okay?' said Lizzie, watching her closely.

Megan nodded, then started to shake her head, and then changed her mind and nodded again. 'I had an idea,' she said slowly. 'For the business. This business.'

'Oh, right,' said Lizzie, promptly checking that she wasn't frowning. She wanted a nice, neutral expression for whatever was about to come out of Megan's mouth.

Lizzie was glad and grateful that both girls seemed to be taking an interest in Moore Bikes rather than just dismissing her dream out of hand - but it was taking a bit of getting used to.

'You don't mind, do you?' said Megan quickly.

'Course not! Let's hear it!' said Lizzie.

'Well… I was thinking… this shop is obviously a great idea,' said Megan slowly.

'Erm, thanks?' said Lizzie.

'It's just a fact. You're not even officially open yet and you've got work coming out of your ears. So much so, that you've already had to hire someone.'

'Right,' said Lizzie.

'And I was thinking… it would make a great franchise business!' she said. 'You could sell the Moore Bikes way of doing things to other people, train them up, charge them through the nose for a business package that works - and rake in the cash.'

'Uh huh?' said Lizzie, doing her best not to look as poleaxed as she felt.

'I mean - you'd need a Franchisee Manager. Someone who's got business experience - someone who can help you set up a website, and social media, and actually sell the franchises of course!' Megan paused and fiddled with one of her rings for a moment. 'I could do it. I know how to do that sort of stuff... I've got great contacts. Web designers. Graphic designers. The lot! I mean, I'd need a decent wage - but the first sale of a franchise would sort that out.'

'It would?' said Lizzie, still feeling completely lost.

'Definitely,' Megan nodded. 'I can pull a bunch of figures together for you first if you'd like. And I can find you a decent accountant - and set up all your social media?'

Lizzie nodded really slowly. She didn't want to react straight away. After all, Jenna's ideas had sounded completely nuts – but there had been a lot of possibilities once she'd had the chance to think everything through properly. She wanted to afford Megan the same respect.

'Amazing ideas, Meggie,' said Lizzie slowly.

Megan instantly beamed at her, looking thrilled.

'Can you give me a little while just to let it all sink in, and then we'll talk some more?' she said.

'Of course!' said Megan.

'Great. And... do me a favour while I'm doing that?' she added. She needed to be soooo careful how she worded this next bit...

'Anything,' said Megan.

'Have a think if this is what you really want,' she said gently. 'Do you really want to work with me... in Seabury... and with this business?'

'Of course I-' started Megan.

'Long. Slow. Thinking,' said Lizzie, shaking her head.

'Right. Yep... yep, okay,' said Megan with a sigh.

'Cool,' said Lizzie.

'Cool?' laughed Megan, getting to her feet. 'You've been hanging around teenagers too much!'

'Wait... before you go, what was the second thing you wanted to talk to me about?' said Lizzie curiously.

'Well,' said Megan. 'I was wondering if you'd be up for me redecorating the living room for you next?'

CHAPTER 5

*L*izzie ducked her head as she wheeled one of the hire bikes out of the shop. She might be her own boss these days but skiving off for the afternoon was making her feel super guilty.

It really was far too early to be closing up so that she could go off on a jolly - but Lizzie couldn't resist. She needed to feel the wind in her hair... or at least her helmet! She'd started to drive herself mad keeping a constant watch for Liam's arrival... and what better way to distract herself than to go for a ride?

Leaning the smart blue bike against the wall, she turned the key in the lock before pulling on her helmet. She'd deal with the lights and all the rest of it when she dropped the bike back on the way home.

'I'm sure the boss won't mind!' she breathed as she clambered onto the saddle.

Lizzie sighed. She really missed her old bike. That thing had been her pride and joy, and she'd been heartbroken when it was stolen from her back garden a couple of weeks before she'd moved.

'Sorry... you're just not the same,' she whispered as she kicked off and started to pedal. The bike might be unfamiliar, but cycling itself... well, that was her happy place - and she simply hadn't been doing enough of it lately. It was kind of ironic, really!

The minute Lizzie had waved Megan off after their little chat, she knew it was time for her to escape the shop for the afternoon. With both her daughters' suggestions for Moore Bikes sloshing around in her head, she had a lot to think about! What better way to let the old grey matter chew things over than taking a lovely whizz along the early-autumn hedgerows?!

Lizzie stood up as she began to pedal for all she was worth. She'd decided to take the route up the hill past the allotments and out of Seabury. She didn't want to cycle through the centre of town just in case anyone tried to talk to her. This afternoon was her time. Well... hers and Ted's!

Before leaving Moore Bikes, Lizzie had grabbed his folder of designs and tucked it into her bag. She wanted to pick Ted's brain and she just hoped that he wouldn't mind her turning up unannounced. From what Margie had been saying, though, Lizzie had a feeling he might rather enjoy having a random visitor!

By the time she reached the top of the hill, Lizzie was puffing hard. If she *did* decide to go ahead with Jenna's hair-brained rickshaw plan, she was either going to have to get in better shape or ask Jason if he had a couple of mates who'd like to join the team!

Signalling to the left, Lizzie pulled out and then relished the freedom of freewheeling downhill for a moment - stretching her legs out on either side of the bike. Thank heavens this stretch of road was quiet today because she probably looked like a total idiot!

Lizzie grinned. Pelting along this stretch of road with the wind whipping her cheeks was bringing back memories of childhood. What a wonderful place to have called home for so long!

'Woohooo!'

Lizzie's squeal of delight drifted on the sea breeze as she let her momentum carry her halfway up the next hill. Then, before she knew it, it was time to turn back off the main road and onto the winding lanes that would eventually lead her to Ted Hatherleigh's barn.

Lizzie sucked in a deep breath as the calm of the afternoon stole over her. This was where she belonged! These lanes held so many memories – she'd grown up between these hedges – exploring every dip, corner, and hill on her trusty bike. The other kids had tried to keep up with her, but when she'd got going, they'd never really stood a chance.

Turning down an even narrower lane, Lizzie began to pick up speed again, weaving around the twists and turns, and leaning into the bends at speed as she let the unfamiliar bike carry her along her old stomping grounds.

Suddenly, Lizzie was ten years old again - pedalling as fast as her feet would go. The familiar roar of the wind in her ears was exhilarating. She might be puffing - but she still had a bit of extra energy left in the tanks!

'Yeah!!!' she cried, zooming down a hill and flying over a bump in the road, feeling like she was about to take off.

Uh oh-

Wait... that corner-

Maybe she didn't remember this lane quite as well as she thought! That was a seriously tight bend – and there was no way she was going to make it. If she hit the brakes now, she was definitely going to come off.

'Nooo!' gasped Lizzie.

Hedge or ditch? That was her only choice now.

The ditch looked like a seriously long way down... hell - it was going to have to be the hedge!

'Uh oh!' she yelled as she hit the bend at speed. Panicking, she yanked far too hard on the brakes and promptly flew right over the handlebars into the hedge. The fact that she'd chosen her landing place in advance did nothing to soften the blow.

'Holy mother of... OWWW!' she moaned.

Okay, so it was official - the hedge had been a terrible idea.

Lizzie froze for a long moment, trying to assess the damage. She couldn't see the bike - but she could still hear the front wheel ticking as it spun in circles somewhere nearby. As for her – she was spread-eagled – face first in a pincushion of brambles.

Taking a deep breath, Lizzie closed her eyes for a moment and thought longingly of the ditch. It would have been nice and soggy - probably quite muddy after all that rain. It might even have been a soft landing.

This... definitely wasn't soft.

Lizzie let out a little whimper, trying hard not to burst into tears from the sheer shock of what had just happened. Maybe she needed to look on the bright side - at least she'd missed the sycamore stumps that rose on either side of her. On the not-so-bright side though, she was now wedged between them with her bum in the air, feeling a bit like she'd had every inch of her body pierced.

Still... they were just prickles. She could deal with prickles. Everything hurt, but it didn't feel like there was any kind of *big bad hurt* going on... not as far as she could tell, anyway.

Right - there was no point waiting for someone to

come to the rescue! She needed to get herself out of there... somehow!

Lizzie winced as she tried to shift against the spiny pillow.

'You've got to be kidding me!' she gasped. She could barely move. Not because she was hurt – but because the arms and neck of her jumper were so caught up in the brambles, it felt like she'd been velcroed face-down into the hedgerow.

What on earth was she going to do? She was well and truly stuck!

Trying to calm the rising tide of panic that felt like it was grabbing her by the throat, Lizzie wriggled again. Maybe if she managed to shift her weight around a little...

Nope. That wasn't going to work. In fact, if anything, she seemed to be sinking deeper into the undergrowth every time she moved an inch. Something hot and wet was trickling down her face from somewhere near her right eyebrow. Fingers crossed it was sweat rather than blood.

'Erm... help?'

Lame. Pathetic. Pointless.

The nearest house had to be more than a mile away, and someone standing right behind her wouldn't have been able to hear that puny little warble!

'Help?' she tried again.

At least it came out a bit louder this time...

though she really wasn't sure she wanted anyone to find her in this state anyway! What had she been thinking? She was a business owner... the mother of two grown-up girls... she shouldn't have been racing along the road like a lunatic. At least - not when she couldn't remember where all the bends were!

Lizzie closed her eyes again and tried to calm down. Giving herself a hard time right now wasn't going to help matters, was it?! She took a long, deep breath, trying to ignore the fact that the brambles beneath her were probably infested with spiders!

The thought made Lizzie's eyes fly open again.

'Dumbass!' she muttered. She'd been trying to calm herself down, not freak herself out even further.

'Get me out of here!' she muttered, trying to push herself up again. It had no effect whatsoever. She was trapped in place... and there seemed to be an army of snails heading along the undergrowth in her direction.

'HELP!' she yelled, hoping against hope there might be a kindly dog-walker somewhere nearby.

As if in reply, a low rumbling sounded somewhere in the distance. That *had* to be a vehicle of some sort! The burning question was... were they heading in her direction?

'What if they don't see me?!' she whispered, trying to crane her neck around and completely failing.

They *had* to see her! She was starting to get cold... partly because of the shock, and partly because she'd been sweating buckets from the unaccustomed exercise. Now she had goosebumps rising on her scratched and bruised limbs.

Lizzie shivered. What if she was here all night?!

'HELP!' she yelled again, though she was pretty sure it was pointless... there was no way the driver would be able to hear her over the racket that engine was making.

It was definitely getting closer. Maybe they'd be able to see the bike from the road? It felt like she'd flown meters before crashing into the brambles – but perhaps she hadn't gone quite as far as she feared.

Lizzie heard the engine roar... and then idle.

'Help help HELP!' she yelled as the clap of a door being closed rang out behind her.

'I'd have gone for the ditch, myself!' came a familiar voice.

'Liam?!' demanded Lizzie, struggling to peer behind her again and once again failing miserably.

'Are you hurt?' he said.

'No. I mean... I don't think so,' said Lizzie. 'Not really.'

'Thank goodness for that!' came the cheerful reply. 'You know, I wasn't expecting to find your bottom sticking out of a hedge on my way home!'

Lizzie spluttered, not quite knowing what to say. Part of her was completely horrified... but she was grinning from ear to ear. Not only had someone found her... it was *her* someone.

'Are you sure you're not hurt?' said Liam.

'Pretty sure,' said Lizzie, 'but am so stuck, I've not been able to test that theory!'

'Okay. Let's get you unstuck and go from there.'

Lizzie could hear the barely suppressed amusement in Liam's voice, but she was too happy that he'd found her to care.

'I've got something in the back of the van that might work on these brambles,' he said. 'Don't go anywhere!'

'Oh, har-de-harhar my sides are splitting.' Lizzie's mouth twitched, but she didn't dare let out a giggle in case it made her sink even further into the mess.

'Alright, I'm back,' came the disembodied voice. 'I've got some gloves and a pair of wire cutters… not exactly perfect, but we should be able to get you out of there.'

Liam paused, clearly assessing the situation.

'Right, I'm coming around to your head. Hang tight.'

Lizzie rolled her eyes but then spotted Liam's boots searching for safe footholds just in front of her.

'What are you waiting for?' Lizzie asked the boots.

'Erm… to be honest, I'm trying to work out where to start,' he said.

'Anywhere… please!' begged Lizzie.

'Okay…' he blew out a long breath. 'I'm going in!'

Lizzie did her best not to move as she heard the wire cutters get to work – though it was hard not to jump every time Liam tugged on her jumper as he tried to free her.

'Stop squirming!' he begged. 'You're making it worse.'

'Sorry,' said Lizzie. 'I'm getting pins and needles in my legs.'

'Okay. Just a couple more of these big ones and I might be able to pull you out,' said Liam.

Lizzie grunted and bit her lip, trying to ignore the shooting pains in her legs.

'Okay,' said Liam. 'Do not move. I'm going around behind you and I'm going to try to pull you out, okay?'

'M'kay,' muttered Lizzie.

'Thank goodness you wear dungarees!' said Liam from somewhere behind her.

'Why?!' said Lizzie, holding still.

'Number one - hopefully, they'll have protected your stomach a bit,' he said. 'And number two... they give me handles to work with!'

Lizzie let out a shriek of surprise as Liam took a firm grip of the denim straps and yanked her bodily out of her prickly prison.

CHAPTER 6

'Girls?! Jenna?! Megan?!'

Lizzie winced as Liam's deep voice boomed through the little cottage. He had one arm around her, supporting her weight, and had managed to unlock and open her front door with the other.

'Shh,' she said. 'They'll hear you!'

'That's kind of the point!' laughed Liam.

'Oh... right,' said Lizzie as she snuggled deeper into his arm... then promptly wished she hadn't. The sleeves of her jumper were more chopped-up bits of bramble than wool by this point, and every time she shifted a new scratch or bruise made itself known.

Still, she couldn't resist clinging to him. As embarrassed as she was by the manner of their reunion - Liam was home! She had turned into a Lizzie-shaped puddle of happiness... though she might be an even happier puddle if she could stop the scratch on her forehead from bleeding.

Thundering footsteps upstairs heralded the imminent arrival of at least one of the girls.

'Mum?!' gasped Jenna as galloped down the stairs. 'Oh - *not just* mum!' she added pulling herself up short. 'Erm hi…'

'I'm Liam,' said Liam.

'Yeah… I remember… hi!' said Jenna, her eyes fixed in horror on Lizzie. 'Meggie? MEGGIE GET IN HERE!' she bellowed at the top of her lungs.

'Wow!' laughed Liam.

Lizzie flinched at the volume - and then flinched again as various prickles embedded themselves even further into her poor battered body.

'Sorry,' said Jenna, still staring at Lizzie. 'She's got her headphones in… she's started on the living room.'

'Already?' said Lizzie faintly. She was desperate to sit down, but Jenna was completely blocking the hallway and barring their entrance.

'You know what Meggie's like,' said Jenna. 'But… what happened to you?'

'Had an argument with my bike,' said Lizzie, suddenly feeling more than a bit knackered.

'Let's get you inside,' said Liam, taking more of her weight as the last of the adrenalin left her body and she sagged against him.

'Kitchen,' said Jenna quickly, eyeballing the undergrowth caught up in Lizzie's clothes.

'You called?' said Megan drifting into the hallway, looking much younger with her hair pulled back under a scarf and smudges of dusky blue paint on her cheekbones.

'Alright, dreamy Doris?' said Jenna. 'Mum's had an accident.'

'Oh shit!' said Megan, her eyes going wide as she caught sight of Lizzie, still being held up by Liam. 'Sorry - I mean... sugar,' she amended, eyeing Liam warily.

'Shit just about covers it,' said Liam.

'Into the kitchen,' said Megan, instantly straightening up and taking charge.

'That's what I said!' muttered Jenna.

'Good call,' said Megan. 'Jenna - grab the first aid kit from mum's bathroom cupboard?'

'On it!' said Jenna, pelting back up the stairs.

'I've got a first aid kit?' said Lizzie vaguely as she let Liam lead her towards the kitchen.

'You have since I bought one and put it there a couple of days ago,' laughed Megan. 'I was unpacking your bathroom stuff for you and yours went out of date when I was about ten years old.'

'Figures,' said Lizzie, easing herself gingerly onto one of the wooden chairs.

'Liam?' said Megan, eyeing him again.

'Nice to meet you properly,' said Liam with a grin.

'You too. Pop the kettle on? I'm going to need to bathe all these scratches... once I get all the prickles out. Plus - I'm guessing everyone could do with a cuppa!'

'You don't need to fuss,' muttered Lizzie, attempting to stand up only to be greeted by a duet of protests from Megan and Liam.

'Sit! Stay!' said Megan.

'I'm not a puppy in training,' mumbled Lizzie.

'No...' said Liam gently, 'but you are in shock and bleeding, so...'

'Here!' said Jenna, belting into the room. 'First aid kit, antiseptic stuff, tweezers for the prickles, and a pair of PJs for you to change into, mum. I figure it's best if we de-thorn your clothes out separately... without you in them.'

'Perfect!' said Megan.

'I'm thinking a pair of gardening gloves for whoever undresses your mum might be a good plan, too!' chuckled Liam as he flicked the kettle on.

'You old romantic!' laughed Jenna.

'I've got some in the van,' said Liam. 'Two secs.'

Jenna watched him bustle out of the room and then dropped into a chair next to Lizzie.

'So, what happened, mum?' she said. 'And where did Liam spring from - I thought Liam was away?'

'Bike - meet hedge,' said Lizzie, wishing she could just go and lie down in a darkened room for a moment.

'But you don't have a bike?' said Megan, who was busy laying out an array of plasters, creams and cotton wool balls on the kitchen table in front of Lizzie.

'One of the hires,' said Lizzie. She swiped the back of her hand across her forehead and then examined it. To her horror, the streak of blood mixed with mud and sweat made her sway on her chair.

'Steady!' said Jenna. 'If you're going to pass out, we'd better get you sitting on the floor!'

Lizzie shook her head and took a long breath, feeling like an idiot.

'I'm fine,' she said.

'Add some sugar to her tea!' said Megan. 'It'll help with the shock.'

Jenna hopped up and rushed over to the worktop to make the drink.

'Don't worry about your head,' said Megan gently, sitting in Jenna's newly vacated spot and taking a closer look at Lizzie's forehead. 'It's just a shallow scratch - probably feels much worse than it is. I'll clean that first and see if we can get it to stop bleeding.'

'Okay,' said Lizzie, meekly.

'Then we need to get you out of these clothes so we can see what else is going on,' said Megan.

'Is there anything majorly painful under there?' asked Jenna, placing a bucket of builder's brew in front of Lizzie as Megan snapped on a pair of medical gloves.

Lizzie shook her head and then shrugged. She

reached for the tea and took a sip. It was insanely sweet... but as she took another mouthful, she felt it start to work its magic.

'Nothing too bad I don't think,' she said. 'It's my arms that hurt most. They're tingling and stinging all over!'

'Right, let's see what we can do,' said Megan, dipping a cotton wool ball into a little bowl of warm, antiseptic-scented water.

Lizzie closed her eyes as Megan began to swab at the cut on her forehead. Having both girls fussing around her was oddly relaxing. She felt surrounded by their concern and love, and it seemed to be breathing a bit of life back into her.

'You've not broken anything... have you?' said Jenna.

'No love,' sighed Lizzie. 'I don't think so... other than my pride, maybe.'

'Pfft - don't worry about that!' said Megan. 'No one cares as long as you're alright!'

'Was it Liam who found you?' said Jenna, lowering her voice.

'Yep!' said Lizzie. 'Bottom-up in a hedgerow.'

'Nice, mother!' laughed Megan. 'Sorry, sorry - didn't mean to laugh.'

Lizzie shrugged and then winced. 'It's okay... it *is* pretty funny.'

'Even funnier when I lifted her out by her

dungaree straps!' said Liam, his grinning face appearing in the doorway.

'Oh my goodness!' said Jenna. 'Now that's something I wish I'd seen.'

'Well... just as well it wasn't a bunch of teenagers who found me - otherwise, there'd probably be video evidence,' said Lizzie.

'Can you imagine?' laughed Megan.

'Wait... Liam... there' *isn't* video evidence, is there?' said Jenna.

'I've just been uploading it now,' said Liam.

Lizzie's eyes flew open, and Megan stopped what she was doing to glare at him.

'Joke!' he said quickly, holding up his hands in surrender as he was pinned by three identical glares.

'Phew!' said Jenna.

'Yeah... because you and I would be having words!' said Megan. Then she grinned and shot a wink at him.

Lizzie stared between the pair of them. Well... this definitely wasn't the way she'd been hoping to introduce them all... but it seemed to be working out okay!

'I really need to get out of these clothes,' said Lizzie, shifting on her chair as Megan reached up and carefully extracted a long piece of bramble from her hair. 'I'm sure there are a couple of snails inside these dungarees somewhere!'

'Eew!' laughed Jenna. 'Shall I go and put the hot water on so that you can have a bath?'

'Good plan!' said Megan. 'Then we can make sure all the cuts are properly cleaned up before patching you up!'

Jenna nodded and hurtled out of the room.

'On that note, I'm going to make myself scarce!' said Liam, 'unless you need me?'

'Make me and Jenna a cup of tea before you go?' said Megan, shooting him a sweet smile that made Lizzie laugh. 'Jenna only made one for mum!'

'You've got it,' said Liam, moving towards the kettle. 'Lizzie – do you want me to drop your poor old bike back down to the shop?'

'Yes please,' said Lizzie, trying not to sound quite as pathetic as she felt. 'And my bag with Ted's folder… and can you make sure I turned everything off and then lock up properly?'

'Sure!' said Liam.

'Sorry to be a pain,' she added.

'You're not!' said Liam, firmly. 'I'll send Jason home, shall I?'

'He's not there,' said Lizzie. 'He's sick. I took him home pretty much as soon as he arrived this morning.'

'Oh – poor lad!' said Liam in surprise. 'That's not like him.'

'Trust me, he wasn't putting it on,' said Lizzie. 'He

was all grey and wobbly. His dad's been ill, so I guess he caught it.'

'Sounds like it,' said Liam. 'I wonder if they need anything.'

'I grabbed a few basics for them earlier and left them on the doorstep, but it might be a good idea to check in again,' she said. 'Maybe shoot Jason a text and check they're doing alright?'

'Will do,' said Liam, bringing two cups over to the table and placing them next to Megan's medical supplies. 'Right... I'll get out of your hair.'

'Thanks for rescuing her!' said Megan.

'My pleasure,' said Liam.

'Yeah!' said Jenna, bouncing back into the room. 'You're a hero!'

'Hardly!' laughed Liam. 'Anyway - let's all catch up properly... maybe when there are less prickles involved?'

'Deal,' said Lizzie. She knew it was ridiculous, but she felt her heart sink a bit. This *really* wasn't what she'd had in mind when she'd pictured welcoming him home!

'See ya!' shouted Megan as Liam headed out of the kitchen, closely followed by Jenna.

'Where's your sister going?' said Lizzie, shooting a worried sideways glance towards the door.

'Don't worry, I don't think she's about to give your *lover* the third degree... that's more my style!' chuckled Megan.

'My *lover?!*' laughed Lizzie, before pulling a face as various prickles prodded her sore skin.

'Yeah. And for the record - he's nice,' said Megan.

'He really is,' said Lizzie.

'Now then mother, don't go all mushy on me!' she laughed.

'Sorry… can't help it!' said Lizzie.

'Well, I guess that's fair enough, considering he did just save you from a hedge,' said Megan.

'Not exactly the perfect, swooning heroine though am I, eh Meggie?' said Lizzie. 'Pulling an ageing tomboy out of a patch of brambles is hardly the stuff of romance novels!'

'Oh, I don't know,' said Megan, smiling at her. 'You're pretty cute, you know!'

'Thanks,' said Lizzie, reaching out and giving Megan's hand a gentle squeeze. 'I love you, you know?'

'Okay… you're definitely going into shock,' laughed Megan.

Lizzie stuck her tongue out at her daughter and then glanced towards the door again. 'Where *is* Jenna?!'

'Still with Liam, I expect!' said Megan

'Why?' said Lizzie. 'She'd better not be giving him a hard time out there! The poor guy's only just driven halfway across the country!'

'Don't worry!' said Megan, grabbing her tweezers and angling Lizzie's palm so that she could start removing some of the thorns. 'Right now, my little sister only poses a threat to one thing…'

'What?!'

'Liam's van!' laughed Megan.

'Uh oh,' said Lizzie, her eyes going wide. 'Do you think we should warn him?'

'I'd say he can handle blondie,' said Megan. 'Right, that's the big ones gone,' she added putting the tweezers down

'What next?' said Lizzie.

'Time for me to swap gloves!' she said, removing the thin medical pair with a snap and reaching for the thick gardening gloves Liam had left on the table. 'Right then… time to get you out of those clothes.'

Lizzie sighed. 'See… those are definitely words I was hoping to hear today… just not from you!'

'Mother!' laughed Megan, helping her to her feet.

'Okay, maybe you're right,' said Lizzie, pulling a face as she forced her rapidly stiffening limbs to support her weight.

'About what?' said Megan, unclipping the straps of the dungarees with some difficulty.

'Maybe I am in shock,' said Lizzie with a wink.

CHAPTER 7

Lizzie smiled to herself as she limped towards town. The sun was out, and Seabury was glowing. Sure, she felt a bit battered and bruised after the previous day's escapades - and she could swear she smelled a bit like a walking pharmacy - but Lizzie felt strangely happy.

There was something weirdly familiar about being covered in a layer of antiseptic cream and sticking plasters! The big one Megan had pressed onto her forehead was her favourite. Her daughter's shopping trip for fresh first-aid supplies had clearly leaned heavily towards the children's section, and now Lizzie was proudly sporting a rainbow-coloured teddy bear on her face.

She might be enjoying the fresh air, but Lizzie would be glad to get to the shop this morning. She'd been desperate to head back down to Moore Bikes the previous evening – just to check how much damage she'd done to the hire bike and pick up her car while she was at it - but in an unusual moment of agreement, the girls had both thrown a hissy-fit at the mere mention of it.

Instead, Megan had forced Lizzie to enjoy a long, luxurious soak in the bath before tending to all her cuts and removing as many prickles as she could find. Lizzie had quickly discovered that she was banned from the living room until Megan had finished working her magic - but given how fast she'd completed the kitchen, she wasn't too fussed.

While Jenna cooked everyone a delicious fish pie for supper, Megan had joined Lizzie in her bedroom, and the pair of them had stretched out on the bed, flipping through yet more swanky interiors magazines. The afternoon might have started out as painful, uncomfortable and mildly mortifying... but it had ended up being one Lizzie knew she'd treasure for a long time.

Smiling softly, Lizzie touched the plaster on her forehead again.

Goodness... what were the customers going to think?!

Shrugging, Lizzie did her best to pick up her pace again, wincing slightly as she went. It didn't really matter what anyone thought, did it? Besides, she was considering keeping the doors closed so that she could finish off getting the shop set up. She had some storage drawers and shelving turning up on the morning delivery, and if she could get a wiggle on and get them put together, she'd finally be able to sort and stash all the spares from the Hatherleigh's barn.

'Yoo-hoo? Lizzie?'

Lizzie blinked, coming out of her reverie only to spot Ethel waving at her. She was wandering along the seafront towards her, hand-in-hand with Charlie. Lizzie returned her wave and winced. Blimey – she'd definitely pulled a muscle or two when she'd taken that trip over her handlebars!

'Lizzie lovely!' gasped Ethel, coming to a standstill in front of her, her eyes resting on the teddy bear plaster.

'I heard you fell off your bike!' said Charlie. 'Are you okay?'

'Yep!' said Lizzie, staring at her feet and scuffing the pavement with her shoe before remembering that she wasn't actually ten years old.

'Riding too fast again?' said Ethel.

'Uh-huh…' said Lizzie, glancing up at her.

They were both shaking their heads, clearly amused.

'Nothing changes!' they said in unison.

Lizzie snorted.

'It's true,' said Charlie. 'Your old nan was always patching you up!'

'Looks like you've got yourself some new plasters,

though!' said Ethel, her eyes back on her forehead again.

'That was Megan,' laughed Lizzie.

'Good girl,' said Charlie with an approving nod. 'Glad to hear she's looking after you!'

'They both are,' said Lizzie, feeling that warm ball of happiness bounce in her chest again. The fact that both girls had fussed around her the day before had made her feel so lucky. It was like a calm kind of contentment had descended on the cottage - one she couldn't remember feeling for a very long time.

'Good,' said Ethel with a nod.

'I heard on the grapevine that it was Liam who pulled you out of the hedge, though?' said Charlie.

'Who told you that?!' said Lizzie, her eyes widening.

'Oh you know what Seabury is like,' laughed Ethel.

'Heard he used your dungaree straps as handles!' said Charlie, his eyebrows twitching with amusement now.

'Honestly, ignore this one,' said Ethel. 'He'll believe anything.'

'Erm... it's true,' said Lizzie, feeling a bit bewildered.

Ethel bit her lip.

'We'd better be off,' said Charlie promptly. 'You be careful now - you hear? No more antics.'

'Roger that!' said Lizzie giving him a little salute

as they started to wander away, their heads bent together. She could swear Ethel's shoulders were shaking with laughter.

Lizzie shrugged. There might not be a video on social media to worry about… but Seabury's gossip grapevine was probably even better at spreading the news!

Unlocking the doors to Moore Bikes, Lizzie was just pushing her way inside when her mobile phone started to buzz in her pocket.

'Yellow!' she said cheerfully.

'Boss?' came a rasping voice.

'Jason?!' she said in horror. 'That you?'

'Mmhmm.'

There was a pause which contained an awful lot of coughing on the other end.

'Is everything okay?' she said. 'You sound awful.'

'Fine. I'm fine,' said Jason. 'That's code for "I'm dying of man-flu" by the way.' He paused to cough again. 'I'm not going to be able to come to work today.'

'A week!' came a distant voice at the other end of the line. 'At least a week!'

'Is that your dad?' said Lizzie.

'Yeah,' huffed Jason. 'He said I'm not allowed back for at least a week, even if I feel better before then. He doesn't want me spreading this crap around.'

'That's okay,' said Lizzie quickly, secretly thinking he'd be lucky if he improved that quickly anyway.

'Don't you worry about it. Take your time and feel better. I'm not going anywhere.'

'Thanks!' said Jason, then promptly dissolved into another coughing fit.

'And maybe text me if you need anything,' she said, pulling a pained face. 'Sounds like you're going to lose your voice if you do too much talking!'

'I'm 'kay,' he said.

Lizzie just raised an eyebrow and stopped herself from pointing out that if he was losing syllables, he most definitely wasn't okay.

'What about you?' he rasped. 'We're worried!'

'I'm fine,' said Lizzie with a frown. 'Why wouldn't I be?'

'Bike crash?' said Jason, who'd obviously decided to resort to the minimum number of words necessary to get his point across.

'Oh… that!' said Lizzie, once again at the sensational speed of the Seabury grapevine.

'That!' agreed Jason. 'You 'kay?'

'Fine. A bit scratched and battered… and Megan had to remove a serious number of prickles for me… but I'm fine.'

'Phew,' said Jason. 'Northcliff Road?'

'Yep,' said Lizzie, pulling a face.

'Forget about the corner?' he wheezed.

'Uh huh,' said Lizzie.

'Always go for the ditch,' said Jason with the wisdom only a true local would possess.

'Tell her - nettles over brambles every time!' came the sound of Jason's dad in the background again.

'Hear that?' asked Jason.

'Mmm hmm,' mumbled Lizzie in amusement.

'Cool,' said Jason. 'Going back to bed now.'

'Good plan,' said Lizzie.

'Don't give my job away!' he added.

'No fear,' said Lizzie. 'Feel better - both of you.'

Lizzie was humming tunelessly to herself as she tidied up her workbench when there was a polite tap behind her. Turning, she spotted Ted Hatherleigh peering around the half-open door.

'You open... or... not open?' said Ted with a grin.

'Erm... half and half if that counts?' said Lizzie. 'I'm on my own - but I didn't want to miss anyone if they needed me... so I kind of opened one door and left the other one closed.'

'Very logical!' laughed Ted. 'I've got a couple of boxes for you.'

'Oh blimey!' said Lizzie guiltily. 'Thanks so much - I'm sorry it's taken me so long to pick them up. I-'

'Don't go worrying about that!' laughed Ted. 'They're just my excuse for getting out of the house, to be honest. Margie's mithering on worse than ever this morning. I don't really have much to do out in the barn these days - I'm a bit bored of the mowers - so I thought I'd come and see you instead!'

'Oh!' said Lizzie. 'Well, that's wonderful - thank you! Fancy a cuppa?'

'Don't mind if I do!' said Ted, his whole face lighting up as he limped inside. Lizzie noticed that his walking stick was nowhere to be seen - it was something his wife tended to insist on but Ted abandoned it at every given opportunity.

'Erm... shall I grab those boxes first, so that you can move your car?' she said.

'Nah, I've got them in me pockets,' said Ted, patting his beige jacket. 'The car's parked up already. Didn't want to risk that parking warden. Vicious piece of work!'

'So I've heard!' said Lizzie. 'I've not actually met him yet though.'

'Lucky you,' said Ted, feeling around in his pockets. 'Right - here you go.' With that, he pulled out two of the tiniest boxes Lizzie had ever seen and handed them over.

'Screws?' she said.

'Screws,' Ted confirmed with a straight face. 'I told Margie I'd bring down at least two boxes... and I'm a man of my word.'

Lizzie snorted with laughter and Ted grinned at her.

'Right,' she said, 'I'll shut the door so that we don't get disturbed, and then I'll put the kettle on?'

'Don't you go making special arrangements for me!' said Ted, taking his jacket off, hanging it over her stepladder and then looking around with interest. 'Keep that door open and we'll deal with any customers that come our way. I'll watch the shop while you make the tea? Or do you want to point me towards the kettle?'

'I'm on it,' said Lizzie with a smile. 'Thanks Ted.'

Two minutes later, Lizzie returned from the back room with two steaming mugs and her mind made up. She'd been on her way to see Ted yesterday and got rather... side-tracked. Not today, though – today she was determined to put her plan into action... even if she wasn't quite sure how to broach the subject.

'Ooh lovely!' said Ted, taking the builder's brew from her and taking an appreciative sip. 'Thank you! I say, pity that young lad of yours has taken ill - I've heard good things about him. I'd like to have had a chat.'

'He'll be back before we know it, I'm sure,' said Lizzie, sipping her tea. 'Though that's a nasty bug they've got, so it might be a couple of weeks. Actually... he was in here just yesterday... are you sure you're alright to be around me? Just in case I go down with something...'

'Don't you start mithering too!' said Ted in horror. 'I'm as strong as an ox, me!'

'Fair enough,' said Lizzie.

'Besides - you smell that strongly of antiseptic, I don't think any cold or flu would dare come anywhere near you!' said Ted, grinning at her over his mug.

'I've got my daughter to blame for that... Megan got a bit enthusiastic when she was making sure I was all patched up after I crashed my bike yesterday.'

'Hmm... I heard about that,' said Ted. 'Just down the road from us, weren't you?'

Lizzie nodded, not bothering to ask how Ted knew about it, considering everyone in town seemed to have received the memo!

'Always was a devil of a corner,' said Ted. 'Doubly-nasty if there's been a frost.'

'I don't have that excuse!' said Lizzie. 'I was just going too fast.'

'Nothing changes,' laughed Ted. 'Was your bike alright?'

'It wasn't actually my bike,' said Lizzie, suddenly feeling decidedly guilty. 'It was one of the hires!'

She hadn't even checked it over yet! If it had been her old bike, she'd have been at the shop first thing to start work on any repairs it might have needed. But, because it was one of the hire bikes, she didn't have any kind of attachment to it!

'And is it alright?' said Ted again.

'Honestly? No idea!' said Lizzie, pulling a horrified face. 'I've not even looked at it. Liam dropped it back down here for me last night. There it is... in the rack.'

'The blue?' said Ted, popping his mug down on the workbench and heading straight for it.

'Yes, but don't worry... I'll...'

Lizzie had been about to say that she'd sort it out later, but before she could even get the words out, Ted had it out of the rack. She watched as he cast a practised eye over every inch of it before flipping it over so that he could get to the wheels.

'Two broken spokes,' he said before making a sucking sound through his teeth. 'Bent derailleur hanger,' he added, 'but that's not surprising... and the wheels will need truing up.'

'Could be worse,' said Lizzie.

'Yep,' said Ted with a nod. 'And no time like the present. I'm sure there was a whole box of derailleur hangers in that stuff you brought down from my place.'

'I'm pretty sure you're right,' said Lizzie, feeling guilty again. 'Problem is, I haven't actually managed to sort it all out yet. It's a bit jumbled, I'm afraid. I had some new storage arrive earlier, so I'll soon be able to put it all away. Building those units was my plan for today!'

'I'll help!' said Ted, rubbing his hands together eagerly. 'That's if... if you don't mind?' he added, suddenly sounding unsure. 'Sorry... I don't want to go inviting myself to the party!'

'Are you kidding me?' laughed Lizzie. 'I'd love your help - as long as you really don't mind?'

'Mind? I can't imagine anything better to be doing with my afternoon!' said Ted.

Lizzie smiled. Considering it was only about half past ten in the morning, it sounded like Ted might be with her for the long haul.

CHAPTER 8

'Oh my giddy aunts, what happened to your face?!' demanded Sarah.

The young girl had just ambled into Moore Bikes, flicking her hair and peering around in a way that made Lizzie decidedly suspicious that *she* wasn't the person Sarah was really hoping to bump into. Then she'd spotted Lizzie and had stopped in her tracks.

'Bombing around the lanes and ended up in a hedge!' called Ted helpfully from his perch on a stool behind the rack of hire bikes.

'Oh!' said Sarah. 'Wait... is that Ted?'

'The one and only!' called Ted cheerfully.

'Did you really fall off your bike?' said Sarah, moving forward to take Lizzie's hand so that she could turn it this way and that to inspect the cuts and scrapes on show on her bare forearm.

'Yep. I can't believe you didn't know already!' said Lizzie.

'Why would I know?' said Sarah, looking confused.

'Erm... because I swear the rest of the town heard the news before Liam had even managed to free me from the bramble patch!' laughed Lizzie.

'That's Seabury,' said Sarah with a shrug.

'Yeah... so where have you been to miss out on all the gossip?' said Lizzie, watching Sarah's eyes as they drifted around the shop. 'He's not here!'

'What? Who?' she said sounding dazed.

'Jason,' said Lizzie with a slight smile. 'He's ill – the poor lad's managed to catch that horrible flu his dad's got.'

'Oh, that sucks!' said Sarah, sticking her lip out.

'Yeah - he's going to be missing in action for a while, I think,' said Lizzie.

'I wonder if he needs anything,' said Sarah. She promptly turned bright pink. 'I just meant... from the cafe. It's horrible being stuck at home when you're too ill to cook or anything. At least I've got Kate and Dad to cluck around me – but if Mr Eaves is poorly too...?'

'Well, you could text him?' said Lizzie.

'Don't have his number,' sighed Sarah. 'And we're not friends online... yet.'

'Oh...' said Lizzie, thinking hard. Then a cunning plan nudged its way into her head. 'Hey - have you guys got your soup on the go every day at The Sardine, now that we're heading into autumn?'

'There's always soup - even in the middle of summer,' laughed Sarah. 'Just in case the Chilly Dippers need to warm up.'

'Great. I was going to grab some for Jason and his dad and take it over to their place so that they've got something hot for lunch. Are you working this week?'

Sarah nodded.

'Would you guys be able to deliver soup to their house for me - every day around lunchtime? And maybe a roll each, and a cake or pastry? Then at least they've got something to keep them going. If Kate's willing, we could put it all on my tab and I'll clear it in one go once they're better?'

'Sure,' said Sarah. 'I mean, I can take it up to them even if it doesn't fit in with our usual delivery round timings.'

'That would be amazing,' said Lizzie. 'Thanks. And make sure you just leave it on the doorstep - you seriously don't want whatever those two have got!'

'Right,' said Sarah, deflating slightly. 'How'll they know it's there?'

'Well... I guess I'd better give you Jason's mobile number,' said Lizzie, keeping her face as innocent as possible.

'Cool!' said Sarah. 'Or... you know... whatever!' she added with a shrug.

Lizzie did her best to ignore the sound of chuckling coming from Ted's direction as she scribbled Jason's number on a scrap of paper and handed it over.

'Now… what were you after?' said Lizzie.

'After?' said Sarah, already entering the number into her mobile. 'Oh – right - that! Kate asked me to pop in to see if it's okay to bring Trixie in for a service. She always likes to get it done before winter… and as you're right here…'

'Sure!' said Lizzie, thrilled at the idea of getting her hands on such an important Seabury mascot. 'And you can tell her I've got the tricycle guru on hand if I need any guidance!' she added, grinning at Ted.

'I love that trike,' sighed Ted.

'That's because you made her!' laughed Sarah.

'Too right. I think she's my favourite child,' he said. 'Just don't tell Margie!'

'I promise!' said Sarah. 'So it's okay for Kate to bring her over? I think she was hoping to do it before lunch - while it's not raining!'

'Any time,' said Lizzie nodding. 'We're going to be here until about five. Or… I am, at least!'

'Me too… can't get rid of me that easily!' said Ted. 'Send a couple of cakes over with the old girl, will you?' he added, fumbling in his trouser pocket and bringing out an old-fashioned folding wallet. He flipped it open, grabbed a five-pound note and waved it at Sarah. 'Just-'

'Don't tell Margie?' said Sarah.

'You've got it! And for that, the change can go in your tip jar!' he said with a wink.

Sarah disappeared and Lizzie was suddenly aware that Ted was watching her closely.

'What?' she demanded.

'You're limping,' he said.

'Am not,' said Lizzie.

'Are too... and I should recognise the action!' said Ted.

'I'm fine,' sighed Lizzie, 'just bashed my knee when I went for my prickly flying lesson yesterday. I didn't really notice it to start with, what with all the brambles... I guess it's had a bit of time to swell up.'

'Ouch!' said Ted. 'Well, don't overdo it today - no going up and down that ladder!'

'You sound like Jason!' said Lizzie.

'Good lad, sounds like he's got his head screwed on straight,' said Ted. 'Mind you, not surprised with that dad of his. Eaves is quiet, but a nice enough chap!'

'I've not actually met him,' said Lizzie.

'Not surprised,' said Ted, hauling himself to his feet and stretching. 'The man's a bit of a recluse... or at least, as much as you can be, living in Seabury!'

'That's quite a challenge!' laughed Lizzie.

'You could say that,' said Ted, 'especially with lovely old busybodies like Ethel Watts around.'

Lizzie grinned.

'Anyway,' said Ted, nodding towards the boxes that had arrived just before Sarah, 'shall I give you a hand with putting those storage thingies together?'

'But your fingers?' Lizzie blurted, then wished she hadn't. It wasn't fair to mention Ted's stiff hands when they were the reason he'd given up working on his beloved bikes in the first place.

'They're fine for a bit,' said Ted with a shrug. 'It's just when I'm doing fiddly work for too long they start to give me gyp!'

'Well – in that case – yes please! Blimey - if I get you and Jason working together, I'll never have to lift a finger myself!' laughed Lizzie.

'Just think how bored you'd be!' said Ted. 'Anyway, the sooner we get them done, the sooner we can put away everything you've already brought down from the barn... and then you'll be ready for the last few loads.'

'Sounds like a plan to me!' said Lizzie. 'Shall we shut the door?'

'No! Where's the fun in that?' laughed Ted. 'If we get any customers, you can let me at them... as long as you're not worried an old codger like me might frighten them off!'

'I *definitely* wouldn't call you an old codger!!'

laughed Lizzie, enjoying the company of her twinkly new playmate.

'Well no... maybe that's just the wife!' said Ted with a smirk.

'Let's unbox the first lot and see what's what then, shall we?' said Lizzie, leading the way to the pile of boxes and packages the delivery driver had left in the corner.

Grabbing a knife from her pocket, Lizzie made quick work of the straps and tape. Then, between the pair of them, they started to unpack the various bits.

'Ah ha! Instructions!' said Ted, triumphantly waving a crumpled piece of paper at her. He did his best to smooth out the creases and then peered at it.

"Angle ramrod diagonal down. Twist with the whistlefinger?!" said Ted, pushing his reading glasses up his nose.

'Give that here!' laughed Lizzie. 'It says... what the actual...?'

The instructions appeared to have been translated by someone who'd never even heard English before, let alone spoken it.

'I want to know what a *whistlefinger* is?!' chuckled Ted.

'Let's start with the *ramrod* first!' hooted Lizzie.

'I know what to do!' said Ted.

'Excellent, that makes one of us,' said Lizzie.

'Give that here again,' he said, taking the instructions from her. He promptly screwed it into a ball and tossed it over his shoulder. 'You and I can do a better job without that rubbish throwing us off the scent.'

Lizzie nodded.

Ten minutes later, they already had three of the five units set up. Sure - there was quite a pile of nuts, bolts and washers that didn't seem to have a home… but it didn't really matter because they'd used plenty of extras pilfered from Lizzie's stash, along with some metal brackets to reinforce everything.

'We'll be able to get all those boxes unpacked and put away before the end of the day at this rate,' said Ted.

'That would be ammmmazing!' groaned Lizzie.

'Let's do it, then!' he said, his eyes alive.

'Hey Ted?' said Lizzie, as she made a start on the next unit.

'Yes Lizzie?' he said with a grin, holding the other end of a strut in place without her even having to ask.

'I was actually on my way over to your place yesterday, you know!' she said.

'Oh!' said Ted in surprise. 'I do love visitors - pity you never made it!'

'Yeah, you could say that!' she said, blowing a puff of air upwards as her fringe tickled the edge of the plaster.

'I'm guessing you weren't on your way to pick up boxes,' said Ted, 'seeing as you were on a bike and all.'

'No,' she said, 'though I guess it would have made more sense if I'd brought the car.'

'Sense is overrated, in my opinion,' said Ted cheerfully.

'Man after my own heart!' said Lizzie. 'Anyway - there's two things I wanted to check with you.'

'Lucky I'm here today then, eh?' he said, taking the screwdriver from her and tightening the screws on his side of the unit.

'So… first thing… and please don't take this the wrong way, but…' Lizzie trailed off, trying to figure out how best to word the question. The last thing she wanted to do was offend Ted in any way.

'Spit it out,' said Ted. 'Don't worry about rubbing me up the wrong way… remember who I've got to live with!'

'Right. Fair point,' said Lizzie with a grin. 'So - I just wanted to double-check you're still happy about me half-inching all your stuff?'

'Lizzie, you kno-'

Lizzie held up her hand to cut off his instant protests. 'I'm serious Ted. I was in dire straits and you helped me out… and I'm so grateful. But Margie said you'd been out looking for bits and pieces in the boxes that are still there, and I hate the idea that you didn't really want to get rid of it all.'

'For one thing - you worry too much,' said Ted with a kind smile. 'And for another - Margie talks too much!'

'But–' said Lizzie.

'No buts, Lizzie. You did me a favour. It would have broken my heart if it had all ended up at the tip.' He paused and switched screws. 'I know Margie calls it rubbish, but you and I know better. So – the short answer is - you're still welcome to all of it... and if you try to give it back, I might end up with a divorce on my hands!'

'Better not risk it then!' said Lizzie, grinning at him.

'Indeed,' laughed Ted. 'My only regret with it all is that I wish I could have seen more of those designs through to the end.'

'Is that what you were doing out in the barn?' said Lizzie, raising her eyebrows.

'Nah, I just get a bit bored in the house, that's all,' said Ted with a sigh.

'Well... that leaves me with two more questions if that's okay?' said Lizzie.

'Fire away,' said Ted with a shrug.

'Number one - you know that trike design you were working on,' she said slowly, 'the one with the two back seats for passengers?'

'I know the one,' said Ted. 'I could never quite figure out the balance.'

'Do you reckon it could be turned around as a kind of rickshaw? A backwards trike almost... two passengers up front and a rider behind?' said Lizzie. She grabbed her phone from her pocket and flicked through the photos for a moment until she found the one Jenna had forwarded to her.

'Now there's an idea!' said Ted, peering at it. 'We'd need to have a look at the weight distribution so that it wasn't a complete pig to steer... but I don't see why not!'

'Brilliant,' said Lizzie, feeling a swoop of excitement in her stomach.

'And the second question?' said Ted, who was now eyeballing her with something bordering on suspicion.

'I don't suppose you'd be up for joining me down here in the shop a bit more often?' she said.

'I'm never going to say no to a cuppa surrounded by bits of bikes and tools,' said Ted, looking pleased. 'Especially if there are people to chat to that aren't *her indoors*.'

'Well...' said Lizzie, 'I was thinking more along the lines of you working here.'

'I know!' laughed Ted. 'That's what I thought you meant!'

Lizzie started to giggle.

'Right... so does that make me your official Saturday boy?' he said, looking delighted.

'Or even a bit more often until Jason comes back to work, if you'd be willing,' she said, crossing her fingers in her pocket.

'Lizzie love, I'd set up camp and sleep here given half the chance!' said Ted.

'Definitely *not* necessary!' she laughed. 'But… well, I'd love to work with you on some of those designs… and you can handle chatting up the customers whenever your hands have had enough.'

'Sounds like heaven to me,' said Ted simply.

'Well then, that's settled,' said Lizzie.

'Thanks Boss!' said Ted.

'Wait… that's just weird,' laughed Lizzie. 'Are you sure you haven't been talking to Jason?'

CHAPTER 9

'Hey lady - that'll be a pound for the chair!'

Lizzie cracked her eyes open and grinned up at the silhouette looming over her. One of her favourite people in the entire world was outlined against the washed blue of the perfect afternoon sky.

'I'm sure I've got some money in one of these pockets,' she said, starting to pat at her dungarees - the memory of her first meeting with Liam making her wriggle with pleasure.

How was it so recent? She somehow felt like she'd known this wonderful man forever!

'Don't worry, I'll let you off,' said Liam, leaning down to drop a gentle kiss on the top of her head before sinking into the chair next to her. 'How are you feeling after yesterday?'

'Not too bad,' said Lizzie, 'could definitely have been so much worse. I'm just a bit battered and bruised… especially my pride!'

'Rubbish!' said Liam. 'That corner's been the end of many a joyful cycle… it's where you yanked me out of the nettles and put my chain back on for me when we were kids.'

'Seriously?' said Lizzie.

'Yep… only I had the sense to go for the ditch instead of the hedge,' he smirked.

'I don't know why I thought it was a good idea,' said Lizzie. 'I guess I was hoping it meant I wouldn't have to fall so far!'

'Rookie mistake… you're definitely out of practise,' said Liam.

'Yeah - comes with not having my own bike,' she sighed. 'I'm really going to have to sort that out.'

'But you've basically got an entire shop of bikes at your disposal now,' laughed Liam.

'Yeah - and I'll wreck one after the other if I'm not careful,' she said, sitting forward and readjusting herself slightly so that her various cuts and bumps weren't getting smooshed by the chair.

'The bike didn't look too bad,' said Liam.

'Nothing Ted couldn't sort out in about a second,' she said with a shrug.

'Ted?' said Liam. 'Wait… Ted Hatherleigh?'

'My new Saturday boy,' said Lizzie with a grin that was bordering on triumphant.

'Oh wow! Excellent choice,' said Liam.

'So why are you pulling that face?' said Lizzie in surprise. He looked... horrified!

'I'm just imagining what Margie will do to you when she gets her hands on you!' he laughed. 'She's just managed to get Ted to give up his barn full of bikes, and now you've invited him to hang out in yours!'

'Blimey... I hadn't thought of it like that!' said Lizzie, widening her eyes. 'He just seemed to be so happy - and I'm loving his company. He'll be amazing with Jason, I reckon.'

'Yeah... they'll definitely make a brilliant team,' said Liam with a shrug. 'Just as well... they can run the place when Margie's put you out of action.'

'Oh hush!' laughed Lizzie, reaching over to give him a playful prod, only to wince as her muscles protested.

'Are you sure Megan managed to get all those prickles out?' he said.

'Trust me - you don't know Megan that well yet - but give that girl a pair of tweezers and I can promise you she's extremely thorough!' said Lizzie.

'Doesn't bare thinking about,' laughed Liam.

'You can say that again,' she agreed. 'And I'm sorry, by the way.'

'What for?' said Liam in surprise.

'That *definitely* wasn't the way I'd been planning to welcome you back to town,' she said, pulling a face. 'I didn't even say thank you properly for saving me from the hedge!'

'I'll let you make it up to me,' said Liam wriggling his eyebrows.

'Maybe when I'm sporting fewer plasters and don't smell quite so... medicated?' she said. 'Anyway, how'd it go with Amy? Is she happy in her new place?'

'It was easy as pie, to be honest,' said Liam. 'Until the van conked out on the way home, that is! The new house is massive - so no issues fitting all her stuff in. I even got my own room to kip in while I was there, so that saved me having to deal with the ex.'

'Well... small mercies!' said Lizzie.

'Huge mercies!' muttered Liam. 'I'm not sure I'd have been quite so keen on *dad-to-the-rescue* if it had meant sleeping under the same roof as Lucy.'

'Fair enough,' said Lizzie. 'I mean – it was bad enough having Mark at Pebble Street for a few days!'

'Yeah – and you're on speaking terms with him,' he sighed.

'I am when he's not being a giant knobhead!' chuckled Lizzie.

'Fair point,' said Liam. 'Anyway, that's more than enough about those two! Sounds like you sorted things out beautifully - and I got a whole bunch of unexpected time to hang out with Amy, which was amazing. She had a bit of leave from work – which basically never happens - so I decided to make the most of it.'

'Megan really liked her, by the way,' said Lizzie. 'Apparently, they were on the phone for ages.'

'That's... rare!' said Liam, raising his eyebrows. 'I mean Amy's lovely... but she's not usually one for long phone chats.'

'Megan neither,' said Lizzie.

'Maybe they kind of cancel each other's weirdness out?' laughed Liam. 'How's Megan doing, by the way? Has she chilled out any? She seemed to be on really good form last night.'

Lizzie frowned.

'Oh... not so much, then?' said Liam.

'I don't know. It's like she's at war with herself or something,' said Lizzie. 'One minute, she seems to be happy and relaxed, and the next she's descended into uber-grouch mode again. She seems to do better when she's busy - she painted my whole kitchen in about five seconds, and now she's working on the living room. Whenever she emerges she's totally chilled - plus we had a lovely time talking about colours and lamps and curtains and all those things last night.'

'I didn't know she was into all that!' said Liam.

'Well... nor did I,' said Lizzie. 'To be fair, I'm not sure Megan really did either... I think it's a new thing!'

'Well, it sounds positive,' said Liam.

'Yeah... but then it's like she catches herself at it, gets all grumpy again and disappears off to the caravan.' Lizzie paused and sighed. 'Even Jenna's noticed something's up with her. I keep hoping that if I leave it long enough – if I give Meggie some space - she might open up and tell me what's wrong.'

'Sounds to me like you might need to give her a bit of a prod in the right direction?' said Liam.

'Yeah, you might be right,' said Lizzie, pulling a face.

'I mean... both girls are talking to you at the moment, right?' said Liam. 'And each other?'

'Oh yes!' laughed Lizzie. 'The squabbling has well and truly stopped since my Mafia Boss moment!'

Liam let out a snort of laughter and Lizzie grinned back. When she'd filled him in on the phone about the showdown at The Pebble Street Hotel, his reaction had been to cheer and clap at every single one-liner she'd come up with. He'd also promised to buy her a stuffed toy of a long-haired, white cat if she ever fancied playing the role again in the future.

'Right...' said Liam, slowly. 'So maybe it's time to rope Jenna in. Perhaps if Megan knows she's got both of you supporting her and backing her up, it'll help her open up a bit?'

'Or make her feel like she's being ganged up on,' said Lizzie dubiously.

'I guess it all depends on how it comes up in conversation...' said Liam, scratching his head.

Lizzie smiled. She loved this about him - Liam liked nothing more than to help people. All he wanted to do was fix problems and make life better... what he didn't seem to realise was that just his presence was all that was needed to make her world a much brighter place.

'Well... I *do* need to talk to them both anyway,' said Lizzie. 'They've both come up with a whole bunch of ideas for Moore Bikes.'

She paused and blew out a long breath.

'Uh oh,' said Liam. 'You just said that like it's a bad thing!'

'It's... not? I mean, not necessarily,' she said. 'Some of the suggestions have got me really thinking about the possibilities...'

'But?' said Liam.

'But - both of them say they want to be a part of the business. And although I don't hate the idea in principle... I know it won't work.'

'Because neither of them are staying in Seabury?' said Liam.

Lizzie nodded.

'Jenna definitely won't - she's been clear about that from the start,' said Lizzie. 'I don't know about Megan yet. Obviously, if it was something she really wanted to do, that'd be different... but she just seems to be so lost right now.'

'Right,' said Liam.

'Anyway,' said Lizzie. 'Even if they both wanted to

put down roots here - I want their life to be filled with things they love… and that includes doing work they love. I know they've both come up with these ideas for Moore Bikes because they're trying to support me - but it's not what they want to do… not really.'

'Sounds like the three of you have a lot to talk about,' said Liam. 'And – from my limited experience with these things – I'd say being open and honest is definitely the best way to go'.

'Exactly,' said Lizzie. 'I don't want to stamp on their ideas - there's loads there that I can use, but…'

'This is your dream, Lizzie,' he said. 'It's fine for you to have it exactly the way you want. And the girls need to find their own dreams too.'

'Exactly,' she said again. 'And with any luck - they won't wait as long as I have. Maybe I'll message them now… just to see if they're free to have a meal with me this evening.'

'Do it!' said Liam, nodding as he settled back in his chair and closed his eyes.

'Sorry - this is really rude of me,' said Lizzie, pausing with her phone in hand. 'I came to see you…'

'I'm in no rush,' said Liam with an easy smile.

'Thanks,' said Lizzie. She dashed off a message to both girls and had barely hit send when Megan replied.

> *Sounds good.*
> *I've got questions about the living room anyway.*
> *Bring Liam? I'd like to get to know him better!*

'Megan wants me to ask you to come too,' said Lizzie, the surprise in her voice evident. The phone buzzed in her hand and she glanced down to find another one, this time from Jenna.

> *I'll cook. Homemade pizza?*
> *Bring a bottle – and ask Liam to come!*

'Okay - that's a second request for your presence!' chuckled Lizzie.

'You know I'd love to… but…' said Liam slowly.

'But maybe not tonight?' said Lizzie, nodding.

'Right,' said Liam. 'You need to find out what's going on with them… and they don't know me yet. It'll turn it into something else if I'm there. We can do that another time – I'm not going anywhere.'

'Okay,' said Lizzie. She glanced at him, wanting to crawl onto his lap and wrap her arms around him… but the deckchair would probably eat them both whole if she did that. 'We'll just have a girls night tonight.'

Lizzie blew out a long breath as she felt the first stirrings of butterflies in her stomach. She knew it was ridiculous, but who knew what she was going to find when she started delving into what was really going on with Megan. Even worse... how was Megan going to react?!

'Changing the subject slightly,' said Liam, 'what's Jenna up to at the mo?'

'Mostly cooking for me!' laughed Lizzie. 'I think she's got vague plans to pick up a bit of work while she's here. She wants to save up for a van... though I think it's proving to be a bit of a non-starter so far... mainly because she's so chilled she's practically horizontal!'

'You said she's pretty practical?' said Liam.

'Yeah,' said Lizzie with a nod. 'That's why I feel a bit guilty about not offering her work in the shop... but...'

Liam shook his head. 'You've already got your dream team in place now that you've poached Jason and dug Ted out of retirement!'

'Erm... I think you'll find you practically had Jason gift-wrapped and hand-delivered to the shop!' laughed Lizzie.

'Well, it *is* perfect for him,' said Liam with a shrug. 'No - I was just thinking that Ben and I could do with an extra pair of hands. Jason's off sick even if we could tempt him away from Moore Bikes for a few days... so I wondered if Jenna might be up for it. It's only for a week or two?'

'Oh,' said Lizzie in surprise. 'Do you want me to ask her?'

'If you don't mind - see if she's even slightly interested,' said Liam. 'Make it sound as unglamorous as possible - a bit of cleaning, some pre-winter garden tidy-ups - that sort of thing.'

'Okay - you're on,' said Lizzie. 'Thanks!'

'Don't thank me - we need the help and if she's up for it, she'll be busy busy busy!' laughed Liam.

'That might be a good thing,' said Lizzie, patting her stomach, 'before I have to go a size up from all her amazing cooking!'

'You are perfect,' said Liam, 'and... when we get everything sorted out... maybe we can have our first proper date?'

'I'd like that...' said Lizzie, feeling her cheeks glow at the compliment. 'Though I think we might be past first-date territory, somehow!'

Lizzie yawned and felt her eyelids flutter lazily as the soft sound of the sea lapping at the sand started to work its magic on her. The temptation to lean back in her chair and have a little snooze was almost overwhelming.

'Hey!' she said with a slight yawn. 'You okay?'

Liam had just sat forward in his chair and was looking weirdly uncomfortable. Suddenly, the impending snooze disappeared. Lizzie mirrored him, sitting forward and wincing slightly as one of her many scratches caught on the strap of her dungarees.

Liam glanced at her, looking uneasy. 'It's just... when I was with Amy... she said something that's been kind of bugging me.' He reached up and ruffled his hair. 'Something about you.'

'Oh?' said Lizzie, as a cold finger of fear ran down her spine. She had nothing to worry about… did she? But then, If Amy had some kind of problem with her, Liam's daughter was always going to come first, wasn't she? 'What… what was it?'

'She said you've been waiting so long for this first date of ours… that I needed to make a "grand gesture",' said Liam, making air quotes with his fingers. 'She said you'd probably be expecting it… and it was only fair.'

'A grand gesture?' said Lizzie, staring at him. 'Like what?'

'That's the problem… I have no idea!' said Liam with a sheepish grin. 'I don't want you to feel like you're missing out on anything though… because you deserve everything. Dreams and sparkles… and even grand gestures… whatever that means!'

Lizzie reached out and grabbed his hand. Ignoring the stinging pin-prick cuts from her fall, she laced her fingers through his - relishing the feel of their firm, capable roughness.

'I don't need "grand gestures",' she said quietly. 'Can we agree… to just be us? Because from where I'm sitting, that's more than enough.'

'Just be us?' said Liam, his face splitting into a relieved grin. 'That… that I can do.'

'Good,' laughed Lizzie. 'Bloody daughters – they've got a lot to answer for.'

'Agreed!' said Liam with a long sigh of relief.

CHAPTER 10

'I brought wine!' yelled Lizzie as she slammed the cottage door behind her and hurried through to the kitchen.

'Fab!' said Jenna, turning to her.

Lizzie eyeballed her. There was something about her smile that looked… wrong, somehow. Forced.

'Where's Meggie?' she said, lightly.

'In the caravan,' sighed Jenna. She turned back to the worktop and upended a giant mixing bowl, tipping a large lump of dough onto the surface. Tearing it into three, she started to expertly knead and shape one after the other into perfect pizza bases.

Lizzie watched, mesmerised. Her youngest daughter really was a bit of an eye-opener sometimes.

'I'm guessing she's still joining us for dinner?' said Lizzie, surreptitiously crossing her fingers.

She'd been really looking forward to a girly evening with the pair of them. It was a feeling that was relatively new... but entirely wonderful. Sure, she had some serious stuff to discuss with them - but that was life, wasn't it?

'I think she is,' said Jenna, nodding. 'I expect she's, erm... sorting herself out?'

'What do you mean?' said Lizzie, shrugging out of her coat and hanging it over the back of one of the kitchen chairs as she watched Jenna smearing the pizza bases with herby tomato sauce. 'Is she getting changed or something?'

Jenna shook her head, not quite meeting her eye.

'Jenna - what's going on?' said Lizzie.

'I promised I wouldn't say anything,' said Jenna.

'About what?' said Lizzie.

'Just... go see her?' said Jenna. 'Then I won't have broken my promise, and you'll find out anyway. Maybe take her a glass of wine while you're at it?'

'Okay,' said Lizzie, picking up one of the bottles.

'Red, mum - unless you want to incur her wrath!' said Jenna.

'Right, right,' said Lizzie, quickly swapping the bottles and taking the glass Jenna pulled down from a cupboard for her.

'I'll hold off putting these in the oven until you reappear, okay?' said Jenna.

'Okay... erm... thanks?' said Lizzie, now thoroughly concerned.

'Take yourself a glass too,' said Jenna, 'you might be a while.'

'But... then she'll know I know something's up?' said Lizzie.

'Trust me,' said Jenna with a shrug, 'she won't even notice.'

Lizzie quickly poured two glasses of red wine and hurried back towards the front door. After a bit of juggling in order to let herself out, she made her way around to the caravan. Pausing, she tried to rearrange her hold on the glasses again so that she could knock.

Wait... what was that?!

Lizzie froze. She could *swear* she'd just heard someone crying!

'Megan?' she called, giving up on the idea of knocking.

There was a scuffling sound on the other side of the door, and then silence.

'Meggie, love? I've brought you some wine!' said Lizzie, forcing a smile into her voice. 'Can you get the door? I've got my hands full!'

There was a beat of silence, and Lizzie was just considering facing the consequences of letting herself in when the door swung open. She nearly dropped the glasses in shock.

Megan was a total mess. Her eyes were red and

swollen, her cheeks still shining with tears... and she was back in the same diamanté cat sweatshirt she'd arrived in... *never* a good sign!

'Megan love - what's wrong?' said Lizzie, staring up at her daughter and feeling like her heart might break. Megan stared at her for a long moment before letting out a shuddering sob.

'Alright - I'm coming in,' said Lizzie urgently. 'Make way!'

Megan stepped backwards obediently and Lizzie hopped up into the little caravan. In classic Megan-style, it was immaculate... apart from the bed which was covered with piles of magazines. Torn-out pages were scattered across the duvet like a drift of autumn leaves.

'You said you've got wine?' said Megan, her voice thick with tears.

'Sure love,' said Lizzie, offering her the glass containing the largest dose of red.

'Ta,' said Megan, taking a huge gulp even as more fat tears spilled from her eyes and made their way unheeded down her cheeks.

'Shall we sit?' said Lizzie.

'What about dinner?' said Megan, scrubbing her face with her sleeve and only succeeding in spreading tears and mascara everywhere.

'Jenna's in charge,' said Lizzie. 'It's nowhere near ready yet.'

It was only a little white lie, but there was no way

she was about to hurry. She'd take as much time as she needed to get to the bottom of Megan's tears.

Lizzie perched right on the edge of the bed and pushed a couple of magazines out of the way so that Megan could join her. She sank down looking thoroughly miserable, clutching her glass of wine in both hands.

'What's up, Meggie?' said Lizzie.

As much as she was desperate to pull her daughter into a hug, Lizzie knew it was a bad idea to initiate any kind of physical contact while she was in this state. It had always been the same - even when Megan was really little, she couldn't bear being touched when she was upset.

'I... I... everything's just ruined!' said Megan.

Lizzie watched her chin quiver, and she had to grip her own glass tightly to stop herself from reaching out to grab her daughter's hand.

'What's ruined, love?' said Lizzie. 'Talk to me.'

Megan shook her head. 'I'll sort it. I'll figure it out. I'm... I'm... f...f...f...fine!'

It was clearly as much as Megan could do to get the last word out on a shuddering sob. Then much to Lizzie's surprise, her beautiful, strong, independent daughter crumpled onto her shoulder, crying her heart out.

Lizzie winced as the sobbing girl wrapped an arm tightly around her waist, coming into contact with various scratches she hadn't even realised were there!

Reaching out, she quickly rescued Megan's wine glass. With her daughter still attached to her like a limpet, Lizzie placed both glasses on the bedside table, then moving slowly, she wrapped her arms around her heartbroken daughter.

It took a full five minutes for Megan to cry herself out. As she finally started to calm down, Lizzie half expected her to pull away. It would be just like Megan to realise that her barriers were down and put some distance between them while she pulled her game-face back on – but not this time. It looked like Megan was well and truly broken.

The silence stretched out between them, and Megan just sat there with her head on her mum's shoulder while Lizzie gently stroked her hair.

'Tell me what's bothering you, Meggie,' said Lizzie eventually, realising that one of them was going to have to start speaking first. 'Is it Owen? Or your job… or…?'

'All of it?' said Megan, with a sigh. 'It's all of it.'

'Don't say that,' said Lizzie. 'Whatever it is, we'll sort it out.'

'I always thought I could plan my way out of anything,' said Megan, 'but not this… not this!'

She sniffed, and Lizzie braced herself for another torrent, but it didn't come. Instead, Megan gently pulled away from her and sat up straight. She turned and locked eyes with Lizzie.

'I want kids,' she said.

'Well... that's wonderful,' said Lizzie slowly.

Megan shook her head. 'It's not because... because...'

Lizzie held her breath.

'Because it was in my plan. And then Owen saw my plan... and he dumped me!' said Megan. 'Wine?' she added, making a grabbing motion in mid-air.

Lizzie quickly handed her back her glass.

'Ta,' said Megan, taking a fortifying sip.

'Right,' said Lizzie slowly. She really didn't want to say the wrong thing at this point. 'So - Owen didn't want kids?'

'Not with me!' said Megan, shaking her head. 'He said he didn't want to be with a psycho who knew the best days of the month to get pregnant.' She took a deep, shuddering breath.

'But... had you two talked about kids before?' said Lizzie.

'Nope,' said Megan. 'But... that was in my plan too. I just wanted all the info first... you know what I'm like!'

'I do,' said Lizzie. 'You're amazing. And you will be an amazing mum.'

'Not anymore,' said Megan, her lip wobbling again. 'He dumped me... and then I lost my job... and...'

'Wait. You lost your job?' said Lizzie in surprise. 'I thought you said you missed a promotion.'

'I did. Because they found out I wanted to start a family,' said Megan.

'How?' demanded Lizzie.

'Because Owen dumped me in the middle of the office with everyone listening!' said Megan.

'He did WHAT?!' gasped Lizzie.

Megan nodded.

'Wanker,' said Lizzie.

Megan gave a surprised giggle.

'Sorry,' said Lizzie. 'Sorry.'

'No - don't be,' said Megan. 'I mean, you're right.'

Lizzie nodded, breathing a little sigh of relief. It had to be a good sign that she'd just smiled, didn't it, no matter how briefly?

'It's just... I wasted so much time with him. And I want a family,' said Megan. 'And now I don't even have a job!'

'Back up a second,' said Lizzie. 'If they fired you when they found out you wanted a family, then you're taking them to court for discrimination - pronto.'

'Nah,' sighed Megan, shaking her head. 'It wasn't like that. I walked out.'

'You walked out?' said Lizzie, feeling like she'd just lost the thread again.

'I'm not working in the same company as him,' said Megan. 'And I'm not working for people who won't support women. I'm just... not doing that. I've worked there for *years*. I am... I was... bloody good at my job. And that's the support I get? They can take that job and shove it where the sun don't shine!'

'Shame someone doesn't tell them exactly that,' said Lizzie.

'Mother... don't you know me at all?' said Megan with a tired smile. 'Of course I told them! *All* of it – and trust me, it wasn't half as polite as the version I just gave you.'

'Good for you!' said Lizzie.

'Well... not really,' sighed Megan. 'Because now I don't have a job and I don't have a partner... I'm back to square one.'

'Love...' said Lizzie, 'you might not believe this right now, but both those things mean you're so much closer to what you want than before.'

'How?' said Megan, looking so young and scared that it made Lizzie's heart squeeze for her.

'Well, for one thing - you aren't about to start a family with one of the biggest turds in the UK,' said Lizzie.

Megan raised an eyebrow, and Lizzie quickly changed tack.

'Sorry, that's not fair and if you loved him then-'

'I didn't,' said Megan quietly. 'Love him, I mean. I just didn't want all those years to be wasted.'

'Oh love,' said Lizzie, shaking her head. 'Well in that case - it's a *really* good thing you didn't start a family with him. The fact that he doesn't want kids with you... that should be enough for you to know he wasn't the man you want as your babies' father. The fact that he is an asshat who I'd quite like to help kick in the painful-plums right now has nothing to do with it!'

Megan smirked. 'Physical violence is never the answer, mother!'

'No... but sometimes it's so tempting!' said Lizzie, winking at Megan. 'As for starting a family - you're still young, Meggie. There's time. Time to meet someone and try for babies. Or *not* meet someone, if that's what you choose - you can have babies on your own. Or you can adopt or foster. You can draw a family to you without ever giving birth or doing any of the above. You can have the life *you* want. The life *you* deserve.'

Lizzie paused, breathing hard. Then she continued, her voice growing more earnest. 'Please... don't settle for some berk just because he's already in the picture. Life's far too precious for that. *You* are far too precious for that.'

Megan nodded and leaned her head on Lizzie's shoulder again. 'Thanks mum. You're amazing.'

'You too, kiddo,' said Lizzie with a soft smile. 'As for the job...'

'I was *so* bored,' sighed Megan.

'You were?' said Lizzie in surprise. She felt Megan nod against her shoulder.

'Yeah. But... do you mind if we go in for pizza

before we talk about that,' she said. 'Crying makes me starving!'

'You realise if we go in there, Jenna's going to see that you've been crying?' said Lizzie.

'Erm... I hate to tell you this, mum...' said Megan, 'but little sis has seen me crying practically every day since we've been here.'

'She has?!' said Lizzie in surprise.

'Yup,' said Megan. 'I'm just surprised Jenna's managed to keep her trap shut for so long!'

'Oh,' said Lizzie, realising they'd been rumbled.

'To be fair,' sighed Megan, 'being around Jenna's really helped. Not with the whole *kid* thing, but she's helped me start to see that there are different ways to live.'

'Like what?' said Lizzie. Somehow, she couldn't imagine Megan traipsing around the world in a van that was constantly on its last legs.

'Like... like the way you're building your life now,' said Megan. 'You're building it around your dream. You've found something that lights you up so much that it doesn't matter how many insane hours you spend on it - because you love it! And Jenna - I mean... she does what she wants and then works to support it... though I've yet to see her actually do any paid work!'

'That reminds me,' said Lizzie, momentarily distracted. 'Liam and Ben might have some work for her.'

'See!' said Megan. 'It's stuff like that. She doesn't have a plan... but stuff just falls into place for her to support what she wants to do!'

'Right,' said Lizzie, nodding slowly. 'So... do you know what it is you *want* to do?'

'Not yet,' said Megan. 'I mean, I think I just need to take things one day at a time for a bit?'

Lizzie nodded, barely able to grasp that this was *Megan* saying these wonderful things.

'I'm enjoying helping decorate the cottage, though,' she said. 'I'd really like to carry on... I'd love to do some of the other rooms for you while I'm here. But only if you don't mind?'

'Mind?!' laughed Lizzie. 'The fact that I've somehow landed myself my own personal interior designer with impeccable taste?! I love what you've already done!'

'Cool,' said Megan. 'I just hope... maybe I can prepare for having a family by making sure I look after myself first? Designing my life in a way that means it'll fit around kids... or whatever family I'm lucky enough to end up with.'

'Sounds like a plan,' said Lizzie.

Megan shook her head. 'If there's anything I've learned from all this... I think I'm done with plans for a while!'

CHAPTER 11

2 Weeks Later…

'Wow, wow, wow Boss!' said Jason, his eyes growing wide as he wandered into Moore Bikes and stared around. 'You've been busy!'

Lizzie followed his gaze. The place had really come together in the last few weeks. Her tool wall was set up as she'd always wanted it, and she'd made short work on the storage units with Ted's help. They were lined up along the back of the workshop area and were neatly filled with all the goodies from the barn.

'Okay – that is officially epic!' said Jason, staring wide-eyed at the huge enamel sign that now graced one of the walls.

Lizzie grinned. It had been a gift from the girls –

and it made her smile every time she looked at it. After several long chats with Megan and Jenna, they'd both admitted that they didn't *really* see themselves settling in Seabury long-term. However, the girls had been adamant that they wanted to help with Moore Bikes as much as possible while they were still in town.

The three of them had put their heads together to work on some branding ideas - and Megan had pulled in a favour with a graphic designer who'd freelanced with her old company. Moore Bikes now had this gorgeous logo inspired by Rosie the Riveter... though in this version she looked decidedly like Lizzie and was wearing a pair of denim dungarees! The whole look was a little bit vintage... and seriously cool.

'You know – the logo really suits you!' said Jason. 'I can't believe how much you've managed to do in here!'

'Not just me,' she said quickly. 'Jenna and Megan have helped with loads of ideas, and they've even set up social media for us - and I've got Wonder Ted to thank for sorting this place out!'

'Wonder Ted?!' sniggered Jason. 'Wow, is that his official title?'

'Yes it is,' came Ted's gruff voice from the back of the workshop. 'Two little girls decided that's what I should be called from now on – and I'm sticking with it! Anyway, it's about time you came back to work. You've had far too much time on the sofa with your feet up - playing those computer games, no doubt.'

'More like passed out in bed for a week,' sighed Jason. 'But yeah – I was getting seriously bored there for a bit!'

'Man after my own heart!' said Ted, shuffling over to shake Jason's hand. 'And you're all better?'

Jason nodded, smiling broadly at Ted.

'It's great to have you back, Jason!' said Lizzie. 'We missed you.'

'Cheers,' said Jason, going pink. 'Oh – that reminds me. Dad wanted me to apologise.'

'What for?' said Lizzie in surprise.

'Shutting the door in your face when you dropped me off!' laughed Jason, rolling his eyes. 'He was so poorly, and so worried about getting me to the sofa before I passed out on him... well, he just said he wasn't very polite.'

Lizzie shrugged. 'The poor guy could barely stand!'

'Yeah... and between you and me,' said Jason, 'he's super shy. Or... well... not shy, but not very... people-y?'

'I get it,' said Lizzie. 'And tell him not to worry. Hopefully, I'll get to meet him properly sometime.'

'Maybe,' said Jason. 'Don't hold your breath, though – he definitely prefers bees to people!'

'I won't take it personally, then,' said Lizzie.

'Good,' said Jason. 'Because he's really grateful for everything you've done... are doing... for me.'

'Goodness, this is getting very soppy!' laughed Ted, glancing down at his watch. 'I think we all need a coffee! My treat - but Lizzie - you're getting it.'

'Wait a minute!' laughed Lizzie. 'I thought I was the boss?'

'Exactly,' said Ted. 'You get to go out in the sunshine and sneak a little chat with that man of yours while you're at it!'

'Yeah, and don't pretend you won't!' said Jason with a smirk.

'Go! Enjoy some sunshine,' said Ted, 'and leave us lackeys to it!'

'Well,' said Lizzie, 'when you put it like that - I don't mind if I do.'

Doing her best to make an escape without taking the ten-pound note Ted was waving in her direction, Lizzie sighed as Jason promptly barred her way out.

'Ah man... you two are going to gang up on me, aren't you?' she said with a grin.

'Only when it's for your own good!' said Ted, winking at her as he thrust the money into her hand.

'Don't hurry back,' said Jason.

'Charming!' she laughed. She only managed to get about a dozen paces down the road when Ted's voice rang out behind her.

'Don't forget to buy some buns!'

Lizzie turned and gave him the thumbs up to

signal she'd received his message and then carried on towards The Sardine. It really was a stunning day... though autumn was most definitely showing its true colours now. It might be the morning, but her shadow was long, and the air had a fresh tang to it that hinted at mittens and bobble-hats to come.

Wrapping her arms tightly around herself, Lizzie wriggled with joy. She was glad the sun was out - she had a treat lined up after work, and it would definitely be better if it wasn't raining! A picnic tea on West Beach was always going to be a high point of any day – but especially when she got to share it with Liam, Jenna and Megan.

The four of them had already shared several happy evenings together - something that seemed to happen so organically that it was hard to believe she'd ever been worried about it. It was a regular occurrence for Liam to drop Jenna back from work and nip in for a cuppa, only to end up staying late.

Jenna had jumped at the chance to work with Liam and Ben - though from what Liam had told Lizzie - he had his suspicions that she was just doing it as an excuse to dribble over their vans.

As for Megan, she'd worked her way steadily through the whole of Lizzie's cottage. Somehow, she'd managed to bag herself a home worthy of any interiors magazine. Megan seemed to have a knack for figuring out what was inside Lizzie's head and turning it into a reality.

Not only had she decorated the entire cottage but, with Lizzie's blessing, Megan had also helped her to unpack properly. Liam had helped her to hang shelves, shift furniture, and even polish the floorboards in Lizzie's bedroom. At long last, she was really starting to feel like she was home.

Glancing down at the beach, Lizzie grinned. Liam's chairs weren't out this morning… which just went to prove how unobservant the boys were. She'd not been expecting to see him, though. Liam was off to a local dealership to trade in his old van for a new one – and Jenna had gone along for the ride.

Technically, this wasn't a work day for Jenna - but she'd jumped at the chance to ogle a whole bunch of shiny new vans. Lizzie had left Liam with strict instructions to stop her youngest from trying any wheeling and dealing to get her hands on one. Somehow, Lizzie wouldn't put much past Jenna if it meant getting her hands on a new van!

After a good, long gossip with Lou and a quick cuddle with Stanley, Lizzie made her way back towards the shop, bearing a tray laden with cups and a bag of Ted's favourite sticky buns. She'd just been given the third degree by Sarah, who'd insisted on knowing how Jason looked - and whether he'd mentioned the soup deliveries at all. Lizzie was willing to bet almost anything that they'd be getting a visit from the young baker before the end of the day!

As Moore Bikes came into view, Lizzie squinted. There was a blue pick-up she didn't recognise pulled up right outside. As she got closer, it moved away, heading off towards the allotments.

'Ooh,' she breathed, 'some new repairs, perhaps?!'

Lizzie instinctively sped up... and then slowed back down again. She didn't need to rush, did she? With Jason and Wonder Ted on hand - she didn't need to worry about anything - the shop was in very capable hands.

'Alright boys!' she said, as she bounded into the shop at last. 'Coffee and sticky buns are served!'

Ted and Jason turned to face her... and both of them looked ridiculously guilty for some reason.

'What are you two up to?' she demanded.

'Nothing,' mumbled Jason.

'Nothing at all!' said Ted.

'Uh huh?' she said, eyeing them both in turn. 'So... what's with the large mound of tarpaulin behind you that wasn't there before?!'

'You spoiled the surprise a bit,' said Ted.

'Yeah - you were meant to be out for ages,' said Jason.

'What surprise?' said Lizzie.

'We didn't get a chance to put this on it!' said Ted, fishing around in his pocket and pulling out a length of slightly crumpled blue ribbon.

'On what?!' said Lizzie, completely lost.

'May as well?' said Jason to Ted.

'Yeah,' said Ted. 'What is it you youngsters say? Busted?'

Jason grinned and grabbed a corner of the tarpaulin. Ted took the other.

'Tada!' they said in unison, throwing it back with a flourish.

'A bike?' said Lizzie. She stared at the silver paintwork and the beautiful sweep of a pair of very familiar-looking handlebars.

'Not any old bike!' said Ted, looking excited.

'*Your* old bike!' said Jason.

Lizzie nodded slowly. It was the bike she'd ridden as a child. The one Ted had rescued from a hedge and then given back to her all these years later when it came to clearing his barn.

'I don't understand...' she said. This was essentially her childhood bike - but now it was big enough for her to ride. 'It's... grown?'

'Told you I got bored at home,' said Jason with a shrug.

'But... how?' said Lizzie, running her hand over the new saddle.

'Ted nicked it and brought it round for me,' said Jason with a shrug.

'You did?!' said Lizzie.

'Might have!' said Ted, looking shifty. 'He sent Sarah a message saying he was bored, Sarah told me, and we arranged something for him to do. It wasn't like the bike could catch the flu, was it?! So I left it for Jason just inside their back gate.'

'And the parts?' said Lizzie, in wide-eyed wonder that she'd somehow managed to miss all this going on right under her nose.

'I *might* have half-inched what he needed from the pile from my barn!' said Ted.

'It's beautiful,' said Lizzie, looking it over. 'I mean... this is serious skill, Jason!'

'Thanks, Boss,' said Jason, looking pleased.

'You're missing something, Lizzie,' said Ted.

'What... wait... what's this?!' said Lizzie, staring at a long, black block that ran down the back of the seat post.

'Well... I know you like a bit of speed,' said Jason with a wink. 'This is my super-power... or at least, that's what I'm working on!'

'But what...?'

'It's a battery!' chuckled Ted. 'He's souped-up your ride for you!'

'Wait... what now?!'

'I can undo it if you hate it,' said Jason quickly. 'But I did this course – learning to retrofit regular bikes as e-bikes with a kit.'

'Wow!' said Lizzie. 'Wait... you've got that skill and you're only just mentioning it?' Suddenly an entire new possibility for Moore Bikes opened up before her eyes.

'How's that for a bit different?' said Ted. 'Kid reckons we could add it to your rickshaws too… if you wanted, of course!'

'How do you charge them up?' said Lizzie, completely intrigued.

'Oh, that's easy – just a mains charger,' said Jason. 'But… you could always look at getting solar panels installed on the roof. This place has got loads of space up there.'

'Do you know how to do that too?' said Lizzie, feeling like she'd believe just about anything right now.

'I will soon,' said Jason. 'I'm doing a course on it in the new year – part-time. I figure it'd be a good thing to learn. Plus - I bet there are grants that would help pay for it if you wanted to do it here.'

'Don't know about that,' said Ted, 'but I'm betting those blighters on the council would jump on it. Nice little selling point for the town. Visitors would like it!'

'You're right, Ted!' said Jason with a nod. 'Boss - you could offer solar-powered battery top-ups for tourists in here!'

Lizzie stared at the co-conspirators with her mouth hanging open. It looked like the five-year business plan she'd been working on with the girls' help might need an entire new section! She ran a hand lovingly over her old-new bike again, trying to let it all sink in.

'How'd you get this in here without me noticing?' she asked.

'Dad brought it over in the pickup just now,' laughed Jason. 'He was waiting for me to message and say we'd managed to get rid of you!'

'Charming!' said Lizzie.

'Do you like it?' said Jason.

'Like it?!' said Lizzie, staring at Jason. Was it her imagination, or did he look nervous?

'She's shaking,' said Ted. 'It's usually a good sign, I think.'

'It's amazing,' she breathed. 'And we definitely have the centre-piece for our window display!'

'What - for the grand opening?' hooted Ted.

'Yeah… that!' said Lizzie.

'Grand opening,' said Jason. 'Thing of legend - kind of a mythical beast by this point!'

'Cheeky blighter,' chuckled Ted.

The three of them fell silent again and stood gazing at Jason's incredible work.

'Sorry boys…' said Lizzie at last, 'I'm going to play hooky again - I *have* to try this beauty out!'

Grabbing the handlebars, Lizzie pushed the bike outside, and then paused, suddenly aware that she didn't have a clue how to turn it on.

'Show me?' she said, turning to Jason.

'Here,' said Jason, handing her a helmet which she dutifully pulled on. Then he stooped to turn a key near the battery. 'Then this switch here, and then when you start pedalling…'

'Like this? Oh… Wheeeeeeeeee!' laughed Lizzie as the bike took on a life of its own and she swiftly left Ted and Jason's cheers far behind her.

CHAPTER 12

The sun was low in the sky by the time Lizzie locked the doors to Moore Bikes. Jason had headed home a couple of hours ago having hit an energy slump mid-afternoon. She'd promptly put her foot down and sent him packing.

'Night, Boss,' said Ted. 'You go careful on that new-fangled contraption!'

'I will!' said Lizzie with a smile, before pulling on her helmet and hauling the bike away from the wall. Both her boys - as she was quickly coming to think of Ted and Jason - had warned her that she wasn't to dare ride the thing without a helmet... and after her morning zoom around on it, she could see their point.

It had been the most wonderful day of making plans and talking about the future of Moore Bikes. The shop might not even be officially open yet - but

Lizzie could already see so much potential with her new team of three that it almost took her breath away.

'To the beach!' she squealed, as she started to pedal and Jason's magical power assist kicked in so that she took off like a scalded weasel.

Of course, she didn't actually *need* to cycle - considering she was only heading to the far end of West Beach, but she couldn't resist showing off her amazing old-new bike to everyone!

Lizzie found herself whizzing past The Sardine before she'd even had the time to blink. Glancing towards West Beach, she spotted the other three waiting for her down by the deckchairs, but they disappeared in a blur before she dared to let go of the handlebars to attempt a wave.

Making the executive decision that the bike deserved to stretch its little legs properly, Lizzie continued to zoom towards North Beach, letting out a loud *whoop* of glee as she passed Lionel, who waved his hat at her.

In what felt like mere seconds, Lizzie had u-turned outside the post office and was pelting back towards West Beach. This time, she started to brake gently, giving herself plenty of time to slow down before drawing to a smooth stop right at the top of the steps that led down to the beach.

Panting - not from exertion, but from the sheer amount of adrenaline coursing through her system –

Lizzie hopped off the saddle and leaned the bike against the railings. She unclipped her helmet and left it dangling from the handlebars before running down the steps - straight into Liam's arms.

'Who in their right mind gave you a souped-up bike?!' he whispered in her ear as he swung her around.

'Like it?!' giggled Lizzie.

'I have no idea! You were just a dungaree-and-silver-shaped blur on the horizon!' he laughed, setting her down on the sand.

'Jason made it for me,' she said proudly, 'it's my old bike from when I was a kid.'

'I remember that bike being a lot smaller!' said Liam. 'And I definitely don't remember it having a battery that meant you could basically fly!'

'What can I say,' said Lizzie. 'The kid's a genius.

Liam grabbed her hand and led her towards the deckchairs where both the girls were lounging in the late evening sunshine.

'Did you see my bike?!' she demanded as soon as she drew near.

'Of course!' laughed Jenna.

'Awesome!' said Megan, with her eyes closed and a big smile on her face. Lizzie noticed that her cheeks still held the tell-tale traces of eggshell gloss which meant Megan had been putting the finishing touches to the bathroom. 'I stopped looking when you two started being disgustingly cute though,' she added, cracking an eye open and giving Lizzie a wicked smile.

'Where'd you get the bike, mum?' demanded Jenna, as Lizzie sank down into the sand next to her youngest daughter's feet.

'Jason made it for me. Apparently, he got bored of being ill, so turned my childhood bike into a flying machine!' she laughed.

'What… he did the power and battery and all that shizzle?' said Jenna impressed.

Lizzie nodded. 'Apparently, he did a course on it, and next year he's going to do another one… something to do with solar power and green energy and… a bunch of stuff that went right over my head! She laughed.

'Wow… just imagine one of those rickshaws with a battery!' said Jenna, dreamily. 'That'd make town tours a whole lot easier!'

'And you could shout about the whole *green* thing all over your new social media pages,' said Megan, sitting forward. 'Though… how green are they?'

'Very… if we leave it to Jason!' laughed Lizzie. 'He's got this idea of installing solar panels on the roof of Moore Bikes and providing solar-powered charging points!'

'Wow,' said Liam, 'that's a great idea! Can you imagine… solar-powered rickshaw trips around Seabury?!'

'And that's what happens when you mix genius

ideas,' she said pointing from one girl to the other, 'with my boys!'

'Your boys?' laughed Liam, flopping into a chair next to Megan.

'Ted and Jason. My boys,' said Lizzie, proudly. 'Seems they teamed up behind my back.'

'You've *so* got your hands full!' laughed Jenna.

'Mum can handle it,' said Megan. 'She's had more than enough practise with us two!'

'Amen!' said Liam, making the three giggle.

'Well... it's been a day of gifts,' said Jenna.

'Ooh, yes!' said Lizzie, turning to Liam. 'Did you get your new van?'

'Yep,' Liam nodded. 'Petula is in da house!'

'Petula?!' sniggered Lizzie.

'I like it!' said Liam.

'That's all that matters,' said Megan, biting her lip, though Lizzie could see her shoulders were shaking, so it rather undid the effect. 'Anyway,' she continued mildly. 'I don't think that's what Jenface was talking about.'

Jenna smiled beatifically and shook her head.

'What's going on?' said Lizzie.

'She's relieved Liam of his old van,' laughed Megan.

'You didn't?!' gasped Lizzie.

'They were going to crush her, mum,' said Jenna looking horrified.

'Erm... for good reason?' said Lizzie, turning to stare at Liam.

'There's plenty of life in the old girl yet,' said Liam with a shrug.

'Exactly,' said Jenna. 'She just needs some TLC.'

'But... I thought that repair at the garage was only temporary,' said Lizzie. 'I thought...'

'I've got plenty of time to do her up... and then she's taking me off on a jolly!' said Jenna excitedly.

'And... you just... *gave* Jenna a van?' said Lizzie, turning to Liam again.

'Nope,' Liam shrugged. 'She paid me exactly what the guy at the garage offered me for the scrap value.'

'I did,' said Jenna with a nod. 'All fifty quid of it!'

Megan let out a snort. 'Told you she'd get one from either Ben or Liam before she was done! Seems this one's a soft-touch!'

'Yeah... you might be right!' said Lizzie, winking at Liam.

Liam grinned at her.

'Thank you,' she mouthed.

Liam just shrugged and Lizzie felt herself melt.

'Urgh... you two!' laughed Megan, 'can you stop being so cute for a minute... I've got a favour to ask?'

'Oh?' said Lizzie, turning to face her.

'I think you mean *uh oh!*' laughed Jenna.

Megan stuck her tongue out at her little sister, making Jenna giggle even harder.

'It's not a big deal... well, maybe not,' said Megan,

suddenly looking a bit nervous.

'What's up, Meggie?' said Lizzie.

'Well… would it be alright if I use the bathroom first in the morning?' she said. 'I've got to get going early.'

'Fine by me!' said Liam, his face dead serious.

Jenna leaned across and slapped him on the leg.

'Oi!' laughed Liam. 'I was just joining in!'

'Works for me, Meggie,' said Jenna with a shrug. 'I'm not working tomorrow, so I'll be slobbing around in my PJs for most of the day anyway.'

'Nice, sis,' said Megan with a smirk.

'Yeah, go for it,' said Lizzie. 'Fine by me too.'

'It'll be mega-early anyway, so I should be out of the way before you want to get ready for work,' said Megan.

'It's fine,' said Lizzie. 'Thanks for asking, though.'

Megan shrugged. 'I just wanted to make sure. I don't want to be late.'

'For what?' said Lizzie with interest.

'I've got an interview tomorrow,' said Megan.

'When?' said Lizzie.

'More importantly - *where?!*' said Jenna looking intrigued.

'Erm… well,' Megan looked nervous again. 'I mean… it's not likely I'll get it… but I'm going up to stay with Amy for a few days.'

'Wait… Amy?' said Liam. 'You mean… *my* Amy?!'

'That's the one,' said Megan. 'We really hit it off

and we've been chatting nearly every day.'

'Seriously?' said Liam, looking delighted.

'Yep!' said Megan.

'So... is the job at the hospital?' said Jenna, looking confused.

'Nope,' said Megan. 'That's definitely not my scene! Amy told me some friends of hers have an interiors business, and they're looking for a new member of the team.'

'Wow Meggie!' said Jenna. 'That sounds amazing.'

'It's perfect for you!' said Lizzie, nodding enthusiastically.

'Don't get too excited,' said Megan 'They might decide I'm not the right person for the job.'

'I don't think they'd dare,' said Liam.

Megan smirked at him. 'Thanks for that vote of confidence! Anyway - it's a really junior role. I'd be going in to learn the ropes - doing a lot of the grunt work and the basics.'

'Best way to start!' said Liam.

'Exactly,' said Megan with a nod. 'If I get the job, I'm basically going to start as an apprentice, and pair it up with a college course to get some qualifications.'

'I hope you get a place!' said Jenna.

'Oh – I've already got that lined up,' said Megan, 'I sent them photos of everything I've been doing at the cottage and they said I can start this term. So now... I just need the job to go with it!'

'Wow!' said Lizzie.

'Seconded!' said Jenna.

'I'll take you to the station in the morning if you'd like?' said Lizzie.

'Thanks, mum - but I've checked with Ben and there's an early bus that'll get me there in plenty of time,' said Megan.

'I'm proud of you, love,' said Lizzie. She instantly kicked herself for letting the words slip out. That had been far too soppy for Megan's comfort - especially given that Liam was there and they were basically sitting in full view of the whole town.

Megan scrambled out of her deckchair and dropped down into the sand in front of Lizzie. 'I'm proud of you too, mum,' she said, throwing her arms around her.

'Wait!' squealed Jenna, 'let me get in there!'

Lizzie felt a thud as Jenna threw herself at them. She peeped over at Liam, only to find him with his phone raised, capturing the moment.

'Get in here, Liam!' came Megan's voice, all muffled by Jenna's sleeve and Lizzie's hair. 'You're part of the family now.'

'Whether you like it or not!' added Jenna.

Lizzie watched as Liam pocketed the phone, a smile of pure joy spreading over his face. Striding towards them, he dropped to his knees and did his best to wrap all three of them up in one great big hug.

'Like it?' he said. 'I like it a lot.'

CHAPTER 13

*L*izzie yawned widely. It had been an exhausting day - a *wonderful* day. Still... she had to admit that she was glad to be heading back up the hill towards the cottage. The shop had been insanely busy, and she'd been so grateful to have both Jason and Ted there to help... even if Ted wasn't meant to be in the shop again until Saturday! He'd turned up for a cup of tea and simply not left again until closing time.

Lizzie grinned to herself as the wind kissed her cheeks and the golden hedgerows blurred into autumn rainbows on either side of her. Thank heavens for Jason's wizardry! She didn't really have the energy to pedal home – but now, with just the click of a button, the battery jumped into action and hauled her up the hill. She could see she was going to get decidedly lazy at this rate!

Lizzie had spent some of the afternoon getting to grips with the new social media pages Megan had set up for her. She was under strict instructions to post at least once a day... so Lizzie had started with a picture of her beautiful, enamelled logo sign, along with a vague hint about the long-awaited Grand Opening. Not that she'd set a date yet... or that she was ever going to. Still... it gave her something to talk about!

Marvelling at just how quickly her new bike had navigated the hill, Lizzie arrived at her cottage in record time. She skidded to a halt and had a good giggle to herself at her less-than-graceful dismount. Yanking off her helmet, she let out another ginormous yawn as she leaned the bike up against the caravan.

It was weird to think it would probably be heading over to Ted and Margie's barn soon. She'd become so used to it sitting there, but if Megan got this job and moved north, she wouldn't need it any longer.

Megan had been decidedly nervous when she'd headed off to catch the early bus that morning, but there was no doubt in Lizzie's mind that her go-getting daughter would be moving onto the next chapter of her life before too long. If this was what she wanted to do, then nothing would stand in her way!

Lizzie glanced at her watch, wondering how the

interview had gone. The company had arranged it as late in the day as possible to fit in around Megan's travel... but surely it must have finished by now!

A rumbling from the lane made Lizzie turn, only to spot a knackered white van heading in her direction. It wasn't Liam in the driving seat though - Jenna was waving at her excitedly from behind the wheel. Liam was next to her in the passenger seat, looking bemused.

Jenna pulled the van neatly in behind the caravan and killed the engine.

'Hey mum!' she said, hopping down and bouncing on the balls of her feet, looking like an excited six-year-old.

'So... this is your new van, eh?' said Lizzie, smiling at Liam as he climbed down.

'I'm already regretting selling her!' sighed Liam. 'Petula's not quite broken in yet!'

'As soon as you've scuffed her up a bit and rearranged the back just the way you like it, she'll be perfect,' said Jenna, patting him on the shoulder as she came to stand next to her. 'Anyway - no backsies!'

'Wouldn't dream of it!' laughed Liam, holding up his hands in surrender.

'Mum - is it okay if we do some work on her out here on the drive?' said Jenna. 'I'm not going to be in your way, am I?'

'Go for it!' said Lizzie, shaking her head. 'I'm done for the day – I'm not going anywhere.'

'Cool, thanks,' said Jenna, heading around the back of the van and disappearing inside.

'Are you staying for a bit?' said Lizzie as Liam wrapped his arms around her and pulled her close.

'As long as you'll have me,' said Liam.

'Oi - no commandeering my helpmate!' said Jenna, reappearing with a toolbox.

Lizzie grinned and relinquished her hold on Liam.

'I'll get the kettle on, shall I,' she said

'Yay!' said Jenna.

'Perfect!' said Liam, giving Lizzie a kiss on the forehead and then letting her go somewhat reluctantly.

'Right Liam, get the jacks!' said Jenna.

Lizzie headed for the front door with a broad smile on her face. It looked like her easy-going daughter could be just as bossy as her eldest when there was a van awaiting some TLC!

Letting herself into the cottage, Lizzie drifted through to the kitchen, feeling like she was gliding around on a little cloud of happiness. Somehow, everything felt right with the world.

Flicking the kettle on, Lizzie went to stand at the window and watched Liam and Jenna laughing together as they busied themselves around the van.

The sound of the landline springing to life in the living room made her jump, and Lizzie dashed through to answer it.

'Hello?' she said, grabbing the phone, even as she ran an appreciative palm over the glossy dado rail that had appeared from thin air. Megan had done wonders in here and she felt like she'd wandered into a dream every time she stepped inside.

'Mum! It's me!' squeaked Megan.

'Hey love!' said Lizzie in surprise.

'You didn't answer your mobile!' said Megan.

'Sorry... I only just got home. It's still out on the bike,' she said, realising she'd left it in the little zipped compartment at the bottom of the brand-new basket.

'I got it. I got it mum!' said Megan. 'I've been with them all afternoon. They want me to start as soon as possible.'

'Oh Meggie,' breathed Lizzie, beaming. Could this day get any better? 'Congratulations love, I'm so happy for you.'

'Me too!' laughed Megan. 'I'm so excited. I called the college and they said if I can get up here by next week, I won't even miss enrolment!'

'But... where will you live?' said Lizzie. 'What about your flat in Bristol... and..?'

'You worry too much,' said Megan, though Lizzie could hear the smile in her daughter's voice. 'Owen can deal with the flat. I'll just stop paying my half and he'll just have to sort it out.'

'Least he deserves,' muttered Lizzie.

'Yup!' laughed Megan.

'I can't really imagine you in student halls, though,' said Lizzie.

'Halls? Come on mother,' she laughed. 'This is me we're talking about. I'm moving in with Amy!'

'You are?' said Lizzie.

'Her house is huge and we get on like we've known each other forever,' said Megan. 'And anyway... she's practically family!'

Lizzie suddenly had to swallow down a huge lump of emotion. She hadn't known Liam long... not in the grand scheme of things, anyway... but that was exactly the way she felt too. Liam was already family.

'I'm so happy for you, Meggie!' said Lizzie. 'It sounds perfect.'

'Nothing's perfect,' said Megan softly. 'But today... this feels pretty damn close to it.'

'Amen to that!' said Lizzie.

'Gotta go, mum,' said Megan. 'We're all going out for a drink to celebrate.'

'We'll be raising our cups of tea to you, Meggie!' said Lizzie

'Thanks mum,' said Megan. 'For everything.'

And then, she was gone, leaving Lizzie cuddling the receiver to her chest and staring around the beautiful space her daughter had created just for her.

'You too, Meggie love,' she whispered. 'You too.'

Lizzie had only just made it back to the kettle when the sound of the phone ringing again had her jogging back through to the living room.

'What did you forget?' she panted, figuring that it'd be Megan with a detail or two she'd forgotten to share.

'Oh good, you're home!'

That wasn't Megan!

'Erm... yes?' said Lizzie, desperately trying to place the familiar voice. 'Who's this?'

'Margie. Margie Hatherleigh!' came the curt reply. 'I wanted a private word with you... about my husband and that shop of yours!'

Lizzie swallowed.

Uh oh!

Was Liam's prediction that she was "in for it" about to come true?

'Are you still there?' said Margie.

'Oh – yes!' said Lizzie. 'Sorry. And... sorry I kept Ted for so long today. I had no idea–'

'Stop that this instant!' said Margie.

Lizzie shut her mouth in surprise.

'Please,' said Margie, her voice softening. 'I'm calling to say thank you.'

'You... you are?' said Lizzie.

'Yes, you ninny!' laughed Margie. 'Thank you for getting him out from under my feet.'

She paused, but Lizzie didn't dare say anything.

'Thank you for giving me my husband back,' Margie continued, and Lizzie could swear she sounded almost tearful. 'I've not seen Ted this happy in... well... a very long time. Working with you has brought him back to life. He brought me flowers home tonight. Flowers! For me! And he's taking me out to Pebble Street for a meal after he's finished work next week too!'

'That's… brilliant?' said Lizzie, as a huge smile spread over her face.

'You're blummin' right, it's brilliant!' said Margie. 'Anyway – like I say – credit where credit's due. You've done a good thing.'

'Erm – Ted's the one doing me a favour, working in the shop,' said Lizzie. 'He's amazing… there's nothing he doesn't know about bikes.'

'Don't I know it!' laughed Margie. 'A word to the wise though? Don't go puffing smoke up his behind too often… he'll get too big for his britches otherwise!'

'Noted,' laughed Lizzie.

'Oh… and do me a favour?' said Margie.

'Anything,' said Lizzie.

'Don't let him have too many sticky buns!'

Lizzie was still chuckling as she replaced the receiver and headed back to the kitchen. Gathering three mugs together to make the tea at long last, Lizzie peeped out at the van again. Jenna now had her head deep under the bonnet, and it looked very much like Liam had been given the job of handing her the right tool whenever she snapped her fingers. Lizzie grinned. Maybe it was time to go and rescue him?!

'I've got news,' she called to both of them as she navigated the front path, doing her best not to spill the tea or drop the biscuits she was carrying as she went.

'Oh yeah?' came Jenna's muffled voice from somewhere near the engine.

'Good news?' said Liam, taking his mug gratefully and blowing on the tea.

'The best!' said Lizzie. 'Megan got the job!'

'Amazing,' said Liam.

'No surprises there,' said Jenna. 'What Megan wants, Megan goes and gets... as long as she forgets to be a colossal asshat while she's at it!'

Liam spluttered on the mouthful of tea he'd just taken and Jenna straightened up and grinned at him.

'I apologise for my daughter!' sighed Lizzie.

'Why?' said Jenna. 'She's miles away.'

'Not *that* daughter!' added Lizzie, winking at Jenna.

'So... where's Megan going to live?' said Liam.

'With Amy,' said Lizzie.

'Oh my goodness,' said Liam. 'Those two living together? They'll take over the world by Christmas.'

'So,' said Lizzie, leaning in and peering at the engine, 'what's the verdict.'

'She's going to be as sweet as a nut when she's had some work,' said Jenna.

Lizzie turned to Liam for confirmation, but he just shrugged. 'Don't ask me,' he laughed. 'This one takes after you, I think. She just fixed something I didn't even know was wrong in about three seconds flat.'

'I just need to do a bit of welding underneath,' said Jenna distractedly. 'The garage who patched her up have done a decent enough job, but I want to strengthen up the arches and deal with a bit of the rust before we set off!'

Lizzie stared at Jenna with her mouth wide open.

'You know how to do all that?' she said.

'Of course!' laughed Jenna. 'I'm not completely useless mum - not like dad! Like Liam said - I take after you. Anyway, how do you think I managed to keep the last one going for so long?!'

Liam raised his eyebrows and Lizzie grinned at him. Jenna was happy that she took after *her?* A warm blush of happiness kicked off in Lizzie's chest and it was as much as she could do to stop herself from wrapping her arms around her daughter.

'Anyway, I've already asked Ben,' said Jenna, completely oblivious to the effect her words had just had. 'He knows someone who's got the kit I need to borrow… so I should have her all fixed up before you know it.'

'And then… back to Morocco?' said Lizzie, surprised to feel a pang of sadness that both her daughters would be heading back to their own lives before too long. She'd got used to them being around - and she'd miss their company.

'Maybe not Morocco again,' said Jenna, 'I think I'd like to be able to pop back a bit more often. Someone needs to keep an eye on you two… and I've got friends in Europe I haven't had the chance to visit for ages.'

'Sounds like a plan,' said Liam.

'Oh no!' said Jenna. 'I don't do plans. I do dreams.'

'Something else she gets from you!' said Liam quietly, as they watched Jenna dive back under the bonnet.

CHAPTER 14

'Are you nervous?' demanded Jenna as soon as Lizzie reached the bottom of the stairs.

'No!' said Lizzie, her voice shaking slightly. 'Why would I be nervous?'

'Oh… you know,' said Jenna, shifting the box of cooking implements onto her hip and looking her over from head to toe. 'Official first date at long last…?'

'Oh hush!' said Lizzie, starting to feel decidedly breathless.

'I mean… Liam might make a grand gesture or something!' said Jenna, her eyes wide and serious before a slight twitch at the corner of her mouth gave away the fact that she was pulling Lizzie's leg.

'Well,' said Lizzie, 'that's one thing I know I'm completely safe from. We agreed ages ago that we don't do grand gestures. We're going to just be us and see what happens.'

'Uh huh?' said Jenna, raising her eyebrows sceptically. 'Is that why you're currently wearing a little black dress I've never seen before? And… is that… mascara?!'

'Oh hush, you,' said Lizzie, fanning her face. 'But seriously… do I look okay? Too much? Maybe it's too much… maybe I should go and change!'

'Oh no you don't,' said Jenna, promptly plonking the cardboard box on the floor and grabbing Lizzie's hands before she could make a break for it. 'You look absolutely gorgeous. And I was just teasing.'

'Oh,' said Lizzie.

'Breathe, mum,' laughed Jenna.

'Right. Breathe…' said Lizzie, doing her best to take her daughter's advice.

'Seriously - it's just Liam,' said Jenna.

'Just Liam?' squeaked Lizzie, feeling more than a bit ridiculous.

'You know I didn't mean it like that. I mean… you *know* him. He's lovely… and chilled. And you're going to have a lovely time!'

'He's not even told me where we're going!' said Lizzie.

'Breathe woman!' laughed Jenna. 'I expect you're going to Pebble Street. With your 'no grand gesture' rule, I can't imagine he's about to whisk you away in a private jet or anything.'

'Right,' said Lizzie, nodding and trying to pull herself together. 'You're right.'

'Though… if he did happen to have something a bit more exotic up his sleeve, you definitely look the part!' said Jenna, looking her up and down.

'I just fancied a night off the dungarees,' said Lizzie, starting to feel self-conscious.

'But not the boots?' laughed Jenna, checking out her clumpy black boots, complete with their yellow laces.

'They're my comfort blanket,' said Lizzie.

'They look hot!' said Jenna, approvingly. 'Where did you get the dress?'

'Megan lent it to me before she moved,' said Lizzie, freeing herself from Jenna and peering into the box. 'Hey - isn't that my cheese grater?'

'Erm… yeah… I was going to ask you if I can nab it? Mine's still in the back of the van… in Morocco!' she said. 'And it's not like I can replace it before tomorrow morning.'

'I can't believe you're leaving tomorrow!' said Lizzie straightening up.

'I know - it's come around so fast,' said Jenna.

'Maybe I should cancel tonight… so we can spend it together? I feel awful abandoning you for a date!' said Lizzie.

'Don't even think about it!' said Jenna with a stern frown. 'You, me and Meggie had our last "girl's night" before we got all her stuff moved up to Amy's last week!'

'But…!' said Lizzie.

'No buts, mum,' said Jenna. 'You'd break his heart if you cancelled now.'

'I know, but…'

'Too late!' said Jenna. 'That's him now!'

'Oh no… oh no…!' gasped Lizzie.

'In the words of Meggie… *Mother, you're being ridiculous!*' laughed Jenna, turning to answer the front door after just one knock.

'Hey Liam!' said Jenna. 'Looking handsome!'

'Erm… thanks Jenna?!' laughed Liam, looking rather surprised to find them both loitering in the tiny hallway.

Jenna shuffled back out of the way, and then when Lizzie made no move to greet Liam or even take a step towards him, she pushed her forward.

'Honestly,' chuckled Jenna.

'Wow!' said Liam, his eyes going wide. 'I mean… wow!'

'Thanks?' said Lizzie shyly. 'I think?'

'Definitely!' said Liam. 'You look… absolutely beautiful!'

'Awwwww!' sighed Jenna, earning herself a glare from Lizzie. 'What?! He's right!' she laughed.

'Shall we go?' said Liam. The moment he reached out to take her hand, Lizzie felt all the awkward shyness melt away.

'Yeah. Let's go!' she said, lacing her fingers through his.

'You crazy cats have fun!' called Jenna, standing in the doorway and watching as they made their way towards Liam's van.

'Hey!' said Lizzie, raising her eyebrows. 'Why are you hooked up to the caravan?'

'Awkward!' came Jenna's voice from behind them.

'I thought we could drop it over to the Hatherleigh's... before our date,' he said, ruffling his hair. 'I didn't expect... I mean... your dress... I...'

'It's fine,' Lizzie laughed. 'No grand gestures, remember? Good idea!'

'Cool,' said Liam, visibly relaxing. 'Here!'

Liam opened the passenger door and held it for her while Lizzie clambered up.

'Wait, wait!' yelled Jenna just as Liam was about to close the door.

'What?' called Lizzie.

'Can I have that grater or what?'

'Take the grater, Jenna!' laughed Liam.

Jenna gave him a salute and then blew them both a kiss.

Lizzie let out a long sigh as she relaxed into the seat and waited for Liam to climb behind the wheel. Everything was fine... this was just her and Liam off on an adventure... and the fact that she was wearing a little black dress didn't change anything!

'Are you okay?' he said, turning to her once he'd strapped himself in.

'Yep!' said Lizzie. 'I mean... why wouldn't I be?'

'No reason,' said Liam lightly. 'Just with Jenna off again in the morning and Megan all moved out last week-'

'Thanks again for that,' said Lizzie quickly, as they began to make their way along the lane towards the turning that would take them up onto the main road.

'It's no problem,' said Liam with a laugh. 'Like I said - it was a great excuse to visit Amy again.'

'Yeah... and with both you and Jenna helping, it meant she got it done in one go,' said Lizzie.

'We made quite a good convoy!' laughed Liam. 'Plus, it meant that Megan had decent backup when it came to facing that boiled potato of an ex-boyfriend!'

'Boiled potato?!' hooted Lizzie.

'Sorry,' said Liam quickly. 'That's unfair to potatoes.'

'I'm glad he's out of the picture,' sighed Lizzie.

'He was definitely lacking in the personality department,' said Liam.

'And the kindness department too,' said Lizzie with a frown.

'Yeah well - I wouldn't worry about our Megan anymore,' said Liam. 'She's left her old life in her dust!'

He indicated and pulled out carefully onto the

main road, glancing in his rear-view mirror to check the little caravan was still following behind.

Lizzie nodded – though she doubted that she'd ever stop worrying about her girls. She'd not heard much from her eldest since she'd moved into Amy's massive house, but Megan had sent her and Jenna a couple of photos of her new room - already freshly painted - along with its very own ensuite!

'Well, at least Amy's house is a step up from the caravan,' said Lizzie.

'I think she was quite sad to say goodbye,' said Liam with a shrug.

'That makes two of us,' said Lizzie with a long sigh. 'But... now maybe you and I can spend a bit more time together at last... without the added bossy gooseberries!'

'I've enjoyed being ordered around by both of them if I'm honest,' said Liam with a grin. 'You'll have to take over!'

'Not really my style,' said Lizzie.

'I'll remind you of that when I'm trying to reverse this blasted caravan into Ted's barn,' laughed Liam.

'Don't worry about that,' said Lizzie. 'I'm sure Ted'll do it for you.'

'Nah,' said Liam, shaking his head. 'He's taken Margie out this evening.'

'Out?!' said Lizzie in surprise.

'A party, apparently,' said Liam, glancing in his mirror again.

'Blimey - those two have a better social life than me!' said Lizzie.

'Snap,' said Liam.

Lizzie glanced at him. For some reason, he seemed to be uncomfortable again. She quickly cast around for a random topic – just to keep the conversation going.

'I thought there was still a problem with Ted's driveway?' she said. 'Ted told me he'd been stalling because he couldn't face having to fill all the holes by hand.'

'Margie got bored of waiting,' said Liam. 'She paid me, Jenna and Ben to do the job yesterday behind Ted's back.'

'Oh, he's going to be thrilled!' said Lizzie.

'Yeah,' sighed Liam, 'but now it means I've got to get this blighter down there in one piece! Maybe I should have left it for another day. I don't think there's room to swing it around at the far end without ruining Ted's lawn... so I'm going to have to reverse it in all the way from the road.'

He paused, looking mildly sick at the idea.

Was that all Liam was worried about?!

'Don't worry,' said Lizzie, quickly taking pity on him. 'I can reverse it in if you can't face it?'

'Well... that *was* my sneaky plan but... you're wearing a dress?' said Liam. 'I wouldn't have agreed to do it this evening if I'd have known!'

'Relax!' laughed Lizzie. 'It's just a dress… it's still me underneath!'

Liam shot her a grin, and Lizzie thought she caught the hint of a blush flushing his tanned cheeks.

'Huh,' he said, 'there I was thinking it was your dungarees that gave you superpowers.'

'Nah,' said Lizzie. 'Always the boots!'

'Bingo!' said Lizzie with a triumphant grin as she guided the caravan easily past the doorway and into the newly tidy barn. Parking up, she quickly hopped down and headed around to help Liam unhook it from the van.

'Are we all good?' she said, peering around the caravan to make sure she hadn't managed to sandwich the door right up against one of the walls.

'You nailed it!' laughed Liam. 'No - don't worry, I've got this,' he added quickly, ushering her away from the tow hook, clearly keen to stop her from getting covered in grease.

'Ta!' she laughed, feeling a bit awkward as she stepped back and waited until he was done.

'Right… there's one more thing I need to do before we head off again,' said Liam, wiping his hands absently on his clean jeans and leaving two dark streaks along his thighs. 'Damn it!' he laughed, following her gaze. 'I tried!'

'I know!' chuckled Lizzie. 'Anyway, what is it you need to do?'

Liam took two swift steps towards her.

'Hi!' she said.

'Hi!'

Liam wrapped one strong arm around her waist. Then he took her chin between his thumb and forefinger and tilted her head gently so that he could kiss her.

Lizzie let out a happy sigh against Liam's lips as she stood on tiptoe and leaned into him... not something that was easy to do while wearing a pair of boots... but still, she managed it.

'Ready for our date?' breathed Liam.

'Depends?' said Lizzie, holding his gaze and briefly considering wrestling him right into the little caravan. After all, hadn't he said Ted and Margie were out for the night?!

'On what,' said Liam.

'Whether you've got any ridiculous grand gestures up those suspiciously clean sleeves?' she said.

'Sorry to disappoint,' said Liam with a smile, 'but we're just going to Pebble Street... and I thought we might have a quick return trip to our favourite lamppost afterwards?'

'Now that sounds just about perfect!' said Lizzie.

'There's no rush though,' said Liam, casting a

mischievous look over his shoulder at the caravan and then wiggling his eyebrows at her.

'You're bad!' she said, wondering if he was also a bit of a mind reader.

'I'd be totally up for it-' he said, pausing to drop a kiss on the end of her nose, 'but Margie told me they'd had new cameras installed!'

Liam spun her around and pointed up at a tiny lens set in the corner.

'Thank goodness she told you!' laughed Lizzie. 'That could have been a double-coronary in the making… and now that I've got him, there's no way I can do without Wonder Ted at Moore Bikes!'

'Still… let's give Margie something to gossip about!' said Liam, planting a huge kiss on her cheek before they both waved and blew kisses at the little camera.

CHAPTER 15

'I'm going to head this way into town,' said Liam, taking the narrow turning that led down the hill towards the old ice cream shop.

'Oh,' said Lizzie. 'Okay!'

'We can park up outside New York Froth and wander along to Pebble Street,' said Liam.

'O-kay?' said Lizzie, narrowing her eyes at him.

She wouldn't have thought anything of it, but there was something about the way he'd just mentioned it - *oh so casually* - that made her immediately suspicious that he was up to something.

'What?' said Liam. 'I don't want to run into the traffic warden!'

'You and that traffic warden!' laughed Lizzie, instantly relaxing.

Liam had absolutely no side to him. In fact, she doubted that he had it in him to keep a secret for five minutes, let alone have some kind of plan up his sleeve.

'I swear he's got it in for me,' muttered Liam.

'Why?' laughed Lizzie.

'Because... he's always... there!' said Liam.

Lizzie shook her head. 'I think I've seen him once. Maximum,' she laughed. 'There's way more ticketing to be done over in Dunscombe Sands. I don't think he really cares about Seabury much.'

'Hm... maybe he just follows me around, then,' said Liam, pulling into one of the parking spots and killing the engine. 'Wait right there!' he said, hopping down.

Lizzie sat in the deafening silence, wondering what on earth was going on. The next thing she knew, Liam opened her door and offered her a hand down.

'Wow, thank you,' said Lizzie. 'If I'd have known wearing a dress could cause such chivalry, I'd have tried it years ago!'

Liam grinned and pulled her towards him, kissing her lightly. Lizzie felt her knees wobble. Blimey, at this rate, she'd only manage the first course before begging Liam to accompany her back to the cottage. Jenna would just have to deal with it!

'Dinner,' said Liam, his voice slightly husky as he pulled away from her.

'Right!' said Lizzie. 'Let's go.'

Liam tucked her hand into the crook of his arm

and they drifted along the pavement towards the hotel. Lizzie stared out at the sea, gentle under its blanket of low evening cloud. She shivered slightly as the promise of many wonderful days to come washed over her.

'Are you cold?' said Liam.

Lizzie shook her head. 'Nope. Just happy.'

'Me too,' said Liam, wrapping his arm around her shoulders as she snuggled into him.

They walked in silence, each of them grinning from ear to ear until they were standing in front of The Pebble Street Hotel. Lizzie's stomach promptly gave a loud grumble and she clapped a hand to her belly in horror.

'I heard that,' chuckled Liam.

'Yeah well… a girl's gotta eat!' she laughed.

'Let's do it!' said Liam, taking her hand and leading her inside the sparkling warmth of the reception.

'Oh!' said Lizzie as they came face to face with a girl she didn't recognise. 'Hi! Is Lou not on tonight?'

The girl shook her head. 'I'm Sandy,' she said. 'Lou's off. You must be Lizzie… and Liam?'

Liam frowned and nodded.

'How'd you know that?' said Lizzie, desperately hoping she hadn't met this person before and simply forgotten her.

'Because you're the only people left to arrive for the evening!' laughed Sandy.

'Oh,' said Liam. 'Fair enough. Is Lionel around?'

'No, he's... erm... out,' said Sandy, shaking her head. 'Now, I'm afraid there's a bit of an issue with your booking this evening.'

'Why?' said Lizzie.

She felt all shivery again, but she wasn't quite sure why. It wasn't the same rush of overwhelming happiness that had overtaken her outside. This was more like... there was something out of place... and it bothered her.

'I'm afraid we've had to close the dining room this evening,' said Sandy.

Lizzie watched her closely, but her pretty face was completely calm.

'Right,' said Liam, 'so are we in the breakfast room instead?'

It wasn't unheard of for Lionel and Hattie to use the smaller, more intimate room when they didn't have many bookings. It meant their dinner guests didn't feel like they were rattling around in the cavernous dining room.

'No,' said Sandy, 'no... I've got special instructions for you both.'

'You have?' said Lizzie, the back of her neck prickling. 'Who from?'

'Lionel,' said the girl. 'He asked me to give you this.'

She handed a key over to Liam and he glanced at it.

'Room twenty-two?' he said.

'That's right. Second floor,' said Sandy. 'Why don't you head on up.'

'To a room? I *knew* you had something up your sleeve!' said Lizzie, turning wide-eyed to Liam and batting him playfully on the arm.

'Not me,' said Liam, shaking his head. 'Seriously!' he added when she narrowed her eyes at him.

'I believe Lionel left a note for you up there explaining everything,' said Sandy.

'I'm game if you are?' said Lizzie with a shrug.

'Fine by me,' said Liam. 'As long as there's food involved.'

Sandy nodded.

'Okay... let's go!' said Lizzie. 'Actually, hold that thought!'

Lizzie abruptly changed course and instead of heading for the staircase, she made her way at speed along the hallway towards the dining room. Pausing briefly at the closed door, she took a deep breath before grabbing the handle and flinging it open.

'Oh!' she said in surprise.

The large room was full of shadowy gloom. The lights were off, and the tables all wore fresh, snowy linens, ready for a service that clearly wasn't going to be happening that night.

'What was that about?' chuckled Liam, as he peered over her shoulder.

Lizzie shook her head and rolled her eyes at

herself. 'Nothing,' she sighed. 'Just me being paranoid. For a moment... I don't know... I thought you might be in on some kind of surprise setup or something!'

'Nope!' laughed Liam. 'No surprises in there! So... shall we go upstairs and see what's going on with this whole room thing?'

'Why not?' said Lizzie, shooting him a grin.

Liam grabbed her hand and, leading her back past a slightly bemused-looking Sandy, they took the wide staircase at a bit of a jog.

'Thank heavens I'm not wearing heels!' puffed Lizzie.

'You're telling me!' said Liam. 'I'd have to carry you.'

'Imagine!' chuckled Lizzie as they rounded the tight bend and took the second flight slightly slower. She still had Liam's hand clasped tightly in one of hers, and she trailed the other along the silky-smooth wood of the bannister as they went. 'This place is so beautiful.'

'Yeah,' said Liam. 'Lionel and Hattie have done a gorgeous job with it.'

'Here we are,' she puffed. 'Second floor... room...'

'This one!' said Liam, coming to a halt. 'Shall we?'

Lizzie nodded. Grabbing the key from him, she opened the door to a flood of golden light.

'Wow!' she gasped. 'It's a suite!'

'Blimey!' said Liam, staring around in surprise. 'I

had no idea there was anything *this* grand at Pebble Street!

Lizzie wandered into the smart sitting room and gazed around. There were two soft velvet sofas facing each other across a lovely little coffee table. Beyond that, there was a floor-to-ceiling window with a view out over The King's Nose and the sea. Directly in front of the window stood a linen-clad dining table, perfectly set for two. At its centre was a single red rose along with an ice bucket containing a bottle of champagne.

'Look!' said Liam, grabbing her hand and tugging her through a doorway into a bedroom with a four-poster canopied bed.

'Wow!' gasped Lizzie.

'There's a note - it's got your name on it!' said Liam, grabbing a heavy cream envelope from one of the pillows and passing it to her.

Lizzie frowned as she took it and tore into the envelope.

Dearest mum,

This is a gift from both of us. Thank you for everything you've done for us. Not just on this visit - but always. You're the best. We're both so proud of you for chasing your dreams - and encouraging both of us to do the same.

Go grab that life, mum - you deserve it.

And Liam - we know you're there too. We've agreed that you're pretty okay. Be nice to our mum, or you'll have to answer to us.

Enjoy the suite. It's from both of us - a thank you for letting us crash the cottage for so long and getting in the way of all that nookie!

We love you.

Megan and Jenna

X

P.S We left this on the bed because we figured that'd be your first stop ;)

P.P.S Jenna wrote the P.S! (Meggie x)

'My classy daughters!' laughed Lizzie, handing the card to Liam, who scanned the words and barked out a surprised laugh.

'Wow,' he said, still chuckling.

'No... this is *wow* - check it out!' said Lizzie, who'd just pushed open yet another door only to discover a stunning ensuite bathroom, complete with a claw-footed bathtub.

'We've got it for the whole night?' said Liam, wide-eyed as he peered over her shoulder.

'Yep!' said Lizzie, turning to him with a grin.

'So... do you fancy ordering room service?' he said. 'Or maybe we could have a glass of that bubbly before...?'

'Before what?' said Lizzie, wiggling her eyebrows.

'Before we get you out of those boots?' chuckled Liam.

'What's the time?!' said Liam, leaning back in his chair at the dining table and stretching his arms over his head.

Lizzie watched him lazily, admiring the expanse of bronzed skin that came into view as the fluffy towelling robe he was wearing parted slightly.

'Why?' she said, slowly. 'You in a rush or something?'

Liam shook his head, grinning at her.

Lizzie let out a long, happy sigh. She was warm, cosy and full of amazing food. This was such an amazing surprise from the girls, and both of them had agreed that - even if they weren't "grand gesture" kind of people - the girls deserved some kind of prize for this one!

'Not in a rush,' said Liam, yawning widely, 'but I'd love to go for a wander along the seafront... if you're up for it?'

'Only if I can go in my towelling robe?' she said.

'I think we'd probably have to get dressed first,' he laughed. 'Just imagine bumping into Charlie and Ethel!'

'You do have a point,' smirked Lizzie. 'Do you *really* want to go out?'

Liam nodded. 'I kinda want to visit our lamppost... like on our first non-date!'

'You old softy!' said Lizzie with a smile. 'Okay - I'm game... if you don't mind zipping me back up?'

'Deal,' said Liam, getting to his feet. 'You know... I think Hattie's food just keeps getting better,' he said, eyeballing his empty dessert bowl that had held the mythical Pebble Street pudding just ten minutes before.

'The woman's a genius!' agreed Lizzie. 'C'mon... let's go visit our lamppost!'

∼

The air outside had grown cold. The evening had that inky quality about it - not quite dark, but the shadows had deepened and the lights seemed brighter as Lizzie and Liam strode, hand in hand, along the seafront. Neither of them said a thing, but there didn't seem to be any need for words right now.

Lizzie was so happy, she felt like she might float away... if it wasn't for the three-course meal she'd just inhaled!

Liam glanced at his watch briefly.

'Here we are!' she laughed as he nearly shot right past their lamppost.

'Sorry,' he said, coming to a halt. 'I was miles away.'

'Oh,' said Lizzie, suddenly feeling a bit deflated. 'Oh...'

'Not like that!' he laughed. 'And that was an exaggeration. I wasn't *miles* away... not even a single mile, in fact!'

'Okay... you've lost me,' said Lizzie smiling up at him. She was feeling a bit hazy around the edges – that bottle of bubbly had a lot to answer for!

'Here,' said Liam. 'Let me show you.'

Liam took Lizzie's hands and drew her towards him. After placing a long, slow kiss on her lips, he turned her gently on the spot and pointed in the direction of Moore Bikes.

'What am I looking at... oh!' she said. 'Lights... and loads of people?' Lizzie suddenly became aware that her heart was hammering. 'What's... what... I'm confused!' she laughed.

'Ready for a party?' said Liam, his eyes glittering with mischief as she turned back towards him.

'Party?' she said.

'Your party,' said Liam. 'Or should I say... your Grand Opening!'

'You didn't!' gasped Lizzie.

'Not me!' said Liam. 'Okay... maybe a little bit. But mostly the girls... and Wonder Ted... and Jason... and Charlie... and Ethel... and Lionel... and...'

'The whole of Seabury, then?' said Lizzie.

'Pretty much,' said Liam with a shrug.

'Thank goodness you didn't let me come for a walk in my robe!' laughed Lizzie. 'Is my hair okay?'

'Lizzie,' said Liam, leaning down and kissing her again, 'you're perfect.'

Lizzie clung to him for a long moment, trying to take it all in.

'Ready?' said Liam.

Lizzie didn't answer – she simply laced her fingers through his and let him lead her towards Moore Bikes.

'Here she comes!' cried Ted the minute they were spotted striding along the seafront.

'Who's got the scissors?'

'Lionel!'

'Not me!' said Lionel. 'Megan had them last.'

'I gave them to Jason,' came Megan's shout from the back of the crowd.

'I haven't got them, ask Amy!' said Jason, who was standing next to Sarah.

'Here they are,' said Kate, moving to the front of the crowd. 'Is the photographer here?'

'Ready!' cried a guy from behind an impressive-looking camera.

'Oh my goodness!' laughed Lizzie, squeezing Liam's hand. 'Look, there's a ribbon!'

'And Megan… and Amy!' laughed Liam, waving back at the visitors.

'Here!' said Kate, handing Lizzie the scissors. 'You're going to need these!'

'Wait – presents first!' said Jenna, moving to the front of the crowd. 'No… not for you!' she laughed as Stanley greeted her, his tail wagging frantically as he eyeballed the three parcels in her arms. Kate quickly tempted the furry roadblock out of the way with half a Rich Tea biscuit from her pocket.

'Here's yours, mum,' said Jenna. 'And Jason? This one's for you… and Ted?'

Lizzie beckoned for her boys to join her, and the three of them lined up in front of the ribbon that was stretched across the doorway of Moore Bikes.

'Open them, then!' called Ethel, who was standing with Charlie and a huge group of people from the allotments.

Lizzie untied the denim bow and then peeled back layers of tissue paper to reveal a brand-new pair of slate-grey dungarees. Shaking them out, she started to laugh as she spotted the word "Boss" embroidered across the back.

Turning to watch Jason and Ted open their identical parcels, she grinned as they unwrapped two pairs of overalls. Jason's bore his name and their logo.

'Let's see yours!' she said to Ted, whose shoulders were shaking with laughter.

He dutifully turned them around to reveal the words "Wonder Ted" stitched across the back.

'Brilliant!' chuckled Jason.

'Wonder Ted… I'll second that!' called Margie

from the middle of the crowd, earning herself a titter of appreciation.

'Open the shop already, Mother!' yelled Megan.

'Cut, cut, cut!' agreed the crowd.

Lizzie grinned at them and handed her dungarees to Jason.

'Ready?' she yelled.

'For weeks!' came the reply from Ethel's direction.

'Okay!' said Lizzie. 'Moore Bikes is now… officially open!'

Lizzie snipped and the ends of the ribbon fluttered away from the doors in what felt like slow motion. The crowd cheered and applauded and the photographer took shot after shot of their happy faces.

Lizzie swallowed hard, beaming around her - at her community - the town she'd always loved – all out in force to help her mark her dream coming true.

As Liam wrapped her in a hug, only to be joined by Megan, Jenna, Amy, Ted, Jason and then everyone else in the biggest group-hug Seabury had probably ever seen - Lizzie knew one thing for sure - she really was living the dream.

THE END

ALSO BY BETH RAIN

Standalone Books:

How to be Angry at Christmas

Little Bamton Series:

Little Bamton: The Complete Series Collection: Books 1 - 5

Individual titles:

Christmas Lights and Snowball Fights (Little Bamton Book 1)

Spring Flowers and April Showers (Little Bamton Book 2)

Summer Nights and Pillow Fights (Little Bamton Book 3)

Autumn Cuddles and Muddy Puddles (Little Bamton Book 4)

Christmas Flings and Wedding Rings (Little Bamton Book 5)

Upper Bamton Series:

Upper Bamton: The Complete Series Collection: Books 1 - 4

Upper Bamton Series:

A New Arrival in Upper Bamton (Upper Bamton Book 1)

Rainy Days in Upper Bamton (Upper Bamton Book 2)

Hidden Treasures in Upper Bamton (Upper Bamton

Book 3)

Time Flies By in Upper Bamton (Upper Bamton Book 4)

Crumcarey Island Series:

Christmas on Crumcarey (Crumcarey Island Book 1)

All Change on Crumcarey (Crumcarey Island Book 2)

Making Waves on Crumcarey (Crumcarey Island Book 3)

Fool's Gold on Crumcarey (Crumcarey Island Book 4)

Seabury Series:

Welcome to Seabury (Seabury Book 1)

Trouble in Seabury (Seabury Book 2)

Christmas in Seabury (Seabury Book 3)

Sandwiches in Seabury (Seabury Book 4)

Secrets in Seabury (Seabury Book 5)

Surprises in Seabury (Seabury Book 6)

Dreams and Ice Creams in Seabury (Seabury Book 7)

Mistakes and Heartbreaks in Seabury (Seabury Book 8)

Laughter and Happy Ever After in Seabury (Seabury Book 9)

A Quiet Life in Seabury (Seabury Book 10)

In A Spin in Seabury (Seabury Book 11)

Living The Dream in Seabury (Seabury Book 12)

Seabury Series Collections:

Kate's Story: Books 1 - 3

Hattie's Story: Books 4 - 6

Standalones: Books 7 - 9

Writing as Bea Fox:

What's a Girl To Do? The Complete Series

Individual titles:

The Holiday: What's a Girl To Do? (Book 1)

The Wedding: What's a Girl To Do? (Book 2)

The Lookalike: What's a Girl To Do? (Book 3)

The Reunion: What's a Girl To Do? (Book 4)

At Christmas: What's a Girl To Do? (Book 5)

ABOUT THE AUTHOR

Beth Rain has always wanted to be a writer and has been penning adventures for characters ever since she learned to stare into the middle-distance and daydream.

She has recently moved to a windswept, Scottish island, and it is a dream come true to spend her days hanging out with Bob – her trusty laptop – scoffing crisps and chocolate while dreaming up swoony love stories for all her imaginary friends.

Beth's writing will always deliver on the happy-ever-afters, so if you need cosy… you're in safe hands!

Visit www.bethrain.com for all the bookish goodness and keep up with all Beth's news by joining her monthly newsletter!

facebook.com/BethRainBooks
twitter.com/bethrainauthor
instagram.com/bethrainauthor

Printed in Great Britain
by Amazon